It Came as a Shock to Rory When His Lips Found Hers

She stiffened at first, startled by the contact, the unexpected kiss tearing through her like a flash of lightning. His mouth tasted of wine, so hot, so moist, so seductively sweet. Then what was sweet, what was gentle became fire, the dammed-up passion she had sensed in Zeke breaking free.

And God help her, the fever seemed to have spread to her, licking through her veins with tongues of flame. She buried her fingers in Zeke's hair and caught herself returning the kiss with equal fierceness . . .

ESCAPADE

Berkley Books by Serena Richards

MASQUERADE
RENDEZVOUS
ESCAPADE

SERENA RICHARDS

Escapade

BERKLEY BOOKS, NEW YORK

ESCAPADE

A Berkley Book / published by arrangement with
the author

PRINTING HISTORY
Berkley edition / October 1991

ISBN: 0-425-12957-8

A BERKLEY BOOK ® TM 757,375
Berkley Books are published by The Berkley Publishing Group,
200 Madison Avenue, New York, New York 10016.
The name "Berkley" and the "B" logo
are trademarks belonging to Berkley Publishing Corporation.

PRINTED IN THE UNITED STATES OF AMERICA

10 9 8 7 6 5 4 3 2 1

To my son,
Ricky,
"a totally awesome dude"

Escapade

One

It was a splendid day for a wedding—splendid, that is, if one took no heed of the dark clouds gathering on the horizon. And the ominous rumble of thunder sounding low in the gentle rise of green hills forming the Hudson River Valley. But for most, the warning was lost in other noises emanating from Westvale's fairgrounds—the shrill clamor of the calliope, the circus barker's cries, the laughter and squeals of children, the strange hiss of the hot air balloon being filled with gas.

For hours the yards of silk fabric had lain spread out on the grass. Earlier, it had been a pool of blue, but now the silk billowed, taking on shape, a giant monolith straining against the ropes holding it earthbound. The crowd, which had gathered before noon, eager for the spectacle, could now identify the form of the painting on the balloon's gores. It was a demure young woman holding the flags of both the United States and Ireland in her outstretched hands.

The crowd's excitement mounted and the people pressed closer. Several daring boys ran forward to touch the wicker basket being attached to the netting of ropes that surrounded the hissing monster. Mr. Dutton, the circus owner, grabbed

1

up a bullhorn to warn the people to keep back.

"La-a-adies and gentlemen, your patience please! Very soon you will be witnessing the romantic event of the decade. The airborne wedding of Miss Glory Fatima, our equestrienne star, to the Fantastic Erno, the world's greatest lion tamer. . . ."

Mr. Dutton's voice boomed out over the fairgrounds, reaching the distant canvas of a small tent where Aurora Rose Kavanaugh—also known as Rory—was changing her clothes. Her silvery-blue eyes gleamed with amusement at the circus man's exaggerated patter. She discarded her white shirtwaist, the last of her sensible garb, and folded it neatly beside a straight navy skirt and jacket.

Standing only in her drawers and camisole, she stared at the frothy confection of peach silk she was about to don. Rory's amusement faded. Her features were delicate for such a determined young woman; only the firm line of her chin revealed her strength. The pert tilt of her nose and a dusting of freckles gave an almost pixieish appearance to a face that had no art of concealment. At the moment disgust could have been read plainly as Rory snatched up the silk gown.

Although she grimaced, she eased the folds over her head, careful not to disturb her coiffure. It had taken too much time and too many curses to arrange her thick chestnut hair in the elegant pompadour to have it all come tumbling down now. Enveloped in a cloud of silk, Rory once more caught Dutton's blaring voice.

"Soon, very soon, ladies and gentlemen, Miss Fatima and the Fantastic Erno will exchange their vows suspended one mile above your heads."

"Five hundred feet," Rory muttered, struggling into the gown's sleeves. "I said I wasn't taking them up any higher than five hundred feet."

"All under the auspices of that daring young lady, Miss Aurora Rose Cavenish . . ."

"Kavanaugh," Rory corrected through clenched teeth as she fought with the flounce and nearly lost.

" . . . the daughter of the late, great balloonist, Mr. Seamus Cavenish."

"*Aeronaut*," Rory said. "My father was an aeronaut." Although she spoke only to the small mirror on the dressing table, her voice was filled with a quiet pride and the familiar ache of loss.

It had been over a year since her father's death, but her grief still struck her at odd moments. To avoid the quick stinging of tears, Rory concentrated her loathing for the gown instead.

She couldn't imagine what had induced her to rig herself out in such a damn fool fashion. She rarely agreed with Dutton's idiot notions.

"Please, Miss Aurora," the circus owner had pleaded, "I know you are only going up to operate the balloon, but it would add so much more to the spirit of the thing if you were attired like a bridesmaid."

Rory would have told him to go to the deuce, but her friend Gia had stopped her. Gia had been entranced with the idea of making Rory a new gown. Rory had no delusions about her friend's motives. What Gia, with her own happy marriage and two toddling babes, really desired was to outfit Rory with a wedding gown. But since there was no prospect of that, Gia had settled for second best: the bridesmaid costume. Using her considerable needlework talent, Gia had copied this . . . this *thing* from a fashion plate in *Harper's Bazaar*.

Now that she had the gown on, Rory could see that Gia had wrought a miracle. It was too bad it would be wasted upon her. She didn't have the curves or the graceful carriage to do justice to such a dress.

The puffed sleeves were going to be a great nuisance, Rory thought. She felt as if she were wearing a pair of miniature balloons, one rising off each shoulder, and no matter how hard she struggled, she would never be able to fasten the dress hooks herself. The waist was narrow even for her boyishly slim figure. She supposed she should be wearing a corset, but Rory drew the line at lacing herself into one of those female torture devices.

While she pondered what to do about the hooks, the tent flap was edged aside. A tall young man dressed in blue denim stood silhouetted in the opening. Rory whipped around, flustered, until she saw that it was only Anthony Bertelli. Since her father's death, Tony had become the foreman of the Transcontinental Balloon Company. Her company now.

"Rory?" Tony called uncertainly.

"It's all right. I'm decent," she said.

Tony ducked through the opening, the tent flap brushing the top of his tightly-curling jet black hair. His handsome features were clouded over with a worried frown.

"Rory, the wind's getting pretty stiff. I don't think you're going to be able to go through with this thing."

Tony always thought the wind was too stiff. If he had his way, the balloon would only go up in conditions of dead calm. Accustomed to his gloomy cautions, Rory ignored the warning.

"Come on over here." She beckoned to him with a jerk of her head. "I need your help. I can't get this damn thing fastened."

As Tony started forward, she turned her back to him. She sensed him pause within a few inches of her and wondered why he hesitated.

"Come on. Hurry up," she said impatiently.

After another long moment, she felt him begin to fumble with the fastenings at her waist. Rory sucked in her breath. She did not feel in the least self-conscious making such a request of Tony. She had known him from the cradle. He was Gia's big brother, and as such, Rory had practically adopted him as her own.

Tony secured the gown's waistline. Rory didn't notice anything was wrong until his hands moved farther up her back. By the time he reached the fastenings at her neckline, she could hear his breath quicken.

Rory stiffened. As soon as he was done, she stepped quickly away from him. When she turned back to face him, he had that funny look in his eyes again, that look that she had surprised there too often of late, the look that Rory wanted to pretend didn't exist.

Suddenly Rory felt awkward. "I must look a regular

mark," she said, trying to cover her embarrassment.

"No," Tony croaked. "You . . . you look swell. A real daisy."

Rory picked up a pair of gloves and pretended to examine them for loose threads, anything to avoid Tony's eyes. She didn't want to look like a real daisy, at least not to her childhood friend.

"You're pretty enough to be the bride yourself." Tony's voice took on a teasing note. "Maybe you should make it a double wedding."

"Go on!" Rory gave a toss of her head. "Where would I find the groom?"

"I might do it. Your ma would have approved of me—a good Catholic boy."

"But my father wouldn't have. You're not even one quarter Irish."

Beneath all the joking, Rory detected a vein of seriousness in Tony that made her uncomfortable. Tugging on the gloves, she assumed a brisk manner.

"Is the balloon ready?" she asked.

"Almost." Thankfully Tony had taken the hint and dropped the subject of weddings. He didn't say any of those words Rory feared he would insist on saying, words that would ruin their easy camaraderie forever.

For now, Tony returned to the original source of his grievance. "It's a shame your dress is going to be wasted, Rory, but I really think you're going to have to scrub this one. There's a storm coming."

Rory peeked out the tent flap to see for herself. The sky was looking a little overcast and there was rain in the air. She could smell it. The flags adorning the other circus tents snapped in the breeze. Over the heads of the distant crowd, Rory could see the *Katie Moira* tugging at her moorings. No matter how many times Rory had seen one of the great balloons readied to take flight, it always moved her. Her heart swelled within her breast, and she felt almost dizzy with excitement, the longing to soar free.

Rory stepped back from the flap. "The storm will hold

off," she told Tony. "I'll be back safe before you know I'm gone."

"That's what you always say. That's exactly what your old man said when—" Tony broke off and flushed.

He didn't have to remind Rory what her father had said on that last morning. Every word of it was engraved on her mind forever.

"The eternal optimism of the Kavanaughs," Rory said with forced lightness, ignoring the lump that rose in her throat.

"Eternal foolhardiness."

"That too," Rory agreed with a smile. "But, if I don't go through with this, we break our contract with Mr. Dutton and we don't get paid."

"Yeah, well, there'll be other jobs, other ways to get money."

But his voice carried little conviction. He knew as well as she how badly the Transcontinental Balloon Company was running in the red. Whatever financial backers there had been had vanished after Seamus's death. Not even the most daring speculator was willing to risk capital on a company with a twenty-one-year-old girl at its head.

Rory still had some hope of a contract with the government. The U.S. Army was thinking of reviving its balloon corps. One of their agents was supposed to arrive in New York this week for a demonstration. But it would do little good if the agent arrived to find Rory's balloon company evicted from its warehouse due to nonpayment of the rent.

"Dutton's paying us too much money for this stunt for us to back down now," Rory said. "Besides, Tony, you surely don't want to disappoint a bride on her wedding day."

Before he could object, Rory seized Tony by the arm and steered him toward the tent opening.

"I still don't like it," he grumbled.

"What an old hen you can be sometimes, Anthony Bertelli. Will you quit your worrying? It's not even as though this is going to be a free flight, is it?"

Tony gave a reluctant grunt by way of assent.

"The balloon's going to be attached to a winch the whole

time, for pity's sake. You'll have complete control. If you think the weather's getting too bad, all you will have to do is order Pete and Angelo to wind in the rope and haul me back down."

"Haul you down before you are ready to come? I can imagine what you would have to say to me."

"So it will be the first time all these good folks ever heard a bridesmaid swear. Now be off with you and make sure that blasted Angelo doesn't pump in too much gas again."

The last time she'd gone out, Tony's enthusiastic younger brother had generated too much hydrogen, not allowing for the expansion of the air as the balloon rose. One of the seams had ripped open, making for a very short flight and, for Rory, almost a very short life.

The reminder startled Tony enough into hastening back across the fairgrounds. As he went, Rory heard him muttering that he should wash his hands of all this craziness and go get a real job down at the docks like his mother wanted. Since it was a familiar strain with him, Rory paid no attention to it.

She retreated back into the tent long enough to put the finishing touches on her toilette. Only one last thing remained and that was to fasten the pocketwatch to the belt of her gown. The gold watch had become her talisman. It had belonged to her father.

Briefly she consulted the time. Quarter till four. She snapped the case closed and for a moment cradled the watch's cool weight lovingly in her hand. Engraved on the cover was, appropriately enough, a hot air balloon in full flight.

Rory could not help remembering how her father had consigned the watch to her care that morning last June. She hadn't wanted him to take the balloon up, his proposed flight enough to daunt even her. But for too long had Seamus dreamed of sailing one of his balloons across the Atlantic, a feat that no aeronaut had ever accomplished. It little mattered to Seamus that all his predecessors had met death making the attempt.

And Rory's fears for her father were only increased by

the dream she'd had the night before. It wasn't the first time she had dreamed such a thing—the white faerie appearing from the mists over New York harbor, the dread specter the Irish called the banshee, the harbinger of death. Rory had had the same nightmare once when she was twelve years old. The next day her mother had succumbed to the effects of a prolonged bout with scarlet fever.

Now the dream had troubled her sleep again, and there was her father about to embark on the most dangerous risk an aeronaut could take. But Seamus Kavanaugh scoffed at all the old superstitions. Rory had known it would do little good telling him to abandon his flight because she had had a nightmare.

So instead she had remonstrated with him about the follies of a flight over the ocean until Da had become quite angry.

"Whist now!" he had commanded. "I'll not have me own daughter questioning me judgment. I've been flying balloons since before you were born."

He strode away from her, but he must have noticed the tears glinting in her eyes for he returned almost at once. He had a smile that would have charmed the little people into surrendering their gold, but he was not able to coax Rory out of her fears. He finally resorted to an old trick from her childhood.

As a little girl, Rory had often wept and begged to accompany her father on one of his trips. He had always soothed her by giving her the "important" task of keeping his watch safe. That last morning, it was as though he had forgotten she was a woman grown. He had cupped her hand about the watch, saying, "There now. Don't you be crying, Aurora Rose. You be lookin' after this for me and you know I'll be coming back. I always come back to retrieve me treasure."

He had pinched her chin and smiled into her eyes, and as ever Rory had known it wasn't the watch he was talking about. There was nothing she could do then but watch helplessly as he mounted into the balloon's gondola. The ropes were cast off and he drifted into the sky. Her last vision of her father was of him looking down, the wind whipping back his mane of gray hair as he merrily waved his cap. . . .

"Miss Kavanaugh?" An acrobat lady in spangled tights peered into the tent, bringing an abrupt end to Rory's remembrances. She suddenly realized that the watch she held clutched in her palm had become blurred and out of focus.

Rory dashed the back of her hand across her eyes. "Yes?"

"Are you almost ready?" the woman asked. "Mr. Dutton is getting anxious."

"I'll be right there."

When the woman had gone, Rory tucked the watch away in her belt. It would never have pleased Seamus, this grieving of hers. He would have expected her to give him a fine wake, which she had done. Then he would have told her to get on with her life, with the pursuit of the dreams they had both shared.

"Which, please God, is exactly what I intend to do," Rory murmured.

Shoving the flap aside, she strode out of the tent. The wind threatened to wreak havoc with her hair. But Rory scooped up her skirts and moved determinedly forward.

The crowd had thickened to such a degree that Rory began to wonder how she would get through. But with the aid of some burly circus roustabouts, a path was cleared for her.

As Rory emerged into the open area where the *Katie Moira* awaited her, she saw that the barrel-shaped hydrogen generator had already been disconnected. Pete and Thomas were loading it back onto the wagon. Tony was tying more bags of ballast to the side of the balloon's car as though he were determined one way or another to keep Rory earthbound.

All of her crew were hard at work except for Tony's younger brother. A dark, curly-haired, more slender version of Tony, Angelo lounged near the balloon winch, his nose thrust deep into yesterday's edition of the *New York World*.

Rory glided up behind him. Crossing her arms, she

cleared her throat with a loud "Harrumph!" Angelo slowly looked up from his newspaper, not in the least abashed to be caught loafing.

"Hey, Rory, look here," he said, extending the paper toward her. "John Ezekiel Morrison is giving a party today."

"Who the devil is John Ezekiel Morrison?"

"Only the most eligible bachelor in New York. I hear tell he's what the Bowery dance halls girls call a real 'looker' and rich as Diamond Jim Brady. He lives in what is practically a damned castle. The paper calls him the Mysterious Millionaire of Fifth Avenue."

At first, Rory could make little sense of Angelo's excited chatter. Then she glanced at the paper and realized with some disgust that the youth had been reading the society columns again. It was both amusing and exasperating the way Angelo devoured any news about the lives of wealthy and famous people. When he wasn't collecting cigarette cards of Lillian Russell, he was driving everyone mad with accounts of where Mrs. Vanderbilt had dined last night or who J. P. Morgan had entertained at Delmonico's.

Angelo was now completely oblivious to the balloon roaring above them. "It says here the Whitneys will be there and Mrs. Van Hallsburg. But it don't say nothing about the Vanderbilts." Angelo frowned. "Do you think Mrs. Vanderbilt knows something about Morrison that the rest don't?"

"I have no idea," Rory snapped. "The next time she invites me to tea, I'll ask her. And now, Angelo, if you don't mind—" She broke off the rebuke she was about to deliver, stiffening with annoyance as she stared upward at her balloon. Someone had woven garlands all over the ropes that connected the balloon to the basket.

"Who stuck those damn flowers all over my rigging? I never gave permission for such a thing."

Angelo shrugged. "Mr. Dutton's idea. After all, it is a wedding, Rory. Now about this Morrison fellow? Do you think it's true what the paper hints about his unknown background, that there might be something sinister about him? I read that he punches out any reporters caught nosing around his castle, so he must have something to hide. How does a fellow get to be that rich honestly anyhow?"

"I don't know, but I do know how a fellow gets to be that poor honestly. By losing his job." Rory snatched the paper from Angelo and thunked him over the head with it. "Now get back to work."

Angelo grinned. Although he did grab his precious newspaper back from her, he folded the society section, tucking it into his jacket pocket, then turned his attention to checking the balloon's tether, making sure it was secured to the winch.

Still not trusting Angelo to keep his mind on his task, Rory was keeping a wary eye on him when she was approached by the circus owner himself, Mr. Dutton.

The man's checkered suit was enough to blind her even on this overcast day. He grinned in her face, chomping on a fat cigar. "Ah, here she is at last. The balloon lady."

"*Aeronaut*," Rory grated. She plucked the cigar from his plump fingers, dropped the stogie to the ground and crunched it beneath her shoe.

"Hey! That was an expensive see-gar."

"And that's a bag full of hydrogen," Rory said, pointing at the balloon. "One little spark and they could be picking up pieces of us all along the Jersey side of the Hudson."

Mr. Dutton's eyes widened, and he took a few extra stomps at the crushed cigar himself. Then he stepped back and cocked his head at her admiringly.

"Well, now, don't you make a peach of a bridesmaid!"

Rory was not about to allow her irritation to be deflected by the man's oily compliments. She was still annoyed about all those blasted flowers caught up in the balloon's rigging. But before she could complain, Mr. Dutton dragged her over to meet the minister.

The Reverend Titus Allgood looked very prim, very young and very scared.

"Is . . . is this thing really quite safe, Miss Kavanaugh?" he asked in a quavering voice.

"Completely safe," Rory said.

Tony, who happened to be passing by within earshot, gave a loud snort. Rory glared at him. She still hadn't managed to calm Reverend Allgood's fears when the circus band was heard to strike up a flourish.

An excited murmur ran through the crowd at this signal that the wedding procession was about to commence. The band blared out the strains of Mendelssohn's Wedding March. From the main tent across the fairgrounds, two elephants led the parade, followed by a line of lovely ladies in tights riding white ponies adorned with feathers. Drawing up the rear was a flower-bedecked open carriage in which rode the bride and groom, driven by the ringmaster himself in a red coat and top hat.

As the crowd clapped with pleasure, Rory tried to smile, but it was difficult to disguise a certain chagrin. This had formed no part of her father's dream, this usage of the *Katie Moira* to perform a cheap circus stunt.

Her father's vision for the company had been so much more than that—grand plans of establishing an aerial mail service, a passenger line, even the use of balloons for scientific exploration.

Someday, Da. Someday, Rory vowed silently.

The crowd pushed and shoved, and it was all the roustabouts could do to prevent a general surge forward as the wedding carriage arrived in the clearing.

The groom was the first to alight, doffing his high silk hat to the assembled masses. The Fantastic Erno's handlebar mustache bristled as he flashed a smile. With a flourish, he turned to hand down his bride.

The crowd let out a collective gasp. Rory gaped herself at Miss Glory Fatima's idea of a wedding costume. She was garbed traditionally enough in white, but in the skimpiest pair of tights Rory had ever seen. The skirt of her leotard did not even cover her calves, and the glittering bodice scarcely contained Miss Glory's ample charms.

Mr. Dutton snatched up his bullhorn again, and the crowd had to endure a rather long-winded speech. Just as everyone was getting a bit restive, he finally arrived at his conclusion.

" . . . and now, suspended miles above the earth, Miss Glory Fatima and the Fantastic Erno will exchange their solemn vows, witnessed by that intrepid balloonist, Aurora Kavanaugh."

"*Aeronaut*," Rory said wearily.

Erno helped his bride climb into the balloon's basket. He also assisted the white-faced and noticeably trembling minister. To Rory's annoyance, her skirts hindered her from scrambling into the gondola with her usual dexterity. Tony had to lift her over the edge, and she thought he clung to her a little longer than necessary.

"I heard thunder again," he hissed in her ear. "This better be the shortest wedding on record."

Rory merely smiled sweetly.

"I mean it, Rory. Ten minutes and then I'm telling Angelo to haul—"

She cut off his warning by giving the signal to Thomas that he could begin undoing the lines that tethered the balloon. The *Katie Moira* immediately surged upward several feet, now held back by only the thick rope affixed to the winch. The balloon bucked in the wind as though it resented even that restraint upon its freedom. Miss Fatima gasped and clutched at Erno. The minister looked as though he would have liked to have done the same.

Rory motioned to Angelo to start cranking the winch, but he was too spellbound by Miss Fatima's costume to pay any attention. It took a sharp command from Tony to set him and Pete into motion.

The muscles in the forearms of both young men appeared strained as they struggled to hold in the surging balloon and let the rope out smoothly. As the *Katie Moira* started upward, the crowd gave a great cheer.

Owing to the wind, the ascent was a little rough. Cursing the flowers again, Rory clung to the rigging, setting free a shower of blossoms. She cautioned the others to move about as little as possible, an unnecessary admonishment for Reverend Allgood. The man seemed frozen with fear.

Erno and Miss Fatima peered cautiously over the side, waving to their adoring public below. Soon the faces of the crowd grew less distinct, the mighty elephants and even the circus tents assuming the dimensions of toys. The cheers of the crowd reflected upward with that peculiar clarity Rory had often noted on her flights.

The balloon had not risen much higher when it jerked to a sudden halt.

"Damn you, Tony," Rory thought. He had obviously prevented Angelo from reeling her out the full distance she had planned. But perhaps it was just as well. Much more and they would be obscured from the view of the circus crowd, lost in the scudding gray clouds overhead.

Rory looked expectantly at the Reverend Allgood. It was some moments before the little man would take the hint. At last he managed to pry free of his death grip upon the basket's side and draw forth his prayer book.

"D-dear beloved," he began.

A rumble of thunder sounded and he almost dropped the book. After a deep gulp, he relocated his place in the text and continued.

Although she was supposed to be a witness to this event, Rory's thoughts drifted from the ceremony. The storm was moving closer. She had seen a distant flash of lightning. Although the balloon was fairly stable, she felt the insistent tug. If it had not been for the stout rope and the winch, the wind would have carried the *Katie Moira* away from the fairgrounds rapidly.

She wished there were some way she could force Allgood to hurry. But as though calmed by the familiar words of the wedding service, he was proceeding with all the slow dignity the occasion demanded.

Then, finally, the minister reached his conclusion.

"I now pronounce you man and wife. What God hath joined, let no man set asunder."

As Erno moved to kiss the bride with great enthusiasm, Rory scooped up a red parachute. She tossed it over the side. As it drifted back to earth, it would signal those below that the ceremony was complete.

Rory offered the couple her congratulations, then produced a bottle of champagne from the bottom of the basket.

"On the way down, we'll drink a toast to—"

She was cut off in midsentence as the balloon gave a wild lurch. Dropping the champagne bottle, she pitched against Erno.

Miss Glory gave a little squeal as the balloon began to rise. "What's happening? Why aren't they bringing us down?"

Rory recovered her footing and braced herself against the side. Instantly, she knew that they were not only rising, but also drifting swiftly to the east.

Peering over the side, she saw the green splotch of earth and the mere specks that were the circus vanish from view. The next instant they were enveloped in the eerie gray world of the clouds. It was like being lost in a heavy fog. Rory didn't know how it had happened, but somehow that blasted Angelo had let the rope come free of the winch. The *Katie Moira* was now in a pattern of free flight.

Her passengers looked puzzled, but only a little frightened, until the significance of the balloon's movements dawned upon Erno.

"Why . . . why, we've broken loose," he said.

The Reverend Allgood turned pale and sagged down in the basket. Miss Glory screamed.

"There is no cause for panic—" Rory was cut off by a roll of thunder. A burst of lightning seemed to electrify the entire cloud.

Rory gave up on any attempts to calm her passengers. She had to act and quickly. Snatching up a knife from the basket's floor, she bent over the side and began slicing open the ballast bags, setting free a cascade of sand.

Erno seized hold of her wrist. "What are you doing? That will make us ascend even higher."

Rory wrenched herself free and explained with all the patience she could muster. "We have no choice but to go up. We have to get above the storm."

When she could make him understand, Erno moved to help her.

"That's enough," Rory said. Gradually, the *Katie Moira* lifted out of the cloud cover. The sky above them emerged

in a burst of blue, the sun more brilliant than the most
sparkling summer day. That hushed calm descended, that
absolute quiet which Rory had never found to exist anywhere
on earth.

"Are we dead?" Reverend Allgood quavered. "Is . . . is
this Heaven?"

"No," Rory said, consulting her barometer. "It's only
about fifteen hundred feet."

"We shall have quite an adventure to report when we land
back at the fairgrounds," Erno chuckled.

The fairgrounds? Rory arched one brow but said nothing.
She didn't know where they would be landing. She only
knew it wouldn't be anywhere near the circus. At this
height, the movement of the wind was deceptive, but
Rory knew they were being carried far from their point
of departure. According to her compass, they were headed
in a southeasterly direction. Rory's one concern was that
they should not end up in the Atlantic Ocean just as her
father had done. . . .

A shudder worked through her and she was quick to set
the thought aside, concentrating on her more immediate
problem. Now that there was no shielding of clouds, the sun
was heating the gas in the balloon, causing it to expand. The
falling barometer told Rory they were rising steadily. The
higher they went, the thinner the oxygen would become.

Rory tugged at the valve line, releasing some of the gas
from the balloon. She pulled again and again, letting out
a little more air each time. The balloon's descent became
swifter until they were lost in the cloud cover once more.

Rory was certain they had outdistanced the storm. She
could only hope that below them lurked some decent place
to land, hopefully a nice level field and not the Atlantic.

As the cloud cover parted below them like vanishing
mists, Rory peered downward. When she got her first good
view of the terrain below, she bit her lip. "Damnation!"

Below them it looked as if some giant's toy box had been
upended, scattering rows and rows of little blocks in a dense
hodgepodge.

The rows were actually solid walls of towering buildings,

an endless maze of streets. New York City. The very heart of it. And cooled by the cloud cover between the balloon and the sun, the *Katie Moira* was making a rapid descent.

Rory groaned and grabbed for her knife. Miss Glory stole a peek downward.

"Ooohh, Fifth Avenue. All the shops. Miss Kavanaugh, I don't suppose you could land—"

"No!" Rory slashed at a sandbag, but the balloon was still dropping. There was not much ballast left. At this rate, they were soon going to slam into the rooftop of one of the taller buildings. Reverend Allgood appeared to have fainted, but Rory hadn't time to concern herself over the fact.

"Throw everything out of the balloon," she shouted to Erno and Glory.

Everything was not much, since no equipment or provisions had been loaded for this short trip. But the champagne went, along with Rory's compass, barometer and telescope, even the seats of the gondola.

To Rory's relief, the balloon steadied itself, but she knew it couldn't last long. The bottom of the gondola scudded perilously near the high, sloped walls of the Croton Reservoir, and astonished sightseers on the walkway trained their field glasses toward the balloon.

"Should we make a jump for it?" Erno asked, dubiously eyeing the reservoir's expanse of blue water.

"Are you crazy?" Rory cried. Shading her eyes with her hand, she scanned the distance for some safe place to land. Before her stretched nothing but Fifth Avenue. The balloon's sudden appearance had shaken even the New Yorkers out of their indifference.

Traffic had snarled up on the avenue. Rory could make out horses plunging in terror, the flow of carriages brought to a halt. Heads tipped back as everyone stared and pointed upward. The shrill sound of a policeman's whistle drifted to Rory with startling clarity.

She spared one brief glance for the chaos she was creating, her thoughts snapping to the distance. Perhaps they could come down in Central Park. She grimaced. Rory hated landings in trees. She had broken her arm that way once, been lucky it hadn't been her neck.

In any case, the *Katie Moira* had leveled off enough to give her hope. If her memory served her correctly, the land beyond the park should be a vista of open fields. Crossing her fingers, Rory murmured a brief prayer.

But to her dismay, she saw that it had been far too long since she had been north of Central Park. The area had changed somewhat. No more was it the expanse of green country she recalled. The mansions of the wealthier element of the city now sprawled out even here.

"What a way to scrape up acquaintance with the Vanderbilts," Rory muttered. She tensed, realizing the balloon was losing altitude again, drifting ever closer to one of the larger mansions.

It was a fantastic structure of massive white stone walls and towers, like a chateau that should have been nestled somewhere along the banks of the Seine. Rory thought it looked ridiculous near the bustle of Manhattan, but at least the mansion boasted something many city dwellings did not—a broad lawn surrounded by an iron fence.

"Brace yourselves," Rory warned her passengers. "I am going to try to bring us down over there."

"Th-there?" Erno gasped when he saw where she was pointing. "But Miss Kavanaugh. That's Morrison's Castle."

"So?" Rory started gathering up the length of rope and grappling hook.

"It . . . it's just that I have heard about— Well, that Mr. Morrison. He doesn't like trespassers."

It was the second time that day someone had told her that. Vague memories chased through Rory's mind of Angelo's foolish chatter, something he had been reading out of the papers about a sinister millionaire who hated reporters. But as the *Katie Moira* dipped lower, the recollection seemed of little importance. The balloon was coming down on this Morrison's property whether he liked it or not, whether Rory liked it or not.

And she didn't. The lawn was far from ideal. Blast it all! It was crowded with a lot of damn fool people having

a garden party. Lilting orchestra music wafted upward, but
the strains of the waltz abruptly ceased. As the *Katie Moira*
drifted overhead, some of the party guests started to point
and shriek.

Rory yanked on the valve line and gritted her teeth. She
had a feeling this was not going to be one of her better
landings. As the balloon surged downward, she bent over
the side and tossed out the grappling hook, trying to catch
the iron fence. But she missed, snagging a slender tree
instead.

Rory groaned, watching as the sapling bent double. It
would still have been all right if those idiots below had had
the wit to seize onto the balloon's rope lines and help haul
her down. But most of those gentlemen were doing little
but gaping upward beneath the brims of their high-crowned
hats, the ladies gesturing shrilly with their parasols.

One tall, broad-shouldered man shoved his way forward
and attempted to grab the rope, but it was already too late.
The sapling tore free of the ground, and the *Katie Moira*
lurched onward, dragging the tree, roots and all. Erno and
Miss Glory lost their balance, tumbling atop the prostrate
Reverend Allgood.

Rory clutched the side of the gondola, catching a dizzying
glimpse of the havoc she was wreaking below. Her tree
"anchor" plowed through linen-covered tables, sending
china flying. The orchestra dove for cover, abandoning
their violins. Silk-clad ladies ran shrieking, likely faster
than they had ever moved in their lives.

"Grab the ropes, you fools. Grab the—" Rory's hoarse
cry was cut off as the balloon rapidly lost altitude, causing
the gondola to smack against the ground. Rory lost her own
footing, joining the heap of flailing arms and legs that was
her passengers.

The *Katie Moira* leaped upward, as though making one
last desperate effort to regain the skies. Rory struggled,
elbowing Erno sharply as she clutched frantically for the
valve line. The gondola rocked and Rory tugged harder at
the line than she had intended.

Like a prizefighter doubled over by a blow to the stomach,

the great balloon gave up the last of its air with a mighty whoosh. Someone screamed. Rory was not sure if it was Miss Glory or the Reverend Allgood.

She had no chance to figure it out before the gondola plunged downward. Her breath left her lungs in a rush as the basket slammed into the ground with bone-jarring force.

Cobwebs of darkness danced before Rory's eyes. She thought she was going to pass out. But she fought the sensation. She retained enough awareness of her situation to realize her face was pressed against the ground, blades of grass prickling her cheek.

She had been thrown clear of the gondola. But what of her passengers? Miss Glory? Erno? Reverend Allgood? Rory raised her head, attempted to call out their names, but her voice came out in a wheeze. God, how it hurt to talk, even to breathe. In fact, when she tried to move, everything hurt. She must have broken every bone in her body this time.

Rory blinked, shaking her head to clear it. She managed to get some air into her lungs in a few pain-wracked gulps, then raised herself up onto her elbows. She was distressed to find herself draped by heavy yards of blue silk, but only for a moment. She had crept about beneath the balloon's envelope to attach rigging enough times that she did not feel unduly alarmed at the prospect of being smothered by the *Katie Moira*'s collapsed weight.

Soon she felt recovered enough to begin crawling forward, trying to find her fellow travelers. Perhaps she hadn't broken any bones after all. The chief hindrance to her movement was the damn dress, its folds tangling about her legs. It seemed to take forever to reach the edge of the balloon cover. She did not know whether to feel encouraged or alarmed when she did not encounter the forms of any of her passengers.

Beyond her, she became aware of muffled voices, the thud of running feet. Brushing aside the edge of the silk, she poked her head out and felt the welcome rush of cool air against her cheeks. She was alive. As she struggled to rise, her hand came down upon the toe of a man's shoe. Her nose all but collided with a pair of legs encased in elegant gray trousers.

Hunkering back on her heels, she tipped her head up. There seemed no end to those long legs, but she did come eventually to large fists propped against the flat plane of hips, a silk waistcoat straining across a hard stomach and broad chest, a pin-striped coat set over powerful, squared shoulders.

Rory had a hazy memory of having glimpsed those shoulders, that tall frame before. Of course, he was the one who had tried to help, had attempted to grab onto the balloon's tow line. But as Rory stared upward into the stranger's face, he did not look so helpful now.

In fact he looked very much as if he were ready to murder her.

Two

The breeze tossed sable strands of hair across the man's forehead, but it did nothing to soften the harshness of his expression. Rory took brief note of his inflexible jaw, his slightly crooked nose, his heavy black brows drawn together, but it was his eyes that caught and held her. Dark eyes, magnetic eyes, roiling-with-fury eyes. The mere contact of his gaze made Rory feel as though she had crashed all over again.

He reminded her of a thunder god she had once read about in school—that is until Sister Mary Margaret had caught Rory and rapped her knuckles for studying myths instead of her catechism.

When the man suddenly bent down and reached for her, Rory shrank back instinctively. His hands caught her about the waist and hauled her to her feet, not ungently but in a manner that brooked no resistance.

Rory swayed slightly. She braced her hands against his chest, could feel the fury and tension coiled there and drew back as though she had been scorched.

"You all right, miss?" The question was curt, but the solicitude seemed genuine enough.

Rory nodded, oddly unable to find her voice.

"And where is he?"

"Huh?" she squeaked out, puzzled by the angry question.

"The jackass," the man said, his restrained rage beginning to break through. "The fool who dumped this thing on—Never mind!"

Rory was still struggling to make sense of his words when he abruptly released her. The force of that bludgeoning stare turned elsewhere. As he strode away from her, Rory's gaze followed him. Just ahead several other gentleman were helping the Reverend Titus Allgood to free himself from beneath the balloon. The little minister looked as if he were about to kiss the ground and every one of his rescuers.

"Thank you, Lord, thank you," he said, casting his eyes heavenward. His quavering gratitude abruptly disappeared when he saw the tall, angry man bearing down upon him. Rory watched in astonishment as the man seized the minister by his collar.

"You stupid bastard! If I find you have injured anyone, I'm going to break your neck. I'll give you five minutes to get that damned balloon of yours off this lawn."

Reverend Allgood was too terrified to get out even a squeak of protest. Rory thought the minister looked about to faint again and started to intervene. She winced at a sudden shooting pain in her ankle, but still managed to hobble forward.

She tugged at the angry man's sleeve. "You're making a mistake. He's only the minister who performed the wedding ceremony."

The man's dark eyes flashed at her again, but he did not release Mr. Allgood. "What?!"

"We had a wedding in the balloon," Rory cried, yanking on the man's arm until he let go of the minister.

"Congratulations," the man grated. "Then I collect it's your new husband I want to kill."

At that unfortunate moment, Erno emerged from beneath the balloon, pulling his bride after him. Glory Fatima appeared in blushing splendor, her charms all but spilling

free from her spangled bodice, much to the admiring gasps
of the men, the dismayed cries of the ladies.

Rory was relieved to see the rest of her passengers
unharmed, but the relief was short-lived as the furious
man prepared to descend upon them. What was the matter
with this fellow—charging down upon people like a raging
bull without waiting for explanations?

Rory limped into the man's path, nearly colliding with
the wall of his chest. "Erno is not my husband. *That* is his
wife and it's not their balloon either. Who the devil are you
anyway to go about threatening everybody?"

"I'm Zeke Morrison and this is my property."

"Oh," Rory said. So this was John Ezekiel Morrison,
the millionaire she had heard so much about. She might
have guessed as much, except that Morrison looked neither
mysterious nor sinister, merely bad tempered.

"Would you mind telling me who owns that contraption?" he demanded.

Rory tipped up her chin. Any fear she felt was lost in
defiance. "It's mine!"

"Yours?" His gaze raked over her in deprecating fashion.
"Well, that explains everything."

"What do you mean by that?"

He bent down so that his face was only inches from hers.
"I mean, little girl, that the fellow who turned you loose to
play in that balloon should be shot."

Now Rory knew why Morrison's nose was a little crooked. At some time in his life, someone must have broken it. Rory felt her own fists tense with the temptation.
"How dare you! I am an aeronaut, sir, and let me tell
you, this disaster is as much your guests' fault as anyone
else's."

"My guests," he bellowed.

"Yes!" Rory gestured toward the assembled crowd, who
were now staring more at her than the fallen balloon.
The ladies in particular, their flowered hats still askew,
seemed to regard her as though she were a weed that had
sprung up on this perfectly manicured lawn. Rory's cheeks
burned.

"Instead of gawking," she shouted at them, "you should have helped to grab the line I tossed down. Then I could have landed the balloon safely."

She got no response except for raised eyebrows and pursed lips. Only Zeke Morrison retorted. "No one asked you to land on my lawn at all, lady. You could see I was having a party here."

"Well, you shouldn't have been having a garden party on a rotten day like this."

"You certainly took care of that, didn't you?" Zeke snarled. "Just look at the damage you did!"

His lawn did appear as though a hurricane had just swept through. Rory knew she was being unreasonable, but she was bruised, she was shaken, she had twisted her ankle and Zeke Morrison was a foul-tempered beast.

"The devil with your stupid party!" she said. "What about the damage to the *Katie Moira*?"

"Oh, she looks just fine to me." Zeke gave a sardonic nod of his head toward the buxom Miss Fatima.

"*Katie Moira* is the balloon," Rory said. "And very likely this rough landing has torn holes in her."

"Pardon me! Next time I'll level the whole house to clear you a smooth field, but for now, Miss . . . Miss . . ."

"Aurora Rose Kavanaugh," she said, drawing herself up proudly.

"For now, Miss Kavanaugh, I am about this short of tossing you and your balloon out into the street!"

"Come ahead and try it then." Her Irish now thoroughly up, Rory raised her fists, assuming a fighter's stance she remembered from when her Da had sneaked her in to see the great John L. Sullivan spar a few rounds.

Morrison took a menacing step toward her. Rory braced herself for resistance. But as he glared down at her, an odd thing happened. The line of his implacable jaw began to quiver. His lips twitched, his mouth curved into a wide grin and he began to laugh. He stole a glance from her to the indignant faces of his disheveled guests, then flung back his head and positively roared.

Rory wanted to punch him more than ever. "What's so

blasted funny?" she started to ask, but at that instant a rumble sounded from the skies as though to match Morrison's own booming voice. The storm seemed to have followed Rory down the Hudson. With another loud clap, the clouds burst, sending rain pelting down.

All about her, Morrison's guests began to squeal and dart for shelter. Only Zeke Morrison remained unaffected. Still laughing, he tipped his head back, the rain beading on his swarthy countenance and dark windswept hair, the lightning itself seemingly caught in his mirth-filled eyes. With his hands on his hips, he defied the elements as though he indeed was the god of thunder whose mere laughter could command the skies.

He exuded a kind of masculine beauty, very raw, very primitive, and watching him, Rory felt oddly breathless. Her fists relaxed, and her arms dropped to her sides without her being fully aware of it.

Morrison finally made an effort to regain control, swiping the back of his hand across his eyes. Still chuckling, he managed to bark an order to the squealing ladies to stop carrying on like a flock of biddy hens and get themselves into the house.

"Wellington," he shouted to a tall manservant who was attempting to rescue the fallen linen across the lawn. "Don't worry about that blasted tablecloth. Help those boys from the orchestra move their instruments."

Butler, footmen, maids, guests—all scurried to obey his commands except Rory. The others jostled past her, including her own passengers, as they all bolted through the double French glass doors that led into the imposing mansion.

Although she was getting drenched, the raindrops trickling down the back of her neck causing her to shiver, Rory didn't budge. She was annoyed with herself for ogling Morrison as though he were some sort of matinee idol and even more annoyed with him. The amused look he cast her way did nothing to soothe her temper.

"Head for the house, Miss Kavanaugh."

She'd be darned if she would, not after the way he had

insulted her, then laughed at her to boot. "I thought you were going to throw me into the street."

"I wouldn't throw a stray cat out in this weather. Get moving."

"How gracious of you," she muttered. Turning her back on him, she limped over to the *Katie Moira*. She stiffened as she heard Morrison coming after her.

"What's the matter with your ankle?"

"Nothing!" She nearly slipped on the wet grass and gasped at the fresh pain that spiked up her bruised limb. Morrison seized her arm to steady her.

"Come on, little girl. Get inside."

"I have experienced quite enough of your hospitality, Mr. Morrison." But her dignified speech was ruined by the way her teeth chattered. Her gown clung to her, now thoroughly soaked, making her miserable.

Morrison appeared in little better shape. His fancy shirt-waist was likely to be ruined, his wet hair was plastered to his brow, but he only laughed. Of course, Rory thought resentfully, such trifles would not bother a thunder god. He slid his arm about her waist, the other swooping behind her knees to lift her off her feet.

"Hey!" Rory cried. The gesture was not in the least romantic. He hefted her as though she were just another chair to be moved into the house at his convenience.

"Put me down!"

He paid her no heed. He was too busy shouting more orders to some straggling servants. She drew back her fist and thumped him hard on the chest. It was like pounding on a brick wall.

As he toted her toward the house, he looked down at her and grinned. "If it weren't for the lightning, I'd stay out here. I forgot how much fun it is to romp about in the rain. My mother used to give me pure holy hell for it."

"So did mine—," Rory began, then re-collected herself. "You put me down right now!"

"What! Right here in this puddle?"

She saw the disconcerting twinkle in his eye and knew the infernal man was fully capable of doing such a thing.

Although she despised herself, she wrapped her arms about his neck in alarm. With gritted teeth, she endured being carried into the house.

She caught a glimpse of the bedraggled guests crowding into a large parlor. Someone was striking a match to the gas jet in the fireplace grating. But Zeke Morrison carried her in the opposite direction.

"Too crowded in there. We'll find some quiet spot to dry you out, then have a look at your ankle."

"Dry me out? I am not a wet dishcloth! And you are not looking at my ankle!"

He still made no move to release her, even when she squirmed in his arms. Far from being furious now, Morrison seemed to find everything she said damned amusing. But as he carried her into the front hall, Rory's struggles abruptly ceased.

As she stared about her, she was awed in spite of herself. The scrolled ceiling that towered over her head was as impressive as the rotunda at City Hall. The crystal chandelier glittered even on such a gloomy day, and the marble staircase seemed to wind upward into eternity.

And at the foot of those stairs, barring Zeke Morrison's path, stood the most elegant woman Rory had ever seen. She had masses of icy white-blond hair and frigid blue eyes. Unlike the other guests, she seemed untouched by the storm breaking outside.

Mrs. Morrison? Rory wondered. Although beautiful, the woman looked too old to be Zeke's wife.

Yet there was something very proprietary in the way she demanded, "What are you doing with that girl, John?"

Morrison should have been embarrassed enough to set her down at once. Goodness knows, Rory felt her own cheeks burn as though she had been caught doing something wrong.

"Please," she hissed. "Put me down. I swear I can walk."

Although he continued to smile, the belligerent tilt of his jaw became prominent again. Yet he seemed to sense something of Rory's own embarrassment at being seen cradled in his arms. He lowered her reluctantly to her feet, explaining to the woman, "Miss Kavanaugh seems to have sustained some injury to her ankle."

"That is hardly your concern," came the cool reply. "I imagine the police will provide her with whatever medical attention she needs. I have taken the liberty of summoning them."

"Police?" Rory gasped at the same time Zeke demanded, "What the devil did you do that for?"

The woman's fine brows arched upward. "These circus people vandalized your lawn, John."

"On the contrary," Zeke retorted. "I have it on the best authority that my lawn vandalized Miss Kavanaugh's balloon."

"I doubt Captain Devery will share your levity, John. There are still, thank God, laws that protect people from the wanton destruction of their property."

"But it was an accident. . . ." Rory faltered, a sick feeling clutching her stomach. She had never expected this misadventure to end with her being thrown into jail. Although she despised herself for it, she could not help casting a pleading glance up at Morrison.

He squeezed her hand, the warm pressure comforting. "Don't worry, little girl, nobody's going to jail. I'll deal with the police." His reassuring smile vanished as he turned back to the woman blocking the stairs. "Sometimes I wish you would not be so confoundedly busy on my behalf, Cynthia."

"Do you indeed? That could be arranged."

"Look, I've got no time for a quarrel now. Could you step out of the way until I see that Miss Kavanaugh is looked after? Then you can snap at me as much as you please."

A faint trace of pink stole into that icy white complexion. The woman's gaze rested for a moment on Rory; then, with an assumption of chilling dignity, she moved away from the stairs and stalked off down the hall.

Rory shivered. No living being's eyes should have been that cold. Rory felt as though the woman could have destroyed her as easily as brushing aside a speck of lint from her gown. An odd thought to have about such a refined-looking lady.

Rory turned to Zeke, who was following the woman's retreat, a frown on his face.

"I . . . I am sorry," she said. "I didn't mean to cause trouble between you and your . . . your wife?"

"Mrs. Van Hallsburg is not my wife!" As Zeke glanced back at Rory, his expression lightened. "I am quite a free man, Miss Kavanaugh. And you . . . you are quite wet."

He studied her as though he were having his first good look, and Rory realized with dismay that he probably was. She noticed herself how her damp gown outlined to perfection her breasts, the curve of her hips.

"Come on," he said. "You'd better get out of those clothes."

The statement seemed harmless enough, merely a civil suggestion. Why then did she have this odd feeling that Zeke Morrison should have his face slapped? He wasn't doing anything, only looking.

Rory crossed her arms protectively in front of herself. "I . . . I don't want to cause you any more bother. I am sure my assistants will track me here from the fairgrounds. We . . . we'll move the balloon and try to set your lawn to rights. Of course I will pay. . . ."

Even as she started to promise, Rory wondered with dismay how she was ever going to do so. She bit down on her lip. The cost of the damages would likely bankrupt her.

"Don't worry about that," Zeke said. "I am sure we can work something out."

His voice softened with the barest hint of suggestion, and Rory drew back in alarm. Just what did he have in mind?

Before she could protest any further, they were interrupted.

"Mr. Morrison," the butler announced. "The police have arrived."

Rory felt her heart skip a nervous beat, and Morrison swore.

"They didn't get here so fast last fall when I caught

the burglar getting into my safe." He gave a sigh of pure annoyance. "Never mind, Wellington. I'll meet with them in my study. You look after Miss Kavanaugh."

"But what about my passengers? And my balloon?" Rory protested. "I really can't. . . ."

"I'll see to everything. You just run along like a good girl and do what you're told," Morrison said, striding away. He paused only long enough to instruct his butler. "Send one of the maids to help Miss Kavanaugh out of her clothes. I'll be right back."

"Mr. Morrison!" Rory said.

But having given out these peremptory commands, Morrison was gone. She wanted to charge after him, inform him that she didn't take orders as readily as his servants did. Yet it hardly seemed prudent to antagonize a man who had gone to confront the police on one's behalf.

Rory raked her fingers through her damp hair in frustration. She sensed Morrison's butler staring at her and whipped about to face him. If the man had been wearing a smirk, he was quick to stow it behind a deferential mask.

"If you would be pleased to follow me, miss."

Rory wasn't pleased, but she scarce saw what else she could do. She had no doubt that Tony was tracking the course of the balloon, probably half out of his mind with worry. But it might be hours before he found her, what with having to bring the wagon back across on the ferry, and make his way through the uptown traffic.

In the meantime, she could scarcely just stand here, dripping water onto Morrison's carpet.

"Lead on," she said to the butler with a gesture of weary assent.

As she hobbled up the stairs after him, Rory had to grit her teeth. The endless sweeping rise of marble did her ankle no good at all. She was almost sorry she had insisted that Morrison not carry her.

She all but sighed with relief when they reached the upper landing. The butler opened one of the imposing doors that lined the hall and bowed her inside.

Rory stepped cautiously across the threshold, schooling her jaw not to drop open at the sight of the mauve and gilt bedchamber sprawled before her. An imposing array of paintings, which would have looked more at home in an art gallery, hung on the walls. At the room's center stood a massive four-poster bed raised up on a dais. It could have been the state chamber of a king.

"Listen," Rory said. "Isn't there any place in this house a little less overwhelming? Maybe I could go down and sit by the fire in the kitchen."

But she discovered she was talking to herself, for Wellington had already disappeared, discreetly closing the door behind him. Rory could only shake her head over the behavior of Zeke Morrison. One minute the fellow had been threatening to throw her into the street, and the next he was having her ushered into a chamber like this as though she were an honored guest. Well, she had always heard that millionaires were eccentric.

Before Rory had an opportunity to take further stock of her surroundings, the door opened again to admit two maids in starched aprons. Rory assumed they had come merely to light the fire in the grate for her, but she quickly realized the young women had other plans.

One bobbed into a brief curtsey and then moved to deal with the hooks on the back of Rory's gown. "Let me help you out of your wet things, madam. Maisie will draw your bath."

Madam? Her bath?

"Wait a minute," Rory said, ducking away from the girl. "I didn't exactly bring a change of clothing with me."

"We will provide madam with a robe while your gown is dried and mended."

"But I'm not one of the guests here. . . ." Rory's protest slowly faded as she caught her first glimpse of the bathroom. The girl called Maisie was laying out thick towels while a cloud of steam rose from the largest clawfoot tub Rory had ever seen. Two people could have stretched out in it, side by side. And the water poured forth from a golden tap.

It was a far cry from her own chipped enamel basin, where she sat with her knees practically tucked up to her chin. Rory bit down upon her lip.

No, she couldn't. She should only be thinking of packing up her balloon and getting out of here. After the way she had wreaked havoc on Morrison's lawn, then quarreled with him, it hardly seemed right to be accepting any favors from him.

Yet what could a bath matter to him? He was clearly as rich as Diamond Jim Brady. He probably had tubs like this in every room. And who knew when Tony would get here? They could scarce move the balloon anyway until the storm passed.

Rory inched nearer the tub, trailing her fingers in the water. The steaming hot liquid felt as seductive as a caress. Every one of her aching muscles seemed to cry out to her, urging her on.

"Oh, what the hell," she mumbled.

She permitted the maid to help her undress without further argument. The two girls gathered up her discarded clothing and left. But Rory hardly noticed their brisk departure as she eased herself down into the bathtub, closing her eyes in pure ecstasy.

"Ahhh!" Rory leaned her head back, resting it against the porcelain rim. She stretched out for a time, enjoying a blissful soak. Even her ankle began to feel better. Then, with great reluctance, she forced her eyes open and reached for the bar of soap.

As she lathered her legs, she couldn't help but still marvel at the size of the tub, how her toes couldn't even touch the other side. Morrison probably had everything in the house designed to fit his own towering proportions.

She had no difficulty at all picturing him sprawling in the depths of a tub like this one, the way the dark damp hair would curl on the expanse of his broad chest, the water lapping against the tautly honed muscles of his belly and lower . . .

At the quickening of her pulses, Rory checked her wayward imagination with a hot blush. What was the matter with her? She didn't usually go about conjuring up images of men without their clothes on.

She began to scrub herself more vigorously, attempting to blot all idea of Zeke Morrison from her mind. But once she had allowed him to invade her thoughts, she couldn't seem to be rid of the man.

What a strange fellow he was. Somehow he didn't fit her notions of a millionaire, the kind Angelo was always reading about to her from the newspaper, who had a house on Fifth Avenue, racing yachts at Newport, a box at the Opera. With his quick temper, his hearty laugh, his burly shoulders, Zeke reminded her more of a stevedore or a wagon driver, rubbing down his horses, hanging about Tony Pascal's music hall, getting into fights of a Saturday night.

From his snapping dark eyes to that rock-hard jaw, the man bore an intensity about him that had made all those sedate guests of his seem as faded as last summer's flowers. And what was his connection to that Van Hallsburg woman, an icicle if Rory had ever seen one?

Obviously some sort of intimacy existed between them. Could she possibly be his mistress? Rory found the thought oddly disturbing. Even more than that—repulsive.

But the woman did seem well enough acquainted with Zeke to attempt handing out orders in his house. Mrs. Van Hallsburg might be belowstairs even now still arguing that Rory should be turned over to the police. Perhaps Zeke might listen. No. Quick-tempered Morrison might be, but somehow Rory could tell there was nothing mean-spirited or vindictive about him. On the other hand, that Mrs. Van Hallsburg . . .

A shudder coursed through Rory and suddenly her bath no longer seemed quite so soothing. The water had grown tepid. Clambering out of the tub, she toweled herself dry. Gingerly she tested her ankle, putting her full weight on it. Still sore, but at least somewhat better.

She reached for the satiny robe the maid had provided and shrugged herself into it, belting the sash about her waist. The garment, with its batwing sleeves, was in pristine condition, likely never worn and purchased solely for the intention of entertaining the casual overnight guest.

Imagine anyone being that rich they could hand out spare robes like bonbons. For a moment, Rory felt a twinge of wistfulness. Not that she envied Morrison the splendors of his mansion or even that fantastic bathtub. But she bet what he had spent furnishing this one room alone would have been enough to save her company.

Indeed Morrison could probably finance a dozen balloon companies if he wanted to. Pity she had made such a terrible first impression on him. She could well imagine what his reaction would be if she attempted to sound him out as a possible investor in the Transcontinental Balloon Company.

Now that you have seen exactly what balloons can do, Mr. Morrison . . .

He would either laugh in her face or toss her into the street for sure. With a rueful grin, Rory banished the absurd notion from her mind.

Making certain the robe was well-secured, she crept out into the bedchamber. Neither of the maids had returned yet, but she supposed it was unreasonable to expect them to have dried out her gown so soon.

Still, as the minutes ticked by, Rory came to regret her decision to part with her clothes. Being decked out in only the robe kept her a virtual prisoner in the bedchamber. The waiting began to seem interminable, and she grew anxious, noting the deep hues of twilight gathering outside the window, the way the rain still pelted against the glass.

What if Tony couldn't . . . No, she was being silly. Tony always managed to track the course of the balloon.

To occupy her time, Rory began to pace about studying the room's pictures, furnishings, especially that mammoth bed beneath its canopy.

Lord almighty, how did anyone ever sleep on such a thing? It would be like cuddling up for a nap inside of a museum. Rory stole a half-guilty glance about her. Although she felt like an urchin sneaking about in a palace, she couldn't resist.

She boosted herself up onto the bed and sat down, testing the springs with a small bounce. The mattress was firm, much more so than her own bed, worn so comfortably to the contours of her body.

Rory stretched herself out flat, arms at her sides, the brocade coverlet stiff beneath her. She stared up at the canopy looming over her head. No, definitely not conducive to a good night's rest.

But having assured herself that the bed was a thoroughly wretched place to sleep, Rory found herself strangely reluctant to move.

She hadn't realized until this moment just how tired she was. What a horror the day had been. She would be lucky if Dutton still paid her for that disastrous balloon flight. She would be lucky if she could mend the *Katie Moira*. She would be lucky if she didn't lose her balloon company after all.

Well, then, if luck was what it would take, so be it. The luck of the Irish, her Da had called it. If she believed hard enough, she would always find a way. The eternal optimism of the Kavanaughs. It was the one legacy Da had left her that would endure forever.

Smiling at the thought, Rory felt her eyes drifting closed and jerked them open. She really should stay awake. She would be embarrassed to death if anyone found her testing out the mattress. What if it should be Wellington or worse yet Morrison himself?

Yes, here she would be curled up in bed, clad in nothing but this clinging robe. The thought disturbed her enough that she struggled into a sitting position. She couldn't help but remember that odd light, that unexpected warmth in Morrison's eyes when he had gazed at her earlier.

What if he had planned this whole thing, to get her upstairs and in bed undressed? What did she know about the man really? No more than the rest of the world. Even the newspapers had dubbed him a man of mystery.

But she knew plenty about Rory Kavanaugh. For one thing, she couldn't imagine herself the object of any man's lust, especially not as she must have appeared to Morrison, about as desirable as a wet mongrel fished from the gutter. And for another, she knew she could handle any masher. Sometimes the lads who hung about her warehouse got a little fresh and she was quick to put them in their place.

Dismissing her fears as ridiculous, Rory yawned and lay back down. The thought did surface that Zeke Morrison might not be so easy to handle as the dockside boys, but Rory gave it only brief and drowsy consideration. Besides, none of that mattered. Morrison wasn't going to catch her in bed. No one was. In another few minutes, she was going to move. In another few minutes, she would thrust her head out into the hall and shout for the maid. In another few minutes . . .

In less time than that, Rory was fast asleep.

Three

The police were gone.

The blue-coated officers had been understandably annoyed to find themselves summoned out in the rain for no particular reason, but Zeke Morrison had placated them with a few jests and an invitation to enjoy the hospitality of his well-stocked kitchen. The policemen left with no further difficulty. Zeke was not surprised.

One thing he had always excelled at, he thought with a wry smile, was dealing with the police. The two-hundred-some guests, the cream of New York's social register, stuffed into his drawing room, were another matter.

Even from where he lingered in the hall, Zeke could hear the hubbub of voices. The accents, normally so well-bred, were raised in pitch, some of them even shrill with outrage and shock. But as flustered as his guests were, Zeke counted it an improvement.

Earlier that afternoon, he had been yawning behind his hand. All those perfect ladies and gentlemen gathered on his lawn had displayed as much animation as the marble statue gracing his fountain, that is until Miss Kavanaugh's balloon had come swooping down.

Since no one had been killed or seriously injured, Zeke could afford to be amused by the disastrous end to his fête. Aurora Rose Kavanaugh might be a spitfire and a little crazy to go flying about in that contraption, but Zeke had to give her credit for one thing. She had certainly livened up an otherwise dull party.

He supposed he ought to march into the parlor and play the urbane host, soothing, calming, apologizing. What he really wanted to do was to go strip out of his suit, and take a long soak in a hot bath. His wet clothes were drying to a state of stiff dampness that was blasted uncomfortable.

The suit was probably ruined, but Zeke hadn't liked it much anyway. His tailor had assured Zeke that the silk striped vest and close-fitting jacket would give him a dapper appearance, just like any of those young sprigs who had gone up to Harvard. But the transformation had never taken place. He had the tough exterior of a prizefighter, and his muscular frame threatened to burst the silk's flimsy seams.

Zeke couldn't wait to toss the suit into a heap in the corner, and get into something more comfortable. Surely he could leave the cosseting of his guests to his redoubtable butler Wellington and the charming Mrs. Van Hallsburg. This infernal party had been all Cynthia's idea anyway.

But even as he considered this appealing notion, Zeke frowned. If he abandoned his role as host, Mrs. Van H. would likely be even more irritated with him. Not that Zeke feared any woman's wrath, but he owed Cynthia Van Hallsburg a great deal for her help these past months in opening the doors to New York society. Zeke Morrison was a man who always paid his debts.

He reluctantly headed for the drawing room, but a situation arose that required more immediate attention. Someone was hammering on the front door. When a harried parlor maid opened it, Zeke was not altogether surprised to see a representative of the press standing on the doorstep.

Nothing of interest could take place at Morrison's Castle without bringing the reporters out in droves, and none of these newsmen was more persistent than Mr. William Duffy of the *New York World*.

Wellington would have been able to bar the fellow admittance, but the bold red-haired reporter easily slipped past the little parlor maid.

Duffy's sharp features lit up as he spied Zeke paused just outside the drawing room. He crossed the hall in three quick strides, his faded brown coat dripping rainwater with every step.

"Mr. Morrison! Just the man I wanted to see."

"I am afraid I can't say the feeling is mutual," Zeke replied. "What the devil do you think you are doing, barging in here?"

"Oh, Mr. Morrison," the parlor maid wailed. "I tried to keep him out."

"That's all right, Maisie. You go help Wellington with the tea. I can look after Mr. Duffy." Zeke spoke softly, but his voice had enough of an edge to it that the reporter took a wary step backward. As the relieved parlor maid scuttled off, Duffy flung out his hands in a placating gesture.

"I'm here on legitimate business this time, Mr. Morrison. I came to cover your party for my society editor." Duffy produced a small notepad and pencil from his inner breast pocket. He moistened the pencil tip with his tongue and affected to write. "Now let me see . . . What did Mrs. Van Hallsburg wear today—puce?"

Zeke glowered with disgust and snatched the pencil away. "Get out of here. Don't you have anything better to do than hang about my house and bother me?"

"No." Duffy grinned. "You are news, Mr. Morrison. The mysterious tycoon of millionaire's row. You can't just breeze into this town, buy up a whole block, build yourself a castle, and expect not to attract attention."

Zeke sucked in his breath with an impatient hiss. Without further ado, he collared the reporter and began propelling him back toward the front door.

"Ow! Watch the coat, Morrison. I still owe money on it, and I already damn near split my pants climbing your fence."

"You're lucky I don't split your head."

"All right then. All right! I didn't just come to cover the party. I was down at the police precinct and heard there was some sort of an accident out here—something about a balloon crash. Did you hire it for your party?"

"No. I don't provide my guests with cheap circus entertainment."

"Hey, what's wrong with cheap entertainment? I like it."

There had been a time in his life when Zeke would have agreed with him. That he had come across sounding like the kind of snob he despised only added to his annoyance.

As Zeke yanked open the massive front door, Duffy made one last desperate plea. "Aw, come on, Morrison. Do a fellow a favor. Give me a leg up in my career. Just one little interview."

He tossed out a spate of breathless questions. "Is it true you made your money running a gambling establishment in Chicago? What about the rumor that you were once a New York boy? How about the story that you were involved with gangs on the East Side like the Dead Rabbits?"

"You're going to be a dead duck if I ever catch you trespassing again." Zeke started to shove him out, but Duffy clung to the door jamb.

"It's raining buckets out there. You wouldn't throw a fellow creature out into a storm, would you?"

Zeke would and did.

Duffy went flying, but managed to regain his balance before he fell. Turning back, he glanced toward Zeke, his grin undiminished by the rain beating down on his head.

"Never mind, Morrison. I'll get my story somehow."

Turning up his collar, Duffy bounded down the steps, his cheerful exuberance quite unimpaired. As irritated as he was, a half-smile escaped Zeke. Duffy might be as annoying as a green-head fly on a hot day, but brashness and persistence were qualities that Zeke had always admired, perhaps because he possessed a fine measure of both himself.

Zeke watched until he made sure that Duffy did actually exit from his property, going through the iron gate and down the street.

Then he eased the door closed. Just as the latch clicked into place, he was startled by a cool feminine voice calling from behind him.

"John?"

He swiveled just enough to observe the woman haloed in the light of the hall chandelier. Everyone else might be damp and disheveled, but Cynthia Van Hallsburg was still a vision of perfection in her silvery-blue frock, the color somehow in tune with her white-blond hair, the pale blue of her eyes.

The Ice Goddess—that was the name the society columns had dubbed one who had long been a reigning beauty among New York's upper set.

There was definitely winter in the stare that she now turned upon Zeke. "What is the matter now?" she demanded.

"Nothing," Zeke replied easily, coming away from the door. "I was merely convincing Mr. William Duffy that I am not at home to callers."

"That reporter." She gave a shudder of distaste. "I suppose this whole unfortunate affair will end up in the papers tomorrow. Exactly the sort of publicity one most deplores."

"Oh, I don't know. . . . With a little digging, I suppose Duffy could find far worse things to print about me."

Mrs. Van Hallsburg frowned. Zeke had learned early on in their acquaintance that the one sure way of ruffling her ice-like serenity was to hint that some elements in his past were less than sterling.

This time she chose to ignore his comment. "You should go in now and attempt to placate your guests. Some of them are still very upset and demanding their carriages be sent for."

"Well, let them. I take no prisoners."

When his quip caused her lips to thin, Zeke relented somewhat, adopting a milder tone. "I'm sorry the party got spoiled. I know you worked damned hard to help me bring it off. But you can hardly blame me for what happened."

"I don't hold you responsible for what happened, merely how you dealt with it. I think you could have found far better employment for those policemen than having them gorge themselves in your kitchen."

Zeke rolled his eyes. So she was still harping on that. "Believe me, Mrs. Van H., there are far more desperate criminals in this city for the police to arrest than a bunch of circus people in a runaway balloon."

"Then what do you plan on doing with that circus girl?"

"She's already gone," Zeke said. "I sent her off with her husband, booked them into the bridal suite at the Waldorf for a wedding present."

"I don't mean her. I mean the other one, the one you had Wellington take upstairs."

Oh, *her*. Miss Aurora Rose Kavanaugh. Just thinking of her was enough to make Zeke want to chuckle. He could picture her so clearly, a little slip of a thing, barely up to his shoulder, yet squaring off, her fists upraised, ready to darken his lights, disheveled strands of silky hair tumbling before her flashing eyes.

Zeke suppressed his smile lest Mrs. Van Hallsburg misinterpret it. "Miss Kavanaugh is only waiting here until her assistant comes to take the balloon away."

"That sounds exactly like the sort of excuse my late brother, Stephen, used to give whenever I caught him with one of his inamoratas."

Inna— Zeke couldn't even pronounce the word, but he gathered the gist of it. "Whoa! Wait a minute. I only just met that girl today. I carried her into the house because she had hurt her ankle. She's only a kid, for heaven's sake."

Even as Zeke made this declaration, he was troubled by a memory, that brief moment at the foot of the stairs when Miss Kavanaugh's clinging gown had outlined some surprising and delectable feminine curves, revealing that she was not quite as young as Zeke had first supposed her to be.

Still, for all that, she had looked like a drowned kitten, certainly nothing to provoke such an outburst from Mrs. Van H. An outburst of . . . of jealousy? Given Mrs. Van

Hallsburg's dispassionate nature, the thought seemed ludicrous, but Zeke hardly knew what else to call it.

"Miss Kavanaugh nearly killed herself in a balloon today," Zeke continued. "I was only trying to be kind to her."

But he saw that all his assurances were fruitless. She clearly didn't believe him.

"In any case, I don't mean to be rude, but I hardly see where my intentions toward Miss Kavanaugh are your affair. I am *not* your brother."

"No, but I have invested a great deal of time in you, smoothing out your rough edges, attempting to bring you on in society."

"Well, Mrs. Van H., some investments just don't pay off."

"I am not accustomed to taking losses."

Zeke's jaw tightened, and for a brief moment, he wished he could be rid of Cynthia Van Hallsburg as easily as he had disposed of William Duffy. Something had been creeping into Mrs. Van H.'s manner of late that disconcerted him. It was as though the woman believed she owned him. Still, he owed the lady a lot of favors, so he strove to check his temper.

He rubbed one hand wearily along the back of his neck. "It's been a long day, Mrs. Van H., and this is getting to be a damned silly argument. Why don't you run along and have yourself a cup of tea with the others before you get me angry as well. It doesn't bother me to have a shouting match in the middle of the hall, but I don't think you would like it."

He forced a smile to his lips. He really didn't want to quarrel with her, but he had a notoriously short fuse. He terminated the discussion by stalking past her, retreating into his study.

The rain was still lashing against the latticed windows, but a cozy fire crackled upon the hearth. Above the mantel hung a serene landscape by Constable. The walls were lined with shelves of books, the spines uncracked. In the center of the study stood a large oak desk and a wing-back chair of green leather. The entire room was a subtle testimony to wealth, that Zeke could well afford to hire someone to decorate for him and had done so. But it revealed nothing of his own personality.

As he stalked over to a small cabinet to pour himself a much-needed whiskey, he realized that Mrs. Van Hallsburg had followed him. She closed the door behind her.

"I don't want to quarrel either, John," she said softly. "But forgive me if I am a little confused. You seemed almost delighted that that circus girl crashed down here, ruining what should have been the best garden party of this season. Even the Whitneys came. That was quite a coup for you.

"I thought you wanted to be something more than a vulgar adventurer who happened to strike it rich. You are so close to being accepted by the best families in New York. But I get the feeling you would throw it all away just . . . just on a whim. Sometimes I don't understand you at all."

Zeke said nothing. Thrusting his hands deep in his trouser pockets, he stalked over to stare out the window at the rain washing the glass. He didn't even understand himself. Yes, it was his ambition to be accepted by New York's sacred Four Hundred, the top of the social register. But he also had an unholy urge to thumb his nose at Mrs. Van H. and all her set, just the way he used to when he was a kid hawking papers on the street corners, making faces at all the fancy Dans rolling by in their carriages.

On days when he thought about it too much, he didn't even know why he had built this costly barracks of a house on Fifth Avenue, why he was trying so hard to be agreeable to people he held mostly in contempt. Perhaps because it was a challenge to see if he could get those blasted snobs eating out of his hand, a hand most of them at one time wouldn't have let shine their boots. Perhaps because having obtained all the money he could desire, he needed another goal. He had to keep running toward something. If he stopped for too long, he was afraid— afraid that he would notice the great emptiness that was his life.

What was it that Sadie Marceone had always told him?

Your dreams, Johnnie . . . those dreams of yours. Maybe they're gonna take you far. Maybe they're gonna make you rich, but they're never gonna make you happy.

At the recollection of those words, a crystal clear image rose in Zeke's mind of the careworn face of the woman who had raised him. Abandoned at an orphanage when only hours old, he had never known either of his real parents, so whenever he thought the word "mother," he thought of Sadie. He was unaware that his expression had softened, having forgotten Mrs. Van Hallsburg's presence until she said, "That's a nice smile."

Zeke was quick to wipe it from his face.

She rustled over to him and rested her hands lightly on his chest. "You can be so charming when you want to be. Why don't you ever smile at me that way, John?"

"*Zeke*," he complained. "Why can't you ever call me *Zeke*? You know I prefer it."

"And I have asked you more than once to call me Cynthia."

"It seems neither of us is destined to get what we want." He studied the face of the woman pressed so close to him. The merest hint of lines appeared at the corners of Mrs. Van Hallsburg's eyes. The lovely widow's age was one of the best-kept secrets in New York.

Zeke knew she was at least ten years older than him, and he had seen his thirty-fourth birthday last week. Still, she was undeniably beautiful, her figure quite good. He wondered why he didn't have any of the normal masculine impulses toward her.

He had never once thought of trying to take her to bed. While she fascinated him, something about her repulsed him as well. Perhaps it was her eyes. They were as brilliant as gemstones and almost as hard.

He caught her hands and eased her gently but firmly away from him. "I always thought you were after something more than my smiles, Mrs. Van H. What's in all this for you? You're not the sort of woman whose friendship comes without a price. But you don't need my money. Van

Hallsburg left you loaded. Yet I can't see what else I have to offer you."

"My dear John, you're so cynical and so modest as well. Let us just say that I regard you as an unbroken stallion, wild and rugged, but a thoroughbred for all that. As I have told you before, you remind me—perhaps too much—of my brother, Stephen. You even look like—"

She checked what she had been about to say, turning away from him. A shadow crossed her features, a brief second of rare vulnerability.

Zeke knew little about Mrs. Van Hallsburg's older brother other than that the man had met an untimely death several years ago. The lady did not mention him often.

"You must miss your brother a great deal," Zeke said rather awkwardly. He had never been good at consoling other people in their grief.

"Miss my brother?" Mrs. Van Hallsburg echoed the words as though mildly surprised by them. "Yes," she said slowly. "I suppose I was rather fond of Stephen."

Zeke thought he had never heard affection expressed so coolly. As though she realized that she sounded a little heartless, she hastened to explain, "Stephen could try one's patience to the limits. He was a complete devil with women, you know."

She gave a brittle laugh. "Actresses! Dance hall girls. He couldn't keep away from them. It was my great dread he would actually marry one of the low creatures."

"That would have been unfortunate, I suppose," Zeke said dryly.

"I would have known how to deal with it." She said this so quietly, but something in her manner chilled Zeke's blood.

She appeared to regret having confided even this much about her brother. "Enough of these morbid reminiscences," she said, giving herself a small shake. "I suppose I had best adjourn back to the drawing room, and try to convince everyone that the next party given at Morrison's Castle won't be quite so . . . enervating."

"Thanks, Mrs. Van H., but I should tend to that myself. You have done more than enough for me already."

"I don't mind," she said, moving toward the door and opening it. "Just as long as you do one thing for me, John."

"And what might that be?"

Mrs. Van Hallsburg paused on the threshold to glance back at him. "Make sure you get rid of that circus girl."

And although she smiled when she said it, something in her arctic tones almost made the low-keyed words sound like a warning.

As evening overtook the city, the rain finally stopped. All of Zeke's guests had at last taken their leave, most with polite smiles, some even with a weak jest, but Zeke doubted that many of them would be eager to come back again. At the moment, he felt too tired to care.

When he saw Cynthia Van Hallsburg off in her carriage, he breathed a sigh of deep relief. He and the lady had parted on amicable enough terms, but Zeke had deliberately held himself aloof.

Maybe it was time to start putting more distance between himself and the lady. Cynthia was the sort of a female who could cage a man, body, mind and soul. Zeke had avoided many traps of that kind, although he conceded Mrs. Van H. was more clever than most. He wished he could fathom more clearly her motives for befriending him. The conversation they had had in his study continued to disturb him.

Make sure you get rid of that circus girl, John.

Well, he didn't take too kindly to receiving orders from anyone, especially one that smacked faintly of a threat. Yet he convinced himself that he was making too much of the remark. Likely Mrs. Van H. had merely been exercising a woman's infernal prerogative. Didn't they always have to get in the last word?

Cynthia had been right in one respect. He was going to have to do *something* about Miss Aurora Rose Kavanaugh. When he noticed Wellington ambling toward the region of the kitchen, likely intent upon securing his own supper now that the hubbub had died, Zeke flagged the man down.

"Where is that little gal from the circus? Has she come down yet?"

"Why, no, sir. I put her into your room."

"My room!"

"You did give instructions, sir, to get her upstairs and get her clothes off, so I assumed . . ." Wellington gave a discreet cough.

Zeke stared at him, thunderstruck. His butler had leaped to the same wild conclusions as Mrs. Van H.! Anyone would think that he was some kind of a Bluebeard, ravishing every female that crossed his path.

"Sometimes, Wellington," Zeke said, "you have some very un-butlerlike thoughts."

"I am sorry, sir. If I made a mistake, I will see that the girl is moved at once."

"No, go on downstairs before your supper gets cold. I can take care of Miss Kavanaugh." Zeke sent the butler on his way with a weary wave of one hand.

As Wellington gratefully took his leave, it occurred to Zeke that he hadn't had his own supper yet. He longed for nothing more than to sit down to a nice thick steak and a nickel beer.

But first he supposed he was going to have to go have another look at that moppet of a girl everyone seemed to think he was so hot to seduce.

Four

On his bedchamber door, Zeke gave a brisk knock. "Miss Kavanaugh?"

No answer.

He knocked again. No response again. Maybe Wellington was mistaken. Maybe in all the confusion, the girl had already slipped away. She had sure looked scared enough to run earlier, when she heard that the police had been summoned.

The thought that Miss Kavanaugh might already have gone filled him with an unexpected sense of disappointment. Turning the knob, he shoved the bedchamber door open.

The room seemed dark, deserted, only the light of the lamp on the bureau breaking the gloom. Then something stirred on the bed.

"Miss Kavanaugh?" Zeke tiptoed forward. Yes, she was curled up on her side, nestled against the pillows, apparently fast asleep. He grinned and moved the lamp closer for a better look at her.

The light gleamed upon the silken cascade of her dark brown hair, which tumbled across the covers. Mixed among the strands was a sheen of red he hadn't noticed before. Thick lashes rested against her cheeks, which were pale with fatigue. For the first time, Zeke took note of the pert tilt of her nose, the almost perfect bow shape of her lips.

She was rather a dainty-looking little thing to be risking her neck, performing stunts in a balloon or threatening to mill down a man of his weight and size. Her courage roused Zeke's admiration even if he did think she must be a little insane.

His gaze traveled lower, over the silken robe, which had become disarranged in her sleep. The blue folds parted in a deep V, affording him a glimpse of her small, firm breasts, the dark crest of her nipples. She had cast out one leg, baring the smooth contours up to a shapely thigh, the rest tantalizingly concealed beneath the drapings of the robe. How warm and soft her skin would be to caress, more soft than the silk she wore. She was indeed a little temptress, albeit a most innocent-looking one.

Zeke experienced a familiar tightening of his loins. Damn! It appeared both Wellington and Mrs. Van H. were far more perceptive than he regarding the charms of Miss Kavanaugh. It was time to see about being fitted with spectacles.

He shifted the lamp back to the bureau, half-ashamed of ogling her while she slept on, peacefully unaware. Returning to her side, he reached down and gingerly tugged the robe into a more decorous position, covering as best he could that alluring expanse of limb.

Even at that slight touch, Miss Kavanaugh stirred, but she did not awake. From the tension that knotted her brow, Zeke became aware she was not enjoying the most restful sleep. Perhaps somehow she sensed him hovering and it frightened her. Maybe he ought to retreat, just let her sleep. But when she muttered something, then moaned, it occurred to Zeke she was caught in the throes of a bad dream, a dream that was getting worse, judging from the way she squirmed and thrashed about.

When a tiny whimper escaped her, he perched on the edge of the bed and gently shook her arm. "Miss Kavanaugh, wake up."

"No . . . no. Please!" She mumbled and resisted, flinging out her hand as though to ward something away, whether it was himself or some monster from her dreams, Zeke couldn't tell.

He shook her more firmly. "Aurora. Wake up! You're having a nightmare."

She sat bolt upright all at once, gasping for breath, her eyes wide open, confusion and terror in their depths. Her gaze roved fearfully around the chamber, then locked upon him. She shrank back at once.

"What . . . where . . . ?"

"It's all right," Zeke said. "It's only me. Remember? The idiot whose lawn wrecked your balloon."

Recognition slowly returned to her eyes, but she gave a shuddering sigh and continued to tremble.

"There's nothing to be scared of. You were only having a bad dream."

He couldn't resist pulling her into his arms. She stiffened at first, then clung to him in a way that roused a rare sense of protectiveness in him, a protectiveness he would never have felt toward any of those society misses who shrieked at the sight of a butterfly. But a girl like this one, brave enough to dare the skies beneath a scrap of silk and a puff of hot air—nothing should be allowed to frighten her. Ever.

Zeke cradled her tight against him. "No one's going to hurt you," he murmured into the silky softness that was her hair. "It was just a nightmare. There are no bogeymen here."

"It . . . it wasn't a bogeyman," she whispered, burrowing against his shoulder. "It was the fog and I thought . . . I thought the banshee was coming again."

Zeke had no idea what a banshee was, but he tried to soothe her, saying, "Shh. Forget about it. You're awake now."

"Yes, but . . . but it was so strange. When I peeked beneath the hood, it wasn't the banshee at all." Here she tipped back her head to peer up at him with troubled eyes. "It was your friend, Mrs. Van Hallsburg."

That startled Zeke a little. He had never thought Mrs. Van H. to be the stuff nightmares were made of, but he conceded, "Well, I guess she must have come off seeming a little like a shrew to you, but—"

"No! She's an evil woman."

"Sure. Sure she is." Zeke patted Aurora on the shoulder. "But you don't have to worry about her. She's gone now and so are the police."

This assurance seemed to calm her a little. She relaxed, resting her head against him once more. God, she was every bit as soft and warm as he had imagined. Her womanly curves molded against him as though she were made to be in his arms. Once again he felt his blood quicken. It had been a long time since he had embraced a girl like this one, smelling of springtime and fresh Sunday mornings. Perhaps he never had.

He was beginning to enjoy holding her, consoling her, a shade too much. Perhaps she sensed that herself because she tensed, then struggled to pull free. She bolted off the bed, clutching the robe more tightly about her.

She eyed Zeke in a wary manner, which annoyed him a little. After all, he wasn't making any effort to come after her. He was no masher, and she was the one who'd been caught snuggling on his bed.

"How long have I been asleep?" she asked. "What time is it?"

"Nearly seven."

She winced, then stole a look toward the windows, the pool of darkness beyond. "And Tony hasn't come yet?"

"Your assistant? I'm afraid there has been no sign of him. But I am sure I can make other arrangements for you." Zeke started to rise from the bed, but she seemed so skittish, he remained where he was, leaning back, propping his weight against his elbows.

She nervously fingered the edge of the robe. "Your maids haven't brought my clothes back yet."

"No, I guess they haven't. How's your ankle?"

"It's fine. You don't need to look at it," she said in a rush, retreating another step. "I'm . . . I'm just still a little groggy. I didn't mean to fall asleep."

"I'm glad you found my bed so comfortable."

"Your bed!" Her eyes flew open wide. "This . . . this is your room?"

"Yep."

She appeared ready to bolt for sure, either that or grab up the poker from the fireplace to defend herself.

Zeke didn't know whether to be amused or irritated. "I have only been trying to show you a little hospitality after your accident." He levered himself to his feet. "So I would appreciate it if you would stop looking as though you thought I was about to rape you."

She flushed bright red. "I'm sorry. It's just that this is all a little embarrassing. I usually don't hug strange men."

"Or steal into their beds?"

His teasing comment only seemed to add to her discomfort.

"I never meant to cause you such trouble," she continued. "You have been really nice, letting me use your bathtub and . . . and not turning me over to the police and all." She fretted her lower lip. "And I'm sorry that I shouted at you earlier."

"If it comes to that, I guess I wasn't exactly speaking in dulcet tones either. It's refreshing for a change to meet a woman who bellows back at me instead of bursting into tears."

This coaxed a smile from her. Zeke thought that he might be able to risk moving a step closer. "We got off to a bad start with this acquaintance, didn't we, Miss Aurora Rose Kavanaugh? Maybe we could just start over again."

"S-sure," she said, but she ignored his outstretched hand and took care to keep the dressing table chair in between them. Zeke didn't know what to make of her. She seemed suddenly as shy and innocent as his own stepsisters had been, all those good girls who trooped off to mass, carrying their missalets and rosary beads. And yet as a circus performer, Miss Kavanaugh could hardly be that naive, lacking in experience of the world.

Before Zeke could say anything more, a knock sounded at the bedchamber door. He opened it to find Wellington on the other side, bearing Miss Kavanaugh's gown. The butler's poker expression was more annoying than if he had been wearing a smirk. Zeke took the gown from him and closed the door in his face.

He carried the dress over to Aurora. She practically snatched it from him with an expression of real relief. She inspected the peach silk folds briefly and exclaimed. "Why, it looks almost as good as new. Your maids did an incredible job."

Zeke agreed, though he could not help wishing that for once his staff had not been so damned efficient. He would have liked just a little more time. . . .

A weighty pause ensued in which she stared at him expectantly. It finally dawned on Zeke that she was waiting for him to leave so she could get dressed.

"I'll send Maisie in to help you," he said.

"Yes, I would be grateful. Thank you. Thank you for everything, Mr. Morrison."

He nodded and backed toward the door. Why had it taken him until now to realize how pretty she was? Especially when she smiled, showing an even row of pearly teeth. He liked the way those freckles dusted across her nose; most women fought like the devil to keep the sun off their faces. He liked the quicksilver shade of her eyes, the way she met his gaze head-on, never fluttering her lashes like some fool coquette. And he definitely liked the way that blue silk clung to her curves—

Zeke brought his thoughts up short and reached for the doorknob. It scarce mattered what he liked. In a few minutes she would be dressed. When her assistant arrived, she would gather up her balloon and be gone. Likely he would never see her again. The thought left him feeling oddly let down.

He shoved open the door and stepped out into the hall. He had not taken two steps away, when he halted. He didn't know what was getting into him, but something . . . something just wouldn't permit him to keep on going. He spun on his heel and abruptly reentered the bedchamber.

She had started to remove her robe, but she snatched it back to herself with a cry of alarm.

"Uh, sorry," he said. "I just remembered something I wanted to tell you."

She cocked her head to one side, cautious, waiting. It made it more difficult, for he was not sure himself what he had come to say, but he blundered on, "I was just thinking . . . I haven't had my supper yet and I'll bet you're hungry too. Maybe you could leave instructions for your assistant to take care of that balloon and we could go out for a nibble at some little restaurant."

He could already see the refusal gathering in her eyes, so he hastened to add, "I could take you back to the circus myself after—in my carriage."

"I don't live at the circus."

"Well, wherever—"

"No, thank you, Mr. Morrison. I really couldn't. Besides the balloon, I have my passengers to see safely home and—"

"I've already taken care of them," Zeke interrupted. "The newlyweds are launched on their bridal night, and I even apologized to your little minister. Sent him off with a donation for his church."

"That was very good of you, but as to having supper with you, I still don't think . . ." She trailed off with a slow shake of her head, clearly doubtful of his intentions. He couldn't blame her for that. Hell. He was not sure himself at this moment just what his intentions were.

"Please," he said, groping for the words to convince her. "It would give us a chance to talk. I am very interested in—"

She tensed.

"In hot air balloons. I'd be fascinated to hear how they work. And I've never had the good luck to meet with a . . ." What was it she had called herself earlier? "With an aeronaut before," he concluded.

Zeke wasn't sure what he had said. He only knew it was the right thing, for her head nodded in reluctant agreement.

"All right, Mr. Morrison," she said. "I would be only too happy to tell you all about my balloons."

And her lips quivered with a strangely hopeful smile.

Zeke wasted no time in fetching his evening clothes from the closet and bolting out of the chamber, not giving Rory a chance to change her mind. Before retiring to another room to attire himself for going out, he sent the parlor maid upstairs.

Maisie helped Rory to dress with the same brisk efficiency she had exhibited before. Rory had no thought of resisting the girl's aid this time. She sat as docile as a child beneath Maisie's ministering hands, her mind preoccupied.

"What have you gotten yourself into now, Rory Kavanaugh?" she muttered beneath her breath, already doubting the wisdom of having accepted Zeke Morrison's invitation. To be supping alone at a restaurant with a man she had just met, why, only actresses and Hootchie Cootchie dancers did things like that. Neither of Rory's parents would have approved.

Yet this was the 1890s for mercy's sake. Suffragettes whose writings she read in the *Tribune* assured her that an era of new freedom was dawning for women. She couldn't be bound forever by the old-fashioned standards of her parents. She was the president of the Transcontinental Balloon Company. If there was any chance at all that she could interest a wealthy man like Zeke Morrison in investing in her company, she had to take it. Her father at least would have understood.

But as Rory settled into a chair so that the maid could brush out her hair, she pulled a face. Who was she trying to fool? Da would have already wanted to shoot Morrison for what had happened in this bedchamber, the way he had crushed Rory, half-naked in his arms.

But the man was only trying to be kind, Rory argued with herself, all the while feeling a heated blush steal up her cheeks. Comforting Zeke's embrace had been, the feel of his strong arms banding about her, holding her close. But too close for mere kindness, making her aware of his musky masculine scent, the sheer ruthless power of the man, the intensity of passions held in check within him like the skies restraining the onslaught of a summer storm.

And for one frightening moment, her own heart had pounded in rhythm with his. For one frightening moment, she had not wanted to wrench herself away. . . .

Rory gave an involuntary toss of her head as though even now she were forcing herself to resist Zeke's embrace.

"Did I hurt you, madam?" the maid asked, suspending the brush in midstroke.

"N-no. Please continue," Rory said, feeling herself color more hotly than ever. The girl resumed her work, trying to be gentle, but Rory's hair was considerably tangled from her nap.

It was all the fault of that blasted nightmare, Rory thought. If not for that dream, she would never have done anything so embarrassing as cling to Zeke. She had been foolish to allow herself to be so upset, but it had all been so close to one of her banshee dreams, only even more strange. The fear it had aroused still clung to her like a residue of silt, rendering her palms cold and damp. She retained such a clear image of the moment she had lifted the phantom's hood, only to encounter that woman's cold eyes glittering back at her, their expression hard, empty—like the banshee's eyes, utterly without mercy. Irrational it might be, but Rory could not help believing a little in omens. She was just as glad she would never see that Mrs. Van Hallsburg again.

As for Zeke Morrison, perhaps it would be far better if it were likewise with him. She could go belowstairs, tell Zeke she had changed her mind, that . . . that she had a headache. Except that she knew she would wonder forever if she had thrown aside her best chance to save her company, that she would always despise herself for a coward.

And surely she had been in far greater danger when she had been alone with the man in his bedchamber, practically undressed. She had survived that—except for a few disturbing moments. What could happen to her in a crowded restaurant?

The most Morrison could do was train the force of his magnetic dark eyes upon her, devour her with his gaze. And in that case she would make it plain to him he had best satisfy his appetite on the roast turkey.

She wasn't going to be dessert.

Long before Rory finished dressing, Zeke was already on his way downstairs, straightening the cuffs of his white cambric shirt, picking a speck of lint off the lapel of his black evening jacket. He actually caught himself whistling as he took the stairs two at a time, a strange excitement quickening through his veins, an excitement such as he had not experienced for a long time.

Wellington awaited him in the hall below, holding a silver tray.

"Has Miss Kavanaugh come down yet?" Zeke demanded.

"No, sir, but another caller has arrived."

Zeke afforded this announcement only mild interest. "Really? Who the devil would come bothering me at this hour?" He paced off several steps, glancing impatiently back up the stairs for any sign of Rory.

"It is a gentleman, sir. I took the liberty of showing him into your study." The butler trailed after Zeke, persisting until Zeke accepted the small white calling card laid out upon the tray.

Zeke gave the gilt-edged card but a cursory glance. Then he took a closer look at the name and stiffened.

Charles Decker, Esq.

"That's no gentleman, Wellington," he snarled. "That's a complete bastard. Throw him out on his goddamned ear."

Wellington rarely displayed any reaction to his master's profanity. But this time his brows raised a fraction. "I beg your pardon, sir, if I erred. But I did think that Mr. Decker's name was on the list of people that Mrs. Van Hallsburg said should always be received."

"This isn't Mrs. Van Hallsburg's house. It's mine."

But even as he snapped at his butler, Zeke knew he wasn't being entirely fair. For the past few months, he had allowed Cynthia practically carte blanche in ordering his social life.

Of course, she would say Decker should be admitted. Charles Decker was a prominent banker and an old family friend of the Van Hallsburgs. But like most women, Mrs. Van H. had no real understanding of the world of politics. Thus she was completely unaware of the more unsavory aspect of Decker's character.

Zeke crushed the calling card in his fist, annoyed that he should be plagued with the man tonight, but he said to his butler, "Never mind, Wellington. You look after Miss Kavanaugh when she comes down. Send her to me in the study. I'll see to Mr. Decker myself and it won't take long."

"Very good, sir." At his most wooden, Wellington bowed and stepped aside.

Zeke strode toward the study, trying to remind himself that he was supposed to be a gentleman these days. Gentlemen had more subtle ways of expressing their disapproval than using their fists.

The only problem was, he thought grimly, hurting some bastard's feelings wasn't nearly so satisfactory as giving him a good punch in the nose.

Zeke shoved the study door open. At first, all he saw of Decker was the man's homburg and gloves deposited on the desk's gleaming oak surface. Zeke's gaze traveled round the room.

He caught sight of Decker in the far corner. The man had taken down one of the books and was thumbing through it. Decker was a middle-aged man of medium height, his thinning hair parted down the middle and slicked with oil of Macassar. His pin-check suit hung well upon him in that dapper fashion Zeke's own tailor had tried so hard for without success. Decker's clothes suited him to perfection, but then, Zeke thought, a snake always fit his own skin quite well.

Decker didn't look up until Zeke slammed the door closed. With a deliberate casualness, Decker shut the book and returned it to the shelf. He ambled forward to greet Zeke, a pleasant smile creasing his features.

"Ah, good evening, Mr. Morrison." Decker extended his hand.

Zeke ignored it. "Good evening, Decker. What the hell do you want?"

Decker looked a little taken aback, then emitted a half-nervous laugh. "You don't waste time on the social amenities, do you? Mind if I sit down?"

Without waiting for a reply, he settled himself into an armchair in one graceful, fluid motion. For all Decker's suave manner, Zeke could tell the fellow was ill at ease. One foot, elegantly shod in black-and-white patten, tapped against the Oriental carpet.

Zeke perched himself on the edge of the desk. "Well?" he demanded.

The single barked syllable caused Decker to start. He recovered, his lips twitching as he struggled to maintain his pleasant demeanor. "I know we have our differences, Mr. Morrison. But I had hoped we could sit down like a pair of reasonable men and discuss—"

"Cut line, Decker. Why are you here and more to the point, who sent you? Boss Kroker?"

Decker stiffened with a semblance of affronted dignity. "Mr. Richard Kroker and I are certainly acquaintances. We are both privileged to be members of Tammany Hall. But I am not his lackey."

Zeke sneered, not troubling to disguise what he thought of both Decker's assertion and Tammany Hall. Its members might go prosing on about the defense of liberties and the American way of life, and hold their silly initiation rituals, dressing like Indian braves, but for all that, the Hall was mainly a political machine, efficient, ruthless, controlling New York for the benefit of the sachems. The old days of Boss Tweed were remembered as bad, but under Richard Kroker's rule, the city government had reached new levels of graft and corruption.

But Decker continued to deny that he was influenced by Kroker. "It was my own idea to approach you, Mr. Morrison. I am gravely concerned about a rumor that has reached me, that you have been supporting this man Addison."

"It's no rumor. It's a fact," Zeke said. "Stanley Addison is a bright young attorney, a good Democrat. He'll make a fine mayor, don't you think?"

Decker gave a taut smile. "Not without the support of Tammany Hall."

"There are other Democrats in this town besides your Tammany cronies."

"Not enough to elect Mr. Addison. He is a reform candidate. They never do well at the polls. If you persist in contributing to his campaign, you will be flinging your money away, Mr. Morrison."

"It's good of you to be so concerned about my purse. It's too bad you don't worry more about the city treasury, which you Tammany boys have a habit of dipping into."

Decker flushed a bright red. "That remark, sir, brings me to the real purpose of my visit. Your candidate Addison has been making similar libelous comments, flinging about unfounded charges of corruption and graft. Since receiving your financial backing, he has become even more reckless in his speeches. He has even made some slanders against *me*."

"And you, such an upstanding member of the community," Zeke mocked. "The Commissioner for the Public Weal. A very comfortable little sinecure. Profitable too. I can understand why you find Addison irritating, asking so many questions as he does, about what became of all the funds appropriated for new city parks, why, instead of libraries, the city gets more sweatshops and brothels."

Decker shot dramatically to his feet. "Sir, your insinuations are intolerable. In another era, such words would have been grounds for a duel."

"I'm a very old-fashioned fellow, Decker," Zeke said, edging off the desk, doubling up his fists. "I'd be more than happy to meet you round back."

As he took a step forward, Decker abandoned his blustering attitude. He retreated around the chair, resuming his ingratiating manner.

"Mr. Morrison, I am sure you are too fair-minded a man to accept all of Addison's accusations without proof."

"Oh, we'll get the proof, never fear. We'll dig it out if it takes every last cent of my own money to do so."

A fine beading of sweat broke out on Decker's brow. "I don't know why I should have been singled out for this abuse. I have been an alderman for years and discharged my duties well, I might add. Ask our mutual friend, Mrs. Van Hallsburg. Or . . . or inquire of any of my constituents."

"Such as these?" Zeke asked. Turning, he produced from his desk the one book in his library that showed signs of being well worn—Jacob Riis's photographic essay, *How the Other Half Lives.* Zeke held the book out to Decker, rifling through the pages. Stark images of poverty flipped beneath Zeke's fingers—the slums, the brothels, the nickel-a-cup rotgut liquor saloons. All those pictures in uncompromising black and white—the ragged children in the refuse-littered alleyways, the family of six cramped in one room, the withered old women sitting on stoops outside tumbledown tenements. All those faces so devoid of hope, which seemed to stare at Zeke, haunt him with images of a life he had once known, scenes too well remembered, places he had tried to escape from and just forget. . . .

Decker averted his gaze, refusing to look at the book. "I am hardly responsible for such misery, Mr. Morrison. On the contrary, I and my fellow members at Tammany Hall have done much by way of charity to relieve the sufferings of these poor creatures."

"Oh, indeed," Zeke said dryly. "You hand out turkeys for Christmas while you block any real social reform." He slapped the book closed and dropped it back on the desk. "No, I am sorry, Mr. Decker. I am afraid Mr. Addison will continue saying all those unkind things about you and your Tammany friends with my full support. With a little luck, we may even be able to arrange a congressional investigation into your activities."

Decker ran one finger beneath his immaculately starched collar. "You can't have considered, Mr. Morrison, the advantages you might find yourself from belonging to Tammany Hall. You have shipping interests. Arrangements might be made with customs authorities that you would find beneficial."

What little patience Zeke had had for this interview reached its end.

"Get out of here. Now," he grated. He scooped up Decker's hat and gloves and jabbed them at the man.

Decker took them, his fingers beginning to shake. "On the other hand, Mr. Morrison, if you persist in this course, you may find yourself in a world of difficulties. For instance, I hope your fire insurance is paid up. The volunteer companies can be so slow in answering a call—"

Decker's words were choked off as Zeke collared him.

"Are you threatening me, Decker?"

Decker's eyes dilated with fear, but he still managed to gasp, "Only trying to . . . to give you some good advice."

"You know what you can do with your advice." Zeke started to raise his fist, but Decker was such a pathetic excuse for a man, white-faced, trembling, a look of desperation in his eyes, that Zeke contented himself with hustling him to the door. Opening it up, he thrust Decker through it.

"And give my regards to the boss when you see him," Zeke said.

Decker made a last attempt at potshot valiance when he was out of Zeke's grasp. But he muttered so low that Zeke caught little of it other than something about "would regret" before Decker fled across the hall. Zeke slammed the door behind him. He assumed there was no need to summon Wellington. He doubted Decker would be tempted to linger upon his property.

Zeke turned back to the study instead, pushing aside velvet draperies to fling open the windows. Decker seemed to have left a bad odor in the air.

Zeke had met his share of thieves and con men in his day, shifty-eyed fellows who would slit your throat for a two-bit piece. The kind he most despised were the Deckers of this world, who hid their knavery behind a guise of gentlemanly respectability.

Still seething, Zeke flung himself down in the chair behind his desk and fidgeted with a glass paperweight. He supposed he needed to cool off a little, or he would greet Miss Kavanaugh like a snarling dog when she appeared.

It didn't prove too difficult to curb his anger. The more he thought about the session with Decker, the more he experienced a sensation of triumph. When he had first decided to back Stanley Addison, Zeke had his own doubts about what the young lawyer could accomplish against the might of Tammany Hall. But someone must finally have perceived Addison's campaign as a threat. Why else would Decker have been sent sniffing and groveling?

Addison probably ought to be apprised of Decker's threats. Not that Zeke expected much to come of them. Decker was a paltry fellow, but Zeke wouldn't put it past him to hire a couple of thugs to smash windows and that sort of thing. Scare tactics. But still Addison should be warned.

Zeke had reached for the telephone directory, preparing to do just that, when Rory finally made her appearance. She crept through the open study door with some nervousness, her pulses setting up an odd flutter. What was it about Zeke Morrison that so unsettled her normal sense of breezy self-confidence?

Perhaps it was because she had never had much to do with a millionaire before. But as Rory hovered on the threshold, she knew at once it was not the size of Morrison's bank account that intimidated her, but the man himself. The study was a spacious room, all oak paneling and leather-covered furnishings, but Zeke still managed to dominate the chamber.

He stood by a telephone box mounted on the wall, the receiver held to his ear as he leafed through the pages of New York's slender directory. Garbed in black evening attire, his Prince Albert coat contrasted with the whiteness of his starched shirt and high-standing collar. He looked

strikingly handsome, but the formalness of his suit somehow failed to civilize him. He still presented an untamed
appearance, dark and fascinatingly dangerous.

Detecting Rory's approach, Zeke glanced up with a smile
that seemed to pierce right through her. He beckoned for her
to enter, waving her toward his desk, where some paper and
an inkwell stood waiting. He indicated that she should help
herself while he continued his efforts to get the operator to
connect him to the telephone exchange of a Mr. Stanley
Addison.

Rory seated herself behind the massive desk with unaccustomed diffidence. She reached for a sheet of the paper,
fine cream-colored vellum with the monogram of J. E.
Morrison printed on the top in letters as bold as the man
himself. As Rory picked up the pen, she tried to think
how she was going to explain all of this to Tony, why
she wouldn't be here waiting when he arrived. He wasn't
going to like it, the idea of her going off to supper with a
strange man.

But then Tony often presumed too much on the basis of
old friendship, acting at times more domineering than her
father had been. After all, she was Tony's employer now,
certainly not obliged to account to him for her movements.
Thus assuring herself, she dipped her pen into the inkwell
and began to scratch out her plans for the evening in the
most unvarnished terms, directing him to convey the balloon to the warehouse, where she would meet him later.

As she wrote, it was impossible not to be aware of
Morrison's presence. He was so preoccupied with his telephone call, he appeared to have forgotten she was there,
making it safe to steal peeks in his direction. She didn't
mean to eavesdrop on his conversation, but it was hard
to help it, Morrison was talking so loudly into the speaking piece.

It was not Zeke's intention to shout, but as usual he was
finding the new-fangled invention he had installed in his
home a less than satisfactory means of communication.
Addison sounded far away, as if he were at the end of a tun-
nel, with static causing even more interference than usual.

"I said Decker came by to see me this evening," Zeke bellowed. "I think he's scared. Things could get damned unpleasant."

"What . . . ?" Addison's voice crackled.

"Things could get ugly." Zeke's own voice vibrated with annoyance at his inability to make himself understood. "Your windows could get smashed."

Addison's reply came in a garbled fashion that left Zeke barely able to distinguish every other word. " . . . not surprised . . . been uncovering something new . . . will embarrass more . . . not just Decker. Wait until you hear . . ."

To Zeke's intense frustration, he heard nothing but more static. "This is hopeless!" he said. "Why don't you just plan to meet with me tomorrow. The bar at Hoffman House. Four o'clock."

For a moment, Zeke thought he had been entirely disconnected. Then he heard Addison repeat, "Hoffman House. At four."

"Yes." Recollecting the absentminded Addison's habit of forgetting appointments, Zeke added, "And you damn well better be there."

When he rang off, he slammed the receiver forcibly back onto its hook. The noise startled Miss Kavanaugh, and Zeke vented some of his irritation by complaining to her with a half-apologetic smile.

"Telephones! The most useless device ever conceived. You might as well try to shout across town."

"I wouldn't know," she said somewhat wistfully. "I've never used one."

"They will never replace the telegraph or even a hand-delivered note. And speaking of notes, how is yours coming?"

"Oh, I've finished it," she said, folding the paper in half.

"Good. Just leave it there on the desk and I'll instruct Wellington to make sure your friend gets it when he arrives. Are you ready to go?"

Was she? Rory still wasn't sure, but she nodded, and slowly rose to her feet. His bold gaze raked over her in an appraising stare. She fought down a blush and lifted one hand to the neckline of her gown in a self-conscious gesture.

"Do . . . do I look all right?"

"You look just fine." The words were simple, but he pitched his voice to a low timbre that caressed her as surely as if he had run the warm rough tips of his fingers along her bared flesh. When Rory shivered, he added, "Of course, I know the temperature is dropping, so I thought you might be glad of this."

Turning, he reached behind him for a lady's garment that had been left draped over a chair. It was a black velvet cloak with two shoulder capes, trimmed with braid the shade of primroses. Rory had never seen anything so dainty or so elegant, but she eyed it dubiously. She couldn't imagine how a bachelor like Zeke Morrison would have such a thing in his possession unless . . . unless it had been left here by that friend of his.

When Zeke moved to drape the cloak about Rory's shoulders, she shrank back. "No, thank you. I really don't think I ought to borrow anything that belonged to . . . to *her*."

"Her?" Zeke looked puzzled for a moment, then understanding appeared to dawn on him. "Mrs. Van Hallsburg?" He laughed. "Believe me, I wouldn't have the brass to lend you anything of hers either. No, this cloak is merely a trifle I bought my niece for her birthday. She's a very good-hearted girl and wouldn't mind in the least your using it."

His niece? Even she was not naive enough to swallow that one. But she made no demur as Zeke settled the cloak about her, merely speculating on how many "nieces" a man like Morrison was likely to have. Probably a good many of them. That didn't trouble her as long as he didn't have any notions of adopting her into the family.

But he was behaving like a gentleman so far, offering her his arm in courtly fashion. Only the warmth in his eyes betrayed him. Rory prided herself on her ability to handle any situation, but maybe for once she was straying out of her depth. Yet no Kavanaugh had ever backed down from a challenge.

She allowed Zeke to link her arm through his, meeting his bold stare with an equally direct look of her own. She had had a most eventful day, but she had a premonition. It wasn't going to be anything compared with her night.

Five

The soft glow of incandescent lamps illuminated pristine white tablecloths, gleaming silver, sparkling crystal—all the elegance that marked Delmonico's, New York's premiere dining establishment. Here the fashionable set gathered nightly to sample the excellent cuisine, millionaires rubbing elbows with actors and politicians. No matter what newer, smarter salons opened their doors, it still was considered a matter of social necessity to be seen dining at "Del's."

Or so Cynthia Van Hallsburg had informed Zeke upon many occasions, advice that Zeke for the most part ignored. Delmonico's was a shade too fancy and sedate for his tastes, the food good but overpriced. So he could scarce say why he had chosen to bring Miss Kavanaugh here tonight.

As they crossed the plush carpeted foyer, she hung back a little, her pert nose crinkling in doubtful fashion. "Are you sure we should . . . I mean, don't you have to have reservations to get into this place?"

"No," he assured her. "Del's doesn't take reservations after six. They would keep you waiting even if you were the President of the United States."

With that, he caught the attention of the headwaiter, Phillipe.

"Ah, Monsieur Morrison." Phillipe made a smart bow. "So good to see you this evening."

"Good evening, Phillipe. Table for two, the best in the house."

"But of course, monsieur." The man flattered him with an unctuous smile that was at the same time a little insolent.

It was at this instant Zeke realized to his chagrin what he was doing at Delmonico's. He was showing off. Hell! He hadn't done that since the time he had nearly impaled himself on the schoolyard fence, doing handstands to impress Mary Lou Grosvenor.

Mary Lou had been suitably awed, but then it was easy to dazzle a girl when you were both only ten. Not so easy now. Had he managed to impress Miss Kavanaugh? He stole a glance down at her as they followed Phillipe to their table.

Those remarkable quicksilver eyes of hers registered curiosity at least as she made a study of Delmonico's main dining salon. It was a curiosity that was returned, although the occupants of the other tables were too craven to stare as frankly as she did.

The room was already thronged with black dinner jackets and females sporting more diamonds than could be found in the display case at Tiffany's. Although the hum of polite chatter and the sedate chink of forks against china never ceased, Zeke could sense his progress across the room being followed by a myriad of eyes.

"It's that Morrison fellow," he heard someone mutter. "Who's he got with him? One of the chorus girls from Casino's?"

The speculation didn't bother Zeke. By now he was accustomed to the interest he aroused wherever he went, but as she became aware of the whispers, Miss Kavanaugh appeared disconcerted.

Phillipe showed them to a table at the front, quite close to the large plate glass window. It was an excellent location, giving them not only a view of the square outside, but also most of the rest of the room. Yet Miss Kavanaugh looked flushed and distinctly uncomfortable as they took their seats.

As Phillipe bustled off to send a waiter to fill their water glasses and bring menus, Zeke leaned forward. "You know if you don't like this, Miss Kavanaugh, I could ask to be shown to a private room."

"Oh, no," she cried. "This is just fine." She snatched up the linen napkin and spread it on her lap, as though by laying claim to the spot she would resist any attempts to dislodge her.

Zeke suppressed a smile. So she was still skittish at the notion of being alone with him. Well, she needn't have worried. At Del's, they didn't let you close the doors of the private rooms, not even if you were married. But Zeke let the matter drop.

Settling back in his chair, he appreciated the scene unfolding beyond the window. Outside hansom cabs jostled for position at the curb, trying to deposit their passengers. The trees across the way in Madison Square Park cast mysterious rustling shadows, and beyond them, the lights twinkled, reflections of the great hotels, the theaters, the cafés. . . .

He noted that Aurora had begun to relax, enjoying the view with him.

"This is much better than Del's old location, isn't it?" he said.

She laughed a little at that. "I wouldn't know, Mr. Morrison. Where I come from, we don't mention Delmonico's for fear we might be charged for just saying the name."

"And just where do you come from, Aurora Rose Kavanaugh?" he asked softly.

"Certainly not from Fifth Avenue."

"Where then? I want to know all about you. It's not every day a beautiful woman drops from the heavens onto my lawn."

Both his interest and the compliment seemed to fluster her.

"We probably should place our order," she said, retreating behind her menu. This resembled the thickness of a pamphlet, with page after page of entrées listed in French and mercifully translated into American.

Miss Kavanaugh appeared capable of employing the menu as a shield for an indefinite length of time, so Zeke took matters into his own hands. He beckoned to the waiter and ordered for both of them, his own appetite dictating a list comprising vegetable soup, lobster salad, oysters scalloped in the shell and for the main course tenderloin with Madeira sauce, Lyonnaise potatoes, green peas and stuffed eggplant, with apple fritters for dessert.

"That sound all right to you, Miss Kavanaugh?" he asked, belatedly consulting Rory. From behind the menu, he could just see the top of her head nod.

Zeke quickly dispatched the task of selecting a wine, choosing not only a red Bordeaux, but also a bumper of champagne to be served beforehand. With that the waiter retrieved the menus and Miss Kavanaugh was obliged to come out of hiding.

Zeke shifted a small vase of flowers out of his way so that he had a more clear view of her face. Resting his elbows on the table, he glanced across at her and smiled. "Now where were we? Oh, yes, we were talking about you."

"No," she said. "I thought we came here to discuss my balloons."

"Balloons?" he murmured, his eyes tracing the curve of her lips. She had the most delectably shaped mouth, perfect for kissing. When that same delectable mouth pursed into an expression of impatience, he forced himself to snap to attention.

"Oh, yes, your balloons. Tell me, have you been with the circus long?"

She heaved a deep sigh. "Only one afternoon. I told you before, Mr. Morrison, I am not a circus performer. I have my own balloon company."

As a waiter trundled the ice bucket with champagne forward and began to discreetly fill their glasses, she reached for her beaded purse. The reticule had been retrieved for

her from the balloon's soggy depths. Consequently both
the purse and the business card she proceeded to hand Zeke
were a little damp.

Zeke was more interested in watching the way the lamp's
glow played against the silken curls of her hair, highlighting
that sheen of red he was sure gave the spice to her temper.
But he wrenched his gaze away long enough to glance at
the card.

Transcontinental Balloon Company

The name meant nothing to him, sounding like mere
fanciful nonsense. But the address of the company startled
him. It was located not far from the dockside where he had
once worked in his youth. He passed quickly over that,
moving onto the last printed line on the card.

"Seamus Kavanaugh, President," he read aloud with an
inquiring glance at Aurora.

"My father," she said, the word laden with a mixture of
sadness and fierce pride. "I never had the cards changed
after his death last year."

"I'm sorry," Zeke said awkwardly. "Not about the cards.
I mean about your—"

"I know." She cut him off quickly as though she did not
want her grief touched upon. He could understand that. He
had more than a few pain-filled memories of his own he
didn't like paraded in the sunlight.

She continued in a brisk businesslike manner. "I am
the president of the company now. We have been manu-
facturing and flying balloons for nearly seven years, Mr.
Morrison."

"How interesting." Zeke tucked the card carelessly away
in his coat pocket. "But do we have to keep on being so
formal? Why don't you call me Zeke?"

"Well, I . . . I . . ." She had seemed so self-assured a
moment ago discussing her balloons, but his request had
discomposed her again. While she fortified herself with a
gulp of champagne, Zeke pressed his advantage.

"And wouldn't it be all right if I called you Aurora?"

She made a face. "Good heavens, no! If you must—that
is, I am usually called Rory."

"But I think Aurora is a lovely name."

"You wouldn't if you had had to endure years of the neighborhood kids teasing and chanting 'Aurora Borealis.' "

Zeke grinned. "I will admit it doesn't sound very Irish. How did you ever come to receive such a moniker?"

"It was all my Da's idea." Rory paused and stole another sip of her champagne. This was not what she had come here to talk about tonight. The waiter was already serving the soup, and hardly a word had been said about her balloon company. Still, she supposed she must engage in some polite conversation, so she permitted Zeke to coax from her the story of her birth and christening, of how long her parents had waited for a child, of the pain and disappointment of so many miscarriages, of how her coming had been awaited with so much hope, so much fear.

Her father's worst dread was realized when it appeared she had been stillborn. Then she had taken her first breath, let out a lusty cry. At that moment, her Da had always told her, the dawn had been breaking over the city, the sunlight flooding his heart as well. Rose she would be called after the grandmother she would never know, left resting beneath the peaceful hills of Kilarney, but as for her first name, it could be nothing else but Aurora.

Rory picked up her soup spoon, feeling half-embarrassed by the time she had concluded this sentimental tale. She was surprised to detect a softening in Zeke's rather flint-hard features.

"Aurora Rose," he repeated. "Yes, your father was right. It suits you." ·

Rory blushed under the steadiness of his regard. She started to reach for her champagne glass and checked the movement. No, she must go easy. She had drunk enough of the bubbly liquid at Gia's wedding to know that champagne did odd things to her, made her quite light-headed. Why, she'd almost let Jim Petry, the butcher's boy, kiss her, and him with a face that could stop an ice-wagon mule in its tracks.

The next she knew she would be ready to embrace Zeke Morrison. Her eyes drifted involuntarily to the lean contours of Zeke's face, the sensual outline of his mouth. Yes, it was much easier to think of kissing Zeke than Jim.

Appalled by her own thoughts, Rory pushed the champagne glass farther away and concentrated on her soup. "And so what about your name, Mr. Morrison? I mean, Zeke," she chattered on to cover her own confusion. "Were you named after your father?"

It seemed the most harmless question, but one look at Zeke and she knew she had asked the wrong thing. A stillness came over his features.

"No," he said. His reply was curt, yet somehow bleak. Rory didn't know why, but she had the feeling that Zeke had never been regaled with joyous tales of his own birth. She had a sudden urge to reach across the table and press his hand. She checked the impulse just in time, squeezing her fingers into a fist and tucking it against her lap.

It would seem she had already had too much champagne. To presume that a wealthy, powerful man like Zeke Morrison needed her sympathy was ludicrous. By the time the waiter had removed the soup dishes, Zeke had already recovered himself.

"It's a dead bore talking about me," he said as though trying to excuse his previous abrupt response. "Let's hear more about you."

Rory felt she had said far too much about herself already. Instead, she steered the conversation back to her balloon company. All through the course of salad and hors d'oeuvres, she discoursed earnestly upon the potential of hot air balloons. Not only could they provide a pleasurable pastime, but they also could be used for voyages of scientific discovery into the atmosphere, or employed for military purposes, spying missions.

"During the siege of Paris," she said, "they actually used balloons to airlift important people in the government over the lines of the Prussian army to freedom."

"Really?" Zeke said, although his attention seemed more fixed upon the sizzling beefsteak set before him. Rory was obliged to suspend her enthusiastic lecture long enough to do justice to her own tenderloin. She was relieved to see the champagne being removed from the table, only to sigh when it was replaced with a sparkling red wine.

She knew she oughtn't to touch the stuff especially not on top of the champagne, but she didn't want Zeke to find her totally unsophisticated. Just a few sips, she assured herself, then took a large swallow to clear her throat.

"Of course," she said, "in our own country, balloons have been used extensively to—"

Zeke interrupted her with a laugh. "Do you ever think of anything else, Aurora Rose? What do you do with yourself when you are not risking your neck in a balloon?"

"Why, I-I-that is—" The question took Rory so much aback, she had to take another drink of wine to martial her thoughts. What did she do when she wasn't ballooning? No one had ever asked her such a thing before. It took her a moment to realize she had no answer. When she wasn't flying, she was planning flights, designing new balloons, thinking of ways to raise money. Except for her company, there wasn't much else in her life. Especially since her father had died.

This sudden revelation both startled and saddened her. She took a sip of the wine in a rather melancholy fashion. When she didn't reply, Zeke continued to prod. "A pretty young lady like yourself . . . you must have some other interests. Perhaps you walk out on occasion with—er, one particular fellow?"

Aha, Rory thought. So that's what he was getting at. She peered at Zeke owlishly over the rim of her glass. "I'm not promised or anything if that's what you mean."

"Good."

Rory blinked. The man was nothing if not direct, but she rather liked that about him. Still she had a feeling she was drifting into dangerous waters, that she needed to steer back to the safer ground of her balloons. Yet somehow she could not resist asking after a pause, "And what about you? Are you . . . are you and that Mrs. Van Hallsburg . . . ?"

"No. I'm not the marrying kind."

"Neither am I," Rory replied.

He smiled an odd kind of smile and held up his glass. "Then let's drink to that."

Rory obediently complied, clinking her glass against his although she was not exactly sure what they were toasting. But he had a glint in his eyes that made her feel more tingly than the champagne bubbles. She drained her wineglass and warmth coursed through her to the very tip of her toes. It was a most delicious sensation.

I'm getting a little drunk, she thought. She had enough sense to realize that, but not quite enough to resist. Zeke began to question her again, about her home, her family. She found herself telling him the most absurd things about life on McCreedy Street, how she slept on the fire escape when the weather got too hot, about spearing fresh pickles from the big barrel in front of Hoffmeier's Deli, how she liked to ride her bicycle on Riverside Drive of a Sunday.

She knew she was talking too much, but he seemed so interested, drinking in every word. Interested . . . and something more. That odd sad stillness had crept into his eyes again, a look almost of longing.

When her dessert was placed before her, Rory left it untouched. She had drunk too much and eaten too little, but she didn't care. She was feeling exceedingly mellow and strangely tender toward Zeke Morrison. When he urged her to tell him more about ice skating in Central Park with her father, she shook her head.

"You can't really want to know about all the simple things I do. Why, it must be completely different from life on Fifth Avenue."

"Yes, it is," he said. "It all seems so far away."

Far away? That was a peculiar way of describing it. But she let that thought go, more touched by how sad he sounded.

"It doesn't have to be that way," she said. "You're a millionaire. You can do anything you want to. You don't have to waste all your time in places like this—"

She broke off, horrified. Lordy, she didn't want him to think she was ungrateful, criticizing. But he was quick to take her up on her unfinished remark.

"You mean Delmonico's? You don't like it?"

"Well, it's . . . it's very grand," she said, feeling her face flush as red as the wine. "But . . . but the waiters do tend to hover a lot and all the other people . . ."

"Yes?" he prompted.

"They . . . they remind me of a flock of turkeys all stuffed and dressed for Christmas."

She feared he might be offended, but he laughed, his eyes twinkling with amusement.

"You are an astonishing little imp, Rory Kavanaugh. I thought all girls dreamed of being wined and dined at Delmonico's."

"No, that's not what I dreamed of," Rory said, then blushed again to admit that she had ever had fantasies of doing the town squired by a handsome beau, but she had. And Zeke would give her no peace until she told him.

She propped her chin on her hand, saying dreamily, "I always imagined supping at some quiet little restaurant, then going to the theater to see a melodrama. And after, perhaps going to one of the music halls, dancing my feet off until the sun came up."

"The night is still young yet, Aurora Rose."

The suggestive note in his voice snapped Rory out of her fantasy with a start. "Oh, no, I couldn't stay out any later. I have to get down to the warehouse. Tony, my balloon . . ."

But Zeke didn't appear to be listening. He signaled the waiter to bring him the check, then stood, extending one lean, bronzed hand down to her. But it wasn't his fingers that beckoned so much as the smile lurking in his eyes.

"Come on, Aurora Rose," he said. "Let's get out of here."

The dance hall that Zeke escorted Rory to was located at the lower end of Twenty-second Street. It was not one that he had ever frequented, but close enough to his former haunts to render him a little edgy. Chances were good he might run into someone who would recognize him from the old days.

So what, he thought with a shrug. He was hardly a wanted criminal or anything. As he leaped down from the carriage, he stared at the dance hall's brick frame structure, the light and laughter spilling through its open windows on the second floor. Zeke squared his shoulders like a prizefighter about to enter the ring.

He turned to help Rory down, only to discover she had already leaped from the steps herself and stood at his side. He wanted to tell her that maybe this wasn't such a good idea after all. But the lamplight haloed the radiant contours of her face, her eyes so bright and eager. He hated the thought of disappointing her. It had been a long time since he had wanted so badly to please anyone as he did this whimsical sprite of a girl. He already felt bad that he hadn't been able to gratify her wish of attending the theater.

Most of the plays on Broadway were well into their third act by now. He had thought of buying out one of the theaters, hiring the actors to start the show all over again, but he supposed that too would be showing off. The theater would have to wait for another night, but for now at least he could give her her dance.

Inhaling a deep breath, he offered her his arm. "Well, here goes. I probably should have warned you. It's been a long time since I did any dancing. I'm likely pretty rusty."

"That's all right," she confided in a stage whisper. "I'm not so very good at it either."

The night breeze tickled the curls alongside her cheeks, which were already flushed. Zeke suppressed a smile. She was a little tipsy from the wine at Delmonico's. If he had any conscience at all, he would take her home right now, but the thought of doing so caused him to feel strangely empty.

Instead he tucked her arm through his, tightening his grasp as though he feared she was some wayward Cinderella who might disappear at the stroke of twelve. He led her beneath the striped awning and into the dance hall. The restaurant on the lower floor was already closed up, the waiters upending chairs upon tables. But up on the second floor the sound of thumping feet could be heard, the strains of a band blaring out a polka.

As Zeke ascended the stairs with Rory in tow, he wasn't prepared for the wave of nostalgia that washed over him. Stepping across the threshold, he felt he could have closed his eyes and still mapped out that room. He'd been in dozens like it before with its bare-board floor, a little bar tucked at one end, the platform for the band. No, they weren't exactly Landers orchestra, but they could belt out a tune that set Rory's toe to tapping.

And beyond the couples prancing across the floor, making the rafters shake, were a group of young lads lined up along the wall, trying to look so smart in their straw hats, their slickly shined shoes, their best coats cleaned and pressed. Zeke had held up the wall in that same fashion himself once, ogling the pretty girls, casting contemptuous glances at the swells in the black tailcoats who sometimes came downtown to see how the lower orders went on.

Only now, Zeke thought wryly, he was one of the stiff-necked swells and the scorn-filled glances were for him.

"Zeke?" Rory's voice cut into his reflections. "Hadn't we better dance before we get trampled?"

With a start, he realized he had led her out so far they were interfering with the dancers.

"Yes, I'd guess we'd better," he agreed with a laugh, clasping her hand, placing his other at her waist. As they circled the room once, Zeke felt awkward, even though some of the movements were coming back to him.

As for Rory, she was poker stiff in his arms. It amused him to note her intense look of concentration as she counted out the steps. Amused him and opened the floodgates of another memory as well, a rainy afternoon in the sitting room of the old apartment on Pearl Street.

All gangly arms and legs, he had been trying to master the polka under the tutelage of his youngest adopted sister, Agnes. So sweet, so patient, lisping out the count in her childish treble while the eldest sister, Caddie, thunked out the song on the old piano, badly out of tune.

The middle sister, Theresa, had been reclining on the sofa, critical as always. "Hah! You'll never get the hang of it, Johnnie. You've got two left feet."

But Sadie Marceone had hushed her daughter, encouraging him. "You never mind what Tessa says, Johnnie. You just keep trying. You'll learn."

And so he had, going at it with that same dogged determination he threw into achieving every goal he set.

"A-one and a-two and a— ow!"

An outcry of pain from Rory snapped his attention back to her. It would seem he hadn't learned so much after all.

"Sorry," he said, apologizing for having stamped on her foot. He paused a moment to let her rub her ankle. When they attempted to resume the dance, they were more miserably stiff than before.

"Aw, the hell with the steps," Zeke said. "Let's do it our own way."

Rory glanced up at him, surprised at first, then flashing an answering grin. Surprisingly enough, they fared better bounding across the room in their own style. Rory matched him step for step.

By the time the music ended, their mad romp was accorded a smattering of applause from the other dancers. Rory's cheeks flushed a bright pink. Breathless and laughing, Zeke led her over to the bar for a drink.

Zeke tried to order a lemonade for her, but the bartender looked at him as though he thought he'd lost his mind. He had to settle for two champagne cocktails instead. He watched in some alarm as the thirsty Rory gulped hers down as if it were water.

"Hey, take it easy," he said.

"It's all right. We Irish have 'credibly hard heads," she assured him, then hiccuped. He smiled. Taking the glass from her, he prepared to lead her back out onto the floor as the band struck up a waltz.

It was then that the inevitable happened. He spotted someone from the old neighborhood. He could hardly pretend he didn't know her, for he nearly walked dead-on into the woman. She was one of Sadie Marceone's neighbors, living in the house on the opposite corner.

"Good evening Mrs. Jiannone," he said, suppressing a grimace. "And how have you been?"

She stared straight into his eyes. There was no doubt but what she knew him, but she turned and walked away without a word. Zeke didn't like to admit it, but the snub hurt more than any slight Mrs. Van H.'s fancy friends could have dealt him. Perhaps the pain came from knowing what Mrs. Jiannone must be thinking.

It's that worthless boy, the one poor Sadie Marceone took into her home, the one everyone said would turn out bad, the one everyone predicted would break her heart.

And they had been right. He had.

"Is anything wrong, Zeke?" Rory asked. She wasn't so tipsy that she hadn't noticed what had happened. Her eyes were wide with concern.

"No," he said. "I just made a mistake, that's all." He swept Rory into his arms and into the movement of the dance. After the abandon of their previous romp, she seemed suddenly shy, dancing at this slower, more seductive pace.

She tried to keep him at a safe distance, but as the night wore on, she let him draw her closer and closer, until if he had bent down, he could have laid the velvety curve of her cheek against his own. He was aware of nothing but how soft and warm she felt, the scent of her hair sweet and fresh even in the hall's stifling atmosphere. He wanted to bury his face against the silken strands, lose himself in her, lose all painful past memories as well.

As her slender frame swayed in perfect rhythm with his, she roused fierce desires, and a gentler emotion he refused to examine more closely. He only knew he could hold her like this forever.

He didn't want this night to end. But why did it have to? He had sacrificed a great deal on the road to accumulating his riches, lost the respect of the only people he had ever cared about, lost the only real home he had ever known. If being wealthy couldn't get you what you wanted, then what was the good of it anyway?

And he wanted Aurora Rose Kavanaugh. A voice inside him cautioned him to go slow, to take it easy. But he had never been a patient man. If life had taught him one thing, it was that nothing was given freely. If you wanted something, you had to go after it, take it.

Rory was too caught up in the magic of the music herself to be aware of the tension coiling in Zeke. She hummed along with the band. As Zeke whirled her in a circle, a warning sounded in her mind that she should not let him hold her so close, but the warnings were getting fainter all the time.

Zeke's arms were so sure, so strong, the only secure place in a world that spun giddily before her eyes. They might have been alone, dancing together in the dark, everything else so far away, the other couples, his mansion on Fifth Avenue, her balloon company. Only this moment seemed real, this man who held her so tight.

Tipping back her head, she stole a glance up at him. Even in the dim light of the dance hall, she could tell he was smiling at her. The lines about his eyes crinkled, the eyes themselves dark pools of mystery.

Rory stumbled a little, then giggled. "I'm awfully sorry. I guess my head's not so hard after all. You must think I'm a fool."

"What you are is a breath of fresh air."

"Pooh," she said. "More like a big wind, flattening your lawn."

He laughed and the rich deep sound seemed to echo through her heart. "No, you are the best thing that has happened to me in an age."

"You didn't think so at first. You wanted to toss me into the streets, remember?"

"That was because I was getting stuffy, as stuffy as those swells mincing about my lawn."

She could not help but laugh at that, and when he spun her about in another slow, languorous circle, she felt absurdly happy. She scarce knew when the band finished up its last melody, or how Zeke guided her from the dance hall back to the street.

To her astonishment the sky over the city was already lightening to a hue of pearly gray.

"The sun's up," she crowed. "Zeke, we made it. We danced all night."

"So we did." His voice was laced with indulgence as he handed her up into his awaiting carriage. The landau was one of those open sporting vehicles, but Zeke had the folding top raised into position.

Rory settled back gratefully beneath its shadowy depths. Zeke vaulted inside, but he did not sit decorously opposite as he had earlier. He squeezed beside her, and she was glad of the warmth emanating from his long, muscular frame. Even with her cloak, the morning air was chill and her head suddenly felt so heavy.

Zeke's shoulder was just the right height for nestling, and she didn't even try to resist. As she settled against him, he wrapped one arm about her.

The carriage sprang into motion, and swayed by the gentle rocking, Rory closed her eyes. She sang softly snatches of "My Wild Irish Rose," only stopping to murmur, "Dawn comes too soon over New York."

"Yes, it does," Zeke agreed. He gathered one of her hands into the warmth of his own. "Rory, there . . . there is something I want to say."

He paused to exhale a deep breath. "I have a proposition to make to you."

Proposition? The word sounded so businesslike. Vague remembrance drifted through Rory's head of her original purpose in coming out with Zeke tonight. But she had spent very little time talking about her company. She supposed she had tossed away any chance to recruit him as an investor. Therefore he surprised her greatly by saying, "I am willing to make any settlement upon you that you would name."

"Settlement?" she repeated. "Is that the same as . . . as money?"

"Well, yes. . . ."

Money? Money for her balloon company. It would seem she had made an impression upon Zeke after all. Despite the champagne still fuddling her brain, she managed to pull herself into an upright position.

"Oh, Zeke," she cried. "You've made me so very happy."

Overcome with her joy, she flung her arms about his neck. Zeke was not slow to respond, straining her close.

"Not nearly so happy as you have made me, Aurora Rose," he murmured, pressing light kisses against her hair.

It came as a shock to Rory when his lips found hers. She stiffened at first, startled by the contact, the unexpected kiss tearing through her like a flash of lightning. His mouth tasted of wine, so hot, so moist, so seductively sweet. Then what was sweet, what was gentle became fire, the dammed-up passion she had sensed in Zeke breaking free.

And God help her, the fever seemed to have spread to her, licking through her veins with tongues of flame. She had buried her fingers in Zeke's hair and caught herself returning the kiss with equal fierceness when she broke off, panting.

In some dim corner of her mind, it occurred to her that this was not the usual handclasp with which business contracts were sealed. But it was difficult to reason anything clearly with Zeke continuing his assault. His lips grazed against her temples, her cheeks, her chin, moving down to caress the column of her throat.

"Oh, Rory," he said. "I'll give you anything you want. A flat in Morningside Heights, your own carriage, a box at the theater, an account at Bloomingdale's."

"I . . . I don't need all that," she managed to quaver. "Just enough to keep me from being evicted from the warehouse."

Zeke's lips paused, a breath away from claiming hers again. "Warehouse?"

"Yes, and Zeke . . ." She stared deep into those fathomless dark eyes and managed to say somewhat unsteadily,

"I . . . I'm not sure prospective business partners should behave this way."

He frowned, drawing back. "Warehouse? Business partners? What are you talking about?"

"Why . . . why, I'm not so sure. What are *you* talking about?"

"I am asking you to become my mistress."

His mistress! Rory jerked away, thunking her head against the back of the seat.

"We did agree that neither of us is the marrying kind," Zeke said.

"Yes, but mistresses . . . marriage." Rory rubbed her eyes, feeling as if she were groping her way through a fog of confusion. "But . . . but I thought . . . what about my balloons?"

"You don't have to bother about them anymore. I wouldn't want you to keep on risking that beautiful neck." He stroked his fingers through the fall of her hair, brushing it back from her face. "Look, Rory, I know I'm no good at saying all the words a woman needs to hear. I guess I've been too blunt. All I can tell you is that I want you, possibly more than I've ever wanted any woman before."

"Possibly?" she echoed, the full import of what he was saying finally sinking in. It had the sobering effect of a cold water bath. She did not know what outraged her more, the brusque manner of his proposal or his careless dismissal of her balloon company.

"Of all the . . . the gall, the . . . the conceit." She spluttered, unable to find words strong enough to convey her indignation. "What the devil makes you think I would give up my balloons to become your mistress?"

He smiled at her then and began to draw her back into his arms. His expression was tender, but smug enough to snap Rory fully to her senses. Before he could kiss her again, she punched, clawed and kicked to be free. He released her so suddenly she toppled to the floor of the carriage.

Her lips still felt branded from the heat of his first kiss, even more so by her own response. What was the matter with him, behaving like this with a woman he'd just met, practically a stranger? More to the point, what was the matter with her? Even now, in the midst of her anger, she felt drawn to him.

He reached down to haul her back onto the seat. "Come on, Rory," he said, his voice cool, but the fire still smoldering in his eyes. "There's no sense being coy about this. That first kiss told me all I need to know."

Rory struck his hand away. "You . . . you're crazy!" she gasped, glaring at him through the tangle of her hair.

At that moment, the landau was obliged to give way to another vehicle crossing the intersection. Rory saw her chance and took it. As the carriage slowed, she flung open the door and rolled out to the pavement.

Encumbered by her skirts, she barely managed to land on her feet. Regaining her balance, she hiked up her hem past her ankles and tore off down the sidewalk.

"Rory!"

She heard Zeke shout her name, but she didn't look back. The sound of pounding feet told her that he was coming after her. She pushed harder, lengthening her strides although she was no longer sure whom she was running from, Zeke or herself.

He'd have done better to have pursued me in the carriage, Rory thought. Ever since her grammar school days, she had been able to outdistance any boy on her block.

But luck turned against her as she whipped round the next corner. A loose cobblestone caused her to stumble, twisting the same ankle she had injured earlier. She let out a cry and a curse as the familiar throbbing pain shot through her limb.

Gasping for breath, she glanced wildly along the vacant street. Not a horsecar in sight at this time of morning. Not much of anything in sight but a milk wagon making its rounds.

Rory hobbled forward, hailing the driver, a genial-looking old man with side whiskers. "Hey, mister. Could you give me a ride?"

The man appeared surprised to be accosted by a young woman in a silk gown and evening cloak, but he replied good-naturedly, "Well sure, but . . ."

"Thank you." Rory wasted no time scrambling up on the box. "Can we please go? I'm in something of a hurry."

At that instant Zeke came charging round the corner, looking as mad as thunder. The milkman nodded as though in comprehension of the situation.

"Why, the dirty masher! We'll give him a run for his money. Pestering innocent girls." The old man clicked both his tongue and the reins. The ancient brown nag hitched in the traces took off with an astonishing burst of speed.

So did Zeke. For one awful moment, Rory thought he might catch up to them. He managed to race alongside, his face flushed with the exertion, his lower lip caught in grim determination. In another second, he would be able to catch hold of the wagon, haul himself aboard.

In desperation, Rory loosed the cloak from her shoulders. Just as Zeke's hand closed over the wagon's wooden side, she flung the garment, catching him neatly over the head. Tangled in the cloak's folds, Zeke lost his grip, staggering back.

By the time he managed to extricate himself, he had lost any chance of overtaking Rory. Her last glimpse was of him standing planted in the middle of the road, hands propped on his hips. She couldn't make out what he was shouting at her, but that was likely just as well.

Rory sank back against the wagon seat, heaving a tremulous sigh of relief.

"There, that's all right, missy," the old wagon driver chuckled. "We diddled that young spark real proper. You won't be bothered by him anytime soon, I'll wager."

Rory said nothing. She didn't feel like betting on that. A presentiment stole over her, stronger than any of her banshee dreams. Somehow she knew she had not seen the last of Zeke Morrison.

Six

It was late afternoon by the time Zeke arrived at the Hoffman House Hotel for his meeting with Stanley Addison. One look at his face and most of the bellboys had the sense to stay clear of his path. Behind him, Zeke heard two of them whispering.

"Say, what d'ya think is the matter with Mr. Morrison? That scowl on his face is enough to wilt the daisies."

"Aw, you know these big tycoons. Fretting about their money all the time. Probably one of his deals went sour. I'm glad I got no such worries."

"Yeah, ain't we the lucky ones!"

The pair of them clammed up at once when Zeke turned and shot them a killing glare. With nervous smiles, the bellboys hustled off to their task of gathering up the baggage of the incoming guests.

Which was just as well, Zeke thought, or he might have been tempted to bellow at the nosy pair. No, fellows, his problem wasn't money. It was that other root of all evil—a woman.

As Zeke crossed the hotel's plush lobby, heading for the bar, his black mood showed no signs of lifting. He never figured himself for the kind of fool that would waste much energy in moping over some female.

When Rory had escaped from him earlier that morning, he had sworn and said good riddance. If she didn't want him, all she had to do was tell him no. She didn't need to go haring off as if he were Jack the Ripper.

He had taken himself off home and gone to bed. But after a few hours' restless sleep, he had arisen, still irritable but more angry with himself than her. What an ass he had made of himself. Why, he'd never chased a woman through the streets before, not even in the wild days of his youth. For the first time, he began to entertain the suspicion that he might be the one to blame for the disastrous end to what had otherwise been an enchanted evening. Perhaps he had misinterpreted her response to his kiss. Perhaps he had misunderstood her remark about not wanting to be married. Perhaps. . . .

Oh, what difference did it make? Zeke adjured himself wearily. Rory had exited out of his life as abruptly as she had made her entrance. It was best just to forget her. He ought to be thinking of nothing but his upcoming appointment with Addison.

Shoving open a large door, in which was an oval of frosted glass, Zeke entered the hotel bar. He was already having misgivings about his choice of a site for the meeting. If Addison did have some explosive new information about Decker and his cronies, as the garbled phone conversation had indicated, then it might have been better to talk in a more private place.

Mrs. Van H. had always told Zeke he should join one of the exclusive gentleman's clubs. They afforded excellent settings for discreet business chats. Zeke had actually gone so far as to put in an application with the Union Club, but after he had punched out a fellow down on Twenty-second Street for smacking some poor girl, Zeke's application had been politely refused. It seemed the club's august members didn't approve of brawling in the streets, not even for the most chivalrous of motives.

The hell with them then, Zeke had thought. As he glanced

around the Hoffman House bar, he saw that it would do just as well. The crowd that usually flocked to the place to sample the bar's sumptuous free lunch—well, free except for the cost of a beer—were all long gone.

Two men lingered in a table by the corner, drummers by the look of them, with their natty attire and overstuffed valises full of sales samples. Other than that, the place was empty except for the bartender polishing glasses behind the counter.

The tips of his handlebar mustache waxed to perfection, a red garter banding one sleeve of his shirt, James P. Mulgrew flashed Zeke a welcoming smile.

"Afternoon, Mr. Morrison. Been a long time since we've seen you in here. How's life in the castle?"

"Tolerable, Mulgrew." Zeke leaned up to the bar, resting one foot on the brass railing.

"Your usual, sir?"

Zeke nodded, and the man scooped up a mug, turned on the tap, filling it up to the rim with a frothing cold beer. He slid it in front of Zeke with a practiced efficiency.

"Thanks," Zeke muttered. He drew forth his pocket watch and consulted it. Quarter after four. He was a little late, but trust Stanley Addison to be later still, he thought with a frown.

Mulgrew seemed to sense that Zeke was not in the mood for idle chatter. He busied himself at the other end of the bar, for which Zeke was grateful. Funny how the bartender at Hoffman House could still read his moods. It had been over two years since Zeke had lived at the hotel while his house on Fifth Avenue was under construction.

He had rented a suite of rooms on the fifth floor when he had returned from his self-imposed exile in Chicago. He had been gone a long time—eight years. New York had changed a lot and so had he. He hadn't been at all sure of the reception he would get back at the little flat on Pearl Street.

But Sadie Marceone had wept with joy to see him, a joy that hadn't lasted long. You would have thought she would have been glad to see him returned so successful after the mess he had made of his life in New York. Far from being impressed with his wealth, she had been almost frightened of it. He had to assure her he hadn't been robbing banks or anything. No, he had made a killing on the market, several good speculations that had paid off. He didn't tell her he had gotten his initial stake from working a gambling salon in Chicago. She would neither have understood nor approved of that. Instead he outlined his future plans, a real estate investment that he had gotten wind of that promised to double his wealth.

The little he did confide made her less than happy. "Money. God help you, Johnnie, that's all you talk about. It's made you so hard, driven, like nothing else matters, like getting more money is all that life is about."

"Well, I know a man can die from the lack of it," he had retorted. *Or a woman.* She had gotten much older since he had left, more worn, more gray from her own struggle with poverty. He had wanted then and there to take her away from that wretched flat, install her in a grand house on the avenue. All she had wanted was to go to the church, light a candle, pray for his soul. . . .

Zeke drained his mug, trying to shrug off the remembrance, which was as bitter as the dregs at the bottom of his glass. He called for a refill, then noticed that someone else had entered the bar while he had been lost in his memories. Unfortunately it wasn't Stanley Addison.

Zeke stiffened at the sight of the shock of red hair that was becoming like a beacon for trouble. Bill Duffy lounged up against the bar only a few feet away from him. When he caught Zeke's stare, the reporter had the brass to grin at him.

"You're getting to be a nuisance, you know that, Duffy?" Zeke growled.

"Hey, this meeting is purely coincidental." Under Zeke's skeptical gaze, Duffy abandoned his look of wide-eyed innocence. "Would you believe I trailed you here from Forty-ninth Street?"

Zeke gave a snort of disgust. While Mulgrew refilled his glass, Duffy also put in an order for a beer. The bartender plunked it down in front of him, but apparently wary of extending the reporter any credit, he demanded instant payment.

Mulgrew's caution was justified. Duffy turned out his pockets. Except for a stray button, he came up empty-handed.

"Oh, just set it down to Mr. Morrison's account," he said.

When Mulgrew cast a dubious glance at him, Zeke grimaced, then nodded his head. Duffy was an infernal pest, but his sheer bravado roused a grudging admiration in Zeke.

He was less than pleased when Duffy grabbed up his mug and edged closer.

"All right, you've got your drink," Zeke said. "Now go sit down somewhere. I warn you now I am in no mood to be badgered with questions."

"No questions, just a friendly chat. I thought you might want to see this." Duffy dropped a folded newspaper on the bar in front of Zeke. From the banner at the top, Zeke could tell it was the afternoon edition of the *New York World*.

"My story's in there about that little excitement at your party yesterday. *Balloon Girl Invades High Society*. Not exactly front-page stuff, but they let me have a whole column."

Duffy started to unfold the paper, but Zeke checked the motion. The last thing he wanted was to see anything that would remind him of Aurora Rose Kavanaugh. Zeke started to thrust the edition away, then stopped, his eye caught by a headline on the front page.

Reform Candidate Promises Congressional Investigation. Above the caption was a grainy picture of Stanley Addison. Despite the stilted pose, the photographer had managed to capture the young lawyer's idealistic expression.

"What the—," Zeke said, snatching the paper closer.

"My story is on page five. What are you looking at?" Duffy crowded in closer. "Oh, that story Baxter did on Addison? Not bad. I mean Baxter's a nice enough fellow, but the editor always has to clean up his copy. I taught him all he knows."

But Zeke ignored Duffy's chatter, concentrating on the article.

In an interview yesterday, Stanley Addison stated he has uncovered startling new facts in his investigation of slum conditions in the area known as Five Points.

"Deeds have come to light, revealing true ownership of a series of sweatshops, brothels and gambling houses on Grant Avenue," Addison informed this reporter. "I also now have definite proof that the illegal activities of these operations were financed by funds misappropriated from the City treasury and protected by payoffs to the police department."

Although Addison declined to name any names at this point, he hinted that his evidence would incriminate several government officials and some respected members of society as well. He declared that he would demand a special judicial committee be formed to examine his documents and hand down indictments.

Mr. Addison, who has declared his candidacy in the upcoming mayoral race . . .

The rest of the article merely went on to discuss Addison's political aspirations and his legal background. Zeke skimmed through it, then crunched the paper in his hand.

"Why, that young jackass!"

"Who? Baxter?" Duffy asked.

"No, Addison!" Zeke slapped the paper back down on the counter. Whatever had possessed the fool to go spouting off to a reporter before he had had his talk with Zeke? Addison was a good man, but an idealist, tending to get swept away. He hadn't yet learned that it was seldom wise to let your opponents see all your cards before you played them. True, he had been sensible enough to mention no names, but Charles Decker would know who was meant. Decker and his friends would have plenty of time to dive for their attorneys, start preparing a defense.

The more Zeke thought about Addison's folly, the more it angered him, and he swore.

"I don't see what was in that story to get *you* so mad," Duffy said. "I thought Addison was a friend of yours. You're backing his campaign, aren't you?"

"I'll be more likely to break his neck."

Duffy's eyes lit up with speculation, and his nose practically twitched, as though he were scenting a story here. Zeke could almost see the headlines chasing through Duffy's mind. *Millionaire Backer Threatens Reform Candidate.*

That was the last kind of press Addison needed. Zeke could see he had a problem here. The meeting between himself and Addison already promised to be heated enough without Duffy hanging about, all ears. He needed to be rid of the reporter before Addison arrived.

Yet Duffy was a shrewd fellow. Sending him off without arousing his suspicion would be difficult. Zeke attempted simply to turn a cold shoulder on the man, becoming taciturn, but Duffy was more persistent than a horsefly.

He badgered Zeke with questions about Addison and about Zeke's own background. Zeke's patience was wearing thin when help came from an unexpected corner.

Mulgrew snarled that if Duffy didn't cease pestering the hotel's customers, he'd summon a policeman. "I'll have you run in for . . . for loitering and panhandling drinks."

"Bah!" Duffy said. "If there was a law against that, half of Manhattan would be in jail."

But when Mulgrew made a menacing move to come round the bar, Duffy flung up one hand in defeat. "Ah, don't get riled. I'm going."

He tossed off the last of his beer and ambled toward the door. He paused on the threshold long enough to call back to Zeke. "See you around, Morrison. I'll get a good story out of you one of these days yet. You just see if I don't."

As the door closed behind Duffy, Mulgrew snatched up the empty mug and vigorously scrubbed the counter in front of the spot where Duffy had stood drinking.

"I always said this hotel should be more careful, only allow gentlemen into this bar," Mulgrew muttered.

"Then I wouldn't be able to come in," Zeke said.

"Oh, no, you're a gent all right, Mr. Morrison. I always say it takes more than fancy manners and blue blood to make a proper man."

Zeke looked away, pleased but a little discomfited by the tribute. He took out his watch again. He was startled to see it was past five and still no sign of Addison. He expelled an exasperated sigh. It wouldn't surprise him in the least to discover that Addison had forgotten. When absorbed in preparing one of his legal briefs or writing a fiery speech, the man didn't even remember to eat unless that pretty wife of his took away his pen and put a fork in his hand.

Zeke resolved to give Addison another half hour, then he would wait no longer. As the minutes ticked by, he stared into his beer mug, letting the drink get warm as he became increasingly more morose.

This waiting was giving him too much time to think, and not about Addison. Much as he willed it to be otherwise, his thoughts kept returning to last night . . . Rory.

Like the true sprite that she was, her image popped into his mind—the fetching way her hair curled in tendrils about her cheeks, the rest forever a silken disarray, the saucy curve of her mouth, how bright her eyes were putting the city lights to shame, how lithe her figure was, with all a young girl's slenderness, with all a woman's soft charms.

Was it possible to miss someone so much, to feel that you knew them so well after only one night? Zeke had never thought so before. But certain endearing habits of hers already seemed ingrained on his memory. The way she liked to hum with the music when she danced, her tomboyish manner of leaping down from the carriage without waiting for his arm, her obvious dislike of green peas, how she spread them about on her plate to make it look as though she had eaten more.

One minute she seemed such a child, all wonder and delight, the next a woman, alluring him with the promise

of passion. He still didn't understand about that kiss. There
had been no resistance on her part. Far from it. The desire
he had tasted upon her lips had all but driven him wild.
No, it was a longing that went deeper than mere desire,
some force that sent mad thoughts of "meeting his match"
and "meant to be" tumbling through his brain.

He wasn't good enough at examining his own emotions
to explain it any better than that. He only knew that she
had wanted him as he wanted her. Then why had she run
away?

Funny how much it all reminded him of an incident
from his boyhood, a question that he had once asked his
stepmother. He'd come home sporting a shiner. Mary Lou
Grosvenor had slugged him for hugging her and stealing a
kiss at the back of the school yard.

"What'd she want to go and hit me for?" he'd howled
indignantly while his stepmother attempted to apply ice to
his eye. "I know she likes me."

Sadie had chuckled. "Ah, Johnnie, you just can't go up
to a girl and grab her like she was a sack of flour. You
have to be more gentle, woo her a little."

Woo her—it was a funny old-fashioned expression, but
he had taken heed of Sadie's advice. He never had much
luck with Mary Lou, but over the years he had learned a
little more finesse with the ladies—a little dining, a little
dancing, some sweet phrases whispered at just the right
moment.

Then why had none of that seemed to work with Rory?
Had he in the end waxed too hot with impatience, too blunt
with his desires? He didn't know, but it scarce seemed to
matter. Even if he wanted to start all over again, "woo"
her more gently, it wouldn't be so easy to find her. Like
the fabled Cinderella, she had vanished, without leaving
him so much as a slipper to track her down. Her balloon
had been removed from his lawn sometime last night. He
hadn't even thought to inquire what circus she had been
flying for, and that newly wed couple he had put up at the
Waldorf were likely already gone. No one was left even to
ask about her.

Zeke expelled a heavy sigh and shoved his glass away.

"Can I get you anything else, Mr. Morrison?" Mulgrew asked.

"No, thanks." Zeke checked his watch. Six o'clock. He had waited for Addison long enough. Likely Zeke could track him down later on. Occasionally Addison did remember to go home to sleep.

Reaching into his coat pocket, Zeke pulled out his wallet. He drew forth enough to pay for his shot and leave a large tip for Mulgrew as well. As he did so, a slip of paper fluttered to the bar.

No, not a slip, a card. Zeke turned it over and read, *Transcontinental Balloon Company*.

Damnation! He was getting as forgetful as Addison. Suddenly he could see Rory so clearly handing him the card, himself tucking it away without another glance.

As Zeke left the hotel, all thoughts of calling upon Addison fled from his mind. Outside in the street, he summoned the nearest hansom and read off the warehouse address. Giving himself no time to reflect, he leaped inside the cab, astonished by the level of excitement coursing through his veins.

As the vehicle lurched forward, Zeke leaned back with a contented sigh, his lips curving into a slow grin. Maybe, just maybe the fates had offered him one more chance to lure Aurora Rose Kavanaugh back into his arms and into his bed.

No, Cinderella hadn't left him a glass slipper, but she had gone one better.

She had left him her business card.

Seven

McCreedy Street had settled into a state of late Sunday afternoon somnolence. By the time Rory trudged down the steps from her second-story flat, shadows were already lengthening along the narrow street threading through rows of tightly packed brownstone buildings.

Nothing stirred on this quiet side street except an ancient buggy that creaked past and Miss Flanagan's overfed bulldog from across the way. When Rory opened the screen door, the cur set up a fearsome barking. And when Rory wheeled out her bicycle from where she stored it in the corridor, the dog went into an absolute frenzy, tugging on the chain keeping it affixed to a wrought-iron rail.

"Oh, be quiet, Finn MacCool," Rory muttered, maneuvering her bicycle down the stone steps to the pavement. Her head still throbbed from her revels of the night before, and the dog's yapping seemed to tear right through her.

Finn was Miss Flanagan's eyes and ears, alerting the nosy spinster to any movement in the neighborhood, so that she could peer past the lacy curtains adorning the tall windows of her first-story apartment. Not that it was necessary in this instance. The gangly woman was already perched on her front stoop, her long nose poked in Rory's direction.

"Ye missed mass this morning, Aurora Rose Kavanaugh," Miss Flanagan called out. "And ye be preparing to ride that contraption of a Sunday. Yer paving the way to hell, me girl, that's certain sure."

"So I am," Rory shouted back over Finn's barking. "I went dancing with the devil last night."

The old lady gasped and crossed herself. Hiking up her skirts, Rory swung up onto her bike, her lips pursed in a grim smile. And what would Miss Flanagan say if she told her the devil did not have horns and a pitchfork either? Only eyes as black as night, a grin as wicked as sin and a kiss that could fire a woman's blood hotter than any flames.

No, it was best to keep that to herself. Likely she had already shocked Miss Flanagan enough. The spinster huffed to her feet and stomped back into her house. Rory pedaled off, the sound of the bulldog's continued displeasure fading as she got farther down the street. She felt a little ashamed of herself. She usually made an effort to be polite to Miss Flanagan no matter how tiresome the woman could be.

But at the moment, Rory just wished the whole world would go away and leave her alone. She had danced all night and paid the price all day. By the time she had made her way home, the excitement of her escape from Zeke had faded, the miseries setting in. Queasy all afternoon, she had spent her day dozing on the sofa. Only an hour ago had she managed to choke down a little toast and some weak tea. A half hour later she had been able to dress. She had finally stirred herself to face the light of day, but the sun would be setting soon.

Disgraceful!

She was never going to touch champagne again. Or Zeke Morrison either.

The thought caused Rory to pedal faster, as though the man were still in pursuit of her. She turned up Second Avenue, heading northward toward that part of the city where the warehouse of her balloon company was located.

As she cycled along, last night's events took on more the aura of unreality. It was like some sort of strange dream. Had she really dined at Delmonico's, swayed to the music in the arms of a handsome stranger, been asked to become the mistress of a Fifth Avenue tycoon? She, Rory Kavanaugh, the hoyden of McCreedy Street?

It all seemed incredible back in the light of day, back in her own part of New York. The streets she traversed were by no means part of Manhattan's notorious slum district, but it was a very workaday world all the same. Wash was strung along lines running between fire escapes; children played stickball on the pavement; plump housewives lingered on their front stoops, shelling peas for Sunday dinner; men, their hair slicked back into a holiday shine, wandered into the local corner saloon.

In such familiar, simple surroundings, it should have been easy to convince herself to dismiss all thought of Zeke Morrison, to imagine the entire episode had never happened. Easy and . . . and utterly impossible.

Her mind kept replaying that moment when he had breathed kisses and promises against her hair. *Anything you want, Aurora Rose . . . anything.* It had not been the words themselves that had moved her, so much as the raw sincerity in his voice, the yearning that had touched some answering chord deep within her.

That combined with the headiness of his kiss, and Rory was ashamed to admit that she had been just the wee bit tempted to yield to his desires. It was fortunate that Zeke had also been impossibly arrogant, dismissing her balloon company as though it were a child's plaything. Otherwise she might have had more than missing mass to offer penance for at her next confession.

The best thing that she could do was just forget the man as surely as he must have forgotten her. Her fear that he would seek her out again now seemed absurd. A rich man like that, so handsome, so important. Likely he was already off on some other round of pleasure with his wealthy friends, such as that elegant Mrs. Van Hallsburg.

Instead of being relieved, the thought left her feeling as though her world had suddenly been deprived of all color and excitement. She tried to concentrate on her cycling instead, picking up the pace, steering round some horse droppings and taking care to avoid the path of an oncoming hansom cab.

She didn't usually cycle to the warehouse, which was many blocks away, the distance from her flat a little over two miles. But after being cooped up indoors for the better part of the day, she was grateful for the exercise. A soft breeze fanned her cheeks, and she could almost feel her color being restored.

The farther north she headed, the less pleasant became her surroundings. Snug brownstones disappeared, dilapidated tenements with broken windows taking their place. Between the close-packed buildings, Rory caught glimpses of the East River, its dank smell assaulting her nostrils like the odor of stale fish. Overhead the El thundered, the rushing trains spewing ashes and sparks, the tracks casting sinister shadows on the street below.

The warehouse was not located in the best of places, dockside areas rarely being the gentler side of New York. But it was safe enough to travel there in the daytime. Rory had merely learned to turn a blind eye to the increasing number of cheap saloons or those other tawdry establishments with heavy curtains at the window, frowsy young women lingering about the stoop.

"Er, boarding houses for seamstresses," her Da had always told her, rolling his eyes heavenward.

"Ha! Boarding houses for night chippies," Tony had whispered under his breath.

Whatever the case, Rory was prudent enough to suppress her curiosity about those brazen females. She always made purposefully for her warehouse and had never been bothered by any of the local denizens, except for a few occasional remarks.

Some of the lads who hung out at the billiard parlor across the street could never seem to resist shouting at her. Even on Sunday, there always were one or two who appeared to have nothing better to do than lean up against the lamppost, smoking and whistling at the girls.

As Rory wheeled her bicycle to a halt on the pavement and dismounted, one called across to her, "Hey, Rory! Purty ankles. Woo! Woo!"

Rory realized that she had forgotten to wear her gaiters again and likely had revealed too much when her skirts swirled upward. Her usual response would have been to shout back, "Aw, go chase yourself," but she felt in no mood for such banter today.

To the boy's obvious disappointment and confusion, she ignored him, groping in her pocket for the key to the side door. Her warehouse was sandwiched in between a shoe factory and a textile merchant's receiving dock. A large, weatherbeaten structure, the Transcontinental Balloon Company's wood frame showed signs of rot, the sign her father had erected so proudly years before now chipped and faded. Just like all of Da's dreams would be, if she didn't find a backer soon.

Rory thrust that depressing thought aside as she unlocked the door and wheeled her bicycle into the warehouse's gloomy interior. It was one vast chamber, three stories high, large enough to inflate a balloon inside to test it if need be. The small, grimy windows far overhead let in little light, so that the bales of silk, the boxes of iron filings and coils of rope were all little more than mysterious shadows.

As her eyes grew accustomed to the dimness, Rory could make out the form of the wagon and hydrogen generator where Tony must have returned it the night before. The bag of the *Katie Moira* had been spread out to dry.

Somehow the sight of the deflated balloon weighed upon Rory's spirits. That and the almost unnatural silence of the vast, empty warehouse. It had been far different on other Sundays, when her Da had been alive. Then the warehouse had been all life and bustle, filled with her father's booming presence, readying the balloon, packing the wagon. That had always been their "fun" day, the day on which they had bundled up the *Katie Moira* and taken her out into the country, launched the great balloon for no other reason than that the skies were blue, the clouds beckoning like distant white-capped mountains waiting to be conquered.

It was always Sunday afternoons now that seemed the longest, the time she missed her father the most. A tiny sigh came from Rory, which seemed to echo round the great cavern of the warehouse. As though to escape the sound, she turned and skittered up a narrow flight of stairs.

They led to a small office that overlooked the rest of the warehouse. Rory had reached for the knob when she suddenly stilled. A noise carried to her ears, one that had nothing to do with the scrape of her own shoe on the stair. Holding her breath, she listened intently. All was silent. She must have been imagining things. But just as she released the air from her lungs, she heard it again.

A slight stirring on the other side of the office door. Her heart gave a discomfited thud. Inching closer, she stole a peek through the door's small glass window. Someone was there. She could make out a pair of boots, a masculine form sprawled on the floor behind her desk.

It would not be the first time some old vagrant had managed to sneak into the warehouse to sleep. Angelo was always so careless about locking up. Last time, Rory had gotten a real fright, tripping over a body at the foot of the stairs, but the poor old man had meant no harm.

All the same, Rory had prepared herself in case the like should ever happen again. Groping underneath a loose floorboard beside the door, she located a section of lead pipe she had squirreled away there. Hefting the heavy weapon, she inched open the door, her pulses thundering.

This was foolish. She should go get help, summon a policeman. But if it was only that poor old tramp, she didn't want him arrested. She would take just one peek, and if the sleeping intruder looked at all dangerous, she would . . .

Steeling herself not to tremble, Rory tiptoed inside the office. She craned her neck, weapon at the ready, until she could see over the desk.

The interloper was definitely male, his long limbs uncomfortably disposed on a makeshift bed of silk material. His jacket hunched about his shoulders, Rory could just make out a profusion of jet-black curls.

"Tony!" Rory breathed.

Almost weak with relief, she nearly dropped the pipe onto the battered old desk. With shaking hands, she managed to light the oil lamp. Neither the sudden glow nor any of the sounds she made were enough to rouse Tony.

Coming round the desk, Rory stared down at her friend, wondering what he was doing here asleep on the office floor. Worse yet, how long had he been there? Had he waited up for her all night and through the day too?

As Rory's heartbeat slowed to normal, she was stricken with remorse. During the past hours, she had scarce given her old friend a single thought. She had wondered vaguely why he hadn't come to the flat earlier looking for her, but she had been too grateful to be left in peace to give the matter much consideration.

Bending down, she brushed aside his dark tumble of curls, her fingers skimming lightly over a cheek roughened with a morning's growth of beard. Her lips quivered with a sad smile. It still seemed odd to note signs of manhood on one who in her mind would forever be the boy who used to tie her braids together, swing off her fire escape, share his peppermint sticks.

At her touch, Tony stirred at last. He rolled onto his back, his eyes fluttering open. Their brown depths clouded with confusion, then cleared as he focused on her.

"Rory!" He jerked upward. Too close to the desk, he banged his head on the corner and swore. As Rory straightened, he struggled to his feet, rubbing his crown.

"What time is it? When did you get here? Where the devil have you been?"

"Which question do you want me to answer first?" She stretched, flexing her own back muscles like a lazy cat. She tried to keep her voice light, sensing a quarrel coming, wanting to avoid it.

When he glared at her, she settled on the most harmless question and replied, "I think it must be close on five o'clock."

"Five o'clock! And you're just now getting back here?"

"No-o-o-o." Her gaze skated away from his accusing one. "I . . . I've been at the apartment all day."

"No, you haven't. I sent Angelo round to look for you early this morning."

"He must have just missed me. Look, Tony, I . . . I am sorry I wasn't here to help with the balloon last night. I hope you managed all right."

"Oh, I managed all right—to go half out of my mind worrying about you."

Rory winced. Sinking into the chair behind her desk, she used the scarred surface as a barrier between them. "You needn't have fretted so much about me. I can take care of myself. I hope you haven't been waiting here all day."

"All night and all day, until I fell asleep! I didn't know what you were up to, where to find you, but I was sure this would be the first place you would come."

His words only added to her discomfort, for he was right. Ordinarily that would have been her one thought, to get back to the warehouse, to examine the damage to the *Katie Moira*. It was the first time in her life, anything, anyone had ever managed to distract her from her work with the balloons.

"I . . . I had something more important to attend to," she said.

"You mean this?" He drew a crumpled paper from his pocket and tossed it on her desk. She recognized the remains of the note she had left for Tony at Morrison's house.

"I spend all day tracking you from those stupid fairgrounds, thinking this time that you must have broken your fool neck for sure. I finally locate where the balloon went down, only to be told you have gone flitting off with some strange feller."

"I wasn't flitting," Rory started to snap, then checked herself. She hated it when Tony assumed this badgering, dictatorial tone. But she also hated the deep shadows beneath his eyes, the look of hurt lurking beneath the anger. She resumed in gentler accents, "I had a business meeting with Mr. Morrison. He took me to supper at Delmonico's."

"It took you all night to eat?"

"No, afterward, we went dancing and—" Rory broke off. As the hot tide of color surged in Tony's face, she could tell she was only getting herself in deeper.

"Dancing! That sounds like a precious funny kind of business to me."

"I was spending as much time with Mr. Morrison as I could, trying to persuade him to invest in the balloon company."

"And did you?"

"N-no. After all, it seems he was not interested."

"Damn right. I could have told you what he was after. I thought you had better sense than to set yourself up as a mash date for some rich swell."

Rory felt her own temper begin to fray. "It wasn't like that at all."

"No, I suppose he was a *perfect gentleman*," Tony sneered. "He didn't even try to get fresh."

Rory didn't want to blush, but she couldn't help it. The memory of how it felt to be in Zeke's arms was too real, too strong. Tony stared deep into her eyes and looked as though she had just kicked him in the gut.

"Gawd, Rory. You . . . you didn't let him kiss you?"

Rory wished she could glare back at him with defiance, even deny it. Instead she said quietly, "That's really none of your business, Tony."

He whirled away from her and slammed his fist against the wall. "Damn it!" he choked. "I don't care how rich or powerful the bastard is. I'm going back there and break his face."

"Don't be so silly. You will do no such thing. Honestly, Tony, you are worse than my Da ever would have been. Sometimes I think you have been trying to take his place."

"No, it's not your father I want to be." He was regarding her with that hungry look again, the one that made Rory both ache for him and want to shake him as well.

Please, Tony, don't. Don't say anymore, she begged silently. Seeking any kind of distraction, she yanked open the desk drawer and produced a well-worn ledger book. But it was impossible to make sense of any of the rows of neatly inked figures, not with Tony hovering over her desk, his hands jammed into his pockets.

"We have more important things to worry about than Zeke Morrison," she said. "Like how I am going to pay the rent on this warehouse. I don't suppose you collected our fee from Mr. Dutton before you came looking for me yesterday?"

"No, I didn't. Since I was expecting to find you dashed to pieces over New York, the money somehow slipped my mind. But I guess you can always have another go at that rich friend of yours." The bitterness in Tony's voice was as scalding as acid. When she didn't reply, he demanded, "Are you going to see him again?"

"Who?"

"You know damn well who. That . . . that Morrison."

It would have been so easy to set Tony's mind at rest, assure him that she never expected to keep company with Zeke again. Hadn't she already decided as much? Instead she surprised herself by murmuring, "I . . . I don't know."

"Don't you ever read the papers, Rory? The *World* calls him the mysterious millionaire. Everyone wonders where he came from, how he got his money."

"Not everyone. I never gave it much thought." Rory tried to sound indifferent, yet she could already feel herself begin to tense, ready to rush to Zeke's defense, and Tony had not even accused the man of anything yet.

But Tony was working up to it. He braced both hands on the desk and leaned over her, glowering. "You might be interested to hear that Angelo knows this fellow who says that Morrison—"

"Doesn't Angelo always know someone? Your brother is a worse busybody than Miss Flanagan."

"Angelo knows this fellow name of Julio from the old neighborhood," Tony said, raising his voice to drown her out. "And Julio says there's nothing mysterious about Morrison. He's nothing but a bum that used to work down on the docks, an orphan kid who ate out of garbage cans and picked pockets until he was adopted by this widow."

Rory pursed her lips in exasperation. "How many dockworkers do you know that could earn enough money to live on Fifth Avenue?"

"None that could do it *honestly*. Julio also said—"

"Oh, stop it, Tony!" Rory slammed the ledger book closed. "I don't care what Julio says. And as for you and Angelo, I think you could find better use for your time than to gossip like a couple of old hens. I begin to wonder what I am paying the lot of you for."

Tony straightened, a bright flush stealing beneath his olive skin. "You don't have to pay me for nothing anymore 'cause I quit."

"Good!"

Spinning on his heel, he stomped toward the door. Their arguments always ended this way. If she didn't end up by firing Tony, he would resign. But he always came back; they always patched up their disagreement.

Somehow, though, it was different this time. An almost panicky sensation seized Rory as the door slammed shut behind Tony. Their quarrels had always been over trivial matters, mostly concerning some aspect of the balloon company. Tony had never left her looking almost as hurt as he was angry.

Perhaps she should go after him. She rose from the desk and had half started across the room when the door was flung violently open. Tony stood framed on the threshold, his rage fading, but the beseeching look he wore was far worse.

"I'm sorry, Rory. I don't mean to make you mad at me. You know I wouldn't be saying all these things if . . . if I didn't care so much about you."

"S-sure. I know you do. Why don't we just forget this whole thing and—"

Her heart sank with dismay when he caught up her hands in a hard grip.

"Rory, I . . ."

"Oh, no, Tony, please." She tried to retreat, but she saw clearly there was no stopping him this time.

"I love you, Rory. I always have."

"Of . . . of course. Like a brother you do."

"No, not like a brother!" He yanked her into his arms. "I go just about crazy with jealousy thinking of you being with any other feller, not just this Morrison. And to let him kiss you! Why couldn't it have been me, Rory? Why not me?"

"Tony, stop!"

But he pressed his lips hard against her mouth. It was useless to resist. He was far too strong for her. All she could do was hold herself rigid, unresponding. It was all wrong, and Tony was quick to sense that himself. He drew back, his eyes twin mirrors of longing and despair. Her own swam with tears as she struggled to find the words to let him down as gently as she could.

But she didn't have to speak. After staring into her face, he released her, his shoulders slumping.

"Tony, I . . . I am so sorry," she whispered.

He swallowed hard and nodded, an awkward silence descending. In those endless moments, Rory could feel something precious dying, another piece of her childhood slipping away.

She retreated behind the desk again.

Tony gave a harsh laugh. "There's no need for that. I won't try to touch you again. I'm through making a fool of myself. You have nothing to fear from me."

"I know that, Tony."

Somehow her assurance only made things worse. He picked up the jacket that he had forgotten before and moved toward the door again. "I guess I better be getting home. Ma'll be ready to skin me for being late for supper again."

Simple words, the sort of easy remark he might have tossed off as he left any evening, only now it all sounded so strained.

Her own voice came across as too hearty when she agreed. "Goodness yes, I don't want your mother mad at me again for keeping you. You run along. I'll lock up here."

"Don't you stay late either. It's getting dark."

Rory promised she wouldn't. She thought he meant to go without another word, not even good-bye. But he looked back one last time to ask with a wistfulness that nearly broke her heart, "Is it because of that Morrison fellow? Is that why I don't have a chance with you? Did you fall in love with him?"

"Heavens, Tony, I only just met the man yesterday."

"Sometimes that's all it takes. There's something different about you. I can tell."

"I'm a day older." She tried to smile, but couldn't manage it. Only a day. Why did it suddenly feel like years?

Tony drew himself more erect, some of the fire returning to his eyes. "Well, I'm not going to stand by and let you get mixed up with some stranger. I'm going to find out more about this J. E. Morrison."

"Tony . . ."

"And if he does turn out to be a bad one, you are going to stay away from him, you hear?"

"Tony, please. Just go home."

But she could tell from the stubborn look on his face, her plea would go unheeded. When he let himself out, she sagged down onto the chair. Folding her arms upon the desk, she buried her face against her hands, her heart feeling too battered even for tears.

"Damn you, Tony," she mumbled. "You've ruined everything." She wanted to curse him and Zeke Morrison too. The pair of them had somehow robbed her of her tranquillity—Tony, with all his talk of love, spoiling their friendship; Zeke with his kisses, stirring desires inside of her she had never dreamed of.

Strange that for all her grief for her father, her worries over the fate of her company, she had still managed to stay relatively carefree. She had known exactly who she was, Seamus Kavanaugh's daughter, Tony's friend, Rory Kavanaugh, the hoyden of McCreedy Street.

Now she felt so unsure of herself. Everything was so . . . so blasted complicated—most of all her confusing feelings about Zeke Morrison. Why hadn't she told Tony she never expected to see the man again? Why had she been so ready

to fly to Zeke's defense when Tony had begun hinting things
about him?

If she had given Tony the reassurance he sought, he
would have let the matter drop. Now she knew he would
never do so. He would keep prying until he got himself
into trouble or else found something damning to tell her
about Zeke.

And she had a feeling that might not be so hard to do.
Zeke carried an aura about him, of ruthlessness certainly,
but also hauntings of a past that she sensed had not always
been pleasant.

Yet whatever Tony might uncover, it wasn't going to
matter. Rory's instincts had never failed her, and she had
looked into Zeke's eyes enough to know that he was not a
bad man.

An odd judgment to pass on someone who had, after all,
tried to seduce her, lure her into the very sort of wickedness
that Tony warned her against. Zeke himself would likely
admit that his intentions had not been honorable.

But there had been a tenderness in his voice that spoke
of more than mere lust. Zeke Morrison had needs, needs
Rory doubted the man was even aware of himself. The
trouble was he made her too much aware she had needs
of her own and . . .

And blast Tony anyway! She had been struggling to put
the entire encounter with Zeke from her mind. Tony had
stirred up all her memories of last night, raised questions
she had not even thought to ask.

Did you fall in love with him?

What an absurd idea. Absurd and extremely troubling.
Rory pressed her fingertips to her temple. Her head had
begun to ache all over again with all these tormenting
speculations chasing through her brain.

Curse all men to hell anyway . . . all men except for her
own Da. Rory leaned back in her chair and wished it could
be yesterday again, when all she had had to worry about
was going bankrupt.

She thumbed through the ledger, knowing she should put
some energy into going over the accounts or go belowstairs

and make a stab at repairing the damage to the *Katie Moira*. But somehow she could not summon the energy to do either.

To her disgust she caught herself daydreaming of night-dark eyes, a strong, square-cut jaw, rich waves of brown hair framing a man's face too bold for her peace of mind.

Daydreaming? No, it was going to be more like night dreaming if she continued to hang about the warehouse, mooning over Zeke in this idiotic fashion. Rory cast a startled glance toward the window and realized that she had done exactly what she had promised Tony she wouldn't.

She had lingered at the warehouse until the sky beyond had inked to a dark shade of purple. Scrambling to her feet, Rory cursed herself.

"Idiot!"

As if she hadn't done enough imprudent things in the past twenty-four hours. Even without Tony's warning, she knew it was sheer folly to be caught in this part of town after dark. Of course there was no question of riding her bicycle home. She would take the El, but even that was a good two blocks' walk to the nearest platform.

Hastening downstairs, Rory took one last look around to make sure that all the doors were secured for the night. As she let herself out onto the street, she noted with dismay that it was even later than she thought. All trace of the sun had gone, the moon a pale distant sliver in a cloudy night sky.

The street lamps had been lit, glimmers in the murky darkness. Up the street, honky-tonk piano music spilled out from one of the saloons, along with coarse, drunken laughter. But it was not those noisy denizens of the night that Rory had to worry about, but other silent shapes, which might be lurking in the doorways ahead.

Her fingers shook a little as she locked the side door, and she despised herself for a coward. As she set off down the pavement, her shoes made a solitary clatter, heading away from the raucous doings of the saloon, whose bright lights seemed a veritable haven compared to the darkness ahead of her.

Passing the textile dock, she could just make out the East River, a mysterious moving shadow. She could not help thinking of tales she had heard, of bloated bodies fished from those chilly depths.

"Drowned" was always the official verdict, ignoring obviously slit throats. In this part of town, even the police had a habit of avoiding trouble, conveniently looking the other way.

Quickening her steps, Rory chided herself for a fool. As if this walk wasn't bad enough, without allowing her thoughts to wander to such things as murder. She nearly jumped from her skin when she heard a footfall behind her.

Whirling about, she caught her breath, certain that someone was following her. But the street behind her was dark and empty. Swallowing hard, Rory told herself not to panic. She'd be damned if she would allow herself to be spooked by a shadow, run from nothing but the excesses of her own imagination.

Forcing herself to maintain a brisk but steady pace, she could not control the thudding of her own heart. For the worst was yet to come. Ahead of her loomed the wooden posts supporting the tracks of the El itself. To reach the platform, she had no choice but to cross beneath, where the darkness deepened into impenetrable shadow, where the support beams offered a dozen places of concealment.

She had just reached the dreaded spot when she heard it again, the hollow echo of a footstep not her own. Glancing nervously over her shoulder, this time she was quick enough to catch a form melting behind one of the wooden pillars some ten yards behind her.

Wouldn't it be just like that Tony to have waited and tried to play watchdog without giving himself away? Just as though she were a baby and couldn't look after herself. Rory tried to summon up a feeling of anger, but what she experienced was more in the nature of a desperate hope.

"Tony?" she quavered. "Come on out. I know it's you."

No answer.

In that instant, she saw other shapes moving. Dear God, whoever was out there, it was more than one. Without another thought, Rory turned and ran.

She raced along, weaving between the pillars. The tracks overhead let in brief patches of light, guiding her toward the platform stairs. She thought she heard feet pounding in pursuit, but she could scarce discern anything above her heartbeat thundering in her ears, the sound of her own ragged breathing.

What would she do even if she gained the platform? It might be minutes before a train came by. Yet to keep racing along beneath the tracks was madness. It did not even occur to her to try to scream. They were not deaf in this part of town, merely indifferent. She had no choice but to make her way up.

Grasping the handrail, she fairly hurled herself up the steps, stumbling in the process. A soft cry escaped her, so certain was she that she would be overtaken at any moment. But when no monstrous hands reached out of the darkness to snatch at her, she recovered her footing and staggered on.

When she had nearly gained the relative security of the platform, she dared pause long enough to catch her breath and listen to determine the whereabouts of her pursuers. She heard no dreaded pounding on the stair behind her, only other sounds echoing from beneath the tracks.

Strange sounds—a loud crack, a thud, a low grunt. It took her a moment to reach beyond the curtain of her own panic and identify the source. A fight. Someone was having a fistfight down below the stairs.

For the first time it occurred to Rory that the chase had had nothing to do with herself. Feeling still much shaken and slightly foolish, she summoned enough courage to bend down and peer beneath one of the openings in the stair.

Below her three men engaged in a deadly conflict, two of them raining blows upon a larger form. Before Rory's horrified gaze, the big man went down and she caught the glint of something in one of his attacker's hands. A knife.

A cry snagged in her throat as she realized she was about to witness the murder of some hapless stranger. The big man tried to roll clear, but the other two were upon him again.

Enough lamplight filtered through the tracks to briefly illuminate the face of the victim. A face that beneath the smear of blood was incredibly and heart-stoppingly familiar.

Rory froze with the shock of recognition. With all the helpless sensation of being caught in some nightmare, she watched the deadly blade arc downward before she was able to scream.

"Zeke!"

Eight

✻ ✻ ✻

From far away, Zeke heard Rory cry his name. But he was aware of nothing but the feel of sharp rocks grinding against his back, the weight of his assailant bearing him down. A shaft of light piercing the tracks above streaked across coarse features, an ugly raised scar bisecting the chin, thick lips almost slavering, like a mad dog scenting the kill. One meaty hand flashed a butcher's knife toward Zeke's throat.

Zeke caught his attacker's wrist, deflecting the blade just in time. Every muscle in his forearms strained upward to put distance between that sharp cutting edge and his flesh. Gritting his teeth, Zeke tasted his own blood from the blow that had felled him in the darkness. He sensed his second opponent nearby—a short, squat man, watching the deadly contest, wheezing to get his breath.

Christ, Zeke thought. This was a little more than he had bargained for when he trailed Rory from the warehouse. He had been off the streets too long, allowing two clumsy thugs such as these to catch him unaware.

But like a fish tossed back into water, Zeke felt the old

119

moves coming back to him. Managing to get his other hand free, he struck, gouging his fingers into the deep pockets of flesh surrounding his opponent's eyes. As the scarred one yelped with pain, Zeke drove his knee upward, square into the man's groin.

With another howl, the rogue rolled off Zeke, doubling over. "So much for you, Chin Scar," Zeke muttered. Getting to his knees, he tried to raise himself. When he regained his footing, these two cutthroats were going to be mighty sorry they ever singled him out for their mark. But from the shadows came the other one, his thick boot catching Zeke hard in the chest.

Zeke grunted with pain but grabbed the squatty one's leg. With a vicious tug, he upended the man on his buttocks. Using one of the railroad pillars for a support, Zeke drew himself upright just in time to see Chin Scar going for his knife again.

Zeke rammed his heel down, crushing the man's hand, forcing him to release the weapon. After that, all descended into a mayhem of flailing fists, gouging, biting, kicking.

Zeke received another hard knock to the head, but he gave better than he got, taking a keen satisfaction when his knuckles connected against bone and flesh. Caught up in the battle, it took him a moment to realize reinforcements had arrived. Out of the corner of his eye, he caught the blur of furious movement that was Rory.

"Get the hell out of here," he gasped at her, but the wiry little hoyden was doing all right for herself. Snatching up a broken segment of railroad tie, she rained blows down upon the hapless head of the pudgy one.

Just as Zeke rammed his fist into the most vulnerable part of the Chin Scar's stomach, a shrill whistle pierced the night. Zeke's attacker fell back, and as the police whistle sounded again, he whirled and took to his heels. Clutching his head, the squat one staggered after him, the two of them soon swallowed up by the darkness.

Old instincts died hard. At the call of the police whistle, Zeke had to suppress a strong urge to bolt himself. Instead he sagged back against one of the pillars, panting for breath.

"Oh, Zeke, are you hurt badly?"

Rory's features swam before his gaze, her face as pale as the moonlight, her eyes silvery pools of fear and concern. She wrapped one arm about his waist, trying to shore him up with her own slender frame.

"Are . . . are you all right?" she asked.

"Just . . . fine now, little girl." He ached in a dozen different places, his jaw was swelling, but none of that seemed to matter as he draped his arm about her shoulders, drawing her close.

She glanced up at him, wariness beginning to replace her initial concern, but before she could say another word, the law descended upon them in the form of a trim blue-coated officer, a lean face and trim mustache shadowed beneath his gray helmet. Zeke winced at the all-too-familiar sight of the thick billy club the policeman swung in one hand.

"Now then, what's all this disturbin' of the peace?" the man demanded in a thick brogue. "Why, it's the little lady from the balloon company. Has this villain been botherin' you, Miss Kavanaugh?"

"No, Sergeant O'Connell. I was up on the platform to catch the train when I saw this gentleman being set upon by thieves. They ran back down that way toward the docks." Rory gestured vigorously. "If you hurry, you might still catch them."

But O'Connell showed no inclination to bestir himself. He spared a glance up the street, then shrugged. "Sartin the rogues are long gone, more's the pity. Were they after takin' your wallet, Mr. Morrison?"

Zeke shook his head, still too winded to reply. Once a trifling skirmish such as this would have been but a prelude to a rollicking night, which often ended with a trip in the paddy wagon. He must be getting old.

"Poor lad." O'Connell edged closer, but his commiserating smile didn't strike Zeke as being very genuine. "You'll be needing a doctor, I'm thinking. Don't you fret, Miss Kavanaugh. You've done your duty as a good citizen. You run along and catch your train. I'll be lookin' after the gentleman."

"Not necessary," Zeke started to say, painfully straightening. But to his surprise, Rory stepped between him and the officer, a small but fierce barrier. In the glow of the street lamp, Zeke could almost see her bristle.

"You needn't put yourself to any further *trouble*, Sergeant. Mr. Morrison is a friend of mine. I will take care of him."

"No trouble a'tall, Miss Kavanaugh," the sergeant protested, but Rory stood her ground. O'Connell eyed them both for a moment, his fingers twitching, running along the length of his nightstick.

But at last he gave way, saying, "Well, if you are sartin I can be of no help, I will bid you good night."

The policeman shuffled off down the street, pausing once to look back. Zeke was only too pleased to be rid of the officer. With a grateful sigh, he wrapped his arm about Rory's shoulders. But she pulled away from him.

"I have a feeling you are quite capable of standing on your own power, Mr. Morrison."

"Mr. Morrison?" he repeated. "What happened to *Zeke*?"

He could feel more than see the heat of her glare. Spinning away from him, she stomped back toward the steps leading up to the platform. Zeke hobbled stiffly after her. This was getting to be quite a habit, chasing this woman through the streets of New York.

As he mounted the steps behind her, he called, "Lucky for you I happened along, wasn't it? You little fool! Don't you know better than to go traipsing these streets after dark?"

A few steps above him, she whirled about, hands on hips.

"You didn't just happen along, Morrison. You were following me."

He thought of trying to deny it, but he saw the absurdity of such a course. In a swirl of skirts, Rory vanished up the steps. By the time he caught up with her, she had flounced down upon the platform bench, her arms crossed over her chest in a most forbidding fashion.

With a heavy sigh, Zeke sank down beside her, grimacing at the pain in his side. He hoped he hadn't managed to crack his ribs again. Rory scooted farther down until she was almost falling off the edge of the bench.

"I did follow you," Zeke admitted at last. "I still had the business card you gave me and came out to have a look at your warehouse. I never thought I'd be lucky enough to find you here, but I caught a glimpse of you passing by one of the windows. I decided I'd just wait until you left and see where you went."

"You put yourself to a great deal of bother, Mr. Morrison."

"I wanted to find out where you lived and . . . and after the way we parted this morning, I was afraid you wouldn't tell me."

"You were quite right."

When he attempted to drape his arm along the back of the bench, she sprang up like a scalded cat.

"Please, Rory," he coaxed, "I only wanted to see you again, just talk to you."

She gave a small sniff. "I suppose you are wanting to tell me some blather about how sorry you are, how much you regret that outrageous proposal you made me."

"I am sorry," Zeke began contritely enough, but was unable to repress his grin, no matter how much his jaw ached. "I am sorry you wouldn't accept it."

Rory expelled her breath in a furious hiss. "You are impossible! I'd hit you myself if you weren't already so black and blue."

She stalked a few paces away, assuming a posture of affronted dignity that Zeke found completely adorable. "If you will excuse me," she said. "I have a train to catch."

"What? Are you just going to leave me like this to collapse on the platform?"

"I see no danger of that. I am sure someone as clever as you will have no difficulty finding your way home."

"Well if that is the way you feel—," he started to say, then doubled over, emitting a groan that was only half-faked.

He had at least caught Rory's attention. She shot him a look of contempt. But when he began to slump down on the bench, clutching at his forehead, the hardness of her expression wavered.

"Oh, stop that," she ordered, but her voice was laced with uncertainty. She inched a little closer, saying stalwartly, "I know you weren't hurt that bad. Nothing could dent that thick skull of yours."

"N-no, of course not." Zeke moaned. "Don't concern yourself. Just a few broken ribs, I guess. A little concussion. I doubt I'll black out before someone else comes along."

"Morrison, if you are faking . . ." She hurried over and bent down to peer at him. He permitted a spasm of pain to wrack his features.

"Zeke?" She placed one hand tentatively on his shoulder. "Oh, the devil! The train's coming. Come on. I'll help you. Are you dizzy? Lean on me."

With a heroic nod, he struggled to his feet, only too willing to encircle the softness of her shoulders, burdening her with just enough of his weight to be convincing without crushing her.

As she helped him toward the tracks, he gazed down at the baby-fine strands of her hair tossed into that gypsy-wild tangle that was already becoming so familiar to him. His mouth curved into a tender smile, a smile he was quick to erase when she chanced to glance up at him.

Although she regarded him with suspicion, she made no effort to draw away. The El clattered forward in an ear-shattering rumble, the whistle blasting as the train hissed to a halt in a cloud of acrid steam and sparks.

A few passengers disembarked as he and Rory eased their way through the narrow door. Zeke sank down onto the nearest empty seat, Rory nearly lurching on top of him as the train jerked into movement once more. In another few seconds they were lumbering off through the night.

Zeke supposed he must look as disreputable as a tomcat that had strayed down one alley too many. Besides the bruises swelling his cheek, his Chesterfield coat was torn and blood-stained. But he drew only a few curious glances from the other passengers. For the most part, New Yorkers tended to mind their own business. Rory drew a plain linen handkerchief from her pocket and wrapped up his bleeding knuckles. Something in her manner of brisk efficiency told him this wasn't the first time she had tended the wounds of a man after a bout of fisticuffs.

Mrs. Van H. would have taken one look at him, given a shudder of distaste and ordered him to return when he appeared more like a gentleman. But Rory did not seem in the least shocked by his condition or the fight she had just witnessed.

In fact, she said with grudging admiration, "You handled yourself real well back there. I guess you didn't need my help. Not at all what I would have expected from a Fifth Avenue swell."

"Swells don't last long in this part of town," he returned dryly.

His remark caused her to glance sharply up at him, but she made no comment, merely finished knotting the handkerchief. "There. That's the best I can do until I get you home."

Home . . . that had a nice sound to it, Zeke thought, allowing his head to rest back against the seat. He had to admit he had had his doubts earlier when he had been tearing along in that hansom cab, Rory's card clutched in his fist.

Even then he hadn't been sure what sort of madness had come over him, setting out in pursuit of a woman who had already rejected him once. But now that he had seen Rory again, he understood. It was indeed a madness, but of the sweetest kind.

One touch of her hand and he felt the full force of his desire for her gathering all over again. When she stroked her fingers along the line of his jaw, earnestly examining the extent of his bruise, he didn't even flinch. Instead he had an urge to cup her hand, press a kiss against the warm center of her palm.

But he restrained himself. He could scarce try to make love to her on the El, and he didn't want her running away from him again.

Gently, Zeke. Go gently this time. Even the clack of the train wheels seemed to admonish him. So he bided his time, allowing his eyes to drift half-closed, soothed by her feather-light caress and the monotonous clatter of the train.

It had been a long time since he had ridden on the El. He had forgotten how the tracks seemed to cut through the very pulse of the city. It was as if one could thrust out one's hand and reach into the upper stories of the tenement windows.

Vignettes flashed by like scenes from a play: a lodging house where some pathetic old men were bedding down on the floor; the topmost room of one of those hellish sweat-shops, young girls growing old before their time hunched over sewing machines; a dingy parlor where a haggard lad was swilling rotgut and shooting dice.

Yet in the midst of this, there was an occasional room with a plump motherly woman darning socks or standing over a steaming iron while a brood of children romped like puppies at her feet. It never failed to amaze Zeke, the strength of such women, their ability to fashion a place that could be called home even in the midst of such wretched poverty.

It never failed to remind him that he had known such a home once, such a woman. . . .

"Zeke?"

Rory's voice recalled him from his thoughts. He was a little surprised to discover that he was no longer leaning back, but sitting bolt upright and staring out the train window.

Finding Rory's troubled gaze upon him, he forced himself to settle back.

"Is your pain getting worse?" she asked. "You had such an odd look in your eyes just now."

He forced a smile. "I guess over the years, I have taken a few too many knocks to the head."

No, Rory thought. More likely too many knocks to the heart. This wasn't the first time she had seen that haunted look shadow Zeke's face. Although outwardly she accepted his explanation, she could not help but wonder what ghosts he had glimpsed out the windows of the train.

She caught herself studying the man who had erupted back into her life. Earlier today she had tried hard to dismiss Zeke as though he had been some figment of her imagination. But she saw now it had been Delmonico's and that castle on Fifth Avenue that had seemed like a dream, but not Zeke.

His broad shoulders solidly filled the seat opposite her. He was far too real, his presence too strong. There was nothing dreamlike about the man. Even his bruises, his torn collar, became him in an odd sort of way, more so than any silk ruffled shirt would have.

She thought she would be reliving the fight scene for weeks in her nightmares, that horrible moment when it had appeared as though Zeke were about to have his throat slit. All dressed in his elegant clothes, he must have seemed an easy victim to those two thieves.

What a surprise Zeke must have given them! Her lips started to curve, only to lose her smile in a perplexed frown. The more she thought about the fight, O'Connell's sudden arrival, the more some elusive memory niggled at her, a memory of something out of the ordinary, something not quite right.

Perhaps it was nothing more than that Zeke had fought with such unexpected ferocity. She could not help recalling what Tony had hinted earlier, that Zeke's origins were no mystery, that he hailed from the East Side, "the old neighborhood." By that, Rory knew Tony meant that part of New York his own family had inhabited before the Bertellis had moved on the block adjacent to hers. The "old neighborhood," that colorful noisy tenement district known as Little Italy.

Not as dangerous a place as the notorious Five Points, but a man still had to be tough to survive there. Rory had no doubt Zeke possessed such toughness. He had fought off those two street thugs with all the ruthless savvy of any dockworker. A man didn't get muscular forearms like Zeke's from a lifetime spent in playing croquet on the front lawn.

Of course, such impressions weren't facts. She could not

say for sure that Tony was right. But instinct told her that whatever Zeke's past life, it hadn't been an easy one. Her curiosity was roused, yet she hesitated to ask any questions. Somehow she didn't want to know anything that Zeke wasn't ready to tell her.

Even now she could sense him squirming under her scrutiny. He closed his eyes. Whether he was only feigning sleep, she couldn't tell. She only knew he didn't look quite so formidable in that position of repose, dark lashes resting against his cheeks, that rock-hard jaw for once relaxed. It roused strange feelings in Rory, the urge to stroke back his hair, tuck a quilt beneath his chin.

She almost hated to disturb him, but the train was rapidly approaching her stop. It took no more than a touch to urge him to his feet. By the time he followed her down from the platform to the street below, he appeared to have forgotten his injuries and had taken to scolding her.

"I hope you don't make a habit of this, little girl, walking the streets after dark. The Lord knows, you certainly can't rely on the coppers hereabouts for protection."

"The police in our precinct are much better than Sergeant O'Connell," she started to assure him, then stopped. The mention of the policeman's name struck off a sudden realization. With startling clarity, she recalled that elusive something that had been troubling her earlier about the fight. It had nothing at all to do with Zeke's prowess in fending off the thugs, but rather with what had transpired after the arrival of the police.

"Zeke! O'Connell knew you."

"What?"

"He did. He called you by name. I remember clearly now." Rory halted in the flickering shadow of a gaslight. Troubled, she stared up at Zeke, remembering Tony's other insinuations, that to become so wealthy, Zeke must have done something shady. He might be on most intimate terms with the police for the wrong reasons.

Although Zeke looked startled by her words, he said, "I can assure you I never set eyes on O'Connell before tonight."

Rory could not say why, but she believed him.

"Maybe he saw my picture in the papers," Zeke suggested.

Rory shook her head. O'Connell wasn't the sort to delve into the society columns. Besides, in his battered state, no one would have recognized Zeke as J. E. Morrison Esquire of Millionaire's Row, not even his dear friend Mrs. Van Hallsburg.

"Then O'Connell must have heard you say my name." Zeke gave an impatient shrug. Taking her gently by the elbow, he forced her into movement once more.

"I suppose that must have been the case," Rory agreed, but she didn't feel quite satisfied with that explanation either. The more she considered the matter, the more she thought that O'Connell could have done more to apprehend Zeke's assailants if he had chosen. She had seen the policeman bring down a malefactor with one expert flick of his nightstick tossed between running legs.

And when O'Connell had tried to send Rory on her way, offering to guide Zeke to a doctor himself, she had been beset by a vague feeling of alarm.

It was almost as if. . . .

Rory drew herself up short, cutting off the thought. It was almost as if Rory Kavanaugh was letting her imagination run wild again. She tried to put a shivery feeling of foreboding behind her, directing Zeke's steps toward her own block.

McCreedy Street was as quiet as ever, the gaslit lamps like a row of miniature beacons heralding the way to the snug row of brownstones. Front parlors glowed with that after-Sunday-supper contentment, families settling down to make an early night before the next work week began.

Mrs. Flanagan had even taken in Finn for the evening, although as Rory led Zeke up her front steps, she noticed the spinster's lace curtain stir. By this time tomorrow, it would be all over the neighborhood that Rory Kavanaugh had brought a man home with her.

"It's only the devil, Miss Flanagan," Rory muttered under her breath so that not even Zeke could hear. She felt a quiver of unexpected nervousness run through her.

Outside the corridor to her flat, she noted her fingers had gone a little trembly. She fumbled with the keys until Zeke removed them from her grasp and unlocked the door himself. His muscular frame seemed to dwarf the narrow hallway, casting a looming shadow on the opposite wall.

What was she doing, bringing Zeke Morrison up to her flat? By now she knew danged well he was faking much of his misery. Whatever the extent of his hurts, they didn't prevent him from regarding her with that wicked gleam in his eyes.

Still, the bruise swelling his jaw did need attention. She couldn't have just left him that way. All her life she had gathered in strays—abandoned baby birds, wounded kittens, lost puppies. But she knew Zeke was scarce so domesticated, far more dangerous.

The wolf was back at her door, but instead of barring the way, she preceded him, lighting the gas jets so he could see his way to come inside. With the soft glow of the lamps, her parlor seemed to surround her, as it always did, like a pair of loving arms. Little had changed about the place since the days when her mother had kept it all so neat and tidy. The rose print wallpaper had faded a little, but the overstuffed sofa and chair stood in their customary places next to the dark oak of the parlor table. Velour curtains fringed with tassels shut out the night, while the wobbly corner shelf all but collapsed under the weight of bric-a-brac, wax flowers under glass domes, Da's stuffed owl, Mama's precious collection of teacups and saucers, Rory's own wooden music box.

She turned to invite Zeke to enter, but he already had.

"Do come in and make yourself at home, Mr. Morrison," she murmured wryly as Zeke strode about the room, inspecting everything with an approving eye.

"This is real nice. You live here all alone?"

Zeke could make the most innocent questions sound fraught with seduction.

"Yes, but I have neighbors just across the hall," she said

quickly. "Aren't you still feeling dizzy? Perhaps I should fetch my smelling salts."

Her sharp reminder caused him to waver, to recollect that he was supposed to be on the verge of collapse.

"Uh . . . I am still feeling pretty groggy." He made a great show of rubbing the back of his head. "If I could just rest here for a while."

With a soft groan, he sagged down into the depths of the armchair. Rory pulled a face at this bit of melodrama, but all she said was "I'll go get you a compress for that jaw."

Retreating to her tiny kitchen, she chipped some ice out of the icebox and wrapped it in clean linen. Searching through the pantry, she found what remained of her Da's store of Irish whiskey and poured some into a tumbler.

By the time she returned to the parlor she was a little dismayed to see Zeke had already removed his coat and the collar of his shirt. It was a natural enough gesture, considering both garments were stained with dirt and blood, but it left Zeke's shirt open at the neckline. Rory's gaze was drawn by the intriguing dusting of dark hair, a glimpse of deeply tanned chest.

Her cheeks firing, she nearly thrust the icepack and whiskey at him.

"H-here," she said somewhat unsteadily.

As Zeke held the ice to his jaw, she perched primly on the sofa opposite him. He seemed grateful for the compress, even more grateful for the whiskey. It seemed so strange and somehow so natural to see Zeke sprawled in the old armchair, as though he had been there every night of her life.

As he sipped the amber liquid, he stared at her over the rim of the glass, his eyes dark, dangerous. A silence settled over the room, weighted by the memory of that passionate kiss they had shared barely twelve hours ago. Rory thought she could count every beat of her own heart.

Seconds ticked by without Zeke making a move or saying a word. Why had he taken such pains to find her again? She didn't think it was merely to sit and stare at her. She could sense a tension in him as sharp as the crack of a whip. When

he finally did clear his throat to speak, she caught herself
holding her breath.

"Is that your father?"

"What?" The question was so far from anything she had
expected, she could make no sense of it.

"In that photograph over there." Zeke indicated a small
oval-shaped portrait resting upon the parlor table. From
within the frame, Seamus Kavanaugh peered proudly out
at the world, a mere stripling all but swallowed up in an
overlarge blue jacket, the uniform of the Union Army. "Is
that your Da?"

Rory had a feeling that that was not what Zeke had
originally intended to say, but she nodded eagerly, grateful
for any diversion.

Zeke scooped up the photograph, examining it closer.
"You favor him a little. You both have those laughing
Irish eyes." Zeke's lips quirked into a smile. "He looks
damn young to have been a soldier."

"My father got recruited practically the moment he
stepped off the boat from Ireland. He told me once that he
hadn't even known what the Civil War was about, but if there
was any fighting going on, he wanted to be part of it."

"How thoroughly Irish," Zeke drawled.

Rory shot a glance at the bruises yet darkening Zeke's
jaw. He need not have looked so smug. She couldn't imagine him hanging back either when any kind of a battle was
waging.

"Anyway," Rory said as Zeke replaced the photograph on
the table. "The enlistment turned out to be a fortunate thing
for Da. He was assigned to the army's balloon corps for
a while. That's where he got his first experience at flying,
and he never got it out of his heart again."

"So that explains it. I wondered what would cause a
man to do something so farfetched as founding a balloon
company in the middle of New York."

Rory stiffened at the amusement lacing Zeke's voice.
"And haven't you ever had notions that everyone else
thought were a little crazy? Haven't you ever chased after
a dream?"

"No, the only thing I've ever pursued is money." His smile became hard, even bitter.

But Rory looked deep into his eyes and saw past the self-mockery, once again glimpsing the wistfulness, the pain.

"I don't believe you," she said softly. "You must have some other purpose in life."

"Oh, I guess I dabble in politics a little. I've been backing Stanley Addison in his bid to be mayor."

"Is that the man you were shouting at on the telephone yesterday?"

"That's the one. Now there's a dream chaser for you. The idealistic Mr. Addison believes he can rid our fair city of all its misery, the sweatshops, the slums, even unhelpful policemen like your good Sergeant O'Connell."

"You must believe it too," Rory challenged. "Or else why are you helping Mr. Addison?"

"I have to spend my money on something." Zeke stirred restlessly. If he did have any dreams, any ideals, he appeared too embarrassed to admit to them, perhaps even to himself.

He lapsed into silence again, and Rory wondered what topic he would seek to introduce next. He seemed to be avoiding the real purpose of his visit, but all of a sudden he shot to his feet. Steeling his jaw as though he had come to some resolution, he closed the distance between them in one long stride.

Perching on the sofa beside her, he captured both her hands. The assault came too swift, too unexpected for her to resist. The mere touch of his hand sent a warm current rushing through her, his nearness enough to leave her breathless, unable to speak.

"It's no good, Rory," he said, his eyes more somber, more serious than she had ever seen them before. "Ever since I walked into this parlor I've been searching for the right words to say to you and I can't seem to find them. I guess I'll just have to blunder along like I always do."

"G-good heavens. I can't imagine anything you have to tell me would be that difficult." She wanted to pull her hands away. Then maybe this mad thundering of her pulses would stop. But she felt powerless to move.

"It's always hard when a man has to admit to a woman that he lied."

"Lied? About what?"

"When I said that I possibly wanted you more than any woman I had ever known."

"Oh." Rory swallowed, conscious of a hollow feeling of disappointment. "Well, I never supposed you did mean such nonsense—"

"There was no *possibly* about it," Zeke cut in, his grip tightening, his voice dropping low, intense. "I have never desired any woman before like I do you. I thought I was angry when I chased you through the street, but in truth, I was almost desperate. I just can't get you out of my mind."

Rory had always thought she would feel something of a fool if a man made such passionate declarations to her. Her cheeks did fire, but not with embarrassment. Zeke's words sent a thrill through her that seemed to vibrate to the core of her soul.

She heard herself whisper in reply, "I haven't been able to stop thinking of you either."

A foolish admission, even a dangerous one, causing Zeke to steal his arms about her waist. But it was no more imprudent than what she did next, tipping back her head with Zeke's face hovering so near to her own, his mouth a breath away.

He kissed her, his lips gentle, tentative, giving her every chance to retreat if she wanted to. But she didn't.

She had to know if she would find the same magic in his arms as she had known before. Maybe it had only been the champagne. But as the kiss deepened, she knew it hadn't been. Zeke's mouth, whiskey-warm, grew more insistent, more demanding. Her lips parted in a soft, shuddering sigh as his tongue invaded her mouth. She gasped at the sensation, strange, erotic, at once seeming to steal her breath away and to gift her with fire.

When Zeke's hand moved upward to cup her breast, her protest came so weakly she could scarce hear it herself.

Beneath his caress, she could feel her nipple grow taut, straining against the fabric of her gown.

Desire stirred inside her, like embers banked upon the hearth flaring into a roar of flame. She returned Zeke's fevered kisses, hardly knowing what she did. Her fingers slipped inside his shirt, his flesh hot to the touch, his heart seeming to thunder beneath her palm.

With a low groan, Zeke pressed her back upon the sofa, pinning her under the hard length of him, the strength of his desire evident even through the layers of their clothing. The force of his passion should have frightened her, but it didn't.

The taste, the scent, the feel of him near drove her wild with longings she barely understood. Longings to touch and be touched by him, to sweep all barriers aside, to draw him as close as possible, then closer still, feel him bury himself inside of her.

His mouth hot upon hers, Zeke only drew breath to murmur her name. "Aurora . . . Aurora Rose." Never had she known anything could sound so sweet.

All fear, all reason slipped away from her as she arched against him, baring the pulse at her throat to his questing lips. When his mouth found that sensitive hollow, she closed her eyes, emitting a long, quivering sigh.

A thundering sounded in her ears. Lost in the fiery wonder of Zeke's caress, it took her a moment to realize the hammering did not issue from her own racing heart.

The sound echoed from the door of the flat. Someone was knocking. No, more like pounding, startling even Zeke into awareness.

"What the—" His head jerked up, his weight shifting so suddenly he tumbled off the sofa, dragging Rory with him. She fell squarely on top of him and felt the laughter rumble deep in his chest.

His eyes dark mists of desire, he tightened his arms about her, murmuring, "Let 'em go to hell. We're not at home."

As his mouth captured hers again, warm, teasing, slowly rebuilding the fire, Rory would happily have agreed with him. But the knocking sounded again. Even in the midst of her desire, she could not help wondering who could be so persistent.

Her friend Gia? Miss Flanagan, the Lord forbid? Or what if it was her parish priest? Father Grogan had said last Sunday that he would be calling upon parishioners to enlist aid for the upcoming charity bazaar.

It was the thought of the priest that did it. Cooled Rory's passion as effectively as being doused with holy water. When the rapping came again, this time rattling her door with the force of a sledgehammer, she wrenched herself out of Zeke's arms.

"I . . . I think I'd better answer it."

He cursed softly, but made no move to stop her. Rory managed to struggle to her feet. Flushed and somewhat unsteady, she patted at her hair, attempting to set her gown to rights.

"J-just a minute," Rory called, fearing that in another moment the person on the other side of the door would put a fist through it.

Zeke moistened his lips as though still tasting her kiss, collapsing back onto the sofa with a frustrated sigh. Fortifying herself with a deep breath, Rory crossed the room with all the primness she could muster.

Throwing back the bolt, she inched the door open a crack. Peering into the corridor beyond, she stifled a groan. A thousand times worse than Father Grogan! It was Tony. At this moment, the flush of passion barely fading from her cheeks, she thought it would have been easier to face the Pope himself rather than her friend's suspicious and belligerent stare.

"About time," Tony growled. "I saw the light coming up and knew you had to be in here. What took you so long to answer?"

"I . . . I was already getting undressed for bed. What do you want, Tony?"

A smile tightened his lips, not like Tony's usual generous grin, but thin-lipped, taut with a harsh kind of triumph.

"Let me in, Rory. I have to talk to you."

She kept herself firmly wedged in the doorway, shielding the flat's interior and Zeke from Tony's view. "I . . . I am too tired. Can't it wait until morning?"

"No, I told you I wasn't going to rest until I found out about that Morrison feller. I've done better than that. I brought someone to see you who can tell you everything about him."

Rory cast a half-nervous glance over her shoulder, wondering if Zeke was hearing all this. "This is ridiculous, Tony. I told you I didn't want you to—"

But Tony was already beckoning to another figure, who emerged from the shadows of the corridor. Rory tensed, not certain who she expected to appear, some tough-looking hoodlum perhaps. Certainly not the prim middle-aged woman who joined Tony on the threshold. Garbed in a plain black gown, the woman had dark hair veiled beneath a shawl. Her sharp features could never have been described as pretty, but it was the bitterness lurking in her eyes that robbed her face of any charm she might have had.

Rory had to fight down a strange urge to slam her door and bolt it against this grim stranger. Instead she said, "I don't know what this is all about, Tony. You've made some mistake. This lady doesn't look in the least like anyone who would be acquainted with Mr. Morrison."

"I am afraid you're wrong, my dear."

Zeke's voice coming so close to her made Rory start. She realized he had stolen up silently behind her, peering over her shoulder into the hall. Tony flushed and swore at the sight of Zeke, but the reaction of the strange woman was far more spectacular.

She blanched. Her eyes glittered with a hatred so strong it was as though a chilling wind swept through the hall, seeping into Rory's flat.

Bewildered, Rory glanced up at Zeke. "Then you . . . you do know this lady?"

He nodded, his eyes gone dull with remembered pain, but no more so than his voice when he replied.

"Of course I do. She's my sister."

Nine

Rory never remembered stepping aside, allowing her door to swing wide, but somehow the four of them ended up in her parlor—herself, Zeke, Tony and the woman with the dark hair and bitter eyes.

Zeke's *sister*.

An astonished silence had followed Zeke's statement, though it did not shock Rory so much to discover that he had a sister, or even that by contrast, the woman's clothes appeared plain and worn next to Zeke's expensive suit. What mostly stunned Rory was the depth of hatred contorting the woman's face. Although she had consented to enter, she lingered near the door, retreating deeper into the depths of her shawl as though she could not bear the sight of Zeke.

Rory's parlor had always been more cozy than spacious. With the undercurrents of emotion crackling in the air, the room seemed stifling. The woman said nothing, merely fretting the ends of her shawl. Tony hovered near Rory, glaring at Zeke like a jealous dog guarding a bone. As for herself, Rory felt at a loss as to what to say or do next. Only Zeke maintained a semblance of calm.

Leaning up against the mantel, he crossed his arms over his chest. His gaze remained steady, never wavering from his sister's face. "Well, this is a most unexpected reunion, Tessa. Permit me to introduce you to Miss Kavanaugh. Rory, this is my sister—"

"You are no brother of mine!" The woman spoke at last, her voice low, charged with loathing.

Only the flicker of an eyelid betrayed that her harsh words had any effect on Zeke. "So you have always told me, Tessa. On many occasions." He continued with deliberate emphasis. "This is my *sister*, Theresa Marceone."

He tipped his chin to that pugnacious angle, as though challenging her to contradict him again. When she did nothing but compress her lips, he turned to Rory. "And your friend?"

It took Rory a startled instant to realize that he was inquiring after Tony. "Oh . . . uh . . . this is Tony. Tony Bertelli."

"Ahhh. The long-lost balloon assistant."

It was as well Zeke didn't offer his hand, for Tony would never have taken it. Rory held her breath as the two men sized each other up, the hostility overt at least on Tony's part. Odd, but she had thought that Tony had grown to be such a man of late. But standing in the breadth of Zeke's shadow, he appeared no more than a sulky boy, and Rory sensed that Tony was miserably aware of that fact.

"Well, Mr. Bertelli, I missed some of what you were saying outside." Zeke's pleasantness was deceptive, never reaching as far as his eyes. "Perhaps you'd like to explain again why you have brought Tessa to call upon Rory."

"If I had known you would be here," Tessa spat out, "I wouldn't have come."

"I have no doubt of that. But forgive me, Tessa. I was addressing Mr. Bertelli."

Tony washed a dull red, but he thrust his hands in his pockets, adopting that belligerent stance Rory knew too well. "I don't like Rory going out with no strangers. I told her I'd do some checking. My brother Angelo has this friend who—"

"Oh, please, Tony." Rory gave a weary sigh. "Not that bit with the second cousin again."

"Anyhow," Tony continued doggedly, "I was lucky enough to track down Miss Marceone here, ask her some questions. I told her I had this friend who was getting involved with this Morrison fellow. She was nice enough to come with me to see Rory. To . . . to . . ."

For the first time, Tony faltered, looking a little uncomfortable beneath Zeke's hard stare.

"To warn her?" Zeke filled in softly.

Rory tried to intervene. "This is all very melodramatic and quite silly."

"Perhaps not, my dear," Zeke said, shifting his attention back to his sister. "What about it, Tessa? You've come a long way. Aren't you going to speak your piece? Don't hold back on my account."

"I don't intend to," she said.

"Good for you." Zeke gave a harsh laugh. "I'll say this much for you. You never were a backbiter. You always were willing to abuse me quite freely to my face."

Tessa ignored him, turning instead to Rory. Peering from beneath the layers of that black shawl, the woman made Rory think of a strange play Da had once taken her to see, something about the old days in Greece. A group of women had acted like a chorus chanting dire predictions. Theresa Marceone reminded Rory of just such a harbinger of doom as she gestured toward Zeke with a shaking hand.

"Miss Kavanaugh, you don't want to have anything to do with my broth— with this person here who calls himself Zeke Morrison. He's a bad man."

Rory opened her mouth, then closed it. What on earth was one supposed to reply to such a statement? She didn't want to insult the woman, nor did she wish to listen to Tessa's venomous remarks about Zeke either. Rory cast an appealing glance toward him, seeking some sort of reassurance, guidance on how to handle this extraordinary situation. But Zeke appeared to have retreated behind a wall of detachment as though none of these proceedings concerned him.

Tony tugged at her elbow, urging in a low voice, "You listen to Miss Marceone, Rory. She ought to know. She can tell you everything."

Tessa nodded in grim agreement. "My mother took that man off the streets when he was seven years old. She used to call him Johnnie, raised him up like her own son. He repaid her with nothing but heartaches. In and out of trouble until he had to flee New York. He finally returned, a rich man, though God alone knows how."

Tessa paused to cross herself. "That was when he finally broke my mother's heart, turned his back on her."

"That is not true," Zeke interrupted quietly. "I would have given that woman heaven and earth."

"Mama didn't want heaven and earth." Tessa whipped about to face Zeke, her eyes burning. "All she ever wanted was some small sign of love from you, just once to hear you call her 'mother.' All your lousy money and you couldn't even give her that."

Zeke's detachment crumbled. He paled, looking as though he had just taken a kick in the gut.

"You killed Mama with worrying over you," Tessa shrilled. "And then you didn't even come to see her buried."

Rory waited breathlessly for Zeke's words of denial, but none were forthcoming. He lowered his eyes.

Tessa flushed, saying to Rory with a kind of angry triumph, "So you beware of loving him, Miss Kavanaugh. He has no heart. He'll destroy all your dreams just as he ran roughshod over mine. I . . . I was engaged to be married until he drove my poor Marco away. Flashing his money around, he bullied and bribed Marco, forced him to desert me."

"I never meant to hurt you, Tessa," Zeke said. "I was trying to help—"

"By making certain that I stayed an old maid forever?" she cried accusingly. Her lips trembled, her eyes filling with tears. "For the rest of my life, I will be alone."

"Tessa, for the love of God!" Zeke stepped away from

the mantel, tried to rest his hands on her shoulders. "There is no reason that has to be true."

She struck his hands away. "Don't you touch me. I told you once I'd never forgive you and I meant it. You ruined my life. You ruin everything you touch." Her voice broke on a sob, her tears spilling over, streaking her cheeks. "There now. I have s-said all I mean to say."

Backing away from Zeke, she wrenched open the door to the flat and raced out into the corridor.

"Tessa!" Zeke's outcry was part curse, part plea. He rushed forward, and for a moment Rory thought he meant to run out as well. But he pulled up short on the threshold, dragging his fingers through his hair in frustration. He snapped at Tony, "Don't just stand there gawking. Go after her."

"Damned if I will," Tony said. "I'm not leaving you here alone with Rory."

"You brought my sister here and you are bloody well going to see that she gets home safely. I would myself but . . . ."

"But she doesn't want a thing to do with you," Tony said with a vicious satisfaction.

"Oh, shut up, Tony," Rory cried. "Zeke is right. Get going."

"Rory!" The look Tony gave her was one of stark betrayal, but Rory was beyond caring.

"I said, get out of here! You've caused enough trouble for one evening."

Hurt and anger warred in Tony's eyes. "Right! Well, you don't have to worry. I won't be causing you trouble anymore."

Whipping about, he left, deliberately shoving against Zeke as he rushed out of the flat, slamming the door behind him. But Zeke didn't even seem to feel it. He hurried to the windows that fronted the street and parted the curtain, peering out anxiously.

Rory joined him. In the pool of light cast by the street lamp, she could see Tony handing up Theresa Marceone into a wagon. Angelo was in the driver's seat and must have been waiting all this time. Apparently he was in on this too. At this moment, Rory would have given much to have boxed both their ears, Tony's and Angelo's.

Zeke let out a deep breath of relief as the wagon clattered off down the street. "Thank goodness for that or I would have had to take Tessa home myself, by force if necessary. And the devil knows she already has enough grudges against me."

Zeke let the curtain fall back in place, his shoulders sagging. Rory thought she had never seen any man look so drained. Her Da had told her once that words often inflicted more damage than fists. She'd never believed him until now.

Zeke appeared to have taken a worse battering from the confrontation with his sister than the one with the two street toughs. They had only roughed him up, bruised his jaw. It had taken Tessa to bring that look of utter misery into his eyes. And Zeke had raised scarce a whisper to defend himself, just letting her hammer away at him as though he somehow deserved it.

Rory rested one hand gently on Zeke's arm. "You don't have to worry about your sister. For all his temper, I know Tony will make sure she gets home."

"I'm certain he will." Zeke did not attempt to pull away, but he didn't respond to her touch either. "You never told me I had a rival, another suitor in the offing."

"He's not a suitor. He's . . . he's just Tony."

"I see." And Zeke did appear to, more than she would have thought possible, for he added wryly, "Poor fellow."

He walked slowly back to the armchair and gathered up the coat he had discarded before. A rush of alarm shot through Rory as he moved toward the door.

"What . . . what are you doing?"

He spared her a weary glance. "I was going to save you the trouble of asking me to leave."

"Why would I do a thing like that?" She rushed across the room. Although she did not do anything so dramatic as flatten herself against the door, she did get between Zeke and his exit.

"Come now, Rory. You're a sensible girl. And Tessa has seen to it that you have been most thoroughly warned."

"As if I would credit anything she had to say without . . . without . . ."

"Giving me a chance to defend myself. I can't. All that she said was basically true."

Was it? Rory wasn't so sure. Perhaps it was enough that Zeke believed it to be. No matter how bitterly or how much Tessa accused, no one condemned Zeke any more than he did himself. Rory could read it in his eyes, a sentence of eternal damnation.

"I still don't want you to go," she said in a small voice.

"Forgive me, Aurora Rose, but I fear I am in no humor to take up where we left off when we were interrupted."

His dry reference to that passionate moment on her sofa caused Rory to blush hotly. "I never expected you to. I . . . I only wanted to . . ." She faltered. How could she explain to him what she hardly understood herself? That she just couldn't let him leave this way, in a far worse case than when she had brought him home.

"It's . . . it's a long way cross town. You look so tired. I would offer to let you use my Da's bed, but I already gave it away to Tony's grandpa. But you could spend the night on my sofa. It's quite comfortable, and I am sure everything will seem so much better in the morning."

As his brows arched upward in surprise, she blurted out, "I can't bear the thought of you going back to that great empty house of yours."

"It's not empty. I have twenty-three servants." Despite the irony of his reply, his lips curved into the semblance of a smile. His eyes softened with something akin to gratitude. Retreating, he dropped his coat back on the chair.

Rory let out a long breath of relief.

He was going to stay.

Rory had actually tucked a blanket around him, Zeke thought with some bemusement as he lay flat on his back on the sofa, staring up at the ceiling. And she had pressed

a shy kiss to his forehead before turning down the lamps
and retreating to her own bedroom at the back of the flat.

Now the parlor was lost in shadow and silence, only
the moonlight providing patches of illumination, the only
sound an occasional clatter of coach wheels from the street
below. The darkness, the quiet, oppressed Zeke, and he
wished he had been more responsive to Rory's kindness.
She probably thought him damned ungrateful, which was
far from the case.

No matter how great his misery, he only had to think of
her and he found himself able to smile. She was a bit of a
hoyden, his Rory. A mad tomboy, taking crazy risks up in
the sky and on the streets of New York. Imagine walking
alone through that warehouse district after dark! Still, she
had fairly brained that one ruffian who had attacked him.

Yet for all her toughness, she had her more womanly
side. He could almost still feel the gentleness of her hands,
pulling the blanket more snugly about him, softly bidding
him good night. Funny, he'd never given it much thought
before, but he could picture Rory as a mother, raising up
a brood of kids.

Oh, she would be quick to deal a smart slap to sticky
fingers caught raiding the cookie jar, or to box the ears of
squabbling siblings. But he could also imagine her mend-
ing scraped knees, brushing back tousled hair, bestowing
fiercely tender kisses to soothe away childish woes.

He'd made a mistake when he believed all her nonsense
about not being the marrying kind. That's exactly what she
was. She ought to be wed to someone like that Tony. For
all the trouble he had caused Zeke, dragging Tessa here
tonight, Zeke could tell Tony was a nice boy, an honest
one with Rory's best interests at heart. It was painfully
obvious the kid was crazy in love with Rory, half-mad
with jealousy.

And Zeke Morrison, once known as Johnnie Marceone?
Well, he was nothing but a selfish bastard. Thinking back
to that scene earlier on the sofa with Rory now only filled
him with self-loathing. Ever since meeting Rory, he hadn't
given much consideration to anything but his own desires.

Tessa had been right to come here and warn Rory. Exactly as she had said after her own simplistic fashion—he was a bad man.

Zeke tossed restlessly, nearly dislodging the blanket Rory had tucked so carefully about him. He had to bend his knees, the sofa not quite matching him in length, but he had slept in far worse places. It wouldn't have mattered if he had been ensconced upon the world's downiest feather bed. No matter how exhausted he was, he knew he would get no sleep tonight.

It had been a shock seeing Tessa again. A year had gone by since he'd seen her last and she still looked ready to spit in his eye. Time had done nothing to dull her tongue. Sharp as ever, she could be more cutting than any blade that had ever nicked him in a street fight.

Maybe that was as it should be. Sadie Marceone had always been too gentle, never rebuking Zeke half enough. Perhaps it was good that she had always had Tessa to do it for her.

All Mama ever wanted . . . just once to hear you call her "mother." All your lousy money and you couldn't even give her that.

Zeke flung one arm across his eyes. He could shut out the patterns of moonlight spilling through the curtains, but he couldn't shut out those accusing words or the pain-filled memories they spawned.

He could still see that day so clearly, he might well have been a kid again, all of seven years old. He had been fighting as usual. Some bigger boys had been picking on Buck Tooth Willy again, ever an object of ridicule because of his prominent front teeth.

Zeke had been stupid to challenge the older boys. He was big for his age, but they were so much bigger, members of that dreaded street gang, the Plug Uglies. But something in him had never borne much tolerance for bullies, so he rushed to Billy's rescue, fists flying. Billy had escaped, but the two youths had damn near busted Zeke's head open.

They had left him on his knees in the street, blood spurting from his nose. That's how Sadie Marceone had found him. That was the first time he ever looked up into her plump, careworn features. Even then the lines had crisscrossed a face forever old, yet her eyes, remarkable blackcurrant eyes, had been forever young.

She had fussed over him, clucking her tongue in that motherly fashion she had, then scooped him out of the gutter, taking him back to the settlement house where she did volunteer work.

While the other ladies doled out soup to the vagrant poor of the city, Sadie took him back into the kitchens, cleaned up his nose and applied ointment to his cuts.

Looking back on it now, Zeke was surprised that he had let her, half-wild little savage that he had been, subsisting mostly off the leavings of garbage cans like some stray dog. Perhaps it had been because Sadie was the first woman he remembered ever being kind to him. Most ladies had eyed him askance, as though they thought he meant to steal their purse, or, worse yet, chased him with the business end of a broom for bringing his dirty person too near their own pampered darlings.

As she tended his hurts, her work-roughened hands had been gentle, her broad smile warmer than the fire blazing in the coal stove.

"That was a fine thing you did standing up to those bullies," she said. "I saw how you rushed to help that other boy."

"Naw, I didn't neither," he growled. "I just like to fight."

"Well, I think you're a brave boy all the same. Your mama must be real proud of you."

"Not my mother!"

"Nonsense. All mothers are proud of their sons." She patted his cheek, but he wrenched away from her.

"That shows all you know, lady. My mother thought I was garbage. When I was a baby, she dumped me in the trash bin behind the orphanage."

Sadie's eyes went real bright at that. She looked away for a minute, dragging the cuff of her sleeve across her face. She sniffed like a person catching a cold, and when she turned back, her smile was even more gentle.

"What's your name, child?"

"John Doe!" he declaimed promptly. That's what he told most everyone since running away from the orphanage. The matron there, being of a Biblical turn between bouts of drinking, had named him Ezekiel. But Zeke only shared his real name with his most trusted companions. And at that juncture, he had hardly known what to make of Sadie Marceone, let alone trust her.

If she smiled at the clumsiness of his lie, she managed to hide it from him. "John. That's a good strong name," was all she said.

When she had done patching his hurts, she gave him something to eat. But the extent of his trust had been stretched to the limit for that day. He snatched away the chunk of bread and meat and bolted with it, out of the soup kitchen, disappearing down one of the alleyways as he already knew so well how to do.

But after that, he had taken to hanging about the settlement house on the days when he knew she would be there. Sometimes he only drew near long enough to wrench the food from her outstretched hands. Other times he lingered long enough to talk, even let her brush the hair back from his eyes, although he always groused, "Quit that, lady." Pretending to be so tough, all the while he had been secretly pleased by the small gesture.

It couldn't have been more than a few weeks that passed in this fashion before she confessed to him, "Johnnie, I . . . I went to visit that orphanage you told me about."

He glared up at her, his whole body trembling with the pain of imagined betrayal. "You snitched on me. You told them where I am."

"No, Johnnie, of course I didn't. I only needed to find out some things about you." A troubled look came into her eyes, which quickly cleared as she beamed down at him. "You see, I want to adopt you, Johnnie. I want to bring you home with me . . . to be my own boy."

He did not believe her at first. But she meant it. Things seemed to happen quickly after that. His memory contained only fragmented images of standing up before a judge and being told his name was now John Marceone.

Far clearer was the day he had been taken home to the cozy warmth of an apartment, garbed in the first new clothes he had ever owned—knickers and a sailor middy. The cloth was cheap, but the stitching impeccable, set in by Sadie's own clever hands. He had barely had time to take in his new surroundings when he was confronted by three girls in calico dresses, all with long, dark braids. They rose like stair steps, the youngest about his own size and age, the eldest, Caddie, at that time seeming to tower over him. All three regarded him with solemn, critical eyes.

"Girls." Sadie placed her hand on his shoulder. "This is Johnnie. He's come to live with us, the brother I promised you."

Caddie softened enough to give him a shy smile, while Agnes, the little one, let out a delighted whoop and planted a kiss on Zeke's cheek. She didn't even seem to mind when he scrubbed it away. But Tessa, the one nearest his own age, glowered with resentment, muttering low enough so that Sadie couldn't hear, "We don't need any boys around here."

If the little girl with the dark, scornful eyes had been a boy, Zeke would have socked her for making it so plain that he didn't belong here any more than he had ever belonged anywhere else in his short life. Instead he assured himself it didn't matter. He didn't want to live in a houseful of silly girls either. First chance he found, he would get the hell out of there.

His moment came after supper when Sadie shooed the girls off to clear the table. Settled into her rocker, she appeared absorbed with darning a pair of Tessa's stockings. Zeke backed toward the door.

Without glancing up from her work, Sadie said softly, "You can run away again if you want to, Johnnie. But I hope you won't."

Somehow her giving him permission to flee dulled his desire to do so. He squared up to her, saying, "Well, I might hang out here—for a day or two. But I don't want any more mushing over me, see? And don't expect me to start calling you Mama."

Her eyes were sad, but filled with understanding. "You don't have to, Johnnie. But if the day ever comes when you want to, that'd be just fine with me."

Even after all these years, those patient words still echoed through Zeke's mind, more bitter than any reproach that Tessa could have heaped upon him. He tried to shake off all these troubling memories and snap himself back to the reality of tossing upon the sofa in Rory's tiny parlor.

But with Rory asleep in the next room, there was little distraction, only the lonely ticking of the clock upon the mantel. Remembrance of Sadie's wistful expression continued to haunt him.

What had she seen in him anyway that had impelled her to such a rash step, taking in a half-wild street kid to be her son? It wasn't as though she were some wealthy woman given to philanthropic impulses. Far from it. A poor widow, she had labored long and hard, plying her needle, already burdened with the care of three young daughters. Still she had found time to do charity work, at the settlement house, for her church.

Had he been just another of her charities? She had never made Zeke feel that way. More like the son she had always wanted, but never had. But in the end, he had proved a disappointment to her.

True, with time, he had mellowed somewhat from the young savage he had been, learned to wash once a day, not to get into fights more than twice, to bow his head when grace was said, even if he was too stubborn to pray along. But the one thing he had never learned was how to show her his love. Long after he had come to think of her in his heart as his mother, he had continued to call her Lady. After all, tough fellows didn't show their feelings, didn't do anything so embarrassing as go around bleating "Mama."

And when he was finally old enough to know better, it had been too late.

With a heavy sigh, Zeke struggled against the sofa pillows, levering himself into a sitting position. Christ, he would never get to sleep this way. The stillness in the flat seemed to reproach him like the silence of Sadie's grave.

It was so close in here, he could feel circles of dampness gathering beneath his arms. Maybe he had made a mistake staying here tonight. Sadie had never wanted anything to do with his mansion on Fifth Avenue. Her ghost rarely haunted him there.

But Rory's place was too reminiscent of that old apartment, the home Sadie had carved for her family in that concrete wasteland that was Little Italy. Zeke had had difficulty, after so many nights huddled in some alley, in sleeping there too. His temperature had always seemed to run a shade hotter than Sadie's and the girls'.

Flinging off the covers, Zeke finally got to his feet. Surely Rory would have no objection if he opened a window. He approached one of the side ones and tugged at the sash. It stuck. Didn't they always? He was obliged to put a little shoulder into it before the window creaked upward. But the welcome rush of cool air was worth the struggle.

Just outside loomed the familiar metal rungs of a fire escape, making it possible to descend or mount up to the roof. A smile tugged at Zeke along with a memory, one of his few pleasant ones. On those really hot nights, Sadie had always let him sleep up on the roof. It was a good place for privacy, to get away from the chattering of Caddie and Agnes, Tessa's endless scolding. Only him and all those stars to count. Somehow up there it had been easier to relax, to stop being so tough, to harbor a few tender dreams hidden away beneath the moon's shadows.

Zeke leaned up against the window frame, a rare mood of nostalgia sweeping over him. A sudden impulse seized him, or was it the night itself that beckoned? He didn't know, but the next instant he eased himself through the window onto the fire escape. He peered down through the grating to the street below. It was only two stories down, but Zeke felt a familiar churning in the pit of his stomach. He had always had a fear of heights, ever since he was a kid and two of the Plug Uglies had dangled him by his heels from on top of the old cotton warehouse. It had been one of the few times in his life anyone had ever gotten him to cry uncle.

After all this time, Zeke knew the fear to be irrational, but there seemed to be no ridding himself of it. He coped now as he had always done as a boy. Taking a deep breath, he forced himself to look up, never down. Clambering along the metal rungs, he finally reached the flat surface of the roof.

He had almost been afraid he would find the experience not at all as he remembered, changed somehow, but it wasn't. The night was like velvet, the sky still as vast as he recalled, the stars just as far away and mysterious. Keeping a prudent distance from the edge, Zeke sat down, drawing up his knees. Of course it had not been that long ago that he had done this, only two years. But he hadn't noticed much of anything then.

The last time he had been with Sadie. A hot July night, he helped her up above to seek some relief, but no air was stirring, not even on the rooftop. And still Sadie shivered. She was already sick then. If only he hadn't been so stupid, he would have noticed that. But he had been too caught up describing to her the wonders of his castle on Fifth Avenue.

"I'll get you away from this wretched tenement at last, lady. The kitchen is going to be bigger than your whole apartment. You'll love it."

Sadie only gave a sad shake of her head. "I don't belong in such a place, Johnnie. I wouldn't know how to go on."

"You'd learn. My friend, Mrs. Van Hallsburg, has undertaken to teach me to be a gent. I'll get her to help you become a grand lady."

Zeke flinched now at the recollection of his own crudity, his incredible ignorance. As if there had been anything that Mrs. Van H. or any woman could have taught Sadie. The mention of the wealthy widow had only served to spoil that night with his mother, his last, if he had only known it.

On parting, Sadie's eyes had been shaded with trouble. She had always looked that way, ever since he had first told her of his acquaintance with Mrs. Van Hallsburg.

"I wish you would stay away from her, Johnnie. She's

not a good woman. She comes from bad blood—all those Markhams. Cold, uncaring people."

Zeke had been surprised that such a remark would come from Sadie, who ever saw only the good in people.

"But you don't know the Markhams or Mrs. Van H.," he had protested.

"I know enough," she began and then stopped. He had the feeling she had meant to say more, but she complained suddenly of dizziness, begging him to take her inside.

Although he had been disturbed, Zeke had managed to dismiss Sadie's warning. After all, she had only ever seen Mrs. Van H. once. He had pointed the elegant widow out to her during a Sunday drive through Central Park.

But remembering the incident, it now struck him as strange, especially considering that Rory had also taken a strong aversion to Mrs. Van H. on first sight. What was it Rory had said when Zeke had awoken her from that nightmare in his bed?

She had been dreaming that Mrs. Van. H. was some sort of a monster. "She's evil," Rory had insisted.

These women and their peculiar instincts. Zeke wished he could dismiss them that lightly, but the memories continued to trouble him. He was still pondering the matter when he heard the scrape of metal behind him. Someone was mounting the fire escape.

A half-formed hope seized him that Rory might have awakened, found him missing. If she had noticed the window open, perhaps she had guessed where he had gone and decided to join him. Earlier he had only wanted to be alone, lick his wounds from the scrap with Tessa. But now he welcomed the thought of Rory.

He glanced over his shoulder, but his smile froze on his lips. For the second time that night shadows fell across one of the ugliest faces he had ever seen, the man with the scarred chin.

"What the devil?" Zeke started to exclaim, tensing for battle, but this time his reflexes were a shade too slow.

A heavy club swished down through the darkness, catching him hard on the side of the head. The stars above him seemed to explode, a thousand pinpoints of white hot light.

Then they vanished and there was nothing but unrelenting black.

Ten

Rory awoke from a deep, dreamless night with a headache niggling behind her eyes, oppressed by the feeling that something was wrong. Her mind yet fogged with sleep, she remembered that she had gone to bed troubled, but her thoughts were not collected enough to recall what that trouble had been.

Whatever it was, it had sent her to sleep hugging her pillow as she always did when beset with some worry. Even now that downy cushion was crushed close to her breasts. Thrusting it away from her, Rory rolled onto her back, rubbing the haze from her eyes. She blinked at the sunlight streaming across the oak railing at the foot of her bed.

Morning . . . and well advanced past sunrise judging by the sounds emanating from the sidewalks below. She had left her window open a crack, allowing the clatter of passing horse carts to invade her bedchamber, the shrill voices of children marching off to school, shouting and scuffling, the milkman cursing at Finn MacCool for nipping his ankle again, Miss Flanagan hollering back it served Mr. Peaby right for forgetting her second bottle of cream.

Just the normal Monday hubbub on McCreedy Street. Why then did something seem so different? There was always enough noise on a workday to wake the dead.

Or Zeke.

Rory sat up with a start, memory flooding back to her. That's what was unusual. She was not alone in her apartment. Zeke Morrison had spent the night on her sofa, was likely still lost in slumber.

She must have been crazy, insisting that he stay. Yet when she recalled that hollow look in his eyes, that lost, empty expression, she realized she could have done no differently.

In truth, part of her regretted she had not led him to the warmth of her bed, cradled him in her arms, offered him comfort.

Comfort, Aurora Rose Kavanaugh? A stern voice echoed in her head, sounding not unlike the old nun who had taught her her catechism. Are you sure that was all you wished to offer him?

Rory refused to answer that question, even to herself. A guilty flush stole over her cheeks as she scrambled out of bed and pulled a dressing gown over the white muslin of her nightgown. She caught a glimpse of herself in the mirror, a pink-faced gypsy of a girl, her thick chestnut locks in wild disarray. And she scarce knew who she was. Not hoyden Rory, but some other strange creature, a young woman trembling with frightening, but alluring, desires.

She shouldn't even be thinking about such things as having Zeke in her bed. Hadn't she come close enough to being a sinner last night? All recollection of what had nearly happened with Zeke upon the sofa should have shamed her. She should have been grateful Tony arrived when he did, interrupting Zeke's lovemaking.

Instead she felt curiously bereft. It was like hearing the opening notes of some lilting melody, only to have it cut off, being left yearning, wondering whether one would ever hear the rest of that haunting refrain.

What romantic nonsense. Rory tried to give herself a swift mental shake as she reached for the comb on her nightstand, tugging it through her tangle of curls. Nonsense it might be, but she still felt angry at Tony for his intrusion, dragging Zeke's sister to Rory's flat, inadvertently setting off that grim confrontation.

Zeke Morrison is a bad man.

How childish, how spiteful Tessa Marceone's words had sounded. And yet no matter how it was worded, the woman's warning was not so different from those that Rory had repeated to herself. Hadn't she tried to run away from Zeke, determined never to see him again? Tessa's accusations should only have reinforced Rory's own qualms about the man.

Instead they had had the opposite effect. Rory found herself wanting to spring to Zeke's defense, claws unsheathed like a wildcat. She sensed that Zeke had been brutalized enough in his life without his stepsister pouring acid into old wounds. Strange that someone like Zeke, so street-toughened, so ready with his fists, should have stood so helpless against the mere cut and thrust of a woman's tongue. Stranger still that Rory should feel so tenderly protective of a man large enough to crush her slender frame with one blow.

Even the thought of being alone with him in her flat no longer frightened her. It disturbed her in an odd shivery kind of way, but it didn't frighten her. In fact, she caught her heart racing as she contemplated slipping into the parlor, rousing him from sleep.

They had never eaten supper last night. She bet he'd be hungry. She derived immense satisfaction from the thought of leading him into her tiny kitchen, bustling about getting the coffee ready, setting before him a plateful of eggs and toast.

She pictured him sitting opposite her, his hair mussed, his jaw shadowed with pricklings of dark beard. He would regard her over the rim of his cup with that languid manner of appraisal that set all her skin a-tingle.

Maybe their hands would meet. Maybe, just maybe, he would feel like talking, opening a little that locked vault that was his heart.

This domestic scene in her imagination grew so strong that Rory slipped eagerly into a pair of carpet slippers. She was still forcing her heel into one as she limped through the bedroom door and down the short hallway.

She tiptoed beneath the arch that led into the parlor.

"Zeke?" she called softly.

Her gaze tracked to the couch, and she frowned a little to see crumpled on the floor the coverlet she had tucked about him. The pillow bore the indentation made by his head, his coat was flung over the chair, but the tiny, cluttered parlor seemed curiously empty.

Somehow Rory knew there was no use searching for Zeke in the kitchen or tapping upon the door of the narrow closet that comprised her bathroom.

He was gone.

A numbing feeling of disappointment washed over her, and for a minute, she just stood, staring at the vacant sofa as though if she looked long and hard, she could conjure out of thin air the solid frame of steely muscle that was Zeke.

Eventually she was roused from this gloomy contemplation by a clacking sound. The side window had been left flung wide open, and the brisk morning breeze was causing the curtains to billow out, knocking against the étagère, threatening to dislodge some of the knickknacks.

Rory moved almost lethargically to close the window. As she struggled to do so, she glanced into the street below. Perhaps he had only stepped out for a moment to . . . to what? Pet Finn McCool? Pass the time of day with Miss Flanagan? Foolish thoughts. There was no one down there except a mother pushing a perambulator, some clerkish-looking male sprinting past her, obviously late in catching the horsecar uptown.

Rory forced the sash closed and drew the drapes. "Well, Mr. Morrison," she murmured. "It would seem this time it is you who has run away."

But from whom? Her? That hardly seemed possible, no, not after the determined way he had been pursuing her, tracking her to her own part of town. More likely it was memories that he fled, those ghosts of the past that forever seemed to be looking over his shoulder.

"Damn Tony anyway," Rory muttered. "And that Tessa too." She took an angry pleasure in imagining the tongue lashing she would give Tony the next time she saw him, her thoughts interrupted only by the sound of a knock at the door.

"Oh, the devil," Rory swore, wondering who could be plaguing her at this early hour. But a sudden hope stirred within her, irrational but irrepressible all the same. Yes, it just might be the devil, with his wicked dark eyes and lazily sensual grin.

Rory rushed across the room and flung the door open.

But it wasn't Zeke come back to her, full of apologies and explanations. Only Tony, shuffling his feet, looking awkward.

"Uh, g'morning, Rory."

Her lips thinned. "After all the trouble you caused last night, Tony Bertelli, I don't have much to say to you." She started to shut the door in his face.

He jammed the heel of his hand against the frame, preventing her.

"Aw, come on, Rory, please. I ain't here to fight with you anymore. I only want to tell you I am sorry."

She hesitated, but she could see that he meant it. The hollows rimming his eyes told her that he'd had a bad night, Tony who always slept with the imperturbability of a granite boulder.

Not that he didn't deserve to pass a sleepless night after what he had done, interfering when she had told him not to, embarrassing her with that fierce protective air as though she were still nothing but a kid. But how could she keep her heart steeled against him when he stood twisting his cap in his ungainly hands, looking at her so wistfully?

Grudgingly, she stepped back, allowing him to enter. He stepped just inside the door, making no move to come any farther into her parlor, shuffling his feet as uncomfortably as any stranger not sure of his welcome—Tony, her friend, her brother, the kid from the next block, the boy whose heart she was breaking.

A small sigh escaped her. "Oh, stop acting like such a goose, Tony. I'm not going to bite you."

"No? The look in your eyes when you opened the door reminded me of Miss Flanagan's dog." He tried to smile, but his joke fell flat. He took in a deep breath. "I am sorry about what happened last night. I shouldn't have brought that woman here."

"Indeed you shouldn't have. You caused a great deal of upset."

"You're telling me!" Tony rolled his eyes. "That Miss Marceone cried all over my jacket the whole way home. She told me some more about how that fellow Morrison stopped her from marrying. Mother of God, that fool woman was going to run off with Marco Duracy."

Apparently the name conveyed something to Tony, but Rory merely shot him a blank look.

"Marco Duracy? You never heard Angelo talk about him? Well, see, Angelo knew this fellow from down on the docks whose uncle's third wife's daughter—"

"Oh, Tony, please." Rory groaned, clutching her head. "It's too early in the morning for this. Just make your point."

"Anyway, this Marco Duracy was a real worthless piece of—" Tony broke off, with a cough. "Er, he was a bounder, lazy, good-for-nothing. Mean tempered. I wouldn't let any sister of mine get near him."

Rory folded her arms and regarded Tony with a taut smile of triumph. "Then perhaps whatever Tessa might say, Zeke's actions were justified."

"Mebbe." Tony's chin jutted stubbornly. "But it don't make me like this Morrison guy any better. There are still some things about him that are real doubtful. But I didn't come here to get you all riled, talking about him again."

He crumpled his cap some more, staring down at the threadbare carpet. "What I really came to say is that I know I was acting beyond the limit. No matter how I feel about you, I got no business meddling. You have the right to love whoever you want to even if it isn't me."

"Oh, Tony." She touched his sleeve, her eyes glistening.

"No, I mean it, Rory. You should be free to choose for yourself, no matter what kind of bum you pick, no matter how rotten—"

"*Thank you*, Tony," she intervened sharply, before he went on to ruin the whole effect of his apology and make her angry all over again.

"I just wanted you to know that I'll always be here if you need me. I understand I can never be anything more to you, but we have been friends for a long time. I still want that."

"So do I."

She wanted to fling her arms about him, give him a big hug, but the longing in his eyes was yet keen. She couldn't risk it. Instead she gave him a poke on the arm, which he returned, the gestures stiff, awkward, rather than playful. But it was a beginning. . . .

Tony settled his cap back on his head, exhaling a deep breath of relief. "There! Now that we got that all cleared up, maybe we can be heading for the warehouse. Did you eat breakfast yet? We could . . ."

His voice wavered as for the first time he appeared to notice the rumpled coverlet on the floor by the sofa and Zeke's coat lying over the chair. Tony swallowed, looking a little sick. "He . . . he's not still here, is he?"

Rory shook her head.

Tony frowned. He appeared to be biting his own tongue off in an effort to keep from haranguing her any more about Zeke. It was a heroic struggle, but he won it.

"You better get dressed," he said gruffly. "So we can get to work."

"Well, I . . ." Rory hesitated, feeling strangely reluctant to leave the flat. There was always a chance that Zeke would come back here looking for her.

And how long do you propose to wait, you fool? a voice jeered mercilessly inside her. All of the morning, the day, the rest of her life perhaps? She was being idiotic, but somehow she had never felt less like going to the warehouse, dealing with the problems of her floundering company.

"I don't know if I'm feeling up to going in to work today," Rory said.

"Rory! You can't have forgotten, this is the day the government man is coming to look over our operation, to decide about giving us the army contract."

Rory let out a low groan. She had forgotten. She couldn't believe that she had let such an important happening slip her mind. The truth was that ever since meeting Zeke, she had not been giving her full concentration to the Transcontinental Balloon Company. She cast a guilty glance to where Da's picture stood on the parlor table. The youthful soldier that had been her father seemed to bristle with reproach, a reproach that Tony should have been heaping on her.

It was not only her own future tied up in that company, but Tony's as well, Angelo's, Pete's and the handful of other young men who had given up good, steady jobs down at the docks in order to work for her.

Not only was her behavior stupid, it was incredibly selfish. For one day at least, she needed to get Zeke Morrison out of her head.

"You have a seat, Tony," she said. "It won't take me more than a few minutes to get ready."

She was as good as her word. Darting into her bedchamber, she scrambled into a navy-colored Newport suit—a gored skirt with matching jacket, constructed of sensible repellent cloth, plain and businesslike. She managed to knot her unruly mane of hair up into a neat chignon.

Barely a quarter of an hour later, she and Tony left the flat. It was a lovely spring morning, a little brisk, but the sun was shining, warming the front stoops of the brownstones. Even Finn MacCool looked mellowed. Basking in the rays, asleep, he merely opened one eye long enough to growl at Tony and Rory as they passed.

It was like so many other mornings when Tony had dropped by to join her in catching the El, heading for the warehouse, talking balloons. This morning they speculated on their chances of getting that government contract.

If Tony lapsed silent a little more than usual, if he often avoided looking at her, Rory supposed that was to be expected. And if her own thoughts frequently wandered to a certain brash Fifth Avenue tycoon, wondering where Zeke was, what he was doing, what he was feeling, why, that couldn't be helped either.

Since neither she nor Tony had breakfasted, they took a detour by way of Grand Street as they often did, lured by the prospect of lox and cream cheese sandwiched between fresh-baked bagels.

The Jewish quarter of the city had always fascinated Rory, the narrow streets with their endless rows of pushcarts, selling everything from newly-killed chickens to violins. Bearded peddlers haggled with their female customers, whose hair was bound up in kerchiefs. Scholarly-looking men, wearing eyeglasses and skullcaps, lingered on corners, lost in what Rory was always certain must be deep discussions, although she understood not a word of that mysterious language called Yiddish.

After she and Tony had made their purchase, they planted themselves atop a couple of herring barrels to enjoy their breakfast. Rory didn't realize how hungry she was until she bit into her bagel, but as usual Tony had already demolished his before she was half-done.

Licking his fingers, he glanced around, preparing to perform that other daily ritual, the purchase of the morning paper. Although on Grand Street many of the papers for sale were printed in those strange Hebraic symbols, the ubiquitous *New York World* still made its appearance. Tony flagged down a newspaper hawker and secured one.

Usually he would have taken a few moments to glance through it. But with the government man due to arrive that afternoon, neither he nor Rory dared linger too long. There was much to be done to get ready at the warehouse.

As they set off, retracing their steps to the nearest El platform, Tony folded up the paper and tucked it under his arm. But Rory caught enough of a glimpse of the front page headline to make her freeze in her tracks.

"Tony, let me see that a minute."

She didn't wait for him to comply, but snatched the paper from beneath his arm. She unfolded it, her pulse already setting up a thrum of apprehension.

A bold headline jumped out at her.

Millionaire Wanted by Police.

Rory felt her heart turn over. She tried to read the accompanying article under the byline of a Mr. W. Duffy, but it was difficult with Tony crowding so close and the words blurring before her panic-stricken gaze.

"What's the matter, Rory? What are you reading? Holy damnation!"

To her intense frustration, Tony grabbed the paper from her to gain a better look. She had not been able to make out more than the words "J. E. Morrison . . . wanted concerning disappearance of Stanley Addison."

"Tony!" Rory bounced on tiptoe, trying without avail to read over his shoulder. "What does it say? About Zeke? It all has to be some sort of ridiculous mistake. Zeke was with me most of last night. How could he tell them anything about the disappearance of Mr. Addison?"

Tony lowered the paper, looking at her with wide, troubled eyes. "Rory, this paper doesn't say Addison just disappeared. He's dead.

"And your Mr. Morrison . . . he's wanted for *murder*."

Eleven

Zeke Morrison felt as if the top of his skull were going to explode. But considering the pain that thundered like the strokes of a hundred hammers, the loss of his head might prove a blessing. For what seemed an eternity he had been conscious of nothing but mind-numbing agony, mists of darkness webbing his eyes the few times he tried to open them. The effort to do so had proved so great, he had given over trying.

But slowly the pain receded enough to allow him awareness of other things—the feel of silk beneath his cheek, the heavy odor of cheap perfume, so strong it made him want to retch. He remembered enough to know he had sprawled out on Rory's sofa to spend the night. But such a cloying scent had nothing to do with the riot of springtime, the freshness that was Aurora Rose. Something wasn't right.

He managed to raise his hand to his head, flinching as his fingers came in contact with a huge knot swelling on his scalp. He eased his eyes open, a fraction at a time. All was a dizzying blur, but eventually the room stopped spinning. He found himself surrounded not by the cozy warmth of Rory's parlor, but an atmosphere far different.

167

Moth-eaten velvet curtains blocked out most of the light, for which Zeke was grateful. His gaze roved around the chamber, taking in the tawdry flocked wallpaper, the cheap gilt trim on the bedposts and dresser. Somehow it all fit well with the stink of the perfume.

Zeke blinked in recognition, not of this particular place, but of similar establishments he had frequented enough to know a bedroom in a brothel when he saw one.

He could almost hear the echo of Sadie's voice scolding. *Johnnie, why must you have anything to do with bad girls like those?*

"This time, lady, I swear I'm innocent," Zeke murmured. How had he come to be here? Not by his own power, of that he was certain. He couldn't even remember leaving Rory's flat.

He shifted slightly on the lumpy mattress, his head throbbing with the effort to remember. It had been too warm in Rory's parlor. He had opened the window, climbed up to the roof.

The roof! Footsteps behind him, the thug with the jagged scar, the heavy club crashing down . . . It all came back to Zeke in a blinding flash. A soft groan escaped him.

Attacked by the same man twice in one night? It made no sense. Obviously, the Chin Scar had trailed Zeke to Rory's flat, lurked in the street below, waiting for him to leave. When Zeke had climbed up to the roof, the thug must have spotted him and followed. In Zeke's experience, pickpurses usually weren't so persistent. He didn't know what this was all about. He was only sure of one thing—he had to get out of here.

Beads of sweat and pain gathering on his brow, Zeke struggled to raise himself. But at that moment, he heard the scrape of a heavy boot, the chink of a key as someone unlocked the bedchamber door.

Too weak to risk further conflict, Zeke instinctively felt it might be better to lie still. Closing his eyes, he feigned unconsciousness as the door swung open. The floorboards creaked, and Zeke sensed someone standing over him.

He risked peering beneath his lashes enough to see who

it was—two men, undoubtedly the same two who had assaulted him earlier.

The ugly one with the scarred chin leaned closer. "Hey, I thought I saw him move. I better give him another thunk."

Zeke tensed, keeping himself motionless with great difficulty. To his relief the second man intervened. "Naw, stupid. He's supposed to wake up."

"Yeah?" the Chin Scar grunted. "Well, I don't like none of it, all this play-acting and games. This feller's too dangerous. Damn near broke my jaw before. I shoulda just slit his throat the first time we jumped him."

"Good thing you didn't. The boss man would've been mad as hell. Might not have paid us. He wants him alive . . . for now."

The voices faded and Zeke heard the door close, telling him he had been left alone again. He tried to clear his disordered thoughts, make some sense of what he had just heard. *The boss man wants him alive . . . for now.*

So he had been right. This series of attacks was no coincidence, no minor attempt at thievery, but part of some more sinister plan directed by a person who had not as yet revealed himself.

It would seem you have an enemy, Zeke, my boy. There was nothing new about that. In the old days, he could have taken his pick of any number of rival gang members who might have wanted to see him dead. Now that he was a respected pillar of the community, that was supposed to be all behind him. In fact it had been a long time since he had even been threatened. Not unless one counted Charles Decker's pathetic bluster.

Zeke's lips curled in contempt as an image of the politician rose in his mind, the weasly fellow sitting in Zeke's office hemming and hawing, while he had hinted that Zeke should drop his support of Stanley Addison or else he would be sorry.

All bluff. Or so Zeke had thought. He still had difficulty picturing Decker, in his natty checked business suit, dealing with street toughs like the Chin Scar, arranging something so desperate as abduction, possibly murder.

Yet Decker had been hard-pressed of late. Any rat when cornered would bite. Maybe, just maybe, Zeke had been foolish to underestimate the man.

Only one thing was clear. He would find out nothing lying here in some night chippie's bed. Nothing except how they intended for him to die.

Luckily his captors had not taken the trouble to bind him. Whoever was paying the Chin Scar wasn't getting much value for his dollar. The thug wasn't that good in a fight, nor was he overburdened with brains.

This time when Zeke struggled to rise, it still hurt, but his head didn't swim so bad. He made it to a sitting position, the ache behind his eyes settling to a dull throb. Hell, he always had had a hard head.

Swinging his legs off the bed, he planted his feet on the floor. And nearly stepped on someone.

Startled, Zeke drew back, glancing down, realizing he was not the room's only captive. Sprawled on his back lay a young man with waves of wheat-gold hair, staring at the ceiling, glassy-eyed, the sensitive contours of his face gone rigid.

Zeke's throat tightened with recognition. "Addison!"

The shock of seeing the attorney somehow numbed Zeke's own aches. Shaking off what remained of his confusion, he sank down to his knees beside the man.

He didn't need the absence of a heartbeat or even the sight of the dark red pool on the attorney's slender chest to know. Addison was dead.

Addison, with all his muddleheaded ideals that Zeke half-admired and was half-driven crazy by. Addison, his blue eyes empty now, with all his dreams snatched away.

He rocked back on his heels, feeling sick. It was not the first time he had confronted death, even in its more violent forms. Why did this one wrench so hard at his gut? He barely knew Stanley Addison, yet he felt pierced with a sense of loss. He was actually shaking. His fingers trembled as he moved to close those gentle, unseeing eyes.

As his hand dropped back to his side, Zeke struck against something hard, half-protruding from beneath the bed. Grasping it, Zeke pulled the object out, only to find his fingers curling about the thick handle of a knife, the blade encrusted with blood. His sorrow gave way to lashings of anger.

"God damn it. God damn it all to hell!" He didn't know who, but someone was going to pay for this.

At that moment, the door to the room swung wide. Zeke would have given every last cent he possessed for it to be the Chin Scar, or better still the mysterious and cowardly "boss man" who had yet to show his face.

Instead he stared upward into the haggard features of a buxom woman, clad in a scanty negligee. She gasped, her gaze tracking round-eyed to the body of Addison, then to Zeke, the knife still poised in his hand.

From then on everything seemed to happen by prearranged cues. The girl backed out of the door, screeching with a melodramatic flair that would have done credit to Maude Adams.

"Oh, help. Murder! Police."

Flinging her hands into the air, the girl vanished, still screaming. Zeke dropped the knife, ready to plunge after her, only to hesitate. It seemed somehow obscene to abandon Addison, leave him in a place like this.

A ridiculous qualm, for there was nothing he could do for the young man now, only live long enough himself to see the murder avenged. With one last look at the attorney's absurdly youthful features, Zeke staggered out into the corridor. It was already filling up with women, ladies of pleasure in all stages of undress, straggly hair, pale cheeks devoid of rouge, purple hollows beneath their eyes.

The first girl had already raised the alarm, and they all fluttered about, shrilling like a flock of frightened starlings.

"Oh, there he goes. The murdering fiend!"

Zeke's appearance set off a fresh series of shrieks. He wanted to clutch his ears as he bolted down a rickety flight of steps. He expected at any moment to come up against the thug with the scarred chin, or some other burly rogue bent on preventing his escape. But he encountered no one until he reached the small foyer below. Then the front door was flung dramatically open to admit a blue-coated officer.

Zeke gaped at the sight of the dapper Sergeant O'Connell. He would've been prepared to wager that the policeman had never responded to a distress call so fast in his life. He was glad for once the copper was doing his job.

"O'Connell. Good thing you're here. There's a man dead upstairs and—"

To Zeke's astonishment, O'Connell leveled his pistol at him. "Halt or I'll shoot." Not waiting for Zeke's response, he began cocking the hammer.

Although startled, Zeke was quick enough to duck. Instead of plugging him through the head, the shot whistled harmlessly past his ear, shattering a gilt-framed mirror behind him.

No need to ask O'Connell what the hell he thought he was doing. The copper's intent was obvious. Zeke didn't give him a chance to take aim again. By the time the second shot sounded, Zeke had plunged beneath an arched doorway.

Another small passage led him back to the region of the kitchens. A lusty-looking female hovered near the coal stove, looking undisturbed either by the screams or the sound of gunplay. She calmly poured herself a cup of coffee, only glancing up long enough to give Zeke a knowing leer.

"What's a matter, honey? Your old lady catch you here? The back door is that way, handsome."

Zeke couldn't even pause long enough to thank her. Finding the door, he hurled himself through it, almost into the arms of another policeman. The copper fell back with a grunt of surprise as though he really hadn't expected Zeke to make it this far or to be so full of fight.

Before the man could draw his weapon, Zeke sent his fist crashing against the copper's jaw, felling him to the ground. The action took no more than the space of a heartbeat, which was just as well, for he had no time to hesitate, to reflect, only to run.

He plunged down an alleyway behind the brothel, weaving past the rear entrances of tenement buildings. Where was he going to go? He was not even sure where he was, only that if this was O'Connell's beat, he had to be back in the warehouse district. Zeke was a little familiar with the area. The problem was that O'Connell was even more so.

In no time at all, the sergeant was hard on his heels. Another shot rang out, and Zeke felt a burning sensation in his right arm. Bloody hell! He'd been hit.

He stumbled a little and heard a heavy footfall—O'Connell closing in for the kill. Mustering what strength he had, Zeke upended a row of garbage cans, causing the policeman to curse and lose his footing.

As O'Connell went down, Zeke half-buried him in the refuse, then tore off running. But as he clutched his arm, his fingers sticky with the warmth of his own blood, Zeke knew he couldn't keep up this pace. His breathing came in labored gasps.

Somehow he got himself over a fence, squeezing down the narrow space between two buildings. He had eluded O'Connell for the present, enough that he could lean up against the crumbling brickwork, panting, drawing gulps of air into his tortured lungs.

He was weakening and he knew it. The shocks to his system in these past twenty-four hours had been too much; only that ages-old instinct for survival had kept him on his feet this long. Just ahead of him loomed the main street, but from the sound of police whistles, he knew the place had to be crawling with O'Connell's minions. Risking a peek round the corner of the building, he saw that he was right. Blue coats, at least half a dozen of them, their guns at the ready, paced the length of the pavement.

Zeke ground his teeth, fighting off a wave of dizziness, the sensation of falling into a trap, a most well-prepared trap. It was no good reminding himself he was no longer Johnnie Marceone, but J. E. Morrison, a tycoon with a mansion on Fifth Avenue. Under ordinary circumstances, the prudent thing to do would be to surrender to the police, demand to see his lawyer.

But these weren't ordinary circumstances. His lawyer was dead, and Zeke knew if he tried to surrender to O'Connell, he'd never make it as far as the precinct house. Not alive.

He had to get out of here, find some place to hide and quickly. But where? He might be able to make it as far as the docks, take the risk of jumping into the East River, but chances were he would lose consciousness, drown.

The street out there already seemed to be shifting, threatening to give way beneath his feet. He could barely bring the building opposite into focus other than to tell it was a warehouse of some sort.

A warehouse . . . Zeke squinted his eyes, forcing his vision to clear. Yes, he had seen that place before. Had it been only last night that he had lingered outside, staring up at one particular window, as moonstruck as any raw kid, waiting for Rory to come out?

The Transcontinental Balloon Company. Then he had regarded that faded sign with wry amusement. Now it beckoned to him with all the comfort and assurance of a smile on the face of an old friend.

Likely Rory wouldn't even be there, but with luck he might manage to cross the street unseen, find a way inside the warehouse, seek shelter within its shadowy depths.

And the way his arm burned, his head reeled, luck was about all he had left.

At the area back of the warehouse, Rory watched the *Seamus* being prepared for the demonstration as soon as the man from the government arrived. It was the first time the pale blue balloon had ever been inflated, and the gas bag hissed, suspended a few feet above the rough dock boards, like a piece of the sky held captive, pulling against the rope's hemp cords.

Tony and Pete rushed about attaching the gondola, slinging the sandbags over the basket's side. Rory knew she ought to be helping, but a strange lethargy seemed to have overtaken her, borne of the shock she had received earlier that morning. She still clutched the edition of the *New York World* in her hands. On the El, she had read the article about Zeke over and over again until she could nearly recite the lurid details by heart . . . Stanley Addison knifed to death in a brothel, Zeke Morrison seen fleeing the scene.

It was all a nightmare, some hideous mistake. It had to be.

While Pete began hooking sacks of ballast onto the balloon, Tony stepped back, wiping the perspiration from his brow.

"Glad you didn't strain yourself helping out, Rory," he grumbled.

Rory shot him a look of reproach. "How do you expect me to calmly go about my business after seeing this?" She practically shook the paper under his nose.

Tony batted it aside. "There's nothing much else you can do. You got any idea where Morrison is?"

"No . . ."

"Then how you gonna help him? We been over and over this, Rory, and I'm tired of talking about it."

They had been having the same useless argument ever since leaving Grand Street. There was no way to make Tony understand. She just felt so blasted helpless and scared. God help her, she had never felt so scared for anyone in her life as she now was for Zeke.

"You gotta be sensible, Rory," Tony chided. "You just have to forget about Morrison. Did you ever stop to think he might be guilty?"

"No!" Her reply waxed a shade too vehement, perhaps because there had been one awful moment when she had wondered. She couldn't help recalling Zeke's angry phone conversation with Stanley Addison. Zeke did have quite a temper. In the heat of his rage, she could picture him slugging someone perhaps a little too hard, but never, *never* could she envision him sticking a knife between someone's ribs.

Rory fingered the paper again, the page already much creased and worn with her handling. "You just won't listen to me, Tony. There's something wrong about this whole thing. For instance, the *World* says the fight took place last night. How could it have? I am sure Zeke was at my flat at least until eleven o'clock."

"There's plenty of night left after eleven, Rory," was Tony's sobering response.

Rory only set her lips into a stubborn line. "You're asking me to believe Zeke got beat up by two street thugs, had that grim reunion with his sister, then sneaked out of my flat, looked up his friend Addison, took the man to a brothel and killed him?"

"So Morrison has a lot of stamina. Look, Rory, I don't know what happened. All I know is what it says there in the paper."

"Since when did you start believing everything you read, Bertelli?"

Tony swore, flinging his hands wide in a gesture of frustration. "I told you, Rory. I'm done arguing. I gotta go help Pete. Someone needs to worry about the fate of this company since you don't seem to care anymore."

He strode away, with Rory biting down upon her lip and glaring after him. His remark stung, all the more so because he was right. Not that she didn't care anymore. That wasn't true, but for the first time in her life something took precedence over her balloons.

Zeke Morrison. Ever since she had met him, the man never strayed far from her mind, especially not now when he was in such terrible trouble, when she was left wondering when she would see him again . . . if ever.

That last thought was so chilling, she thrust it away. Tony barked an order for her to fetch some more iron filings for the hydrogen generator, and she was getting ready to do so when she heard a footfall on the concrete floor of the warehouse.

Tony's younger brother emerged through the double doors, slipping out onto the dock with a sheepish expression on his face. Angelo clearly expected a rebuke from Rory for being late and looked agreeably surprised when none was forthcoming.

"Morning, Rory," he said, sparing a glance toward Pete and Tony, the balloon looming overhead. "Geez, looks like all of you have sure been busy."

He stripped off his jacket. His dark eyes so like Tony's gleamed with curiosity and excitement. "Say, Rory, what's all that hubbub out on the street? Coppers are prowling everywhere. I never saw O'Connell so stirred up since the time that street kid tossed a firecracker under his horse."

"I don't know what it's about," Rory said. She felt her heart seizing up with apprehension at the mention of O'Connell's name. Of course, she was being absurd. Simply because Zeke was a wanted man, she needn't suppose every activity of the police was now connected with him.

Yet she couldn't shake her forebodings, the same vague fears that had troubled her last night. It still struck her as odd that O'Connell had identified Zeke so readily. Perhaps she ought to take a casual stroll on the street, just to see what was going on.

While Angelo rolled up his sleeves and prepared to help with the generator, Rory moved toward the warehouse.

"Don't forget those filings," Tony bawled after her, and Rory replied with an absentminded nod of her head.

She slipped inside the warehouse's darkened interior. Even with the sun streaking through the small grimy windows, the building was gloom-ridden and Rory had to pick her way with care. She had just reached the deeply shadowed area by the steps leading up to her office when she heard a strange noise.

She stopped, her scalp prickling at the sound. Someone was behind her, someone breathing hard. Before she could move or cry out, an arm shot out of the gloom, seizing her about the waist. The newspaper she had been carrying flew out of her grasp.

Rory drew breath to scream, but the sound choked off in her throat as a voice rasped in her ear. "No, Rory. Don't! It's me."

"Zeke?" she quavered, her heart pounding, torn between hope and disbelief. She whipped about, her hands colliding with his chest. His face loomed above her, streaked with dirt and sweat, his dark hair disheveled, his eyes tired but glittering bright at the sight of her.

"Oh, Zeke." She half-sobbed, half-laughed his name. "I've been so worried about you."

She flung her arms about him, catching him in a fierce hug. Instead of returning the embrace, he flinched, sucking in his breath.

"Zeke, what's . . ." Her voice trailed off as she drew back, staring at her hand. It was streaked with blood. Horrified, her gaze flew to his crimson-soaked sleeve.

"Zeke! You've been hurt."

"Shot. By the police." His lips pulled taut with a valiant effort to smile. "It's been a helluva morning, little girl."

"Don't try to explain anything now. Just let me look at your arm."

He shook his head, motioning her back. "It's all right. The bleeding's nearly stopped. I think the bullet passed through."

Despite his protests, she tore away a section of his sleeve, working as gently as she could. He paled, clamping his teeth together. To her relief, she saw that he was right. Likely the shot had gone clean through, leaving a relatively neat hole through the fleshy part of his arm. Still he seemed to have lost a fair amount of blood.

"We have to get you to a doctor."

"Not possible," he said. "The police are looking for me everywhere. I'm in a lot of trouble, Rory."

"I know. I read about it in the papers."

"The papers?" Despite the pain and exhaustion hazing his eyes, Zeke managed to look startled.

"Never mind about that now. I guess I'll have to do what I can to bind up your arm myself. You stay right here."

A foolish thing to say, for Zeke didn't appear as though he were likely to go anywhere. She had no idea where he had been all this time. She only marveled at the strength that had brought him this far.

Hastening, she fetched water from the washroom behind the office upstairs and some strips of the silk material she used in sewing the balloon panels. When she returned, Zeke had sagged down on the bottommost stair.

But at her approach, he straightened, his eyes still keen, aware. He frequently clenched his jaw and cursed under his breath as she proceeded to clean the wound. But that didn't stop him from asking questions.

"What'd you mean before . . . about the papers?"

Rory told him about the article that had appeared in the morning's edition of the *World*.

Zeke grunted. "Damn that Duffy! How'd he get such a story and so fast? Someone's not wasting much time."

Rory ordered him to stay quiet while she bound up his arm. But it did no good, for Zeke continued. "Rory, I don't know who is behind all this, but I swear to you, I am innocent."

"Hush, Zeke. You don't need to tell me that."

"You ought to know all the dangers if you are helping me. Even the local police are involved."

"O'Connell?"

Zeke managed to nod. "I should've listened to you last night. I think he plans to kill me, make it look like I was shot running away."

"What are you going to do?"

"I don't know, but I need to get away from here."

Rory fully agreed with him, but as she observed Zeke's drained features, she didn't know how he was going to move one more step, let alone escape the police pursuit.

Before she could even begin to think what to do next, she heard Tony coming through the warehouse, shouting for her.

"Don't bother hunting for those filings no more, Rory. We don't need them."

Rory tensed, instinctively moving to cut Tony off before he could see Zeke, but it was already too late. Tony sauntered toward the stairs, only to draw up short. He stared first at the bloodied clothes littering the floor, following the trail to Rory, then beyond to Zeke.

"Christ!" Tony muttered. "Where the devil did he come from?"

"Zeke is trying to get away from the police," Rory said, her words tumbling out in a rush. "They . . . they shot him."

"Guess that's what they usually do to runaway murderers."

"Tony! Zeke is not a murderer. Only a suspect. And O'Connell is shooting to kill."

Tony relaxed some of his belligerence, but he still said, "Well, whatever kind of trouble Morrison is in, it's his problem. He shouldn't be getting you involved."

"Tony!"

But Zeke spoke up. "For once I agree with Mr. Bertelli. I should never have come here."

"No, you should have just collapsed on the street out there so O'Connell could shoot you again." Rory stomped her foot, tears stinging her eyes. "And if neither you nor Tony have anything sensible to say, I wish you would both be quiet so I can think what to do."

Tony lapsed into a dour silence, but Zeke murmured, "If I only could make it back to Fifth Avenue, out of O'Connell's precinct. I have powerful friends that can help me get clear of this mess."

"There's no way at all," Tony said, shaking his head. "My brother says the police are all over the streets. They'll probably start a building-to-building search soon."

"Right," Zeke gasped. "Then I shouldn't be found in here." He braced himself with his good arm, struggling to his feet. Rory placed one hand on his shoulder, gently but forcibly restraining him.

"No, stop, Zeke. Tony is wrong. There is a way, a very good way to get you out of here."

She glanced back at Tony. The boy seemed to comprehend what she was thinking instantly, for he paled, immediately protesting.

"Oh, no. You just forget it, Rory. It's completely out of the question."

But Rory caught Tony's arm, pulling him a distance

away from the steps. They got into a heated discussion with much gesturing of hands, but Zeke could not hear one word. He leaned wearily against the step rail, feeling his mind going hazy again.

What had he been thinking of, creeping into Rory's warehouse like this? If he had been more himself, he would never have done such a thing, never risked bringing the danger to her door. He had staggered in here almost out of a blind instinct, a wounded animal going to ground in the first familiar place. Now he would have given all his strength to be able to stagger out again.

Rory rushed back to his side, Tony hard after her. Whatever she had been saying to the boy, he still looked unconvinced, but resigned.

"Zeke, we have a plan," Rory started to say, but she was interrupted by a loud hammering on the warehouse door. The three of them froze, not moving, barely breathing, like a trio of startled deer caught in the sights of a ruthless hunter.

The knocking raged louder, a voice calling out in O'Connell's unmistakable brogue, "Open up in there. This is the police."

"Let him in," Zeke said, his shoulders slumping in defeat. "Tell him I broke into the warehouse. He can hardly shoot me down in front of witnesses."

"No, he'll just wait and do it later." Rory moved purposefully forward and began to drape Zeke's arm about her shoulder. "Come on, Tony. Help me."

After a heartbeat of hesitation, Tony complied. Linking his arm about Zeke's waist, he and Rory managed to lead Zeke forward. Zeke cooperated as best he could, although he was not sure that he should.

He didn't know what Rory had in mind, only that he now wished she were out of it. In another minute, O'Connell would be kicking in the door. But all resistance was fast draining out of Zeke. It was all he could do to plant one foot after the other, leaning heavily on Rory and Tony, following wherever they were taking him.

He squinted against the bright flood of sunlight as they

emerged onto the dock. A roaring rang in his ears, so loud he thought he was passing out. It took him a moment to realize the loud hiss came from one of Rory's floating monsters.

Glancing upward, Zeke stared at the mammoth balloon casting a shadow over him, and suddenly Rory's plan struck him with crystal clarity.

"Oh, no," he groaned, halting in his tracks. "I would rather take my chances with the police."

"So would I," Tony said, for once in sympathetic agreement with him. But that sympathy didn't cause Bertelli to thwart Rory's order to help Zeke climb into the gondola.

Two other lads rushed forward, looking astonished, but they scrambled to ease Zeke's weight from Rory's shoulders. Zeke never knew quite how, but he found himself standing beneath those billowing yards of silk, clutching the side of a wicker basket.

Rory scrambled in beside him. "Cast off, Tony," she cried, her voice shrill with urgency.

The warehouse beyond echoed with shouts, trampling feet. Zeke realized the police must have broken through the door and were coming through to the dock.

The three young men worked frantically to cast off the lines. Zeke felt the basket shudder and begin to rise. He took one look down as O'Connell and the other coppers came barreling onto the dock.

But then Zeke was aware of nothing but the solid earth falling rapidly away. His stomach clenched, his head reeling, but not from his wound this time. He let go of the edge of the basket, sagging to the floor of the gondola.

Rory continued to peer downward, chortling with grim satisfaction. "Zeke, you should see O'Connell. He looks mad enough to eat his hat. Zeke?"

She glanced around, suddenly aware of his prone position. She hunched down beside him, her storm-gray eyes wide, anxious.

"Zeke, what is it? Are you passing out? Is your wound bleeding again?"

He shook his head, gritting his teeth. It was worse than being shot again to have to tell her, but somehow he got it out.

"No, damn it. I'm afraid of heights."

Twelve

Rory tugged at the valve line to ease the *Seamus*'s rapid ascent. A loud hiss sounded as though the great balloon itself had shuddered in disbelief. Afraid of heights? It was difficult to imagine Zeke, so tough, so bold, being afraid of anything.

She could tell what the admission had cost him, as an angry, shamed look darkened his eyes. He no longer appeared in danger of passing out, as though having a fresh peril to contend with had roused all his senses to peak alert. Tension corded his entire frame; his jaw clamped rock hard. Reaching one hand upward, he gripped the basket's side but made no move to raise himself and risk another look below. He closed his eyes briefly as the balloon dipped downward.

"It's all right," Rory said. "All I have to do is release some ballast, get the balloon to level off."

"Do whatever you have to do," he snapped. "And don't waste time explaining."

Bending over the side, Rory sliced into one of the sandbags. Far below her, the city fell away, the tightly packed buildings, the busy streets now diminished to the size of some cunningly wrought miniatures. Working between the valve and the sandbags, she managed to bring the *Seamus* to a state of equilibrium.

Wisps of clouds drifted by. Rory knew they would soon be lost in the midst of a comforting blanket of white, making it difficult for anyone to track them.

Her gaze shifted anxiously back to Zeke. "You can hardly see the ground for the clouds. Does that make it any better?"

He grimaced. "Nothing will make it any better until I get my feet back on solid earth. Just land this thing on my lawn and try to do it a little more gently this time."

Rory squirmed, not sure how to break it to him. "Uh . . . I can't exactly do that."

"What! You can't land safely?"

"No, I mean I can't land on your lawn at all. There's no way to steer a balloon. You just go where the wind takes you."

Zeke stared at her, then swore. "And just where the hell is the wind taking us?"

"Well, I thought I caught a glimpse of the Statue of Liberty awhile ago. That was off to the right, so I think we're heading more in the direction of the Hudson, toward Jersey."

"You think? Don't you even carry a compass in this blasted thing?"

Rory flushed. "I don't have *any* instruments on board. This flight wasn't exactly planned, Mr. Morrison."

Some of the irritation faded from Zeke's eyes. "You're right. I'm sorry, Rory. I don't mean to sound so damned ungrateful after the risk you've taken for me."

"Oh, hush," she said. Balancing carefully, she hunkered down to sit beside him on the basket's floor. "Considering what you've been through, I guess you've got a right to be surly."

"No, I don't. Not with you." He caught her hand, brushing his lips against her fingertips. "I owe you my life, you and your friends back there. I just hope Tony and those other boys don't get arrested for helping me escape."

Rory felt her heart miss a beat. In her concern for Zeke's safety, that was a possibility she had not considered. But she rallied. "Oh, you don't know the Bertelli brothers. They can talk their way out of anything. No one can look more innocent than Tony, not even when he's been up to the worst mischief. And as for Angelo, if he starts off on one of his stories about uncle's aunt's cousins, O'Connell will be damned sorry he ever broke into my warehouse."

Zeke smiled a little, some of his tension easing. Rory wished she felt as confident as she sounded regarding the safety of Tony and the other two boys. She tried to put the fear from her mind, bending down to examine Zeke's bandaged arm.

She was relieved to discover the wound had not broken open again. She worried a little about the possibility of infection and fever, but Zeke's brow was cool to the touch.

"How are you feeling?" she asked.

"I've had better days," he murmured, but he seemed less concerned with his wound than staring upward at the crisscross of rigging that connected the balloon to the load ring.

"No way at all to steer, huh?" He frowned. "Then what was all that talk at Delmonico's about establishing a mail service? It wouldn't do much good sending a letter to a fellow in Albany only to have it wind up in Canada."

"My father was working on that very problem before he died. He had planned to do some experimenting with rudders, sails, possibly even a small engine."

"An engine. That's a comforting thought," Zeke said glumly. "Anything besides just a puff of air to keep us from plummeting. How long do we have to be up here?"

"Not long. I just want to make sure we get far enough away to be safe. After we land in Jersey, I figure you can surrender to the authorities there and set about proving that you didn't kill Stanley Addison."

"But I did."

"W-what?" Rory froze, certain she hadn't heard him right. A shadow seemed to pass over Zeke's face, his eyes intent as though no longer seeing her or the balloon, but focused inward on some darker image that caused his lips to thin with torment.

"I did kill Addison," he repeated. "Just as sure as if I plunged the knife into his heart myself. I knew there had been threats, but I never took them serious enough. I should have cautioned Addison more strongly."

"You can't blame yourself for that," Rory said softly. "Mr. Addison was a politician, wasn't he? Pressing pretty hard for some drastic reforms, making accusations. He must've realized the dangers. . . ."

"He didn't realize anything. His head was stuffed too full of starry-eyed dreams, notions about honor and fair play, expecting the whole world to be the same. He didn't know any better. But I did."

Rory stroked the hair back from Zeke's brow, wishing she could as easily caress away the bitter self-reproach from his eyes. Hadn't she experienced a similar misery over her father's death, torturing herself with speculations, how she might have prevented the unpreventable? Nothing could ease the guilt, the pain, the shock of a sudden death. Nothing . . . only time.

"It's no good thinking about it now," she said. "You'll only make yourself crazy when you should be trying to rest."

"I probably should. I've never been so damned tired in my life. But I don't think I'll ever be able to rest again until I find Addison's killer. Just five minutes alone with the bastard—that's all I ask."

"Do you have any idea who—"

Zeke nodded grimly. He proceeded to tell her about a weasel of a man named Charles Decker, his connections with the corruption of Tammany Hall, the threats he had made. Zeke figured that Decker had O'Connell working for him, along with the two thugs who had attacked Zeke beneath the El tracks.

When Zeke finished up his tale by explaining how the same two characters had trailed him to Rory's flat, knocked him unconscious and abducted him to the brothel, her eyes flew wide in astonishment.

"But . . . but what in the world were you doing up on the roof?"

Zeke looked a little embarrassed. "I always used to sleep on the roof when I was a kid. It was great as long as I didn't get too close to the edge. Last night it just got a little too hot in your apartment."

Too hot, Rory wondered, or too crowded with memories, the echoes of Tessa's bitter words still lingering in the air.

"I noticed the parlor window left open," she said. "But I would never have dreamed of looking for you up on the roof. I just thought . . ." She was unable to keep the traces of the hurt and the disappointment she had felt out of her voice. "I thought you had just gone away."

"Without saying good-bye to you, Aurora Rose?" The warm way he pronounced her name made it sound like an endearment. "I would never do that, though you would be better off if I did. My sister Tessa was telling the truth when she said that I tend to ruin all that I touch."

"What nonsense—," Rory began.

"Is it? Look at this trouble I have dragged you into."

"Let me tell you, sir, I am very good at getting myself into trouble without help from anyone else."

Her feigned indignation was meant to provoke his smile, that heart-melting grin that always left her feeling so delightfully flustered. But instead of lighting up with amusement, those dark eyes remained sober and lines creased his brow.

"I am serious, Rory. Tessa made me think about . . . about how selfish I was being. It would be better if I didn't see you again."

The pain his quietly spoken words roused in her cut sharper and much more deeply than she would have expected. Tears stung her eyes and she glanced away, still trying to jest.

"What! No more chasing me through the streets?"

"No. No more."

"J-just when I was starting to get used to it." One tear escaped, splashing down her cheek. She straightened fiercely. "Well, it won't do you a bit of good, Zeke Morrison, trying to go all noble on me now."

"Rory . . ." So gently, he brushed away the moisture, his callused fingertips warm, feather-light against her skin.

She sniffed, thrusting his hand away. "If you stop chasing me, I . . . I'll just have to pursue you. And I warn you, I can run much faster than you can."

A reluctant chuckle escaped him. He regarded her with a mixture of incredulity and hope.

"Rory, I never realized that you had come to feel so . . . I hardly know what to say."

"Don't say anything. You talk way too much."

She knew she shouldn't. The man was wounded, exhausted. But she couldn't seem to stop herself. Bending over him, she pressed a hard kiss to his mouth. It was the first time in her life she had been the one to initiate an embrace, so she was a little rough, a little awkward with embarrassment.

But she must have done something right, because Zeke was not slow to respond, for the moment forgetting all his recently acquired noble impulses. Tangling his hand in her hair, he returned the kiss with an intensity that left Rory weak.

Amazing . . . considering what he had recently been through, that he should still be able to kiss that way. It hardly seemed fair. She was now clinging to him, her pulses thrumming, her mind reeling as though she had been the one knocked over the head and shot—straight through the heart.

Breathless, she had the sensation of falling, tumbling head over heels through the sky. . . .

Suddenly, mid-kiss, her eyes flew open, startled. She found herself staring into Zeke's own wide, dark ones. Their lips parted, both seeming to realize at once that the giddy sensation of descending was not entirely due to the fervor of their kiss.

"What . . . what the devil's happening?" Zeke removed his hand from her hair to clutch at the basket's side.

"The air must be cooling. We're coming down faster than I thought." Rory scrambled to her feet and peered over the edge of the gondola. She paled.

"Oh, damn, damn, damn," she muttered under her breath and began slashing at the few remaining ballast bags with frantic energy.

Ever since first being lifted into the sky, Zeke had been fighting off a knot of tension. Neither Rory's words nor her actions were calculated to ease that.

"What are you swearing at?" he shouted, bracing himself for the worst. "Are we going to crash?"

"Uh, no. . . ." Rory moistened her lips. "There just doesn't seem to be a convenient place to land."

By now Zeke was familiar with Rory's mastery of the art of understatement. Horrific images filled his mind of the terrain below—tangles of trees, jagged rocks, closely packed houses. Although his stomach lurched, his head already beginning to spin at the mere thought of doing such a thing, Zeke forced himself to his feet.

Momentarily he closed his eyes to take a deep breath. Gripping the edge of the basket until his knuckles were white, by sheer force of will, he got his eyes open and stared downward.

The world below was nothing but a blur of gray, and Zeke cursed, despising himself for his own weakness, which had him on the verge of fainting like any of those hen-witted debutantes he'd met at Mrs. Van H.'s parties. But as he strove to steady himself, he realized it was not his vertigo causing the scene below to go gray.

It *was* gray, a shifting, eddying, chilling gray breaking into waves crested with whitecaps.

"It . . . it's the Atlantic," Rory said in a small voice.

"I know the ocean when I see it," Zeke growled. "Though before I've always had the good sense to view it from a boat, not dangling above it a hundred feet in the air."

As though to dispute his measurement, the balloon dropped several more yards. The roar of the sea carried to his ears. Zeke had always thought it such a pleasant sound, so soothing, but now it caused a chill to strike through him as though he could already feel the lick of those ice-cold waves.

He never thought he would hear himself say such a thing, but he bellowed at Rory, "So do something. Take us back up."

But Rory stood frozen, just staring over the side, her delicate features a blend of horror and fascination as though she had been hypnotized by the eternal lure of the sea.

In desperation, Zeke reached for a rope that he had seen Rory tugging at earlier.

His movement snapped Rory out of her trance. "No!" she shrieked. "Don't touch that!"

But her warning came too late. Zeke had already given a tentative tug. As soon as he heard that god-awful hiss, he knew what he'd done, even before the balloon started to descend.

"Damn it all to hell!"

He let go the rope and grabbed for Rory, expecting that at any moment the pair of them would be plunged into the sea. Miraculously, the balloon leveled off, but now some of the higher waves were fairly lapping at the bottom of the basket.

Rory wrapped her arms about Zeke's neck, her silvery eyes gone as gray as the ocean, her face nearly as white as the crests.

"Oh, Zeke, I . . . I can't swim. Tony tried to teach me, but I always sank." She made a valiant attempt to smile. "He s-said it was because I have rocks in my head."

"He's right," Zeke said, but took the sting from his words by straining her close. Desperately, he scanned the distance, making out the edge of the shore, but it had to be a good quarter of a mile away. At full strength, he might have been able to make it, even towing Rory.

But as though to remind him of his own weakness, his injured arm throbbed. Zeke cursed under his breath. He had never felt so helpless, so caught up in circumstances beyond his control. If they managed to come through this alive, Zeke vowed, he would never set foot in one of these damned contraptions again, and he wouldn't allow Rory to do so either.

The wind current seemed to be carrying them closer to shore, but Zeke could tell they were never going to make it. A spray of water dashed over the basket, wetting his face, dampening Rory's hair. He could already taste salt upon his lips.

"Rory," he spoke desperately into her ear. "Isn't there anything you can do to bring us up a little?"

She shook her head. Her lips were set and she was trying to conceal her fear. Only her eyes betrayed her. She called back above the ocean's greedy roar, "We've got nothing left to throw overboard, nothing to lighten the load."

As Zeke's gaze roved frantically round the empty basket, he saw that she was right. There was nothing in the gondola except Rory and . . . himself.

The thought struck him like the slap of a wave. Yes, himself, some two hundred pounds of dead weight. Without him, Rory might have a chance. A desperate one, but a chance all the same.

But if he was going to act, it had to be now. He had no time to debate the wisdom of his decision. With a sudden forcefulness, he thrust Rory away from him. Steadying himself by gripping one of the balloon cables, he moved quickly before Rory could divine his intent and try to stop him.

He had only worked one leg over the side of the basket when she screamed. "Zeke! Stop. What are you doing?"

She launched herself at him, her eyes wide with terror. She managed to catch his arm. He tried to shake her off, but she hung on with a strength borne of desperation.

"Rory! Damn it! Let go."

"No! Zeke, you fool—"

He started to give her a rough shove, but it was already too late. The balloon lost altitude, the gondola hitting the ocean surface with a hard smack that toppled Rory over. As a wave crashed over the side, the basket tipped precariously, some of the cables snapping.

Zeke lost his balance and felt himself falling. He gasped as he plunged into the ocean's chilling depths, the sea foam dissolving over his head. Taking in a mouthful of ocean, he choked, the salt water burning his throat, stinging his eyes.

Kicking, he fought his way back to the surface, drawing in a welcome lungful of air. Treading water, he battled the waves, blinking his eyes, searching frantically for a glimpse of Rory and the balloon.

He spotted her some yards away, clinging for her life to the side of the overturned basket. The deflating balloon, still connected to the gondola by the few remaining ropes, was acting like a sail, dragging the basket through the water.

"Zeke!" Above the wind, the waves, Rory's cry came, faint and desperate like the phantom call of some poor soul long ago lost beneath the sea.

Drawing in a deep breath, Zeke struck out after her, swimming as hard and fast as he could. Ocean water seeped through his bandage and salt got into his wound. His arms and lungs seemed to be on fire as he battled both the waves and his own weakness.

Twice he drew near Rory and the balloon, only to have them wrenched tantalizingly out of his reach. His muscles ached with the effort it took to keep kicking, extending his arms for just one more stroke.

Rory was so close, so close, but he knew it didn't matter. He was never going to make it. Panting, choking on the briny waves, he was all but spent. Rory risked her tenuous hold upon the gondola, stretching out her arm to him.

Her fingers seemed to drift upon the water, like a slender thread, all that stood between him and going under one last and final time. With a tremendous effort, he forced himself forward. Rory's hand clamped upon his wrist, her fingers not so fragile, far stronger than he would have imagined.

Somehow he found himself beside her, clutching at the rim of the basket. But the ordeal was far from over. The remaining buoyancy in the balloon kept the soaked gondola from sinking, but with the great monolith pulled by the breeze, Zeke and Rory were left at the mercy of the wind and the waves.

Zeke knew neither one of them could last long at this rate, taking such a buffeting. Rory looked white with fatigue. When she showed signs of loosening her hold, he used the length of his body to shore her up, keep her hanging on.

It was going to take a miracle to save them, a blasted miracle. Zeke, who put no faith in such things, scarce recognized it when it came.

But suddenly a small dinghy loomed before them, two men in oiled cape coats and yellow sou'westers pulling at the oars, fishers by the look of them.

Zeke thought he must be hallucinating until Rory also lifted her head, a choked cry of gladness escaping her. She saw the boat too. It had to be real.

"Help!" Zeke croaked. "Over here."

He wasn't sure if the fishermen could hear him. But they had to be able to see the blasted balloon, the two people clinging for their lives. The dinghy had drifted close enough now that Zeke could observe that the two men were frozen, staring.

"Help!" Rory shouted.

Her cry was shrill enough to have carried. Yet the fishermen made no move to come to their aid although by now Zeke could see the way their mouths gaped open, their dumbfounded expressions. A particularly large wave broke over Zeke's and Rory's heads, causing them to cough and sputter.

Zeke spit salt water and swore. It figured that when he finally got a miracle, it turned out to be a stupid one.

He shouted again and still got no response from the dinghy. Drawing in one final mighty lungful of air, Zeke raised his voice, letting loose enough curses to turn the gray Atlantic blue, not stopping until his throat was hoarse.

The two men suddenly sprang into movement, reaching for their oars. It wouldn't have astonished Zeke to see the dolts start rowing in the opposite direction. But with his string of imprecations, he finally seemed to have made some impression on them, like a stranger in a foreign land finally catching on to the lingo.

Pulling in unison, the fishermen drew alongside, the younger one reaching down weatherbeaten hands. Zeke saw Rory lifted on board before struggling after her and collapsing on the bottom of the boat.

He lay still for several seconds, numb to every sensation but relief at being alive, having Rory safe by his side. He thought she might have fainted, but incredibly he felt her struggling to raise herself to a sitting position.

"The . . . the *Seamus*," she faltered.

Her words made no sense. She was shivering, and Zeke thought she must be in shock from being chilled to the bone, half-drowned. He wrapped one arm about her shoulders, but when she gestured with a shaking finger, he realized she was pointing toward the remains of her balloon yet bobbing on the surface of the waves. The bag was deflated, sagging into the sea, growing more distant with each pull the two men took at the oars.

Damnation! Rory couldn't be so unreasonable as to expect something to be done about salvaging the blasted thing. A wave washed over the gondola, sweeping it from sight.

He pulled Rory firmly against him, trying to warm her, force her to lie still. But as he gazed down, she was still staring forlornly at the cresting waves, and Zeke had an uncomfortable feeling that all the salt droplets trickling down her face did not come from the sea.

Thirteen

❊ ❊ ❊

Darkness overtook the shoreline, the sea becoming a mysterious, moving shadow, white-crested fingers clutching at the beach, raking away particles of sand. But beneath the wooden shingles of the fishermen's shack, the breaking waves were no more than a lulling whisper and Rory felt safe and warm. Wrapped in a blanket, she huddled before the crackling fire kindled on the hearth. She scarce remembered the details of her rescue, how she came to be at the cottage; she only felt grateful that she was.

The place was small, but the oil lamps flickering in the tiny parlor beamed a welcome as powerful as that of any lighthouse. The furnishings were sparse but clean—a couple of rocking chairs, a table covered with a checkered cloth, a few scattered stools. Everything smelled of salt, as though the very lifeblood of the sea had seeped within these walls, perhaps even more so into the person of the woman serving as Rory's hostess.

Rory had never met any female as large as Mrs. Cobbett. Tall with burly arms, she looked almost big enough to heft Zeke over her shoulder, and there had been a point when Rory feared she meant to do so. Although on the verge of collapse when the two fishermen had deposited them on Mrs. Cobbett's doorstep, Zeke had not taken kindly to the woman's ministrations, her gruff demand that Zeke strip out of his wet things.

But even the two dour fishermen had obviously stood in awe of this woman, one calling her "Anchor" Annie, the other calling her "Ma." When she had bade them go about their business, tend to gathering up their nets, they had both snapped to do her bidding, and Zeke hadn't had much choice either.

The last Rory had seen of him, Annie had driven him through a door opposite into a chamber the woman termed her "guest room" with a fierce pride. They could still be battling it out in there for all Rory knew. As for herself, for once she was content to do as she was told, bask by the fire, trying to get the chill of the sea out of her bones.

When the door opened and Annie returned alone, Rory glanced up anxiously. The woman's hair was a steely gray that matched the steel in her eyes. Her face had more crags than a rocky stretch of shore, her skin as brown and weatherbeaten as driftwood. But despite the formidableness of her appearance, there was a bluff kindliness in her manner that Rory found reassuring.

"Zeke?" Rory asked, half-starting to rise from her stool. "Is he—"

"I redid the bandages on your man's wound," she said.

The cup trembled slightly in Rory's hand. Had the woman recognized it as a gunshot wound? Rory hated telling lies, but she could hardly tell Annie the truth, that Zeke had been winged fleeing the law on a charge of murder. At the very least, the woman would fling them both out of her snug cottage with its circle of light and warmth. Rory shuddered at the prospect, her shoulders sagging.

"Well, I . . . he . . ." Rory stammered, trying to come up with some plausible explanation of Zeke's injury.

"Oh, shush, m'dear," Annie interrupted. "I'm familiar enough with menfolk and their scrappin' ways. You don't need to get all flustered trying to explain to me."

Annie took a pull at her cup and smacked her lips with satisfaction. "Fact is, I oughta be apologizing to you for the behavior of my boy Joe. I understand he was a little slow coming to your rescue."

"Yes," Rory said. "It was rather odd considering we were practically drowning."

"The problem is my Joe never saw one of those balloon things before. He took it to be some kind of sea monster. Joe's a good fisherman, but he ain't exactly the brightest one of my boys.

"Now I saw one of them there balloons once. At a circus. You people with the circus?"

"No, I'm an aero—," Rory started to say, then broke off with a tired sigh. No, what was the sense of getting into all that?

"Now you stay by the fire and keep warm." Annie placed one large hand on Rory's shoulder, easing her back down. "Your man is doing fine. A little cantankerous, but I got some of my elixir down him. He's tucked up and sleeping like a baby."

Rory could only gape at her. Upon entering the cottage, although dead on his feet, Zeke had been determined to make his way back to New York tonight. He had been demanding a telephone, the distance to the nearest town.

"How . . . however did you persuade him to—," Rory faltered.

Annie chuckled, a deep sound that shook her ample bosom. She had a booming voice, but not unpleasant. It had a lilting quality, and Rory could picture her raising the rafters of some church, singing in the choir.

"Lord A'mighty, honey," she said. "I've had three husbands and five sons. A woman don't go through that many men without learning something about how to manage 'em."

If she hadn't been so weary, Rory would have been tempted to ask the woman to part with her secrets. But Annie was already bustling about brewing Rory a cup of tea. Rory accepted the steaming hot mug with real gratitude. Annie poured herself a drink into a tin cup. Rory

didn't see what it was, but she would have been prepared
to wager it wasn't tea.

Then Annie plunked herself down onto one of the rocking
chairs. As Rory sipped her tea, she was aware of Annie
studying her, curious but after a friendly fashion. With the
Seamus sunk to the bottom of the ocean, she didn't feel
much like an aeronaut at the moment.

"Yes, we're with the circus," Rory concluded glumly.

"Thought so." Annie smiled with obvious pride in her
own perspicacity. "A cousin of mine a few days ago traveled all the way to upstate New York just to watch some
couple get married up in a balloon. Was that you two?"

"Yes, that was us," Rory agreed before she even thought,
then was a little appalled by her lie. But somehow she
sensed that Annie would be mighty disapproving if she realized Zeke and Rory were junketing about together unwed.

The woman was scowling anyway. "Married in a balloon . . . I'm not sure I exactly hold with that. Don't sound
as legal and binding as being wed in a church."

"People get married on ships, don't they?"

"That's so." Annie appeared much struck by the comparison. She tossed down the rest of her drink. "Well, I
don't mean to sit here jawing at you all night. Poor little
thing. You've had a bad time of it, but you'll feel perkier
after a good sleep. Then, in the morning, I'll get my boy
to hitch up the buggy and drive you into Sea Isle."

Sea Isle? Rory started at the mention of a town far
down the south Jersey coast. She and Zeke had drifted
much farther than she had imagined. They would have a
long, dreary trip back to New York ahead of them. But
she was better off not worrying about that now, or about
the difficulties that would await them on their return.

Annie hustled off to her own bedchamber and returned
with a voluminous nightgown, which she helped Rory to
don. Rory felt swallowed up in it, like a child parading
about in her mother's things, but she was grateful for any
clothing that was warm and dry.

"Off to bed with you now," Annie said, jerking her head
toward the door behind which Zeke had disappeared. "Your

man's likely out so cold, he'll never hear when you creep between the sheets."

Rory fought down a blush at the thought of slipping into bed with "her" man. She barely concealed her expression of dismay as she suddenly realized the full difficulties of the lie she had told Annie. But wasn't that just the way of it every time she told a fib? She always ended up in some kind of bramble.

What was she going to do? It would be far too humiliating to confess now. Annie was already marching about, blowing out the oil lamps. Rory had little choice but to inch toward the door, bidding Annie a nervous good night.

Her fingers trembled as she turned the knob and slipped inside. Closing the door, she leaned up against it, allowing her eyes to adjust to the chamber's darkened interior.

Like the cottage's sitting room, it was small, the chief object of furniture being a heavy wooden bedstead. Moonlight streamed through the open shutters, and Rory could make out Zeke's muscular form draped beneath the covers, his dark head resting on a downy pillow.

"Zeke?" Rory whispered.

But she got no reply. It appeared Annie was right—Zeke was lost in a deep slumber. The wind howled outside the cottage, rattling the panes. There was something unbearably lonely about being the only one left awake. Rory hovered by the bed, shivering, wrapping her arms about herself. It was cold now that she was away from the fire, the boards of the floor chill beneath her bare feet.

Her gaze traveled wistfully to Zeke, so snug beneath the softness of a patchwork quilt, drawn halfway up across the bared expanse of his chest. She took a hesitant step closer.

It wouldn't really be like going to bed with a man, she argued, not if both of them were asleep. Yet she knew what the nuns back at St. Catherine's would have told her. Far better to curl up on the floor, suffer one night of discomfort rather than put her virtue at risk.

But Rory wasn't sure she'd ever had much virtue, and it was difficult for conscience to win out with gooseflesh prickling her arms and her feeling half-ready to drop from fatigue.

"The devil with it," she mumbled. Tugging back the covers, she scrambled beneath them, trying to keep to the edge of the bed, putting as much distance between herself and Zeke as possible.

The bed was as soft and warm as she had imagined, but having allowed herself to become chilled again, it was difficult to stop shivering. She couldn't help staring at Zeke, lying flat on his back, one arm flung over his head. A silvery stream of moonlight outlined his hawklike profile, the muscular contours of his chest. Knowing the heat that radiated from that powerful body, Rory's temptation was great to scoot across, snuggle a little closer.

But she resisted, cuddling the quilt beneath her chin, trying to lie still, not wanting to disturb him. Even in repose the rock-hard line of Zeke's jaw conveyed a certain belligerence, as though daring anyone to challenge him . . . or to hurt him.

She wondered if he really meant what he had said earlier that day, about thinking it best if he never saw her again after they returned to New York. He had talked of being bad for her, causing her harm, but perhaps he was as much afraid for himself, of making himself too vulnerable. She would bet that Zeke Morrison had let many women come close to his body, but none near his heart, and Rory was fast realizing that was exactly where she wanted to be.

Stifling a sigh, she forced herself to roll over and lie with her back to him. She would never get to sleep this way, so tense, so much aware of that masculine form only a pillow's length away.

But by degrees, exhaustion overtook her and her eyes drifted closed. She found sleep, but not a restful one. Tossing and turning, fragments of dreams floated through her mind, tormenting images from events of the days gone by. . . .

Tessa, garbed like a witch, cast some kind of spell, turning Finn McCool into a slavering beastie. . . . Zeke lay sprawled on the street, his arm bleeding, torn open from the attack of a black-winged harpie with beautiful masses of ice-blond hair.

"It's Mrs. Van Hallsburg," Rory tried to tell Zeke, but he only laughed at her, and all the while Tony stood by smirking. "I told you so. I told you so."

Rory moaned, rolling over, but she escaped one dream only to tumble directly into another nightmare equally as tormenting. She was back in the sea again, feeling the icy chill of its embrace, fighting the waves. But this time it wasn't the balloon she was trying to cling to but her father. He was alive. He was still alive if only she could save him.

She had hold of his hand, and Seamus Kavanaugh shouted words of encouragement. "Just try a little harder, Rory, m'darlin'. You can make it."

But as a breaker crashed over her, her father's fingers were wrenched from her grasp. She flailed the water and by some miracle she could swim. It was not she that was drowning but him. She screamed her father's name as he disappeared beneath the waves.

Rory woke up with a start. She sat bolt upright, gasping for breath. As she rubbed her eyes, trying to brush away the last vestiges of the nightmare, she realized she was crying. It wasn't something she did often, but after such a day, such a dream, Rory supposed she was entitled to her tears just this once.

Drawing her knees up to her chest, she rested her face against them and snuffled quietly so as not to awaken Zeke. Such a strange dream. She had seen her Da's face so clearly. The pain was almost as bad as if she had lost him all over again.

Old Miss Flanagan said that when one dreamed about a person dying, it was a sign of guilt, that one had been neglecting him. But her Da was already dead, and Rory was certain she had never ceased to cherish his memory.

Perhaps . . . but she was definitely guilty of neglecting his dream. Thoughts crowded forward that Rory had been trying not to consider, the loss of the *Seamus*, a loss her floundering company could not afford. Even more than that, so much of her hopes had been tied up in the demonstration of that balloon to the man from the government. When that army official had shown up at her warehouse today, he had either found the place empty or else the police and chaos. It was unlikely Rory would ever get him to come back again.

Not that Rory had had any choice. Zeke's life had been in the balance, and Rory knew if she had it to do all over again, she would do exactly the same. But that didn't make accepting her loss any easier.

"Rory?"

Zeke's voice coming out of the shadows startled her. She shifted slightly, dismayed to find him struggling to a sitting position. He knuckled his eyes, regarding both her and his surroundings with obvious confusion.

"Wha— Where the devil are we?"

"At . . . at Mrs. Cobbett's. Don't you remember?" she mumbled. "I didn't mean to wake you. . . . Please, go back to sleep." She ducked her head, embarrassed. She scarce knew how to begin to explain what she was doing in bed with him, and the fact that she was crying only made it worse. She moved to sit on the edge of the mattress, trying to conceal her tear-streaked face.

If Zeke was astonished to awaken under such circumstances, he gave no sign of it. Nor did he take any heed of her request that he return to sleep. Rubbing the back of his neck, he seemed to become more alert. Shifting closer, he tried to peer into her face.

"Rory, are you crying?"

"No," she said and hiccuped on a sob.

Perching on the bed behind her, he draped one arm about her shoulders. "Is it still because of what happened to the balloon?"

Rory tensed in surprise. She thought he hadn't even noticed those few tears that had escaped her when she saw the *Seamus* being sucked beneath the sea. After their lives had been spared, it had seemed so foolish, so wickedly ungrateful to mourn the loss of her balloon. She shook her head in denial, not saying anything, knowing Zeke would never understand.

He drew her back against him. She resisted at first, but the feel of that solid presence behind her was so strong, so comforting. She allowed her head to droop against his shoulder. The quilt was yet pulled up to his waistline, but the curve of his bared chest felt firm and warm to her touch.

He pressed a kiss to her brow and sighed. "Oh, Rory, if it was anything else in the world but one of those accursed balloons, I'd buy you a dozen of them first thing tomorrow."

"I don't need a dozen. I have other accursed balloons," she sniffed. "But . . . but that one was named after my Da."

"I didn't even know it had a name." Zeke wrapped both arms about her, cradling her closer. "Rory, I realize how much you loved your father, but you can't spend the rest of your life pursuing his wild notions. You've got to find a dream of your own."

"But it's my dream too. From the time I've been a little girl, I've always—" Rory broke off, floundering for words, trying to describe for Zeke that sensation she got when she was flying, of total freedom, of a soul entirely loosed from any earthly bounds. A dull ache settled into her heart. She knew this one thing that was so important to her was something she could never share with Zeke. It was enough to make her tears spring afresh.

Although she knew it was useless, she continued to struggle to make him understand. "Don't you see . . . my Da never made me help him with the balloons. I wanted to. If my friend Gia hadn't just had her baby and needed my help, I probably would have gone with Da on his last flight."

She felt Zeke stiffen. "Your father *died* in a balloon crash?"

"Yes. He was attempting an Atlantic crossing, but a storm blew up before he was ten miles out and . . . and I'm afraid Da wasn't much of a swimmer either."

"And you're still flying in those damned things?"

Rory scrambled out of his arms and off the bed. She glared at him through the room's semidarkness, dashing away the last traces of her tears with the back of her hand.

"If my Da had been an army captain killed in battle and I was his son, you wouldn't think it was odd if I wanted to be a soldier."

Zeke started to come after her, then stopped at the edge of the bed, clutching the quilt around him. "But damn it, Rory. You're not a son and you're not a soldier. You're a woman."

"I was never particularly troubled by that fact until I met you!"

Enough moonlight rimmed his features that she could see clearly his frustration, but the hinting of a smile as well.

"Rory, you're tired," he said in a coaxing fashion he might have used with a recalcitrant child. "This quarrel can wait until morning. It must be past midnight. Come back to bed."

"I'd sooner sleep on the floor." But she hugged herself, already feeling a draft tugging at her nightgown, the insidious cold creeping over her flesh.

"Er . . . forgive me, my dear, but I am little unclear as to why you are sleeping in here at all. Not that I have the least objection, but you'd best keep your voice down. I have a feeling that battle-ax of a woman who owns this cottage might toss us back into the ocean if she caught—"

"She knows I'm in here. She thinks we're married."

"Where the blazes did she get an idea like that?"

"I told her so." Rory raised her chin in defiance as a rumble of incredulous laughter escaped Zeke. "It seemed like a good idea."

"Oh, an excellent idea. I'm beginning to appreciate that fact more and more all the time."

She sensed his gaze warm upon her and suddenly realized that the mammoth nightgown had shifted, slipping off one shoulder almost down far enough to expose the curve of her breast. Rory yanked the fabric back up, clutching it together at the neckline. Zeke made a sudden move, and she tensed, almost fearing he meant to carry her back to bed. But something seemed to hold him back, for he checked himself, resorting to pleading instead.

"Come on, Aurora Rose. You'll catch your death of cold. Look, I'll move back to my own side and I won't even try to touch you."

Rory wasn't sure how far she trusted his promise.

"It's a long time yet until morning," he reminded her.

And it might be longer still if she spent it bundled into bed beside a man now fully awake, aroused. But as he retreated back across the bed, she took a reluctant step forward—although she was not certain which lured her more, the prospect of those warm blankets, or that even warmer voice, husky, all too seductive. She gingerly eased herself back down on the bed.

Lying stiffly on her back, she plopped against the pillows, dragging the quilt up to her chin. Zeke rolled to his side, propping himself on one elbow, resting his head against his hand, gazing down at her.

"I can hardly fall asleep with you staring at me," she complained.

"Sorry," he said, but he didn't alter his position a jot. "I was just wondering if this was what it was like to be married."

"I wouldn't know."

"It might not be as bad as I'd always thought, especially not if I awoke to find you beside me."

Rory squirmed. She knew she shouldn't encourage him to keep talking, especially not in this vein, but she couldn't help asking, "Just how bad did you think being married would be?"

"Maybe not that bad, but certainly not a very attractive prospect. With Mrs. Van H. and her friends, it seemed such a cold arrangement, more like a property merger. Back in the slums, it mostly involved a lot of arguing, hollering, smacking, throwing pots and pans."

"It was never like that for my parents," Rory said. "And what about your foster mother?"

Zeke lapsed into a thoughtful silence. Despite herself, Rory shifted to her side to face him. Zeke was never much disposed to talk about his past, so it almost surprised her when he finally answered.

"I guess maybe Sadie was happy in her marriage. She was a widow by the time she adopted me, but she always kept her husband's picture by her bedside, gazed at it kind of sad-like when she thought none of us kids were looking. I believe she missed him a lot."

"It was the same with my Da when my mother died," Rory said. After a heartbeat of a pause, she ventured another question. "What was she like, Zeke . . . your mother?"

He hunched his shoulder. "Sadie . . . she was one of those big, warm-hearted, motherly women. You know, always fretting you aren't getting enough to eat, trying to make you wear a coat when it's ninety degrees outside."

Although he tried to make a jest of it, Rory could hear the threadings of other emotions in his voice—tenderness, regret, a very real sensation of loss.

"You loved her very much, didn't you?" she asked softly.

Zeke sagged back down against the pillows and stared up at the ceiling. "Yeah, I guess I did." He chuckled suddenly. "In some ways that old curmudgeon Anchor Annie reminds me of her, only Sadie was a little more gentle."

Without realizing it, Rory shifted nearer to Zeke, closing up the distance between them. "Is that why you were persuaded to stay here tonight?"

"No, it was because Annie pointed out to me what a selfish bastard I was being, wanting to drag you back out again after you'd been through such an ordeal. That I ought to be ashamed of myself subjecting a sweet little wisp of a girl like you to the dangers of flying in one of those balloon contraptions."

Although she giggled, Rory had the grace to blush. Zeke reached out and twined one strand of her hair about his finger. "I am sorry, Rory. Annie was right. I was being blasted selfish, not considering your feelings. I haven't been looking after you very well, but I fear I have never been much good at that. Tessa always said—"

He broke off, abruptly withdrawing his hand from her hair, the memory of his sister seeming to pass over him, like a cloud obscuring the brightness of that silvery full moon hovering in the sky outside the window.

Rory wriggled closer. She almost could have nestled her head against his chest. She scolded, "I think you fret too much over the things your sister said to you."

"Maybe. Tessa always was able to get to me. Probably because no matter how shrewish, what she said was always essentially true. I never meant to break Sadie's heart, but I did."

A heavy frown settled over Zeke's brow. "I just couldn't be what she expected of me, no matter how I tried. All Sadie wanted was a God-fearing son, content to work, live the simple life. But I seemed to have been born hungry, never satisfied. I couldn't see spending the rest of my life breaking my back down on the docks, watching Sadie and the girls slaving in one of those damned sewing factories. 'It's good honest work, Johnnie,' Sadie would say. But good honest work didn't seem to me to get you anything but an early grave."

He must have realized that Rory was regarding him with a troubled expression, for he said, "Oh, don't look so horrified, Aurora Rose. No matter what Tessa says, I didn't take to stealing or anything. I just got mixed up with one of those East Side gangs."

"You . . . you were a Dead Rabbit?" Rory faltered.

"No, not quite that bad. I became one of the boys working for a Bowery saloon keeper named Silver McCahan. He backed me for a while in the ring, but I wasn't much good at prizefighting. My blasted temper. I couldn't keep a cool enough head."

Rory didn't find that terribly surprising, but Zeke's next admission shocked her.

"So I became sort of an agent for McCahan instead, putting my knuckles to other uses, collecting on bad debts."

"Oh, Zeke!"

"Not a very reputable profession," he agreed, "but don't waste too much of your sympathies on my 'victims.' They were all street toughs the like of that thug that knocked me cold the other night. I would never have agreed to harass anyone weaker than myself, any honest person. That is until . . ."

He paused, tensing a little, apparently with some memory that was not quite comfortable. Rory thought he'd reached the end of his confidences, but he continued with a rush. "Hell, until one day McCahan paid me a lot of money to help him fix an election, see that a candidate he favored won the race. That kind of thing went on all the time in our local ward. All I had do was hang out about the polls, wielding a big club, make sure everyone voted the 'right' way."

A choked sound escaped Rory. Although she said nothing, Zeke shifted to obtain a better view of her moonlight-kissed features. She was looking as disappointed in him as his mother had that night so long ago.

Tessa had found out about his job somehow and of course had promptly tattled. Zeke remembered facing his mother across the kitchen, dumping a wad of money on the work-scarred table.

"Look," he shouted. "There's more there than you could make killing yourself in that sewing factory for a year. You can quit now, lady, because there's lots more where that came from."

"More?" Sadie whispered, angry tears spilling from her eyes. "More money for what, breaking innocent people's heads? Oh, Johnnie, what's happened to you? You used to hate bullies, fight against them. Now you are becoming one yourself."

Zeke shook himself out of the memory, dragged himself back to the present reality of Rory's sad eyes.

"Don't look so grim," he said. "I never went through with the election job. I changed my mind at the last minute, used my club to make sure the voters got to use the polls in peace." He gave a dry laugh. "I'll bet it was the first honest election that ward ever had."

Rory's sudden beaming smile was as bright as the moonlight. "Glad to see that makes you so happy," he grumbled, but he couldn't help feeling warmed by her sigh of relief, the admiration that glowed in her eyes. "I wish I could tell you the whole thing had a better ending, but Silver McCahan wasn't used to being crossed. He didn't even care that I gave him his money back. So what if I didn't exactly hand it to him? If he had been a little quicker, he could have caught it before it blew off the end of the dock."

Rory's delighted gurgle of laughter sounded like music in Zeke's ears.

"Anyhow," he said. "McCahan told me I was a dead man and I knew he meant it. Still, I was stubborn enough to have risked it, stayed, but I was afraid of bringing down trouble, reprisals against Sadie and the girls. So I ran for it, fled New York."

Zeke found himself going on to tell Rory about his years in Chicago, how he had eventually parleyed a small gambling windfall into a fortune, discovering a talent in himself for speculating, choosing the right investments at the right time.

He hardly knew why, but he felt a strong and sudden need for Rory to know everything about him now, even the worst. He didn't spare himself relating the details of his return to New York, how he had become more and more drawn into playing the role of Fifth Avenue tycoon, finding it harder and harder to pay visits back to his old home on the East Side, look into Sadie's sorrowful, worried eyes.

Up until the end, he had tried to get her out of that flat on Pearl Street, but she had always refused, always looking as though she had been waiting, expecting something different from him . . . just the way she had that night he tried to give her the money from the election job.

When he had been summoned by Caddie to attend Sadie's deathbed, his mother had already been delirious, nearly beyond the point of recognizing him.

Yet she had whispered his name over and over again. "Johnnie . . . Johnnie . . . should have let you . . ." Then she had mumbled something about his real mother and father.

You are my real mother, he had wanted to tell her, but he had felt strangled, his voice choked with dammed-up grief.

"Johnnie, forgive me," she had begged with her last breath. "I should have told you. . . ."

He didn't know what she had done to ask forgiveness for. If anyone had left too many words unsaid, it had been him. And now it was too late.

All memory of Sadie's death was too painful for Zeke to speak of, even now. When he fell silent, Rory stirred beside him. She had been quiet all this time, listening, seeming to pass no judgments, asking no questions until he had finished.

Now she said, "But what about your sisters? What happened to them?"

"Agnes married a bank clerk and moved to Brooklyn. Caddie wed some kind of an artist, had three kids. They live in the Village now. And Tessa, well, you heard her story, how I blighted her life." Zeke tensed his jaw into an inflexible attitude. "But I still don't think I'm that sorry I did it."

"Perhaps you did her a favor," Rory agreed. "But, Zeke, you can't always be so . . . so roughshod with people. Even those you care about. Sometimes you have to let them make their own choices, even the wrong ones."

Zeke grimaced. "That's what Sadie always used to say." He twisted back to his side, smiling down to where Rory's curls tickled his shoulder. "She would have liked you. Although she would have thought you could use a little more meat on your bones."

He touched her lightly beneath the covers, his fingers brushing the area of her rib cage just below the swell of her breasts. It was a mistake to do so. When he had awoke to discover himself in this extraordinary situation, Rory in his bed, so warm, so near, he had resolved to act the gentleman for once, not take any unfair advantage.

Maybe that's why he had been blathering on for the past quarter of an hour, to keep his mind off her delectable curves so poorly concealed by that gown half falling off her. He had so much more he could tell her, so much more he wanted to say.

But as he gazed into her face pillowed so near to his own, her eyes quicksilver pools of innocence, her lips so sweet with the promise of pleasures he'd already tasted, his throat suddenly went dry and he ran out of things to talk about.

"Maybe . . . maybe we should try to get some sleep," he said gruffly.

"I don't know if I can. I . . . I just can't seem to get warm."

Zeke nearly groaned aloud. To resist an invitation like that, he would have had to have been a saint instead of the son of Satan that he was.

Taking care not to jar the bandage loose from his arm, he drew her closer, cradling her against the lee of his shoulder.

"Better?" he asked.

She nodded.

Maybe for her it was, but not for him. He was achingly aware of every soft curve, the heat of her flesh seeming to sear him through the thin layering of the nightgown, rousing in his loins a fearsome need.

Damn! He caught his breath as, in an effort to make herself more comfortable, Rory shifted, her fingers brushing along the flat plane of his stomach, lower. . . .

She tensed, snatching her hand away, half-jerking to a sitting position. "Zeke, you . . . you don't have any clothes . . ."

"That blasted woman took them." He ground his teeth, half-hoping that the realization he was naked would send Rory scuttling back to the safety of her own side of the bed.

Instead she hovered over him, releasing her breath in a quavery sigh, her eyes filled with wonder . . . and longing. "I . . . I've never been in bed with a naked man before."

"I'm relieved to hear it," he snapped. "For the love of God, Rory, stop looking at me that way. Maybe you had better . . . had better . . ."

He didn't know what she had better do, but it hardly mattered, for Rory didn't let him finish the sentence. She caught his hand, laying it alongside her cheek.

He could feel the heat of her blush, the way she trembled, but he sensed it was not owing to any embarrassment or shyness. "Rory." Her name on his lips was an anguished plea. He tried to remember that he had decided not to let anything like this happen, that Rory was better off without him in her life. He tried to search deep into his soul for all that noble resolve he had formed, and found himself searching her eyes instead. Searching and discovering a want, a need that equaled his own.

Slowly, she bent to him, so slowly that time itself seemed spun from the silken skein of her hair. Her mouth was but a fraction away from his own. Their lips whispered against each other, a whispering that fast became a clamoring of passion.

With a low groan, he caught his arms about her, pulling her down hard on top of him. His tongue delved deep into the sweet hollows of her mouth, and he could almost feel the thundering of her heart.

Rory was long past considering the wisdom of her actions. She scarce knew at what point she had decided she wanted Zeke Morrison to make love to her. Perhaps it had happened sometime as she lay beside him in the darkness, listening to him open up his heart, share his past, or perhaps back there on the beach when she had rejoiced to find them both alive and realized how fleeting, how precious a thing time could be.

Or perhaps it had happened even earlier than that, much earlier, that minute when their eyes first met.

She didn't know. She only knew that the time, the moment, was now, hers and Zeke's, to find the promise of a desire they had only touched upon before.

When Zeke stripped the nightgown from her shoulders, baring her to the waist, she felt no guilt, no shame, only a shivering delight at the hunger that burned in his eyes. He cupped both her breasts, molding them to the rough texture of his fingers with a gentleness that left her breathless, feeling as though it was her very heart he cradled in his hands.

He followed each caress with his kiss, fire-hot, insistent, as though he would brand her forever as his. With each touch, he evoked new sensations, so pulsing, so warm, Rory ached with the wanting all the way to the center of her passion's core.

Tentatively at first, then growing bolder, her own fingers skimmed over him, exploring the taut contours of his skin, his muscles rippling like tensile steel beneath.

"Oh, Rory," he moaned softly against her ear, " . . . never imagined it could be like this . . . so sweet, so incredibly sweet."

He kissed her again, hard, fierce, but it was a fierceness that was belied by the tender way he eased her onto her back. Poised over her, he panted for breath and Rory could sense him trying to leash the force of the passion that had been building in him.

"You seem so . . . so small," he whispered, caressing back her tangled strands of hair. "Too fragile for me. . . ."

Rory smiled up at him, her mouth trembling with desire. She would have thought that Zeke knew better than that by now. She would simply have to teach him. Gliding her hands over the expanse of his hair-roughened chest, she went lower still, at last daring to caress that most secret part of him.

As Zeke's breath snagged in his throat, she wrapped her arms about his neck, and pulled him insistently downward, kissing him, her lips both pleading and demanding, restoring the urgency of his desire.

There was no fear as she opened herself to him, only a throbbing need, a hushed expectancy as he eased himself inside her. She accepted everything, even the initial pain of his entry. Somehow it all felt so right, so natural that their bodies should join, become one, no more barriers between them, their hearts sure to follow.

As Zeke began to move inside her, that first pain gave way to a most exquisite pleasure. Rory moaned, writhing beneath him, half-closing her eyes, the image of his face flashing before her like streaks of lightning, his eyes dark, storm-ridden. Like the god of thunder she had once proclaimed him to be, he swept her off into a whirlwind of passion. Ever a creature of the skies herself, she matched his every movement, following him without fear.

Zeke strained with all his will to go slowly, be gentle, but sweet Christ, Rory wouldn't let him, this tormenting sprite of a girl who seemed both angel and woman, earth and spirit. Her nails raked his back, her kisses hot, feverish as though demanding he hold nothing back, give all he had to give—not just the power of his body, but his heart, his very soul.

The feeling was too strong to resist, and he was forced to surrender, the sweetest surrender he had ever known. His entire body seemed to shudder with the release as he spilled his seed deep within her.

Long moments after the storms of passion had subsided for both of them, Zeke lay collapsed upon Rory, his face buried against her neck, their thundering hearts still seeming to beat as one. By degrees, his pulse slowed to its normal rhythm, and he shifted, suddenly fearful he might be crushing her beneath his great weight. Gazing down at her, he saw that her lashes had fluttered closed as she strove to take deep, even breaths. She looked so slender, so pale, was likely even bruised from the force of his lovemaking. The first nigglings of remorse ate at Zeke.

"Rory," he murmured, stroking the velvety-soft line of her cheek. "You . . . you were a virgin. I shouldn't have. . . ."

Her eyes fluttered open to regard him anxiously. "Why? Wasn't I any good at it?"

The question, so outrageous, so thoroughly Rory, provoked him to laughter in spite of himself. He rolled over onto his back, pulling her with him, so that she now rested atop him, her hair a curtain of silk spilling across his chest.

"You were . . ." He paused, trying to find the words to tell her all the wondrous things she had been in his arms, but there were none adequate to describe all he was feeling in his heart.

"You were incredible," he finished lamely, tangling his fingers in those glorious chestnut curls. "I . . . I only meant that for your first time, it should have been different for you. In a bridal suite with satin and roses and champagne, on the evening of your wedding day."

"Pooh!" Rory raised herself, splaying her hands against his chest. She arched her head, looking down at him. Although her eyes sparkled with scorn, her voice was laced with a certain wistfulness as she said, "You're starting to sound like my friend, Gia, talking about weddings. Wouldn't I look silly all tricked out in a lace veil?"

"You would look like an angel."

"These are mighty strange remarks, coming from a man who once asked me to be his mistress."

"That was when I barely knew anything except how badly I wanted you."

"And do you still?" Her question came so soft he could barely hear it, the quiver of her lips betraying her sudden fear, her uncertainty.

By way of answer, he tightened his arms about her, pulling her down for a long and very thorough kiss. If there only was some way to make her understand exactly how much he did want her for now and always. One look into her quicksilver eyes was enough to rouse his desires all over again, desire and another emotion that cut so deep it frightened him.

"Ah, Rory," he murmured, breathing kisses against her hair. "There was a moment back there, when we were both in the sea, that I lost sight of you. I thought you were gone from me forever. If . . . if that had happened, I realized I would have lost everything and the sea might as well have taken me."

When she raised her head to look at him, her eyes were misty with tears, but she managed to smile. "What a silly thing for you to have worried about. Didn't I ever tell you that I visited a gypsy on Forty-second Street? She read my tea leaves and said I'm going to have a long life, at least a dozen children."

"Banshees . . . fortune tellers," Zeke grumbled, but he returned her smile. "Is there anything you don't believe in?"

"I like to keep an open mind." After a tremulous pause, she added, "I believe in you."

Her statement made him uncomfortable, as she had feared it would, almost scared. But in the depths of his face, she read a real gratitude as well.

"Then marry me," he said huskily.

"W-what?"

Gathering her into his arms, he rolled to the side so that he could hold her closer still. "I want you to marry me. In a church with a priest, the lace veil, everything."

For a moment she was too stunned to answer, almost too stunned to breathe. Those few times Rory had ever imagined herself receiving a proposal, she had always envisioned some fool dropped to one knee, an embarrassing and daunting prospect. Nothing should have been more embarrassing than hearing an offer of marriage lying naked in Zeke's arms. Yet somehow it seemed so perfect, so right.

As though fearing she meant to say no, Zeke rushed on. "You know I am a wealthy man, Rory. You wouldn't want for anything that money can buy, clothes, jewels—"

"Oh, Zeke, Zeke . . ." she said, trying to stem this tide of reckless promises, half-laughing, half-aching for him that he still did not realize he had so much more than money to give.

"And that big house of mine," he continued. "There is more than enough room for a dozen kids. . . ." His eagerness abated a little, some shadow of doubt clouding his face. "Though I'm not sure how good a parent I can be. I haven't much experience of fathers. I . . . I sometimes wondered what my own old man was doing when my mother was out tossing me into that trash can."

Before Rory could even begin to reassure him, Zeke flexed his jaw with determination. "But I know I can do better by my own kids than that. At least, I promise I'd always be there."

Rory tried not to be swept away by the images his words were painting: herself, Zeke, some cozy cottage spilling over with love, laughter, children. No more loneliness, emptiness. She was helped by the realization that Zeke was not talking about some snug little home, but that vast barracks of a mansion on Fifth Avenue.

"What would all your rich friends think of your marrying someone like me?" she asked. "All those people you have been trying so hard to impress. I . . . I could never fit in, become a society hostess like your Mrs. Van Hallsburg."

"Oh, the devil with Mrs. Van H. and her set. As if I ever really gave a damn about any of them. All I care about is you."

Rory could tell he meant it, and that should have been enough for her, especially when she was ready to swear the same. But something held her back. Maybe because despite all her dreams, she was essentially more practical than Zeke. She could see problems, whispering like ghosts between them, shades of the past not dealt with, both his and hers.

For one thing, there was the Transcontinental Balloon Company. She wasn't sure how it fit into Zeke's rosy picture. She had a sinking feeling that it didn't. He appeared to have forgotten all about it. But she couldn't.

All the same she hated to mention the balloons herself, and stir up the inevitable discord that would follow, not with Zeke so warm, so eager, waiting for her answer.

"You . . . you'll have to give me a little time to think," she stammered. "This is all so sudden."

She had disappointed him, but he appeared to understand. "As long as you remember," he said with a wry smile. "I'm not a man who takes no for an answer, but I appreciate that it wouldn't be too prudent to accept a fellow until you know for certain he's not going to be hung for murder."

"Zeke, no! That has nothing to do with it."

"Yes, it does, everything in the world. You have already become involved far more than I wanted. I would as soon keep you clear of the rest of this mess until I prove my innocence."

"But . . . but you said you thought everything would be all right as soon as you got back to Fifth Avenue."

"I've been doing some thinking about that, Rory. I'm not going home, at least not until I pay a call on Mr. Charles Decker."

Although he spoke lightly, a certain grimness to Zeke's smile alarmed Rory. She knew full well how volatile his temper could be. She feared to see him cleared of one murder count only to end up arrested on another.

"Then I'm going with you," she insisted.

"No, you're not. That meeting will hardly be any place for you. I'm not planning to take tea with the man."

"I know exactly what you have in mind, and you're only going to get yourself into more trouble."

"You misunderstand me entirely, my dear. I intend to be quite civilized, just a little gentle persuasion, beating the pulp out of Decker until he confesses what he had done to Addison."

"It will never work, Zeke. If Decker is the coward you say, he'll shriek for help at the sight of you. With a houseful of servants at his command, you'll be overpowered before you get near him. If not worse."

Zeke stirred restlessly. "Then what do you suggest I do? I don't have any way to prove Decker is behind all this, just a gut feeling. That doesn't hold too well in a court of law."

"Then we must gather some evidence that will."

"And how do we begin to do that?" Zeke asked. "I'm no copper. Neither are you."

"I don't know." Rory sat up, dragging her hands through her hair in frustration. But the glimmerings of an idea came to her. "Zeke, the police aren't the only ones who do investigating. What about that reporter, the one who wrote the story about you for the *World*?"

"Duffy?" Zeke growled. "He's nothing but an infernal pest."

"Yes, but we both agreed it was odd that story should have been published so fast. If we could find out where

Duffy got his information, we might get a link to Decker that way."

"Maybe," Zeke said. Although she got him to agree that her plan had some merits, Rory could sense that Zeke was still more set on pursuing his own plans—the confrontation with Decker.

As he pulled her back down into his arms, Rory sighed. She could only hope she would better be able to persuade Zeke in the morning. Anchor Annie said there were tricks to managing men. Rory wished she had a few of them at her disposal.

She wanted to beg Zeke to be sensible, to stay away from Charles Decker, but it was difficult to say anything with Zeke's lips melding to hers again. His arms closed about her, deepening the kiss, until her mind reeled, unable to think, to remember that anything else mattered except the shattering emotion Zeke aroused in her. The flames of desire stirred, mounted all over again, until both Charles Decker and New York seemed very far away.

Fourteen

Charles Decker had never thought his house on the avenue large or grand enough. Located a few blocks down from Central Park, it compared unfavorably with both the Vanderbilt and the Astor mansions.

But tonight, the hall, with its cold marble floors and tall pillars, appeared almost too looming. A dozen doors led off of the foyer, chambers with exquisite furnishings, tapestries, shelves crammed with ancient vases and Grecian urns. But the glass cases housing the antiquities he collected with such a passion were nothing more at this moment than places for an intruder to hide.

Clad in a satin smoking jacket shrugged over his shirt and trousers, his bare feet encased in leather mules, Decker crept through his own house, half-expecting Zeke Morrison to melt out of the shadows, his large hands lunging for Decker's throat.

Decker gulped, longing to turn up all the gas jets, set the house ablaze with light, but he was too shamed to admit to his own fears, so he took refuge in anger instead.

Damn that fool O'Connell to hell. Decker had conceived a brilliant scheme that would have rid him of two political enemies at one stroke, and that stupid Irish policeman had bungled it, allowing Morrison to escape. Ever since the sergeant had disrupted Decker's dinner to break the news to him, Decker had been bathed in a cold sweat that rendered his palms clammy with perspiration.

"Morrison got clean away, sir," O'Connell had said, in that thick brogue of his. "We had the warehouse surrounded, but he sneaked out."

"What did he do?" Decker had bellowed back. "Sprout wings and fly away?"

"No, saving your pardon, sir. He had a balloon."

A balloon? A balloon for chrissakes! Even now, alone in the vast silence of his house, Decker had an urge to break into hysterical laughter. Morrison had always been known as the mysterious millionaire of Fifth Avenue. This would surely only enhance his reputation. How or why he had been able to arrange such a fantastic escape, Decker couldn't imagine. He only hoped the damned thing would crash, that Morrison would break his neck.

Failing that, he wished the balloon would transport Morrison to the ends of the earth. But that would be of no avail, for Decker feared that even if Morrison touched down in China, he would make his way back to New York with all speed and come looking for him.

As Decker made his way toward the rear of his house, the region of the servants' quarters, he tried to shake off the notion. Such constant fear of Morrison's return was irrational. There was nothing to connect Charles Decker, Esq., to the sordid murder of Stanley Addison or the assault of Morrison by two street ruffians. But somehow Decker sensed that Morrison would know. He would recall the threats Decker had made in his office that day. At the very least, Morrison's suspicions would be aroused.

Pausing outside the narrow hall that led to the kitchen, Decker rubbed his neck and swallowed. It was as though he could already feel the brutal grasp of Morrison's fingers closing on his windpipe. Morrison was the sort that would choke first, ask questions later. Not that it would matter much, for Decker had run out of plausible answers.

When a rapping came at the kitchen door, he nearly started out of his skin, although he had been expecting this late-night visitor. All the same, the thought of unlocking any of his doors when he was alone in the house, unprotected, unnerved him. He could shout his head off for help and no one would hear him through these thick walls, not with all the clatter of traffic out on the avenue. He had always despised guns, so noisy and dirty, but he wished now that he owned some sort of firearm. As he tiptoed through the kitchen, the domain of his superior French chef, he cast his eye over a costly array of culinary weapons, the blades of knives kept razor sharp, gleaming in the glow of the single lamp left burning.

He lingered long enough to possess himself of one . . . just in case. As the rapping came again, a little more impatient this time, Decker moved toward the door. He nudged the curtain aside to peer through the latticed window, but the figure lurking upon the stoop was lost in shadow.

Shooting back the bolt, he inched the door open, his sweat-slickened fingers tensing about the handle of the knife. The night breeze swept in, bringing with it the scent of perfume, the rustle of silk.

Decker exhaled his breath with a deep sigh, some of his tension relaxing as he eased the door wider, permitting his visitor to enter. The willowy form was definitely that of a woman. Her clothing hidden by the folds of a black cape, her face by a dark veil, she seemed to have chosen her garb with a view to blending with the night, a most successful ploy. But nothing could disguise that regal carriage as she stalked across his threshold.

Decker permitted himself a thin smile. He would wager this was the first time in her life that Cynthia Van Hallsburg had condescended to enter anyone's home through the kitchen door, but it had been her idea, not his.

He did not greet her until the door was shut and securely bolted again. "Good evening, Cynthia." He moved to kiss her fingertips as always, but her hands were encased in a pair of black gloves she showed no intention of removing.

"Aren't you quite the figure of romance?" he said. "Asking for a midnight rendezvous, insisting I give my servants the night off. Our dealings in the past have never required this degree of secrecy." He leered at her. "Can it be you have business of a more intimate nature in mind?"

"Don't be any more stupid than you can help, Charles." Her voice came from the depths behind the veil, chilling him.

He flushed at her snub, but told himself it didn't matter. Cynthia had never been his kind of woman. He preferred them younger, warmer, more easily frightened.

Yet when she removed her veil, revealing the aristocratic perfection of her features, the sculpted masses of ice-blond hair, he stared at her with grudging admiration. Nighttime was kind to Cynthia, the shadows soothing away those fine lines revealed too cruelly by the bright light of day. At this moment, she appeared little older than the youthful beauty who had stunned society at her coming-out ball some thirty years ago. Maybe he didn't desire her, but she possessed a mesmerizing attraction for him all the same.

Her cool blue eyes swept over him, and she arched one brow in mocking fashion. "Taking over for your chef, Charles?"

He didn't gather her meaning until he realized he was still clutching the butcher knife. "Why, no, I . . . I found this on the floor. Marceau is so careless." Rather clumsily, he returned the knife to the counter, all the while feeling uncomfortable, as though she could see right through him, as though she knew all the nervous terrors he had been prey to these past few hours.

He attempted to help her remove her cape, but she refused, saying, "Is it your intent to keep me standing in the kitchen all night?"

"N-no, of course not."

He planned to lead her toward his front parlor, but she frowned. "I prefer your study. The windows there open onto the back of the house."

"I suppose they do," he said irritably. "But I don't understand this great need for secrecy. So what if someone should happen to see you calling upon me? All the world knows we are old friends, aren't we?"

She didn't answer him, and he thought he had seen more affection on the faces of some of his enemies. But he gave over arguing, deciding to humor her.

Preceding her into the study, he lit the desk lamp, while she made sure the brocade draperies were drawn tight. The room was a little close, still smelling of his last cigar, but the surroundings were comfortable to him. The shelves were well lined with books, not as many as that oaf Morrison had, but at least *his* were read occasionally.

Strolling over to a small sideboard, he offered Cynthia a drink, but she didn't want it, so he poured himself a tall brandy. He offered her a chair, but she didn't want that either. His nerves near to the snapping point from her cold silence, he plunked down behind his desk, no longer troubling himself to play the host or the gentleman.

"Well," he sneered. "And to what do I owe the pleasure of your company this evening? That request you sent round sounded most urgent."

Request? It had been like a damned command, and he was more than a little annoyed with himself at how slavishly he had complied.

Instead of answering his question, she reached beneath the folds of her cape and produced a newspaper. She laid it face up on the desk before him, the late edition of the *New York World*. She tapped one gloved finger on the headline, an unnecessary gesture for his eyes were already riveted upon it: *Addison Murdered: Killer still at large*.

The story that followed was brief, providing more lurid details of Addison's demise and Morrison's sensational escape from the police. Decker noted that the article mentioned nothing about balloons. Obviously O'Connell had somehow suppressed that detail, finding it either too incredible to be believed or too humiliating.

As Decker perused the newsprint, he was ever aware of Cynthia's eyes upon his face, fixing him like points of ice. He moistened his lips. "I didn't know you subscribed to the

World, Cynthia. It's a working man's paper. I would have thought the *Post* more up to your style."

"I didn't come here to discuss my taste in reading material." She sounded calm, but Decker retained the impression that she was angry, very angry. Yet with Cynthia, who ever could tell? "Perhaps when you have done with your pleasantries, you will get around to telling me what all this means."

For a moment, he felt a wild urge to deny all knowledge of any of it. But he brought himself up short. There was no reason he should lie, not to her. Damnation, sometimes he acted like he was half-afraid of the woman.

Taking a large gulp of his brandy, he hunched his shoulders in a posture of assumed carelessness. "I took a gamble that I could deal with our little problem regarding Mr. Addison. I almost pulled it off, but my plans went slightly awry."

Her finely chiseled nostrils flared. "Your plans? What business had you to be making any plans?"

"Well, damn it. Something had to be done and you seemed to be doing precious little. I warned you how close Addison was getting. He called a press conference the other day. He had evidence pointing to 'that respected member' of society who owned a chain of brothels and sweatshops in the East End, who had been paying off the police, skimming from the city treasury to keep the operations running. That all points to me, Cynthia."

"So it does, my dear Charles."

"You needn't think you would have stayed in the clear for long either, *partner*. I tell you Addison was getting close to uncovering everything."

"So you had Addison murdered. Brilliant, Charles. What a perfect way to turn an insignificant reformer into a martyr, to lend credence to what otherwise could have been dismissed as wild accusations."

Decker flinched under her biting tone, wishing she would sit down, stop hovering above him that way, making him feel like an errant schoolboy called to account before the stern headmistress.

"You fool!" she said. "Didn't you stop to think that the investigation into Addison's death will only raise more questions, make everything twice as bad?"

Decker took another pull at his drink. "That . . . that was the cleverness of my plan. There wasn't to have been any investigation because his killer was supposed to have been caught on the scene. That's why I had Morrison kidnapped as well. If Addison were killed in some sordid brothel fight by Morrison, why that would discredit both of them."

"And you expected John Morrison to oblige you by confessing to this crime?"

"No, I expected him to be shot, escaping from the police."

She received his words with a kind of frozen stillness, her facial muscles pulled taut. Nothing moved but her eyes, which glinted strangely.

"I believe," she said quietly, "that I had intimated to you that I had plans of my own for Mr. Morrison."

Decker squirmed, but he mustered enough belligerence to snap, "So you did. But you never chose to confide in me what those plans were. I never have been able to fathom your interest in that underbred ruffian, all muscle and flashing teeth, his only intelligence in his fists."

"You shouldn't underestimate John Morrison, Charles. That mistake already appears likely to cost you."

"Humph, the way you talk about him, sometimes I've wondered if you haven't been planning to marry the fellow."

When she made no effort to deny his charge, he continued to goad her. "Is that it, Cynthia? You ever were a greedy wench. Attracted by the prospect of marrying all those millions? Well, you should take more interest in safeguarding the investments you've already got."

She paced across the room, thrusting her hands deep into the pockets of her cloak. "I didn't think my investments were in jeopardy until you made this stupid blunder. I told you that I would take care of Mr. Addison, and manage Mr. Morrison as well. You should have waited, Charles."

"Ha!" Fortified by the brandy coursing through his veins, Decker grew a little reckless. "You've never been much good at managing the men in your life. It's well known that old Van Hallsburg had more chambermaids *in* his bed than he had making it. And as for your brother, Stephen, his peccadilloes are legend."

She whipped about to face him, white-faced. "Take care what you say about my brother, Charles."

He should have held his tongue, but he took a certain satisfaction at chipping away some of her icelike facade. It somehow soothed the wounds she had dealt to his self-esteem.

"Not the cleverest boy, your brother, Stephen," he said. "Always fancying himself in love with some opera girl. I've heard tell half the orphanages in New York are populated with his bastards."

"You are changing the subject, Charles," she hissed. "This has nothing to do with your present folly. Your current state of panic has rendered you very undependable, in fact quite a liability to me."

A liability to her? That was rich, he thought, considering it had been he who had included her in the scheme of buying up property cheap on the East Side, forming a lucrative chain of brothels and gaming salons, using his political influence to protect the operations. She would have been nowhere without him. As an old family "friend," he knew full well how brother Stephen had dissipated her dowry, how old Van Hallsburg had never been as wealthy as supposed.

"What are you trying to tell me, Cynthia?" he demanded. "That you want to dissolve our partnership?"

"Yes, that is exactly what I wish."

"That's fine with me. I'll buy you out, write you a check this very night." Yanking open the desk drawer, he drew forth his checkbook. His hands were shaking so badly with suppressed rage, he nearly dumped over the inkstand as he dipped his pen into it.

"But it's going to be at a price I name," he warned. But as he started to write the check, he hesitated. He was acting out of anger and wounded pride. The partnership they had shared was one of such long duration and so lucrative, he couldn't believe she would let it end this way.

When she glided quietly up behind him, he thought she meant to reach down to his hand guiding the pen over the check and stop him.

But she only whispered, "No, Charles. I fear it is I who must decide the price."

He started to look up and felt something cold, hard, pressed against his temple. Before he could move or cry out, a loud report echoed through the room.

Decker's head jerked back, then he sagged in his chair, a trickle of crimson spilling down his cheek, his eyes wide open, surprised.

But Cynthia Van Hallsburg didn't spare him a glance. She stared down at the smoking derringer in her hand and her lips thinned with annoyance.

She had gotten blood on her gloves.

Fifteen

�֍ ✶ ✶

The late afternoon sun streaming through the windows of Grand Central Station made little impression on the throng of people bent on embarking on the passenger trains. Locomotives whistling, brakes hissing, the clatter of voices and rushing feet all combined to make an overpowering din. In such an atmosphere of confusion, Zeke and Rory attracted little attention, descending off the morning train from Jersey.

Her chestnut hair bound up in a kerchief, Rory wore a faded cotton dress, one of Annie's that had shrunk but still fit Rory like sackcloth. In appearance, Rory knew that she was unremarkable, just another weary traveler from coach class. Zeke too was dressed with simplicity—a plain white shirt, denim trousers, his face shielded by a much-battered felt hat that Annie had once fished from the sea.

Why then, Rory thought, did she feel as if everyone were staring at them? Nervously, she ducked her head when a policeman strolled toward them. The blue-coated officer veered aside at the last moment, lingering to trade some jest with one of the clerks at the ticket window. Rory exhaled her breath in a tremulous sigh.

"Stop looking so guilty." Zeke's amused voice rumbled close to her ear. "It's me the coppers are after, not you."

Linking his arm through hers, he guided her away from the platform, laughing aloud at the furtive way she made her way through the crowded station. Rory tossed him a glance simmering with resentment. How could he be so nonchalant about all this? Her own tension had been mounting ever since they left the security of Annie's cottage, growing stronger as they drew closer and closer to New York.

In Zeke's broad grin, she could see the traces of the street urchin he had once been, actually enjoying playing cat and mouse games with the police. But she was on tenterhooks, afraid that Zeke risked being shot on sight if they encountered any more policemen of O'Connell's ilk. When she and Zeke emerged from the station onto the busy street, flooded with sunlight, her heart gave an anxious thud. But it was the same as on the train platform. Pedestrians shoved past them, more concerned with tending to their own affairs than looking too close into the face of any stranger.

The day was warm, and Rory already felt circles of perspiration forming beneath her arms. Her throat felt dry, and when a drugstore across the street caught her eye, she thought wistfully of a cherry phosphate.

"I don't suppose you have any money left of what Anchor Annie loaned us?" she asked Zeke.

"Just enough for fare on the horsecar," came the disappointing reply. He grumbled, "And what do you mean 'loaned'? While you lay abed this morning, my lady, I was up earning that money, cleaning fish for that old sea hag. I'll never be able to face a plate of mackerel again."

Rory laughed in spite of herself and felt better for it, some of her tension easing.

"I'm glad you think it's so funny. I probably even smell like fish."

Zeke raised his arm, taking a cautious sniff at his sleeve. But he smelled just fine, Rory thought, redolent with the clean tang of Annie's soap and his own more elusive musky, masculine scent. He looked just fine too, Rory thought with a sudden skip of her heart.

That weathered hat didn't quite shadow his clean-shaven jaw, or the dark eyes, which sparkled bright and alert. The denims, a fraction too small, hugged the taut lines of his muscular thighs. The warmth of the day had caused him to open his shirt at the neck, revealing a healthy expanse of tanned flesh. He seemed to possess amazing powers of recuperation. If he still felt any discomfort from his wound or the beating he'd taken, he didn't show it. His shoulders squared in that familiar pugnacious manner, he appeared ready to take on the world.

She wished she felt the same, but she was weary from that long trip on the train. She had spent most of the journey arguing with Zeke about their plan of action. He had finally agreed to abandon his notion of confronting Charles Decker, at least long enough to see what information could be obtained from the reporter, Bill Duffy.

Zeke must have noticed the droop to her shoulders, for he chucked her under the chin with a tender smile. "Maybe you should just go home, little girl, get some rest and wait until you hear from me."

"No, you're not getting rid of me that easily," Rory said. Despite all his assurances, she was not sure how far she trusted Zeke to behave with due caution.

She had an awful image of him bursting into some newspaper office and causing a dreadful uproar. At the very least, he ran the risk of being recognized in a place that published his photograph so often.

"Maybe it would be better if you let me find this Duffy and talk to him," she said.

Zeke's darkling glance told her what he thought of that proposal, but she continued to insist, putting forth all her arguments. In the end, they reached a compromise. Rory would go into the building, find Duffy and bring him to Zeke. If the exchange became heated, if Duffy were to whistle for the police, Zeke would have a far better chance escaping if they were outside.

They had to run to catch the horse-drawn trolley that would take them toward Newspaper Row, and they mounted the steps at the last possible second. As Zeke paid the conductor the fare, Rory collapsed on the first seat. Usually as many as twenty people crammed into the cars during peak hours. But at this time of day, they were relatively empty. There was no need to crowd close to the potbellied stove in the center as she did on chillier days, so Rory remained where she was, Zeke edging beside her.

They got down again at Chambers Street and cut across City Hall Park, heading toward Newspaper Row. The park provided a peaceful oasis in the midst of the bustling city, the grass sprouting tender shoots of a spring green, the elms and poplars just starting to bud.

"You can wait on one of the benches," she told Zeke, "and try to look inconspicuous."

"All right," he groused. "I'll give you half an hour to get that jackanapes of a reporter back here."

She nodded, preparing to rush off before Zeke could change his mind. But he seized her by the wrist.

"Wait. I forgot one thing."

The devil's glint in his eye should have warned her. Before she could protest, he yanked her hard into his arms.

"For luck," he grinned and then proceeded to kiss her, so thoroughly her kerchief became dislodged, her hair tumbling about her shoulders.

She swayed against him, her senses reeling. By the time he had done, she was glad of the support of his strong arms keeping her upright. Her face flushed, her breath coming hard.

A nursemaid wheeling a perambulator past on the walkway cast them a shocked glance.

Rory wriggled out of Zeke's embrace. "This . . . this is not exactly what I call being inconspicuous, Mr. Morrison."

"No, but it's a helluva lot more fun." His eyes were warm with the memories of all they had shared the previous night. They had spoken little of it this morning, but always it seemed to be there between them, the remembrance of those passionate hours before dawn when she had been lost in his loving, Zeke's request that she marry him.

She could tell that he was thinking of it too, the way he traced the curve of her lips with his finger, murmuring,

"Mrs. Morrison . . . the sound of that is beginning to appeal to me more and more."

The trouble was it appealed to her too, and she had yet to rid herself of the doubts plaguing her. She couldn't give him an answer last night and she wasn't ready to do so now. She took a step back, putting more distance between herself and the seductive circle of those strong arms.

"I . . . I better be going. You . . . you stay put and behave yourself until I return."

Whirling on her heel, she turned and practically fled, sensing the heat of his gaze following her. She should have been relieved to discover he had his mind on something besides vengeance, but it didn't help to have him befuddling her own senses when she needed her wits clear for the meeting with the reporter.

Coming out of the park, she crossed Park Row, narrowly missing being run down by a smart tilbury, the footman perched on the back so far forgetting his dignity as to shake his fist at her.

But she didn't check her pace. The *World* was not comfortably located on the same block as the other dailies. Rory was obliged to traverse several blocks, heading back toward the approach to the Brooklyn Bridge. The building that housed Mr. Pulitzer's prized newspaper, some twenty-seven stories of it, loomed above Rory in majestic splendor, crowned with the famous gilded cupola at the top.

Slipping inside, Rory found the place every bit as busy as Grand Central Station, reporters and copyboys rushing past, editors bellowing. From the basement below she could hear the thunder of the printing presses, so loud they seemed to make the floor vibrate beneath her feet.

It was hard to get anyone to stand still long enough to listen to her query after the whereabouts of one William Duffy, let alone give her an answer. Finally a cigar-chomping individual barking into the speaking piece of a telephone paused long enough to snap that she should go to the fifth floor.

Daunted at the prospect of climbing so many flights, Rory was relieved to discover the *World* equipped with an elevator. The youthful operator whisked her upward at a speed that caused a fluttering in her stomach.

Stepping out, she peered through an open door into an office full of desks and men in their shirtsleeves. Most of them were crowded round some fast-talking salesman demonstrating the latest in typewriter machines. She eyed the cluster of male faces dubiously, wondering which one it was she sought. But when she mentioned Duffy's name, she was directed to a desk in the far corner.

Behind it sat a young man sporting a startling shock of red hair and a blot of ink on his nose. Oblivious to the salesman's chatter, he scribbled away with an intense concentration. William Duffy's desk was a disaster of scattered papers and partially clipped newsprint. If he did have any evidence useful to Zeke, Rory wondered how they would ever succeed in unearthing it from the chaos.

She hovered, waiting for Duffy to look up, but it occurred to her that she might drop dead on the floor beside him without his noticing.

She cleared her throat. "Mr. Duffy?"

He glanced up, obviously impatient of any interruption. His annoyance faded to surprise, his gaze raking over her. A puzzled frown settled on his brow. Rory had a sudden notion of how odd she must look in the faded sack of a dress, her hair a wild tangle.

She smoothed it self-consciously. "I realize you don't know me, Mr. Duffy. But I need a moment of your time. My name is Aurora Kavanaugh. I have something of vital importance to discuss with you, about a story you wrote two days ago—"

She got no further for she realized he wasn't listening to her. He stroked his chin, musing, "Kavanaugh? Now where have I heard that name before?"

His face lighting with sudden recognition, he came up out of his chair. "Say, I remember now. You are that girl with the runaway balloon from the circus, aren't you? I did the piece about you crashing on J. E. Morrison's lawn."

Rory tried to begin again. "That's why I am here, to talk to you about Mr.—"

"Look, Miss Kavanaugh, if you are here to complain about the article, if your name got spelled wrong or anything, I'm sorry. I'm always careful. It's the copy editors that mess everything up."

"Will you please just listen to me?" Rory exclaimed. "This has nothing to do with the article you wrote about me. I am here to discuss the more recent story you did on Mr. Morrison."

Duffy perched on the edge of his desk, heedless of the stack of papers that cascaded to the floor. He scowled. "Yeah, poor Morrison. He's in the deuce of a fix. I wish it had been anyone but him. A little mule-headed, but I rather like the fellow."

Rory was unable to restrain her indignation. "Then why did you write such terrible lies about him?"

Duffy looked taken aback. "Why, it was all true, though I wish it wasn't." He puffed out his chest a little. "I assure you William Michael Duffy always makes sure of his facts. My information came from an unimpeachable source."

"Indeed? Someone straightforward and honest like Sergeant O'Connell from the warehouse precinct?"

"That grafter? Lord no, it was . . ." He hesitated, a certain wariness coming into his eyes. "What's your interest in all this?"

"I am interested because I know the truth. Even as your story appeared on the streets, Zeke Morrison was waking up to find himself a prisoner in a brothel and Mr. Addison dead by someone else's hand. And that night when Zeke was supposed to be off, committing the murder, he couldn't have been. He was with me."

That was stretching the truth a bit perhaps, but Zeke's case was urgent. Duffy let out a long, low whistle.

"So the wind sits in that quarter, does it?" He subjected her to an another appraising stare which caused the heat to flare into her cheeks. "Morrison must have been quick to take the advantage when you came dropping out of the skies into his lap. Can't say as I blame him."

"My relationship with Mr. Morrison is scarcely important. What matters is that someone fed you that story on purpose to help implicate Mr. Morrison in a crime he didn't commit. You have been made a fool of, Mr. Duffy."

Duffy didn't look very comfortable with that notion. He folded his arms over his chest. "How can I believe you? You'll excuse me for saying so, but my other source is a little more respectable."

"Perhaps it would help if I told you I know who your other source is—an alderman named Charles Decker."

Duffy was too cautious to confirm or deny her guess. "You seem to know an awful lot, lady." His eyes narrowed. "Maybe you also know where Morrison is hiding."

It was Rory's turn to be uneasy. She had come here for the express purpose of leading Duffy back to Zeke, but now she wasn't so sure it was a good idea. The man claimed he liked Zeke, but he was a reporter for all that. Zeke's capture would make excellent front-page copy.

Duffy regarded Rory more hungrily than Tony when he was half-starving and presented with a bowl of his mother's pasta. She was half thinking of retreating when he came off the desk, pressing closer. "What did you really come up here for, Miss Kavanaugh? I don't think it was just to yell at me because you didn't like the piece I wrote about Morrison."

"No. I guess I hoped that you could help him somehow, that if you knew the story wasn't true, you would want to make it right."

"So I would. I don't like making mistakes on my facts. A thing like that could ruin a fellow's reputation. But I need a little more convincing, perhaps to talk to Morrison himself. It was him who sent you, wasn't it? Why don't you take me to him?"

That was exactly what Zeke desired, but still Rory hesitated. "I am not sure I should trust you, Mr. Duffy."

Duffy reached for his jacket, pulling it on. "With Morrison in this much trouble, you haven't got much choice. Besides, whether I believe you or not, I'm a reporter, not a policeman. I write stories. I don't try to apprehend desperate men, especially not ones with knuckles the size of Morrison's."

Rory gave a reluctant laugh. She found something likable about Bill Duffy, even if he was the author of that dreadful article on Zeke. She had only her instinct to go on, telling her to trust him, but it had to be enough, for Duffy was right in one respect. She didn't have much choice. Even if she had changed her mind about taking Duffy to Zeke, she sensed the man would trail her like a bloodhound all over New York.

Returning to the park, Rory noted anxiously that she had been gone longer than she had promised. The sun had dipped lower behind the trees. As it drew closer to the dinner hour, the walkways were nearly deserted. She saw no sign of Zeke. With a thud of her heart, Rory feared that he had gone off to do something rash.

She sighed with relief when she spied him sitting on a park bench, his legs sprawled across the path, a section of newspaper covering his face as though to shield his eyes.

It occurred to Rory he might be asleep, and her relief changed to indignation, appalled that he could be quite that careless when every policeman in New York must be on the lookout for him.

Yet she supposed that she had not exactly given the man the most restful repose the night before. A guilty blush stole into her cheeks. Rory approached Zeke cautiously, Duffy hard on her heels.

Despite how low she called Zeke's name, it was impossible not to startle him. He came awake fast, springing to his feet, fists drawn back. When he realized it was Rory, he expelled his breath in a long sigh. He lowered his arm, adjusting the brim of the battered felt hat, which had nearly flown off.

He smiled even as he complained, "About time you got back here. I was ready to—" His smile vanished when he saw Duffy at her shoulder.

"Hello, Morrison," Duffy said. "I like the hat."

Zeke's hands balled into fists. To Rory's dismay, he took a menacing step forward. Luckily, Duffy understood the better part of valor. He ducked behind Rory, using her skirts as a shield.

"Take it easy, Morrison. You wouldn't want to be arrested for two murders."

"Why not? They can only hang me once."

"Zeke!" Rory positioned herself firmly in his path, splaying her hands against his chest. "Mr. Duffy seems to have been as much a victim as you. He believed that story was true."

"Maybe I should teach him to check his facts."

Duffy peered round her. "I haven't seen anything in your behavior yet to convince me I made a mistake."

With such a beginning, it was all she could do to get the two men to sit back down on the bench and talk. When they did, she positioned herself as a buffer between them.

Although still glaring at Duffy, Zeke was persuaded to tell his entire story, from Decker's threats to O'Connell's attempt to shoot him in cold blood to the escape in the balloon.

"The balloon. That's the first I heard of that." Duffy gave an ecstatic sigh. "What a story! I hope it's all true. With a tale like that the editor would give me the whole front page. Those smart-mouthed reporters from the *Times* would be green." As another thought appeared to strike him, Duffy looked more subdued. "That is if I still have a job. Lord, Morrison, you wouldn't sue the paper, would you, over one little mistake?"

"No, I'd be more likely to bust up your printing press."

Duffy brightened. "Oh, that'd be all right, but my editor hates lawsuits."

Rory tapped her foot, growing impatient with the pair of them. "Before we worry about breaking presses or writing new stories, we need to deal with the problem that Mr. Morrison is still wanted for murder. Mr. Duffy, in a court of law, would you be willing to reveal the name of the man who gave you the false information?"

"Court of law, hell," Zeke said. "All Duffy needs to do is assure me it was Decker, and I'll take care of the rest."

Rory exchanged a glance with Duffy. He apparently understood her unspoken plea, for he began to hedge. "Well, the matter seems more complicated than that. I don't know . . . there could be someone else besides Decker involved. That friend of yours, Addison, was doing extensive investigating, wasn't he? He implied he had uncovered more than one villain. It might be better, Morrison, if you kept a low profile, let me do a little nosing around."

Rory's heart sank as she saw that Zeke was not about to agree to that. Being inactive for this long had chafed him raw. Another argument ensued, but this time she had Duffy on her side.

"At least let me drop by police headquarters," Duffy said. "I have a few contacts there. I can see how their investigation is going, find out whether your place is guarded, if it's safe for you to return home."

As Zeke shook his head, Duffy continued to plead. "Aw, what's a few more hours? Look, I'll lend you a few more dollars and—" He paused to grin. "I never thought the day would come that I would lend money to anyone, let alone the richest man in New York. Anyhow, you could nip off to some quiet restaurant, feed your girl here."

Zeke stiffened. "She's not my girl. She's my fiancée."

Rory nearly choked at that. As usual Zeke was rushing over her with the force of a gale wind. But she had no chance to protest in the face of Duffy's delighted exclamations.

"Another story! I can see the headlines. *Tycoon Weds Balloon Girl*. They'll have to give me a special edition." He looked as though he were about to die and cross the threshold of heaven. "Just remember, Morrison, when this is all over, you owe me. The entire tale of your life, starting with day one, where you were born, who your parents were—"

"I don't owe you anything except a punch in the nose." Zeke felt almost ready to deliver it. But his gaze tracked to Rory's face, her eyes pleading, clouded with an anxiety that hadn't been there when Zeke first met her. She shouldn't have been that pale. Maybe there was some wisdom in letting Duffy pursue a few inquiries.

Zeke gave in with a grudging frown. "Give me the money and get the devil out of here."

Duffy turned out his pockets and managed to come up with a dollar. Folding it into his fist, Zeke was filled with a wry amusement, remembering the night he had taken Rory out to dine at Delmonico's. He had tipped the waiter more than that.

While Duffy disappeared on his mission, Zeke discovered the dollar was enough to purchase ham sandwiches and coffee from a little deli. Afterward, he and Rory returned to the park and lingered on one of the benches, watching the sun set over the rotunda at City Hall.

There was little talk between them. Rory was too tired. Zeke draped his arm about her, nestling her head against his shoulder. Perhaps it was foolish to hang about out in the open so much, but he didn't see much sign of an extensive police search for him. The city was a big place, the locale of many crimes. Maybe the murder of Addison had already passed into insignificance.

Zeke couldn't let that happen. He owed the man more than that. Maybe even the punishment of Decker would not be enough. So what could he do? Erect a statue to Addison's memory? The park was already full of them, just more places for pigeons to roost.

Yet somehow until he settled this matter, there would be no future with Rory. He could tell he had startled her earlier, maybe even displeased her, when he had told Duffy she was his fiancée.

Although she didn't contradict him, he knew she hadn't really said yes. He was trying not to rush her, but it had been hard to hear Duffy refer to her in that disrespectful way.

He supposed it was odd, even inconsistent of him, considering that at one time he had proposed to make her his mistress. But he hadn't known he was in love with her then.

Love . . . the word itself was enough to scare the hell out of Zeke. Yet he could put no other name to the feeling in his heart as he gazed down upon that tumble of unruly curls, the delicate curve of her cheek. He desired her, yes, an undercurrent of that was ever present. But another emotion settled deeper inside him in what he guessed must be his soul. Funny. He had never been sure he had one until he met her. . . .

And how did she feel about him? The same. He was fairly sure of it, could read it in her eyes, taste it in her kiss. Why then did she hesitate to accept his offer of marriage? He didn't think it had anything to do with the warning Tessa had given. Rory had never paid much attention to that, even when Zeke had urged her to do so.

What then? She had never said so, but it was likely something to do with his attitude over her damned balloons. His jaw tightened. He wished he could understand, but he couldn't and it was owing to more than his own fear of heights. He had seen her come through two hair's-breadth escapes flying those blasted contraptions. He was damned if he would risk losing her that way again.

Almost unconsciously, his arms tightened about her. The movement roused her from the half-drowsy state into which she had drifted. She looked up, surprised, noting the moonlight spilling over the pathway.

"It . . . it's getting late," she said. "I wonder what happened to Duffy."

"I don't know, but we can't sit here on the bench all night. That's one sure way to attract the notice of the coppers."

They had agreed to take the chance of slipping back to Rory's flat, when Zeke saw a hackney coach drawing to a halt at the edge of the park. Duffy leaped out, barely taking time to pay off the driver. He came racing through the trees as if the police were after him.

He drew up so short of breath, he could hardly talk, sinking down on the bench. Zeke and Rory barraged him with questions. "Where have you been? What did you find out?"

Duffy held up one hand, imploring them to stop. "Over . . . all over," he gasped.

Zeke frowned, finding no sense in the words. "What do you mean?"

"It's safe, Morrison. To go home . . . no more police. Decker confessed to everything."

"What!" Zeke and Rory exclaimed in one breath. Rory was swifter to accept the glad tidings than he.

"Oh, Zeke," she cried joyously, flinging her arms about him. Zeke patted her back in distracted fashion. After all these harrowing events, somehow this seemed all too easy.

"I don't understand any of this," he said. "I still want to see Decker."

"Impossible." Duffy managed to straighten, fanning his flushed face with his derby.

"Why not?" Zeke demanded. "Even if he's in jail—"

Duffy shook his head. "Not jail, the morgue. Decker's dead. He shot himself through the head last night."

Sixteen

Zeke Morrison had never realized that returning to his own house could feel so strange to him. True, the mansion on Fifth Avenue had never been exactly like a home, but he had gone over the plans with the architect, had been there at every step of the construction, was intimate with every brick, every panel that had been laid.

Why then did the place seem suddenly so alien, so overwhelming tonight despite the welcome he read in the faces of his staff? Footmen, maids, even the cook stole peeks at him and Rory from the shelter of doorways. Their eyes reflected a kind of awe. He supposed it wasn't every servant in New York with a master who had so nearly escaped facing the hangman's noose.

Only the pert one called Maisie dared to step forth and greet him. She curtsied, dimpling with that saucy grin. "So good to have you back, sir. I told and told the rest of these stupids that you hadn't done nothing."

"Thank you, Maisie," Zeke said dryly, but the girl was already being elbowed aside by Wellington.

"That will do, Abrams." While Maisie retreated with a resentful sniff, Wellington made Zeke his best bow.

"Welcome home, sir. When I heard you were coming, I took the liberty of arranging a late supper by way of celebration for the safe return of yourself and . . . ," his gaze skated doubtfully to Rory, " . . . the young lady."

"It was my idea," Maisie was heard to mutter.

Zeke grimaced. While he was rather touched by the notion and hated to seem ungrateful, somehow he didn't quite feel as though he had anything to celebrate.

"That's very considerate of you, Wellington—"

Maisie gave a loud harrumph.

"—but I don't think either myself or Miss Kavanaugh is really hungry. Just damned tired."

Tired? That seemed an inadequate word to describe just how drained he was. And if he felt a little lost in his own house, Rory appeared even more so. She had wanted to return to her own flat, but he couldn't bear to let her out of his sight.

He draped his arm protectively about her shoulders and watched her weary features summon a valiant effort to smile. The devil knows, his staff had enough already to gossip about, but Zeke didn't care. He had every intention of carrying Rory upstairs, tucking her into his own bed.

"Miss Kavanaugh will be occupying my room tonight," Zeke announced, "and I will take the guest room." He ignored the small sound of protest that escaped Rory. "So perhaps you could just send up a bit of that supper on a tray."

"Very good, sir. I shall send Peter up to draw your bath." Turning, Wellington vented some of his disappointment by chastising the staff for standing about and gawking. He sent them about their business, which left Rory and Zeke alone in the foyer.

For a moment, they faced each other in silence. He could tell they were both feeling a little strange, but it was Rory who put it into words.

She gave a half-nervous laugh. "Suppers, baths . . . I guess everything really is back to normal. It's . . . it's just like everyone is telling us we were having a nightmare." Her lip quivered a little. "Only we know it was all real."

Zeke held out his arms, and she walked into them,

burrowing her face against his chest. "Yes, it was real, love," he murmured. "But it is all over now."

They had spent the last few hours at the police station with Duffy, confirming that fact. Charles Decker had indeed killed himself, leaving behind a written confession of how he had arranged Addison's murder and of his plot against Zeke. The document had implicated Sergeant O'Connell's role in the affair, and he, along with the two thugs who had assaulted Zeke, were in jail themselves. Zeke had made positive identification of the two street toughs. He would have liked just a few minutes alone with the Chin Scar, but of course that wasn't granted him.

Zeke was no longer a man on the run, but J. E. Morrison, the millionaire, respected, soothed and patronized by the chief of police.

"Don't you worry about any of these rogues, Mr. Morrison," the chief had said. "The law will deal with them now."

Zeke had had no choice but to retreat. He supposed that was the price one paid for becoming rich and respectable. One lost the luxury of settling one's own scores.

He ought to be grateful it was all over, out of his hands, yet he felt curiously as deflated as one of Rory's balloons. He held Rory close, comforting her with words he didn't half-believe himself.

"I guess what we have to do now, my dear, is just forget the whole thing ever happened."

A difficult task. Whenever he closed his eyes, he could still see Addison's youthful features contorted with the rigor of death. Obviously it was difficult for Rory too. She still seemed troubled, more trembly now than when they had been on the run.

When someone rapped the knocker at his front door, she started in his arms.

"Relax." He smiled, smoothing back her hair. "We know it can't be the police."

She tried to return the smile, but she still looked tense when the knocking sounded again. "Aren't you going to answer that?"

"No, that's what I pay Wellington for. Come on." Guiding her gently, he had her precede him up the curving stair. They were about midway when he heard the butler answering the door.

Zeke didn't bother to look back, sure that Wellington would say he was not at home. To his annoyance, he heard the caller being admitted, the sound of a well-bred feminine accent carrying up the stairs.

Rory appeared too tired to pay any heed. She continued on, but Zeke froze, turning back. He nearly cursed aloud.

Cynthia Van Hallsburg was the last person he wanted to see. He couldn't imagine what she was doing here so late. Garbed in a flowing opera cape of silvery satin, her diamonds winking in the foyer's chandelier light, she appeared to have just returned from some party.

Zeke wished he had had the wit to keep on going, but now it was too late. Mrs. Van Hallsburg had seen him. She stepped to the foot of the stairs, glancing up.

"John," she said softly.

He had no choice but to descend. "Good evening, Mrs. Van H."

For once she made no effort to maintain formality between them. She extended both her hands, which he took. It was the warmest gesture she had ever made toward him, yet still her fingers were cold.

"I am so relieved to see you home safe. I have been through agonies since you disappeared, ringing your house every few hours. When Wellington told me you were returning, I just had to come over despite the lateness of the hour."

Zeke shot Wellington a glare over her head. The butler rolled his eyes and beat a hasty retreat. Zeke turned back to Mrs. Van Hallsburg, summoning up a stiff smile.

"It's very good of you to be so concerned, Cynthia. I have been through a hell— have had a bad time of it. I was just about to collapse."

"I know that, poor boy, and I won't detain you long. I only had to see for myself that you were unharmed and . . . and to apologize."

"For what?"

"Why, for the ungentlemanly behavior of my old friend, Charles Decker."

Ungentlemanly? Zeke nearly choked. "Yes, I suppose murder does tend to place a man beyond the pale. I daresay he would never have received an invite from the Vanderbilts again."

"There is no need for you to be sarcastic, John. You cannot imagine how shocked I was when I heard the things Charles had done. I felt as though he had betrayed my trust as well. When I think of how I introduced him to you, insisting he was an honorable man!"

"I guess he fooled a good many people besides you."

"But I knew him such a long time," she murmured, her lashes fluttering down to veil her eyes. "I should feel more at his death, the way he took his own life, but I can't help thinking that it was better that way."

Zeke had difficulty agreeing with that, but he said, "His suicide was rather unexpected."

"I suppose when you escaped he knew you would return to expose him and couldn't face it."

"The man was such a coward, he seemed to me more likely to bolt than to kill himself."

She gave an eloquent shrug. "Desperate men do the most inexplicable things. I always—"

She broke off suddenly, staring past Zeke, her face going rigid. She dropped Zeke's hands. Glancing behind him, Zeke realized Rory had come back down, emerging from the shadows of the upper stairwell.

Rory paused a few steps above Zeke, unable to tear her eyes from that . . . that woman. It was only the second time in her life she had ever seen Mrs. Van Hallsburg, but the force of her first impression held good. No wonder she had dreamed of her as the banshee. The woman's eyes were like her diamonds, cold, brilliant and hard.

After her initial unnerving stare, Mrs. Van Hallsburg's gaze roved over Rory in a disparaging fashion, making Rory acutely aware that she was still garbed in Annie's old gown. Rory had never given much thought or care to what she wore. But at the moment, she felt as though she would have sold her soul to be dressed in a gown as regally elegant as Mrs. Van Hallsburg's, to appear before Zeke just as beautiful, just as sophisticated. Facing that woman this way was somehow like . . . like confronting an enemy knight without a suit of armor.

For too many painful moments, none of them said anything. Rory experienced a kind of fierce triumph when Mrs. Van Hallsburg was the first to look away.

"What is this person doing here?" she asked Zeke.

Zeke's jaw jutted with annoyance, and he replied with barely restrained civility. "Miss Kavanaugh is my guest."

"I see." Never had two words been so fraught with icy scorn, with patent insult. Rory felt her cheeks burn.

"Not that it's any concern of yours," Rory blurted out. Her retort sounded childish by comparison with Mrs. Van Hallsburg's rigid self-possession. Zeke stepped hastily in between them.

"Miss Kavanaugh is tired. She was just on her way upstairs." Turning to Rory, he touched her cheek, his eyes alight with tenderness, reassurance. He said in a low voice, "Go on, Rory. Don't worry about her. I'll get rid of her."

Although Rory reluctantly complied, she was worried. She had an urge to remain at Zeke's side, to . . . to protect him. A strange notion indeed, for what sort of protection could Zeke possibly need, he such a huge strapping man and Mrs. Van H. such a thin blade of a woman?

All the same, Rory lingered, her troubled gaze following the pair of them until they vanished into the study.

Zeke would just as soon have showed Mrs. Van Hallsburg the front door, but he could tell that Cynthia would not be so easily dismissed. Nor did she intend to enact any scenes within hearing of the servants. It was she who selected the study, obliging him to follow her.

As Zeke lit the gas jets, he grimaced at the sight of the room he would connect forever with what he now thought of as that fatal confrontation with Decker. If only he had known, he could have throttled the little weasel then. Maybe Addison would still be . . .

He suppressed a sigh. It didn't seem fair somehow that the room remained so unchanged, so mundanely normal. Hell, even the Joseph Riis book with its stark images of life on the East Side remained on his desk, right where he'd left it. The text seemed to stare up at him, a grim reminder of Addison and all his dreams, his vows to do something to change all those harsh realities.

Zeke thrust the book to one side, having no desire to linger in the study, so thick with memories that seemed to hang like the dust in the air. He wished Mrs. Van Hallsburg would say her piece and be gone. He knew it was going to be about Rory and he wasn't going to like it.

She paced off a few steps as though seeking just the right words to convey her displeasure. "This was not exactly the reception I had hoped for, John."

"No? Well, if I had more notice I could have arranged for the Astors to be here. Hell, madam, I have been on the run for my life."

"Yet you still found time to be seeking your pleasure with that young female that you assured me meant nothing to you." Her lips pinched in a taut line. "Even my brother, Stephen, never fouled his own house by taking his harlots there."

"Rory is no harlot. I owe her my life. If not for her risking everything to get me away in one of her balloons, I would be stretched out in the morgue beside Addison."

"The balloon? So that's how you managed it. I had wondered." A fleeting smile touched her lips, but it never altered the hardness in her eyes. "I suppose that gives me reason to be grateful to your little circus girl myself. So buy her something pretty, John. Then send her on her way."

"I'm afraid I can't do that. I plan to marry her."

Zeke would have wagered that nothing was capable of shocking Mrs. Van Hallsburg, but she paled, gripping the back of his desk chair.

"You . . . you can't mean that."

He said nothing, but apparently she could read the answer in the implacable set of his jaw. She half-sagged into the chair, then straightened, struggling to recover herself.

"Of course I understand your gratitude to the girl, but—"

"It's not gratitude that I feel for Miss Kavanaugh," he cut in. Mrs. Van Hallsburg's reaction was rendering him acutely uncomfortable. He had expected scorn, perhaps a flash of her icy anger, but nothing like this. Good lord, the woman was actually close to indulging in a display of genuine emotion.

She moistened her lips. "These . . . these passing fancies sometimes happen to a man of your age, John. My brother, Stephen, for instance. There was this actress once he insisted he loved, wanted to marry, simply because she was carrying his child. Your circus girl—she's not pregnant, is she?"

"No," Zeke snapped.

She seemed to find some relief in that. "Good. That will make it easier for you to reconsider. A girl like that . . . she would only drag you down, back to the coarse life you used to know. Is that what you want, John?"

"What I want is to end this conversation before I forget all those fancy manners you taught me."

"Yes, I have taught you, far too much to see you throw it all away on some circus girl."

"All what?" Zeke asked, frowning. "I don't really know what the hell you are talking about, Mrs. Van H. Sure, you polished me up a bit, opened a few doors for me, but—"

"There's been more than that between us and you know it!" To his astonishment and discomfort, she flushed, her face turning a mottled red, her eyes almost feverish. "All my life I have been surrounded by pale imitations of men. I singled you out because I saw something different in you, something hard, strong, ruthless."

As she came round the desk, stalking toward him, Zeke took an involuntary step backward, too stunned to say anything. He had never been backed into a corner by any woman before, but then he had never seen such an expression on one. He was familiar with the look of naked desire, but there was something unsettling about the passion firing Cynthia's eyes, something unwholesome that made his flesh crawl.

Resting her fingertips against his chest, she rasped, "There is a power in you, John Morrison, that matches the spirit in me. I have been watching, waiting for you a long time."

He wanted to thrust her away, but he felt frozen, almost mesmerized. She leaned forward and brushed her lips against his.

It was like kissing cold steel. Revulsion rippled through him. Placing his hands on her shoulders, he pushed her roughly from him.

A guttural cry escaped her. She stared, her eyes burning into his, and for a moment Zeke felt as though he'd caught a glimpse of hell, knew what it must be like to be damned.

Then she turned aside, walking to the window, her back to him. As she drew in steadying breaths, her shoulders trembled. God above, she couldn't be crying, could she? Not Cynthia Van Hallsburg!

He didn't have the damnedest notion what to do. If it had been any other female, he would have tried to offer some comfort. But the mere thought of touching her again made his gut wrench, and he scrubbed the back of his hand across his mouth.

"I . . . I am sorry, Cynthia," he said. "If I ever led you to believe— That is I never had any notion what you were coming to feel—" Hell! Exactly what was it she did feel for him? One could hardly call it love.

She drew herself up and came slowly around. To Zeke's intense relief, she had composed herself, her features settled into those familiar well-bred lines. One glimpse beneath that icy mask had been enough. He had no desire to ever see her lift it again.

"It is quite all right, John. You needn't apologize. I have done acting like a fool. I only wish you would do me the courtesy of forgetting this ever happened."

"Sure," he agreed. But he knew he couldn't, and from the expression in her eyes, he sensed she never would either. The thought left him feeling cold.

Drawing her cape more closely around her, she moved with dignity toward the door. Zeke was almost too swift in his alacrity to open it for her.

"You needn't trouble yourself to show me out," she said, sweeping past him. She paused in the shadows just beyond the door. "About your decision to marry that girl . . . I suppose I should wish you joy. All I can do is hope that you never have cause to regret it."

Without looking back, she walked on, and soon Zeke heard his front door open and close. But her words lingered on like the disturbing scent of her perfume, like a chill in the air.

The old woman down at the fish market where Sadie had shopped was fond of wagging her head, quoting all the trite maxims, ancient proverbs. Zeke had never paid much heed, but one now whispered through his mind.

Hell hath no fury like—

He gave himself a brisk shake. There had been no fury in Cynthia's voice as she'd left, only a cold resignation. The entire incident had been unpleasant, but it was over. He didn't doubt but what the next time he saw Mrs. Van H. riding in the park, she'd snub him most royally and that would be that—the end of their acquaintance.

He blew out the lamp, trying to dismiss the whole ugly scene. But he was beset by a strong urge to seek out Rory, hold her in his arms, make passionate love to her. He suddenly needed it as badly as a man near frozen to death needed fire.

Rory had been left alone in Zeke's bed too long, given too much time to fret and think. She tried to examine her feelings regarding that Mrs. Van Hallsburg, why she so loathed and feared a woman she didn't even know. Maybe the fear stemmed from the fact that Cynthia Van Hallsburg served as a reminder that Zeke was part of a world that Rory couldn't share, didn't even want to.

Her eyes roved about the bedchamber, the expensive paintings, the costly bed hangings, the gilt trim, all the ostentatious display of wealth, and Rory felt little more

at ease here than she had the first time. Being back in
Zeke's mansion only seemed to point out all the differences
between them.

Perhaps at one time, they had come from a similar
background, but their dreams, the things they valued were
not the same.

All Rory had ever desired with her balloon company was
to keep it solvent. Never had she viewed her business as an
end to riches, but rather as a challenge. Even if someday
she were to conquer the skies, she knew it would not
change who she was, make her want to forget that little
corner of the world she came from. But it seemed to have
been different for Zeke. He had struggled to become rich
enough to shut out that part of his life, which had given him
pain. Sadly he appeared to have also set aside the happiness
he had once known with it.

It had been easier to think of marrying him when they
both had been on the run, possessing scarce a dime between
them, only the clothes on their backs and borrowed ones at
that. All they had had to depend upon was each other.

But back in New York, it was just as she had feared.
Life again became . . . complicated.

Despite the doubts tormenting Rory, her heartbeat quick-
ened when the door to Zeke's room opened. Somehow
she had known he would never spend the night in the
guest chamber as he had said. He slipped inside, clad
only in a satin dressing gown, belted at the waist. The
glow of the small lamp he carried illuminated the dark vee
of his chest, the muscular outline of his calves and bared
feet.

"Rory," he called in a soft voice. "Are you asleep?"

"No," she whispered, sitting up and drawing the bed-
clothes around her. As he approached, his lamp cast flickering shadows up the wall, Zeke's face now revealed by
the eerie upward glow. He appeared unusually solemn.

He reminded Rory of a story she had once read, about
some funny old Greek fellow who had gone through the
world with a lantern searching for truth. Looking at Zeke,
Rory had a most melancholy feeling that he had never found

it. As he set the lamp down on the bedside table, she asked, "Is anything wrong?"

"No, I just needed to look at you." The longing in his eyes told her that he needed far more than that. "I have been pacing my own room, trying not to come and disturb you, knowing how exhausted you must be."

At one time she had thought she was. Strange that the feeling seemed to have disappeared. She extended her hand to him, drawing him down to sit beside her on the edge of the bed.

He smiled suddenly, and Rory realized from the direction of his gaze that he had noticed that she was wearing one of his nightshirts, the cotton gaping open at the neckline.

"Funny. It looks much better on you," he murmured, tracing the column of her throat with his fingertips, moving down to caress the swell of her breast, setting her skin a-tingle.

In spite of the delicious sensations he was rousing in her, she couldn't help asking, "Is your friend gone?"

"Friend?" He gave a puzzled frown, then started with the realization of whom she meant. "Yes, a long time ago, thank God."

She heard nothing but relief in his voice. All the same she was beset by a peculiar stirring of apprehension, almost jealousy.

"Mrs. Van H. looked very beautiful tonight." She grimaced, fingering one of the wild tangles of her own hair. "Very different from me."

"The difference between winter and spring," Zeke said.

Yes, Rory thought glumly, the elegant woman did have a way of making her feel like a child, the "little girl" Zeke had such a teasing habit of calling her.

"I suppose I am much younger, unsophisticated," she said.

"And you always will be, even when you are eighty years old." Zeke tucked his fingers beneath her chin, forcing her to look up. His eyes were shining with a glow more soft than the lamp's. "Just as fresh as an April morning. I don't ever want you to change from what you are, Rory. Always be springtime for me."

She thought she would be anything he wanted when he looked at her that way, a dangerous heady feeling as he leaned forward, grazing her lips with the warmth of his own. He pulled her hard against him, and she was content to lose everything, all her doubts, even her very self, in his loving.

When she lay naked in his arms, there seemed no room for any qualms, any questionings between them. Their loving was just as wondrous as the previous night, their bodies melding together in a passionate flame. No matter how soul-weary she might be, his kiss, his touch seemed to gift her with a sensation of renewal. Nothing else in the world mattered but Zeke, the way he could make her feel.

It was only when she lay spent, curled up beside him, her head tucked in the lee of his shoulder, that Rory felt the lack of something, that afterglow of complete satisfaction. She tried to tell herself that perhaps the difference was in this museum piece of a bedchamber, not near as cozy as the one in Annie's cottage. All their whispered intimacies seemed to echo off that vault of a ceiling.

But maybe it had more to do with Zeke, holding her almost too tight, making plans for their marriage. After typical Zeke fashion, he was telling, not asking. He seemed to have forgotten she'd never given him an answer.

Rory listened uncomfortably as he detailed how she could spend any amount she desired redecorating the mansion. When he came to their wedding trip, outlining a whirlwind tour of Europe, she felt she had to stop him, interjecting softly, "It would be difficult for me to be gone that long, with my company on such shaky ground."

She felt Zeke tense, but all he said was, "Oh, we'll find something to do about the warehouse."

The warehouse . . . it was a cold way to refer to the business that to Rory was a rainbow array of silks, gusts of warm wind, the visions of both her father and herself. Zeke's answer was less than satisfactory, but he suddenly showed no more inclination to talk. His eyes fluttered closed, and in a few moments more Rory thought he had fallen asleep.

She wished she could do the same, but the warmth that Zeke's loving had aroused seemed to have fled, leaving her to the cold comfort of all her doubts again. Wriggling away from Zeke, she slipped out of bed and scrambled back into the nightshirt. She ran her tongue over lips that seemed parched and made her way to the bathroom for a glass of water. Although the lamp had been left burning, that portion of the vast bedchamber was lost in shadow. Rory groped toward what she thought was the bathroom door.

But as she turned the handle and shoved it open, she perceived no gleam of porcelain, no looming shape of that mammoth bathtub. She thought she had blundered into a large closet, but her eyes adjusted enough to the darkness to tell that she had stepped into a small sitting room of some kind, a place that she sensed was very unlike the rest of the house.

She should have retreated, but the stirring of her curiosity was too strong. Retrieving the lamp, she carried it into the room. The light spilled off a dainty pattern of floral wallpaper, a braided rug covering a hardwood floor.

The furnishings were few. A small table bore some gilt-framed photographs and a lace tidy that was a little crooked, as though fashioned by childish hands. Next to the table stood a wooden rocker, much scarred with age. It emitted a most comforting creak when Rory touched it.

Setting down the lamp on the table, Rory directed her attention to the photographs. The smallest was of a plump woman garbed in her Sunday best, a suit of stiff black silk, looking not quite at ease dressed thus or peering into the lens of the camera. Yet not even the stilted pose could erase the love and patience etched into that careworn face. Rory had no doubt she was gazing into the eyes of Zeke's foster mother, Sadie Marceone.

Next to her photograph rested an oval frame encircling three young girls in pink gingham dresses with white yokes, the children similar in their dark curls, but their expressions so different. The littlest one who was so bright-eyed, that had to be Zeke's youngest sister, Agnes, while the tallest one with her sweet, placid features must be Caddie. And of course, there was no mistaking the prim girl that was Tessa.

Rory moved to the last picture, obviously one of Caddie grown, a handsome man at her side, three children tucked about her skirts.

After Rory had studied it, she replaced the picture, her hand trembling a little. She cast an uneasy glance about the room, feeling she had strayed into a part of Zeke Morrison's heart not even she had been invited to enter. Reaching for the lamp, Rory prepared to retreat, but it was already too late.

She gasped to find Zeke blocking the doorway, watching her. She feared he might be angry at her prying.

"I am sorry," she began. "I never meant to—"

"It's all right." His voice was a little abrupt as he cut off her explanation. But far from demanding she leave the room at once, he stepped across the threshold himself.

"It's not exactly as though you stumbled upon some kind of skeleton in my closet."

No, Rory thought, only that part of his memories that rendered him vulnerable, that part of himself he tried like death to hide.

He stepped over to the rocker, running his hand along the back. "These are only a few odds and ends I didn't know what else to do with." He gave a lopsided smile. "The rocker was Sadie's. I went by the old flat after Tessa had moved out. She was throwing this away, just because the arm was broken. It seemed so . . . so wasteful. So I carted it back here and mended it."

"And the pictures?" Rory asked softly.

"I never seem to be able to get rid of anything." He added almost defiantly, "Besides they are good pictures, good likenesses."

He hid his face from her as he straightened the photographs, smoothing out the tidy as well, his large callused fingers snagging on the delicate lace. The awkward workmanship was obviously not that of his mother.

"Did your littlest sister make that?" Rory asked.

"No, Tessa gave it to me."

"Tessa?" Rory echoed, startled.

Zeke gave a grudging laugh. "Yeah, I know. It surprised me too. I always thought Tessa more apt to give me the business end of a knife. But the tidy was a present for my sixteenth birthday. To decorate the washstand in my room. Tessa said that Sadie told her she had to give me something. So she wrapped this up in tissue paper and practically bounced it off my head."

Despite Zeke's tone of wry amusement, Rory obtained a new insight regarding his relationship with the sister who seemed so to despise him. Maybe Tessa had to give him a present, but she hadn't had to labor such long hours over the tatting, a task which had obviously been difficult for her. Nor did Zeke have to keep it all these years.

As he stood gazing at the pictures, there was a grim set to his mouth, but a wistfulness in his eyes.

"You don't have any contact with your family now?" Rory asked.

"I send presents at Christmas, birthdays, especially to Caddie's children."

A smile escaped Rory. So he really did have a niece.

He continued with a sigh. "I always wanted to help all my sisters, would've settled any amount of money on them. But they never would take it."

"Maybe they would far rather have a visit from you than the money."

Zeke shrugged. "Tessa's anger makes that difficult. It would put Caddie and Agnes in an awkward position, forcing them to choose sides. It . . . it just wouldn't be worth it."

Rory didn't agree with him, but she kept silent on that head, merely remarking, "These are splendid pictures. It seems too bad to keep them hidden in here. Are you that ashamed of them?"

"No, only of myself." He straightened abruptly. "You had best get back to bed, Rory, before you get cold."

She could tell he wanted her out of that room, wanted out himself. Although she complied sadly, watching him pull the door closed, she had the feeling Zeke was shutting away too much of his life. But it was not something he was willing to discuss, even with her.

She sensed his retreat from her, even before he brushed a kiss on her brow. "You'd best get some sleep while I go back to the guest room and do the same. I have a few details to clear up in the morning regarding the business with Addison."

Rory regarded him anxiously. "I thought you said that was all over."

"So it is, but before we can get on with planning our wedding," he flinched, "I have a funeral to deal with."

Seventeen

✳ ✳ ✳

Zeke Morrison scooped up a handful of dirt in his fist.
He stood over the yawning grave that moments before had
received the earthly remains of Stanley Marcus Addison.
Opening his hand, Zeke slowly released the fine black
grains, watching them scatter over the gleaming surface
of the mahogany coffin below.

Ashes to ashes, dust to dust.

Zeke hated funerals. He would far rather have looked
down the barrel of a gun than into the grief-stricken eyes of
Addison's widow. She stood opposite him, on the other side
of the grave, a delicate woman, too young to be in black,
clutching the hands of her two small sons, one snuffling
against his mother's sleeve.

Zeke experienced a tightness in his throat and cursed his
own folly in coming. He could have made some excuse.
He had even avoided his own mother's burial, although
his conscience had never given him a moment's ease since
for that bit of cowardice. He had vowed never to make that
mistake again.

So this morning he had endured the church service, the
minister's endless eulogy, every word of it deserved by

265

Addison, every word a sharp reminder to Zeke of the kind of man who had been lost. He reflected bitterly that the world would have been better off if that headstone had marked a reprobate like himself instead of the idealist young politician.

As he stepped back from the grave, Zeke felt shamed by his relief that the funeral was almost over. He watched as Rory tossed in a handful of earth. Zeke hadn't asked her to accompany him, but he was glad she had, drawing comfort just from looking into her face, those impish eyes for once sweetly solemn, her bow-shaped lips tremulous with grief for a man she'd never even met.

Zeke was not as pleased by the sight of Bill Duffy. This was one place the press didn't belong, the reporter's flaming red hair somehow an affront to these somber proceedings. Yet Zeke was forced to admit that Duffy conducted himself with decorum, his derby held respectfully in his gloved hands, no sign of the ever-present notebook and pencil.

He edged close enough to Zeke and Rory to murmur, "Damned fine service even if it was a bit long."

"I doubt that matters much to Stanley Addison," Zeke snapped.

"Funerals are not for the dead, only the living," Rory said softly. "Just a way of saying good-bye."

As far as Zeke was concerned, there would have been only one fitting way to bid Addison's memory farewell, and that was to have the man responsible beneath his fists. But that satisfaction had been denied him, his only consolation now to picture Charles Decker roasting in hell, his skinny buttocks seared by the hottest flames.

Zeke fidgeted, trying to quell such thoughts. They didn't seem quite fitting standing in the shadow of a church. The funeral might be nearly over, but the worst part was yet to come, the moment to step up and mutter some final consoling words to the bereaved family. Zeke never could seem to think of anything appropriate to say.

When Rory walked up to Mrs. Addison, Zeke hung back. He couldn't hear all of what she said, something about

Addison resting with the angels. Of course, Rory *would* believe in angels, the conviction in her voice bringing a faint smile to the lips of the widow.

Zeke wasn't sure what he believed in. He only knew that such remarks had never afforded him much comfort. Maybe it was fine and dandy to think of the deceased stringing harps by the peace of the pearly gates, but that sure didn't help those left behind, trying to mend the hole torn in their lives.

He tensed as he realized Rory had stepped back. His turn was next. Clearing his throat, he managed to mumble gruffly, "Very sorry." Which he was, but that didn't bring Addison back. Rather awkwardly, he offered the widow his hand, which she took, her fingers not much larger than a child's.

Zeke had never really taken much notice of Clara Addison, a gentle shadow in her husband's wake. Now he felt appalled by what a wisp of a thing she was, too frail to be left to the task of raising two boys alone.

"If there is anything you ever need—," he began, then broke off, embarrassed. "Though I am sure Addison's trust fund left you well provided for."

"Oh, Mr. Morrison." She pressed his hand, and Zeke had difficulty meeting those brimming blue eyes. "My Stanley had many fine qualities, but being practical, planning for the future, wasn't one of them. I know that trust fund was set up by you two days ago."

Zeke felt his face wash a dull red. "Well, I . . . I . . . yes, but it was money that Addison had invested with me to—"

But she gently shook her head. "It was very generous of you, Mr. Morrison. But I fear I cannot accept such a gift."

Generous? Why didn't she jab a red hot stake through his heart and be done with it. His own conscience was certainly doing so at this moment.

"It's not a gift, madam," he said. "I owe your family that much. I feel a certain amount of responsibility for your husband's death. He didn't understand the risks that he was taking, but I did. I should have never helped him with his campaign, then maybe he would still be alive."

But Clara Addison would have none of that either. "With or without your backing, Stanley would have pursued his reforms. It was what he believed in as much as any soldier who dies for his country on the battlefield. Surely you can understand that."

Zeke didn't. He had always thought men were marks who died fighting for any cause other than their own. Addison's widow was obviously just as starry-eyed as he had been. All the same, Zeke made one more effort to reason with her about the money.

"You should take it," he urged. "If not for yourself, then for your boys. It's no more than I would have spent on your husband's campaign for mayor."

She cast a wistful glance toward her two children, who had wandered off and gathered up a handful of dandelions to bring back to their father's grave. Her lip quivered. "For their sakes, perhaps . . . thank you. But I can only accept a portion of the sum you proposed. The rest I would still like you to put into Addison's campaign."

Zeke regarded her with a tinge of impatience. Didn't she understand that there could no longer be any campaign? One couldn't elect a dead man mayor.

"With your husband gone, I am afraid—," he began.

"Someone else will step forward to take his place. There are other good men who resent corruption as much as he did, who feel there is no reason people should be starving, living in tumbledown tenements, not in a city as bountiful as New York." She unnerved Zeke by staring directly into his eyes. "Yourself, perhaps?"

"Me?" Zeke blurted out, considerably taken aback. "I'm no crusader, madam. I'm only the one who signs his name to the checks."

But she continued to regard him hopefully. "I pray you will reconsider, Mr. Morrison. That is one of the hardest things about Stanley's death, my fear that all his dreams, his ideals, are going to die with him."

Zeke tugged at his starched collar. He was vastly relieved when the widow's attention was claimed by the minister and his wife. He didn't want to add to the woman's grief by telling her exactly what he thought of her crazy notion. He felt he had said and done all that was necessary. Now he just wanted to escape.

When he turned, he was disconcerted to find Rory and Duffy had been hard on his heels and apparently had over-heard the entire conversation. They were both regarding him with that same hopeful expectancy he found so unnerving.

"Say, Morrison," Duffy said, "that was a great idea of Mrs. Addison's. I can see the headlines now. *Tycoon Throws Hat in Mayoral Race.*"

Zeke glared. The only place he wanted to throw his hat was over Duffy's face.

"Go soak your head in an inkwell," he growled at the reporter, tucking Rory's arm through his. "I've had enough of politics and funerals. I just want to get out of here and go have a drink."

"Suit yourself, Morrison. But you can't think this is over because Decker is dead. There's plenty more villains where he came from. I may take over for Addison and do a little more digging myself."

"Dig away, but just don't go down so deep you end up like Addison, six feet under."

Duffy stalked away in disgust, but Zeke took little notice of his departure, being more concerned with Rory. She had volunteered no remarks during this exchange, merely biting down upon her lower lip. Yet it was what she wasn't saying that Zeke found disturbing.

He halted by the cemetery gate, gazing down at her. "Rory, you can't also be imagining that Mrs. Addison had a good idea. Me as a reform candidate, running for mayor!"

"I think you'd make a very good mayor," she said in a small voice.

Zeke gave a snort of contempt. "Oh, yes, I have such excellent credentials. A dockworker, a former gang member, a one-time gambling house operator."

"But don't you see?" she persisted. "That's exactly what makes you so well qualified. You've seen life on both sides of New York, Fifth Avenue and the East Side. You wouldn't be all idealistic and impractical like Mr. Addison."

"No, what I would be is smart enough to know better. It's hopeless to think you can ever change anything over on the East Side. The best a man can hope for is to look after his own interests, get himself out."

"Then why did you ever finance Mr. Addison's campaign?"

"That . . . that was different," Zeke blustered. "It's one thing to give money, quite another to . . . to . . ."

"Give anything of yourself?"

Her words were spoken softly enough, but he felt the sting of them like the lash of a whip. She didn't look angry with him, only unhappy, her silvery eyes clouded with a look of soul-deep disappointment that made Zeke's heart sink. He had seen that expression before. He would count it forever among his most haunting memories of his mother.

He compressed his lips together. "The subject is closed, Aurora. I don't want to talk about it anymore."

"Whatever you wish," she said primly. Her own mouth was taut as he handed her up into his open carriage. He sprang up across from her, and they sat facing each other in tense silence. He tore at his collar, which seemed to be choking him, feeling in a thoroughly bad temper.

He hadn't expected attending Addison's funeral to be pleasant, but he hadn't quite bargained for anything like this either. He dusted his hands as though he could still feel the earth from the grave clinging to them.

He had hoped to put the morning's grim event behind him by taking Rory on a drive through Central Park. Her engagement ring reposed in his front pocket, a huge chunk of a diamond, the biggest Tiffany's had had to offer.

But when he suggested the outing to her, she demurred. "I would rather you just took me home, Zeke."

He gave vent to an exasperated sigh. "Why? Are you still sulking just because I'm not willing to make an ass of myself, following Mrs. Addison's stupid suggestion?"

"No, it has nothing to do with that. I simply have things to do. I have a balloon company to run."

"I have been endeavoring to forget that wretched fact."

The corners of her mouth twitched with irritation, but otherwise she appeared to ignore his angry quip. "I have a lot of preparations to make for Friday," she said.

"Friday?" Zeke stiffened with apprehension. "What happens on Friday?"

"I haven't been idle either since we returned to New York. I have been in contact with that man from Washington who handles the army contracts. He's coming back to New York, to give me another chance."

Rory smiled suddenly, as though she actually expected him to be glad of such tidings. For her sake, he wished he could have been, but he felt nothing but a cold, hard lump of dread settling into his stomach.

"A chance to do what?" Zeke snapped. "Get yourself killed?"

Rory bristled. "The demonstration will be perfectly safe. We've decided to take the balloon out of the city this time, launch it in the countryside past Morningside Heights."

"And where will you end up? Back in the ocean again? Or maybe impaled upon some farmer's fence?"

"Not all my flights end in disaster."

"It only takes once. Damn it, Rory—" It was on the tip of his tongue to inform her that he wouldn't allow it. He wouldn't permit his bride to keep risking her neck in those damned fool balloons. But one look at the stubborn tilt to her chin told him how little effect such an order would have.

Perhaps the time for words was past. Action was needed. Leaning back in the carriage seat, he steeled his jaw, knowing what he had to do. He averted his face from Rory as though half-fearful she might be able to read his intention.

He didn't know precisely what she would do when she discovered his plan. He was only sure of one thing. She wasn't going to like it.

Eighteen

※ ※ ※

The morning after the funeral, Rory awoke to the sound of a commotion on McCreedy Street. She had left her windows open the night before, these first few days of May already proving unseasonably warm, with the promise of a long hot summer to follow.

She awoke feeling miserable, her hair damp with perspiration, her muscles stiff, still aching with the tensions of yesterday. Although she had not been acquainted with Mr. Addison, his funeral had proved a sad affair, and sadder still the way she had parted from Zeke.

He had left her at the door to her flat, brushing her lips with a hard, brusque kiss, a curt promise that he would call upon her tomorrow. She was surprised that Zeke had said nothing more about the balloons. She could tell how much he had wanted to forbid her going up again and had braced herself for a terrific row. Knowing how forceful Zeke could be about getting his own way, his forbearance had been astonishing, almost disturbingly so.

Equally astonishing was the fact that he had not continued to press the idea of marriage upon her. It occurred to her that perhaps he was beginning to have second thoughts.

She had sensed his impatience with her after the funeral, about the disagreement they had had over Mrs. Addison's suggestion.

Perhaps Zeke had good reason to be annoyed. She had no right to be so disappointed because he showed no inclination to pick up Addison's cudgels, run as a reform candidate for mayor. And it wasn't as though she meant to plan his life for him. She only knew that she hated it when Zeke talked as though nothing mattered but self-interest, the power of money. He was capable of entertaining feelings so much finer than that.

Yet never had the differences between them seemed to yawn so wide. Rory supposed if they were that unsuited to each other, it was better to realize it now, but it had been hard to convince herself of that after spending a lonely night in her bed, aching with the need to feel Zeke's arms around her.

With a low groan, she shielded her eyes from the stream of sunlight pouring through her window. As she sat up, coming more fully awake, the clatter in the street below seemed to have intensified. She sprang out of bed, her heart skipping a beat. She had told Zeke that she had to go into the warehouse today, that if he wanted to call upon her, he had best be up early. Wouldn't it be just like him to come pounding at her door before she was even dressed?

Yet when she rushed to the open window, her mouth drooped with disappointment. It was not Zeke's fancy equipage rattling down the street that had caused Finn McCool to set up such a wild barking and all the children to abandon their balls and hoops and come running.

It was nothing but a delivery van, drawn by a set of matched bays. Even pulled up to the curb, it still blocked off half the narrow street. Despite her disappointment, Rory couldn't help gawking herself as she glimpsed the fancy monogram on the van's side. B. Altman and Co., a very exclusive Fifth Avenue department store.

No wonder some of the housewives broke off stringing up their wash to cluster together, pointing and speculating. As for poor Miss Flanagan, she nearly fell out her front

window, straining for a better view as two smartly uni-
formed attendants swaggered around to open up the back
of the van.

Not in living memory had anyone on McCreedy Street
received a delivery from Altman's. Like Rory, most of her
neighbors shopped on the ground floor at Stern Brothers.
As she watched a considerable array of bandboxes being
unloaded, Rory had begun to wonder whose rich uncle had
died, when she was suddenly beset by a sinking feeling.

The van attendants, their arms overburdened, were struggling up the walk leading to her building.

"Oh, no," she murmured. "He didn't . . . he
couldn't . . ." She ducked back from the window and
began scrambling to find her dressing gown. She was just
shrugging into it when she heard the rap at her door.

She fought off a cowardly inclination to pretend she
wasn't at home. Tying the sash about her waist, she trudged
to answer the summons.

Inching the door open, she said, "Yes? What do you
want?"

"Miss Aurora Rose Kavanaugh?"

She could scarce see the little man who inquired after
her name, the boxes balanced all the way up to his chin.
When Rory acknowledged his greeting, he grinned with
relief.

"Delivery for you." He edged his way past into the
flat. She opened her mouth to protest, tell him it was
some sort of a mistake, but the poor man's arms were
fairly breaking with the need to set down his load. The
other attendant, who followed right behind, was equally
strained.

Besides she knew it was no mistake. Nor did she need to
see the arrogantly scrawled name on the order slip to guess
whose signature it was.

Damn the man! Now what was he about? She supposed
she should feel relieved. At least this proved that Zeke was
not that angry with her. Yet with each fresh load of boxes
that was carted into her flat, she became more dismayed.
She wanted to tell the attendants to stop, but she felt much

like a sorceress who had forgotten the words to the magic spell and could find no way to get the genie back into the lamp.

By the time the two men had tipped their caps to her and departed, her settee, the parlor table and all her chairs were stacked to overflowing.

Distractedly running her fingers through her hair, Rory opened a few of the boxes, but soon she had no desire to pursue the activity any further. She winced at the sight of the costly silks, luxurious furs. Good God above! There had to be enough here to outfit every debutante on Fifth Avenue for the season.

Her parlor was crammed so full, she could barely find room to walk across the carpet, and she would have been prepared to wager that half of McCreedy Street still lingered outside, peering up at her apartment window.

It seemed disastrously appropriate somehow that Zeke himself should arrive in the van's wake. The sun glinted off the sides of his shiny landau and the gleaming black coats of horses and liveried servants.

A dark blue Prince Albert coat straining across his shoulders, his top hat tipped to an arrogant angle, Zeke descended to the pavement, swinging a gold-tipped walking stick. The crowd fell back, as much in awe as if he had been visiting royalty. Rory was possessed of a strong urge to drop a flowerpot of geraniums on his head.

It was fortunate she never allowed herself to be much upset by gossip, for Zeke had likely provided the Catholic Ladies Sewing Circle with enough fuel to see them through a summer of meetings. By the time he had made his way upstairs, there was no need for him to knock. Rory already had the door open.

Their gazes clashed across the threshold. Although Zeke removed his hat respectfully enough, his jaw was tipped to that familiar belligerent angle. In that instant, Rory realized neither of them had managed to shake off the tensions of yesterday. Rather like two armies, they had merely fallen back to regroup for a fresh skirmish.

Zeke didn't wait for Rory to greet him, but strode past her into the flat. His gaze skated over the array of packages.

"I see Altman's has already been here."

Rory closed the door. "Been here and nearly buried me. What the devil is all this stuff, Morrison? If this is your way of trying to make up for the misunderstanding we had yesterday, it really wasn't necessary."

"This has nothing to do with yesterday," he snapped back, almost too quickly. "This . . . this is your trousseau."

Her trousseau? Rory stiffened. Now she understood why Zeke hadn't troubled himself to bring up the subject of marriage again. In his usual roughshod fashion, he was taking her assent for granted.

He poked beneath the lid of one of the boxes with the tip of his walking stick. "I told Altman's to send a little of everything. If there's anything there you don't like, just send it back, exchange it."

"I can't imagine there's anything left to exchange it for. I must have the contents of the entire store in here." She placed her hands upon her hips. "Besides, Morrison, I don't recall your ever *asking* me to marry you."

"Then your memory is faulty, my dear." Zeke shoved a pile of boxes off a chair with his cane and sat down. "I intended to make it formal yesterday, but the mood didn't seem to be right." He frowned, then forced his lips into a semblance of a smile. "In any case, I don't want to waste any more time, so come here."

He patted his knee, and Rory choked on an angry gasp, realizing that he had the brass to be suggesting she perch herself upon his knee. He was acting nearly as badly as the night when she had first met him, when he had demanded she become his mistress.

Taking a deep breath, she struggled to keep her temper. It wasn't easy when Zeke stood up flashing a diamond beneath her nose. The thing was blinding, the stone larger than some of the rocks she had skipped over the waters of the Hudson.

"My mother never wore anything but a plain gold band," she said.

"Well, I can do better than that for my wife. Put it on." When she made no move to obey his order, he reached for her hand. Rory whipped both of them behind her back.

"No, Zeke, you are not being fair. You promised to let me have more time to give you my answer."

"I've given you plenty of time and it makes no difference. You know I always get what I want." When she resisted his effort to gain possession of her hand, he pinioned her arms instead, plundering her mouth with a kiss that was rough and demanding, slowly deepening to become fire-hot. Rory strove to hold her body rigid as stone. But she was not a rock. Curse herself how she might, she responded, melting against him.

He traced the curve of her cheek, the line of her temple with his lips, murmuring, "What more does it take to convince you, woman? I'm not the sort to go down on one knee and spout poetry. Besides I never thought you'd be so silly as to want that."

"I . . . I'm not. I just wish that you would . . . you've never even said that you love me."

"I told you that I want you. It's the same thing."

"No, it isn't." She took a tremulous breath, then wrenched herself out of his arms. "Maybe you just want me the same as you wanted to be rich, to own a house on Fifth Avenue."

"That's ridiculous, Aurora Rose."

"Is it?" Her gaze roved to the stacks of boxes, the glinting diamond. "I just wish that I could be sure you believed in something besides the power of your money."

He raked her with a dark, impatient glance. "Are you still expecting me to become the kind of champion Addison was? I'm no dream chaser, Rory. I told you that at the outset."

"But I am," she said, "which is likely the biggest obstacle between us. Now, if you will excuse me, I have to get dressed. I did tell you that I have to go to the warehouse this morning."

"There is no point in your doing that."

Rory had been marching toward her bedchamber, but she paused, taken aback by the terse note in his voice.

"What . . . what do you mean by that?"

"I mean you won't be able to get into the building. I've already been down there myself this morning. The locks have all been changed."

"The locks?" Rory repeated numbly. Locked out of the warehouse? A sick feeling churned inside her, but she was not surprised. Hadn't she been dreading this day for months, knowing she was so far behind on the rent? The warehouse owners had at last reached the end of their patience.

She raised desperate eyes to Zeke. "Oh, Zeke, I have to do something. The government contractor is scheduled to come back tomorrow." It cost her a great deal to frame such a request, knowing how Zeke felt about her balloon company, but she swallowed her pride, touching his sleeve. "Isn't . . . isn't there anything you can do to help me?"

"I'm afraid not, my dear." He lowered his gaze, as though he were unable to meet her eyes. "You see I am the one who had the locks changed. I bought the warehouse."

Rory stared at him with incomprehension. "You? You bought it?" A shaky laugh escaped her. "Great heavens and are you now planning to evict me?"

She wished he would smile, tell her this was all some sort of horrible joke, but the set of his mouth remained grim.

"It won't make any difference, you know," she said with far more conviction than she felt. "I'll simply move my business elsewhere."

"You can't do that either. Hell, Rory, your crazy company is so far in debt to the banks, it won't be difficult to buy up your notes and have your equipment impounded."

Rory could only stare at him, disbelief warring with a feeling of stark betrayal. She could hardly comprehend it. Her worst nightmare was coming true, but it was not some stranger responsible, some cold-hearted banker, but Zeke, the man she loved.

"No," she choked out at last, a knot of bitter tears gathering in her throat, "I suppose nothing is too difficult for the great Mr. J. E. Morrison."

"Rory." He tried to take her hands, but she pulled away from him. "Damn it, Rory, be reasonable. I told you that when we were married, you wouldn't have to worry about that ridiculous company anymore."

"I knew you didn't approve, but at least I thought you understood how much that *ridiculous* company means to me." One tear escaped to trickle down her cheek. She dashed it angrily aside. "How . . . how could you do this to me?"

Although he looked mighty uncomfortable, Zeke folded his arms across his chest. "It's for your own good."

"My own good?" Rory cried bitterly. "No, Mr. Morrison, I don't believe you were thinking about me at all, only what you wanted. Just because you are afraid to have any dreams, you can't bear for anyone else to have them either."

He flinched a little at that, but Rory was too caught up in her own misery to notice. She paced off a few agitated steps. She wanted to fling herself at Zeke, rail at him, plead with him. But Kavanaughs didn't beg, and she could tell from the implacable set of Zeke's jaw that it would do her no good.

"You won't get away with this," she blustered. "I'll fight you." But even as she made the threat, she knew it was hopeless. He had wealth, power on his side, and a ruthless obstinacy she couldn't hope to match. The tears flowed freely down her face now, too swiftly for her to stop them.

In sheer frustration, she gave a stack of the boxes a savage kick, sending them flying across the room. "You can just take your damned trousseau and get out of here. I . . . I never want to see you again."

Zeke swore, but he attempted to gather her into his arms. "Blast it all, Rory, I'm only trying to prevent you from breaking your neck. Stop acting as though I was some kind of a monster."

"You are a monster!" She struggled wildly to break free of his embrace, her grief tumbling out in a rush of bitter words she didn't mean. Striking out as blindly as a child, trying to hurt him as he was hurting her, she cried, "Ev-everything Tessa said about you was true. You d-do ruin people's lives. No wonder your mother died grieving for you."

Zeke's face paled. He couldn't have looked more stunned if she had dealt him a blow to the face, but Rory was beyond the point of caring. When his arms dropped to his side, abruptly releasing her, she sagged onto the chair. Burying her face in her hands, she gave vent to a flood of stormy tears.

A deathlike silence settled over the flat, broken only by the sound of her own sobs. She felt a tentative touch upon her hair, but shrank from it. Then she heard Zeke fling something on the parlor table. His footsteps echoed across the room, and then she heard the slam of the door as it closed behind him.

Rory glanced up, tears yet streaming down her cheeks. Good, she thought savagely. He was gone. But instead of fiercely rejoicing, she only wanted to weep anew, as though her heart would break.

Sniffing, she groped for her handkerchief, her vision clearing enough to attempt to see what Zeke had left behind. If he had had the effrontery to leave that diamond ring, she would—

But she paused, sitting frozen as she focused on the object glinting upon the parlor table. A tiny cry escaped her.

It was not the diamond, but a heavy metal ring of keys.

Nineteen

With a curt command, Zeke Morrison had bade his astonished coachman to whip up the team and go back to Fifth Avenue or hell, Zeke didn't care which. Trembling, the man was quick to obey, leaving Zeke to stalk off down McCreedy Street alone.

Hours later, Zeke was still wandering aimlessly, not knowing where he was going, caring even less. At first, his footsteps had been propelled by anger. Damn Aurora Rose Kavanaugh! And damn John Ezekiel Morrison as well for making such an ass of himself over her.

If she was so eager to break her fool neck, then let her. He should have flung the keys to the blasted warehouse at her instead of just dropping them on the table.

But such a mood could not last for long. His rage soon spent itself, leaving a tight ache in his chest, a sensation of vast emptiness that slowed his steps.

So Rory had rejected him and he was alone again. It always came to that in the end. He had known that ever since the day he first ran away from the orphanage, maybe even from the day he was born, left to die by the woman who bore him.

But he had always managed to convince himself that it didn't matter. He was strong enough to stand alone. He had a talent for survival, a knack for raking in the greenbacks, didn't he? What more did he need?

His shoulders slumped. He also had a knack for lousing up every relationship that had ever mattered to him. First his mother, then his sisters and now Rory. Zeke jammed his hands deeply into his pockets. As afternoon shadows lengthened along the pavement, his thoughts returned to that grim scene in Rory's flat.

Go more gently, Sadie had always tried to warn him, and he had tried with Rory. He honestly had. But for too much of his life, he had been used to coming out of his corner, ready to lead with his right. You never asked, you just took, because if you asked, the answer would probably be no.

So he had heaped Rory with presents, tried to shove the ring onto her finger, closed down her warehouse without telling her first. All he had wanted to do was love, cherish and protect her. His blustering manner had only been to hide his uncertainty, his desperate fear she might somehow slip away from him. Perhaps the disguise had worked all too well.

But God forbid Zeke Morrison should reveal too much of his feelings, let it be known that underneath he wasn't so tough after all, but just as vulnerable as anyone else.

He could only imagine what Rory must be thinking of him now, and none of it was pleasant. Fragments of her bitter words echoed through his head. *How could you do this to me . . . you ruin people's lives . . . no wonder your mother died grieving.*

Zeke grimaced. No wonder indeed. Rory had been wise to tell him to get out, spare herself further misery.

With such thoughts roiling in his mind, Zeke took little heed of where he was walking. He nearly collided with a freckle-faced kid hawking papers on a street corner. But the boy was quick to recover himself. Glancing up hopefully from beneath the brim of his cap, he asked, "Paper, mister?"

Zeke dourly shook his head, but the boy persisted. Waving

a copy of the *World* before Zeke's eyes, the paperboy sang out, "Read all about it. Reporter raises doubts about Decker suicide."

Zeke took a quick glance at the headline. So Duffy had made good his threat to continue the investigation. In his present humor, Zeke wasn't even mildly interested. He gave the kid a dollar, telling him to keep the change and the paper.

The boy's eyes lit up. "Geez, thanks, mister." Gathering up his largess and his remaining papers, the lad scuttled off down the street with an energy that suddenly left Zeke feeling very old.

Snapped out of his musings about Rory, Zeke at last took a look around to gain his bearings. His gaze fell on the weathered street sign.

Pearl Street.

He should've been surprised, but he wasn't. Some part of him had known all along exactly where he was headed. Where, but not why. What could possibly have drawn him back to this place? Nothing lurked on the block ahead of him but old memories, some of them bad, all of them painful.

Yet still he kept going. The row of brick tenements seemed to close around him, packed so close together they blocked out the rays of the setting sun. The street was even more rundown than he remembered, some of the windows boarded over. An old man rooted through a trash can, hunting for something to eat, while a scrawny stray dog barked and nipped at his heels. From an upper story came the shrill sound of laughter, then the shatter of glass as someone tossed a gin bottle out the window. Across the street, a young girl, looking too worn for her years, listlessly hung much-mended stockings out on the fire escape to dry.

All about him were the sights, the sounds of a world he had tried so relentlessly to put behind him. Almost instinctively he turned to the one place that had been a bright spot in the midst of all this poverty and despair— the second-floor flat, third house from the corner.

Sadie's flowerpots were long gone from that windowsill, the curtains that hung there now much dirtier than his mother ever would have tolerated. The place was noisier too. Even at street level, Zeke could hear a man bellowing something in a slurred accent, followed by a smacking sound, then a child's wail.

As Zeke lingered there, a small urchin suddenly emerged onto the flat's fire escape. The boy snuffled against his sleeve, nursing a black eye, but was still full of fire and defiance.

"Don't care whatcha do to me," he shouted back through the window. "I'm gonna run away. Someday I'm gonna have lots of money and live far away from this stinkin' place."

The boy sank down onto the fire escape, drawing his knees up to his chest, staring sullenly up at the sky. Zeke felt strangely chilled watching him, as though he had peeled away too many layers of the past. It might have been himself back up there on that fire escape, so well could he guess what was going on in the child's mind. Brooding over his wrongs, and if he only knew it, dreaming all the wrong dreams.

Suddenly Zeke felt as if he had seen enough. Turning, he strode rapidly away, covering the blocks that led toward the East River. The dockside area was no place to be at dusk, but the size of Zeke, the blackness of his scowl seemed enough to keep any lurking toughs at a distance.

Besides, Zeke thought wryly, he really had nothing on him of any value. As he stood by the water's edge, watching the murky waters lap against the embankment, he thrust his hand into his pocket and drew forth the ring.

Funny. How different the diamond looked to him now. It didn't sparkle near so much as it had in the jeweler's case. In fact, it might as well have been paste, not able to hold a candle to the brightness of the stars . . . or Rory's eyes.

Zeke's fingers folded around the ring, and with a slow deliberation, he drew back his arm and hurled it out across the East River. It landed with a plop, scarce raising a ripple on the darkening waters.

He lowered his arm, feeling worn down, defeated. For the first time in his life, he had no plans for tomorrow, or the day after that. The future stretched before him, an empty succession of years with no meaning, no Rory.

He had never asked anyone's help or advice before. There had only been one person he had even partly needed, but she was gone. Never had he missed Sadie so keenly as he did tonight.

"What am I going to do, lady?" he murmured, tipping back his head, searching the night sky. Even the stars looked cold and remote. It seemed too late to be seeking answers now, too late for so many things.

And then again maybe it wasn't. The thought that came to him seemed borne on the night wind, or maybe it was merely a whisper of hope from the depths of his own heart. For too many years, he had been on a headlong rush down the road to wealth and power, not stopping to count the cost. Perhaps the time had come to pause, to cease charging recklessly forward. Perhaps the time had come at last to turn and go back, begin to recover some of what he had lost upon the way.

The area of the city known as Greenwich Village was a veritable labyrinth of crisscrossing streets. Zeke lost his way several times amidst a maze of artist's garrets, antiques shops, cellar cafés and tearooms. He at last located the place he sought along a side road winding down from Sheridan Square. There was little but a number to distinguish the unpretentious three-story townhouse from a row of others just like it.

Zeke trudged up the steps of the high front stoop and rapped with the brass knocker. Squaring his shoulders, he stepped back, his uncertainty of welcome only betrayed by the way he fingered the brim of his hat.

When the door swung wide, he shrank back from the flood of light and warmth spilling across the threshold. He hadn't been prepared to have his sister Caroline herself answer his summons.

Caddie stood wiping her hands on a dishcloth, brushing

back the straggling ends of her dark hair, which was now
a little flecked with gray. She was still pretty, although she
had grown a little plump after the bearing of three children.
It both disconcerted Zeke and touched some poignant chord
of memory within him. How much his sister looked like
Sadie, the resemblance only growing more marked with
the passage of time.

For a moment, Caddie stared at Zeke. But then her open-
mouthed astonishment gave way to a tremulous smile, a
little cry of gladness. "Oh . . . oh my! Johnnie!"

" 'Evening Caddie," Zeke said sheepishly. He shuffled
his feet on the mat, uncertain what to do next. But he was
not left to debate the matter for long, as his sister fairly
dragged him across the threshold and enveloped him in a
fierce hug.

"Oh, Johnnie." Tears sparkled in her eyes. "What . . .
what a wonderful surprise."

"I . . . I was just passing through the Village. I thought
I would call upon you for a moment."

He made it sound as casual as he could, despite the fact
it had been nearly two years since he had crossed her threshold. Caddie's clear brown eyes gave him a penetrating look
that made him squirm, one of those uncanny soul-seeing
glances that also reminded him too much of Sadie.

But all she said was "I'm so glad you came."

Placing his hat on the hall table, she led him into her
parlor, a cozy nook of overstuffed furniture and the vases
of flowers that had always been Caroline's passion. Still
clinging to Zeke's arm, she called out to a man ensconced
in a wing-backed chair, reading before the fire.

"Phillip, look who's here. My brother, John."

Zeke awkwardly thrust out his hand as his brother-in-law
ambled forward to greet him. Phillip Dawes was an ami-
able man who forever seemed to have paint flecks on his
clothes and a faraway expression as though his mind were
off elsewhere, putting the finishing strokes on some canvas.
It never ceased to amaze Zeke that someone could make a
decent living for his family out of anything as improbable as
painting pictures. But he had to grudgingly admit the fellow

had done well by Caddie. He was almost worthy of her.

Phillip greeted Zeke in a friendly fashion, as though it had been only yesterday that he had seen him. Which, considering the absentminded way Phillip kept track of time, he probably believed it had been.

Zeke found it far more difficult to face Caddie's children, especially without any presents in his hands. They regarded him shyly at first, two curly-headed boys with missing teeth, hanging on the skirts of their sister, Lucy, who had almost grown as tall as her mother.

But it was not long before Zeke found himself surrounded, barraged on all sides with earnest chatter.

"Thank you for the cloak you sent for my birthday, Uncle John," Lucy said with a pretty blush and coy glance. "You're the only one who seems to realize I am quite grown up."

"Hey, Uncle John." One of the boys tugged at his sleeve. " 'Member you said once if you ever came to visit, you would teach me how to fight."

"Me too." The littlest one was already doubling up his fists.

Zeke didn't exactly recall having made such a promise, but he feared he might have.

"I think I only promised to do so if your mother approved." He cast a half-guilty glance at Caddie, who only beamed and shook her head at him.

"You may as well. They are always at the fisticuffs anyway. Just like someone else I remember."

Their eyes met over the children's heads, hers half-scolding, but alight with a tender amusement, shared recollections. Zeke found himself grinning back, feeling very glad that he had come, until a shadow fell across the parlor.

He heard the rustle of stiff silk skirts and looked around, his smile fading as he met the one face that held no warmth of welcome for him. The severity of her black gown was only matched by Tessa's expression, her features pinched white with disapproval, her eyes as ever dark with accusation.

The bright laughter of the children stilled, as even they seemed to sense the change in the atmosphere. Only Caddie managed to retain a most determined smile.

"Tessa, my dear. Isn't it the most fortunate thing? John has just dropped by in time for supper. We must persuade him to dine with us."

"If he stays, I go," Tessa said.

"Theresa—," Caddie began.

But Zeke was already preparing to retreat from the family circle, fade back into the night. "That's all right, Caddie," he said quietly. "I didn't come here to cause any more discord." Suppressing a sigh, he stepped into the hall, reaching for his hat with a weary gesture. He should have known what a mistake this would be.

But Tessa came hard after him. "You needn't make any noble gestures on my behalf," she spat out. "I know how long Caddie has been waiting to kill the fatted calf for you." She snatched her own shawl off the hall peg.

Behind him, Zeke was aware of Caddie shooing her husband and children toward the kitchen. He felt angry with himself, and Tessa as well, for disrupting the harmony of their evening.

"Stay where you are, Tessa," he snapped. "I said I'd go."

Tessa glared at him as she draped her shawl over her head. "I wouldn't dream of—"

"Just stop it. Both of you."

The harsh command from Caddie startled them. She approached them, blocking the doorway, her hands on her hips, her gentle face flushed. "After two years, I have endured quite enough of this nonsense."

Tessa stiffened. "But Caroline, he—"

"Be quiet, Tessa! Now I want both of you to turn right around and march back into the parlor."

When neither of them moved, Caddie actually took a menacing step forward. Zeke's flash of anger dissolved as his sister's stern expression suddenly put him in mind of Sadie those times she had been induced to lose her temper. The incidents had been so rare that even he, ever the defiant one, had scuttled to obey.

The memory now caused him to give way before Caddie, although he had to suppress a twitch of his lips as he stepped back into the parlor. Tessa resisted a moment longer, then flounced after him.

After she had them both securely inside, Caddie announced, "Now neither one of you is coming out again until you have put an end to this silly quarrel."

Before either could guess her intent, she closed the parlor door and locked it. Zeke registered one mild protest, but Tessa rattled the knob, bellowing her sister's name.

"You might as well have done, Tess," Zeke said. "I think Caddie means it."

Tessa shot him a seething look, but she abandoned her efforts with the door. She stomped over to the sofa and plopped down, lapsing into a stony silence. After a brief hesitation, Zeke perched himself on the opposite end of the divan.

The situation certainly was not funny, but he couldn't prevent a soft chuckle from escaping him. He said, "This reminds me of those times when we were kids and Sadie would make us sit out on the stoop until we had patched up our spat. You were so stubborn, I was always afraid we were going to starve to death."

"Me!" Tessa cried. "It was always you—" She choked off with an angry gasp, then averted her face from him.

Zeke slowly inched closer. He managed to get possession of her hand. "Tessa, look at me."

When she wouldn't, he caught her chin, gently turning her head around. Bitter tears sparkled in her eyes, but he forced himself to stare directly into them.

"I'm sorry."

Her lips trembled.

"I know now I shouldn't have done what I did, interfered with your marriage plans in that high-handed way. At least, I should have made you understand why I did it."

She squirmed to get away from him. "You did it to be mean. To get back at me for all . . . all the nasty things I said to you about being adopted."

"You know that isn't so." He hesitated, groping desperately for the right thing to say, to make her understand. "I know you never wanted me, but I was trying to be your big brother anyway, the best that I knew how.

"I broke up your engagement because . . ." He swallowed, the words seeming to form a hard lump in his throat. He didn't think he'd be able to get them out, but somehow he managed. " . . . because I cared too much about you to see you wed some fellow who wasn't fit to lick the sole of your shoes."

Her eyes widened as though stunned by the charge of emotion in his voice. It was as unexpected to him as it was to her. He thought perhaps he had said too much, because she stiffened. But suddenly she dissolved into tears. He watched her in awkward silence for a moment, then draped one arm about her. She tried to twist away from him, but he persisted, drawing her inexorably against the lee of his shoulder. With a great sob, she gave way at last, collapsing in his arms, crying down the front of his waistcoat.

"B-but Johnnie," she wept. "It was so awful. Y-you can't know. When you paid Marco to go away, we . . . we were supposed to run off the next day. He . . . he left me waiting at the door of the church."

"The bastard," Zeke said, stroking her hair. "If I had him here now, I would break his head."

"If he was here, I . . . I would let you."

He rocked her gently until the worst of her grief was spent. She surfaced at last from his shoulder and drew back, sniffing. "I g-guess I always knew what a bounder Marco was, but he was all I had. He was the only man who would ever have wanted to marry me."

"Idiot!" Zeke's lips curved into a lopsided smile as he used his handkerchief to help her wipe her eyes. "Lots of fellows would have been proud to have you. You were always a clever girl, Tessa. The cleverest one of us."

"Clever isn't pretty."

"You were pretty, too. You still are—except when you've been crying. Then you look like hell."

She hiccuped, the sound halfway between a laugh and a sob. "Toad!" she said.

"Shrew!" he shot back.

"Brat!"

They were just completing this tender exchange when the parlor door inched open and Caddie peered cautiously inside. She heaved a sigh of relief. "Thank God. It had gone so quiet in here, I thought you two surely must have killed each other this time."

Zeke stood up quickly, shielding Tessa, giving her time to compose herself. "We are half-dead—from hunger."

Caddie smiled until she dimpled. "The old starvation method. Mama was right. It works every time. Supper is ready if . . ." Her gaze tracked uncertainly from Zeke to Tessa.

Tessa heaved herself to her feet, smoothing out her skirts with an air of wounded dignity. "Then what are we waiting for? I can't recall either one of you ever asking my permission to go and eat."

Zeke grinned and made her a mock bow. "Ladies, permit me to escort you to the dining room." Caddie was quick to take his arm, and after a brief hesitation, Tessa did so as well.

It was a strange feeling to Zeke to be seated back in the midst of a family gathering round a supper table. Caddie was doing her best to set him at his ease, pretend that nothing extraordinary was happening.

But she couldn't quite dim the glow in her eyes nor suppress the tiny catch in her voice as she led them in the prayer. "Bless us, O Lord, for these thy Gifts. . . ." She glanced straight at Zeke, and he was obliged to look away, his own heart suddenly too full.

He barely tasted the excellent roast beef dinner; he was too unaccustomed to entertaining so many emotions to feel quite comfortable. One couldn't do away with all the hurts and the barriers of years, not in the space of one evening. Although Tessa no longer sniped at him, she still refused to meet his eyes or say much to him.

After supper, she retired with the children as though eager to escape his company. Although disappointed, Zeke tried to understand. When Phillip also retreated, up to his artist's studio, Zeke was left alone with Caddie.

As with Sadie, there was something about his eldest sister that induced one to open up to her. Zeke soon found himself telling her all about Rory, the entire mess he had made of their relationship.

"So what are you going to do about it?" Caddie asked.

Zeke heaved a deep sigh. "I don't know."

"Yes, you do. You're going to go find that lovely girl, tell her how sorry you are and tell her how much you love her."

Zeke felt himself tense at the suggestion. Observing him, Caddie smiled. "You said as much to Tessa and discovered it didn't kill you."

Zeke gave a reluctant grin. But it had been easier with Tessa. The reconciliation had been important to him, but not as it would be with Rory, putting his entire heart and soul on the line.

But there was no arguing with Caddie. As she saw him to the door and handed him his hat, she said, "When you've made it up with her, bring Aurora Rose round to see me. I want to welcome her to the family."

Zeke only nodded, not trusting himself to speak, the vision Caddie's words conjured far too agreeable to dwell upon. As he turned to go out the door, Caddie rested her hand upon his arm. Her parting smile was a little trembly, her eyes wistful.

"Whatever happens, John, don't . . . don't be such a stranger, hmmm?"

For answer he deposited a brusque kiss on her cheek before he strode down the steps. He heard her delighted gasp of surprise, then she slowly closed the door, leaving him alone on the darkened street.

Alone? No. It was strange. There wasn't another soul out on the pavement, but he didn't feel alone. A soft smile played about his lips as he glanced back at his sister's townhouse, the welcoming light shining past the lace curtains and making him feel as if he had brought some of that warmth away with him.

Whistling a tuneless song, he leaned up against one of

the gas street lamps and wondered if he should return to Rory's flat, if he had enough courage left to do any more soul-baring tonight. He was just thinking of summoning a cab when the door to Caddie's townhouse suddenly swung back open.

To his astonishment, Tessa burst outside. She was trying to arrange her shawl as she went, but she was in such great haste she let the black wool trail over her shoulder. She glanced anxiously up and down the street and appeared relieved when she spotted Zeke by the lamppost.

"Johnnie. Wait!" she called.

He hadn't moved a muscle, but she came tearing down the front steps as though she expected him to disappear.

As she drew up breathlessly beside him, Zeke said, "What's all this, Tess? You couldn't bear to part with me or you decided you wanted to punch me in the nose after all?"

"N-no," she panted. "This . . . this isn't the time to be funny, John."

The lamplight haloed her pale features, and Zeke could see clearly she was not smiling. Nor was the familiar glare present either. Rather her eyes were filled with an uncertainty, that same troubled look that had rendered him uncomfortable at the dinner table.

"I have something important to tell you, something I should have told you a long time ago."

She seemed so deadly solemn she was starting to scare the hell out of him. He waited, but she was unable to go on, to meet his questioning gaze. She hung her head.

He took hold of her hand to give it an encouraging squeeze and discovered her fingers were trembling.

"What is it, Tessa?" He joked to cover his own growing unease. "Did you pay some gypsy woman in the Village to put a curse on me?"

"Johnnie, please don't," she said hoarsely. "It's . . .. it's about the night Mama died."

Zeke's heart stilled. That was one night he could hardly bear to remember, let alone talk about. He let go of his sister's hand.

"Tessa, if you are going to heap old recriminations on my head, I wish for once you would spare me. I did try to get there sooner that night. I honestly did."

"I know that," she said in a small voice. "I guess I always realized that, but I was so upset for Mama. She wanted . . . she needed so badly to talk to you before she died. She said if she didn't last until . . . she trusted me to tell you—"

"It's all right, Tessa," Zeke broke in, dreading that his sister might begin sobbing all over again, out in the middle of the sidewalk. And damn it all. He could feel his own eyes starting to smart. "Even though I didn't deserve it, I knew how loving, how forgiving Sadie could be. I can guess what she wanted to tell me."

"No, I don't think you can. It was . . . you see . . . she knew who your real family was."

Tessa's halting confession was so far from what he'd expected, her words seemed to slam against his chest with the weight of a powerful fist.

"W-what?"

Tessa bit down upon her quivering lip. "I think Mama must have always known. She said the people at the orphanage told her when she adopted you."

Zeke was stunned to silence. Sadie had known all along who his real parents were and never told him? Sadie, the one person in all the world he had trusted ever to be honest, straightforward, had kept such a thing secret from him? Feelings of betrayal cut through him, sharper than the slashings of a knife.

Tessa stole a nervous glance up at him. "Well? Aren't you going to say anything? Aren't you going to ask who—"

"I'd rather know why," he rasped. "Damn it, Tessa. Why didn't she tell me?"

"Mama was afraid, afraid of losing you. Your real family was wealthy, powerful. All the things you ever wanted. If you had known, you would have gone running off to them."

"To seek out people that let me be dumped in a trash can?" Zeke raked his hand back through his hair, in a gesture fraught with anger and bitterness. He thought that nothing could hurt more than the realization Sadie had lied to him, but something did—that she had apparently believed him capable of turning his back on all her loving kindness, seeking to belong to some cold-hearted bastards simply because they were rich. His pain was the more acute because of his fear that at some point in the shallowness of his youth, Sadie might have been right.

"And after Mama died," Tessa concluded in a voice half-guilty, half-defiant, "I never told you any of this— just . . . just out of spite."

"So tell me now. What's the name of these marvelous beings Sadie thought I would be so eager to desert you all for? The Astors? The Vanderbilts?"

"No, a family named Markham. They had this son named Stephen . . ."

Tessa faltered when Zeke stared at her.

"Have you ever heard of them? I believe it was the maiden name of that friend of yours, Mrs . . . Mrs. Van something."

"I know who the Markhams are," Zeke said. His ears had been filled with enough gossip about the family, even from Mrs. Van H. herself. But Zeke could scarce credit that it had anything to do with him.

"Do you mean to stand there and tell me that *Stephen Markham* was my father?"

Tessa nodded unhappily.

"That . . . that's crazy. From what Mrs. Van H. has told me about her brother, half the unwanted brats in New York could lay claim to being sired by him. What makes you so sure he was my father?"

"Because Mama said so. She even tried to find out more, who your mother was. She went to visit that Mrs. Van Hallsburg."

Zeke flinched. Another leveler. He hadn't been floored so many times since the last time he had put on gloves and stepped into the ring. "Sadie what! When?"

"A long time ago. I'm not sure. Mrs. Van Hallsburg admitted the part about her brother. She said your mother was some sort of an actress, but she wouldn't tell Mama more than that."

Zeke seized Tessa by the shoulders in a hard grasp. "You . . . you mean that Mrs. Van H. *knew* that I was her brother's son?"

"I . . . I guess so."

This was worse than madness. This was a nightmare. Images of Cynthia Van Hallsburg seared his mind, how she had behaved in his study that day, the blaze of unsettling passion in her eyes, her kiss. He could still imagine the brassy taste of it on his lips. He felt like he was going to be sick.

"None of this makes any sense." He gave Tessa a brusque shake. "Go on. Tell me the rest of it."

She squirmed to be free. "There isn't any more. Mama was dying the night she told me. It . . . it wasn't all clear. Please, Johnnie. You're hurting me."

It took a moment for her soft cry to penetrate his haze of confusion and anger. Abruptly he released her, his mind trying to cope with a barrage of information he had never sought. He had always told himself that he didn't give a damn about knowing who his mother or father were. They had left him to die, hadn't they? Then the hell with them. But these half-answers, half-truths . . . It was worse than knowing nothing at all.

Tessa rubbed her arms where he had gripped her. "You are making me sorry I told you. You've got a crazy look on your face, Johnnie."

How did she expect him to look when she had just turned his world upside down? He said curtly, "Go back into the house, Tessa. You shouldn't be out here by yourself."

"By myself? Where are you going?"

He didn't answer her, merely pacing off several impatient steps, scanning the street ahead for the approach of a hack. Of course there was never one around when needed. But it didn't matter a damn. He would walk all the way to Fifth Avenue if he had to.

Tessa trailed after him, tugging at his sleeve. "Come back to the house, John. You're scaring me."

He pulled away from her, his lips set in a taut, angry smile. "You've no need to worry about me, Tess. I'll be in no danger. I'm merely going to pay a late-night call upon my dear Aunt Cynthia."

Twenty

Rarely did Cynthia Van Hallsburg throw open the doors of her white marble townhouse for entertaining. But when she did, her invitations were eagerly sought, her affairs very exclusive.

The dinner party she had arranged for tonight, however, had become almost too exclusive. Half of those invited hadn't put in an appearance, and the rest had only come out of vulgar curiosity. The whisperings had already begun. Mrs. Van Hallsburg was very much aware of that fact as she stood at the entryway to her best salon, but her icy composure revealed nothing of her dismay.

Her guests clustered in polite conversation by the piano, or by the red lacquered Japanese cabinet, or near the decorative sculpture designed by Karl Bitter. The chatter was low-key, well-bred except for the furtive glances occasionally directed toward their hostess.

The rumors were already thick about town, spurred on by the scurrilous articles being run in the *New York World*, written by that barbaric red-haired reporter friend of John Morrison's.

It was all coming to pass just as she'd feared. Charles

Decker's clumsy plot had sparked off an intensive investigation. Not even her clever disposal of Charles had been enough to stop it. She should have shot the fool years ago, not now when it was already too late.

She was obliged to admit she had been less than careful herself. A self-mocking smile touched her lips as she thought of the newspaper article that reported the little detail that threatened to undo her. Decker's death appeared a most unlikely suicide, the paper said. His right hand had been found holding the gun, which made it quite awkward, considering he had been shot through the left side of the head.

She had put the gun in the wrong hand. It was enough to make one laugh, tripping herself up on a tiny detail like that. So clumsy, so careless. Yet that wouldn't have been enough to cause her concern. It was that other report that did it, about someone claiming to have seen a woman slipping away from Decker's house late that night.

No fingers were pointing her way yet, but she feared some sort of evidence might have been found connecting her to Charles's illegal activities. The police had been making discreet inquiries about her bank accounts. She was fast coming under suspicion. She knew it, and, she feared from her guests' uneasy behavior, so did everyone else.

It took all her rigid years of social training to keep her carriage erect, the smile frozen on her lips. She almost wished for once she could be ill-mannered enough to exhibit some of John Morrison's bluntness.

"You've gawked your fill!" she wanted to shriek at her guests. "Now get the hell out." No one was coming to arrest her tonight.

Maybe not tonight, or even tomorrow. But she had to face it. It could come to that. Time was running out. She was going to have to make some plans and soon.

Her anxious reflections were interrupted by the butler appearing at her elbow, forcing his back into a stiff bow.

"Should dinner be served yet, madam?" Chivers cast a dubious glance at the half-filled room.

"We may as well," she murmured. "I doubt anyone else is coming."

As the butler began to retreat, she called him back, adding in a whisper, "And see that half of the settings are removed, the table rearranged."

There was no sense in making her embarrassment obvious. The butler appeared to understand, although he delivered his "Very good, madam" with a slight smirk.

The fellow had never dared show such insolence before, she thought with a frown. Likely he was already on the lookout for another post. She had spent a lifetime maintaining a proper distance from everyone, but now she sensed them all drifting from her, as inexorably as the ebb of the tide. It was hard to admit, but she found the sensation a little frightening.

She was about to encourage her guests to move into the dining room when she heard a thunderous summons at the front door. Perhaps she had not seen the last of the arrivals after all. Although she had never held up dinner this long before, she could afford to wait a few more minutes.

Lingering by the door, she prepared to greet the latecomer more graciously than she would have under ordinary circumstances. But she heard no approaching footsteps, only the unthinkable sound of raised voices in the front hall.

With a slight frown, she excused herself and stepped down the corridor to see who had caused the disturbance. She drew up short. She shouldn't have been surprised. No one would have the temerity to manhandle her butler other than Zeke Morrison. He had the manservant all but pinned to one of the towering Corinthian pillars as he shoved his way past into the hall.

Zeke was ill-dressed as always, his Prince Albert coat rumpled, the tight set of the fabric seeming scarcely enough to contain all that masculine energy straining beneath. Dark strands of hair tumbled across his brow, his eyes darker still, flashing with anger. He was in one of his rages. Distasteful as she found such a display of emotion, she couldn't help a tingle of excitement as well.

Morrison was like a spring of vitality, a slumbering vol-
cano of power, raw and untamed. After their last, humiliating scene, she had never wanted to see him again, yet
now she was glad of the sight of him. Never had she been
so fascinated by any man. Never had she hated anyone as
much.

Although quaking, her butler continued to insist, "Madam Van Hallsburg is not available this evening."

"Then she'd better get available," Zeke said crudely.
"Fast."

The butler had made a dive to summon some footmen to
his aid when she intervened. "It's all right, Chivers. You
may admit Mr. Morrison."

It was an unnecessary command, for Zeke's head had
snapped round at the sound of her voice. He came charging
in her direction.

"Good evening, John," she said, maintaining a calm that
for once she didn't feel. "I thought that I had at least taught
you not to attend a party when you haven't been invited."

"Your party be damned. I want to talk to you."

This wasn't one of his usual blustering rages. His mouth
was taut with some suppressed emotion, his eyes hard,
accusing. She felt a prickling of, if not apprehension, at
least of warning.

"We were just sitting down to dine, but I suppose I
could spare you a few minutes." After a slight hesitation,
she turned, beckoning for him to follow her.

She led him into one of the house's smaller parlors much
favored by her late husband for its dark furnishings and
gloom-ridden atmosphere. She seldom bothered with the
chamber, so consequently the air in the room was stale;
even the lamp she lit did little to dispel the darkness.

Zeke became a little more subdued. Whether it was
owing to the funereal aspect of the room, or to Mrs. Van
H.'s customary chilly demeanor, he couldn't have said. He
had been carried to her doorstep by a fever pitch of emotion. But now face-to-face with the elegant, self-possessed
woman, what Tessa had told him seemed incredible.

He waved aside her offer of a drink. Refusing to be

seated, he paced off a few steps in front of the hearth, no longer so certain where to begin.

"What is so urgent, John?" She favored him with a brittle smile. "Surely it cannot be that you have come to your senses over that little circus girl, that you have been reconsidering what . . . what I offered you?"

"No!" he fairly shouted. The mere reminder of "her offer" sent a shudder of revulsion through him, especially as he considered the possibility that what Tessa had told him was true.

He forced himself to lower his voice. "I only came here because I need some questions answered, questions about some information I received."

She looked wary, but at the same time almost resigned. "I see. You must have been talking to your friend Mr. Duffy."

"Duffy? What the hell has he got to do with this?"

"Why, I thought . . . Then I am afraid I don't understand."

"I've come to you about something my sister told me."

Zeke could find no way to approach the matter subtly. Taking a deep breath, in his usual blunt manner, he laid out for Mrs. Van Hallsburg everything that Tessa had said. She listened in silence, with no more hint of reaction than a flicker of an eyelash. She made no effort to confirm or deny any of it.

"Well, is it true?" Zeke demanded impatiently. "Did my mother ever come to see you?"

"Your mother?" That seemed to startle Mrs. Van Hallsburg. "Oh, you mean that dowdy little Italian woman."

Zeke spoke through gritted teeth. "I mean Sadie Marceone." When she still showed no inclination to reply, he took a menacing step forward. "Answer me, damn it."

"There is no need for you to be coarse, John. I have every intention of answering you." She walked away from him, raising her shoulders in a cool shrug. "Yes, your Mrs. Marceone called upon me. But don't expect me to remember all the details. It was a long time ago, just after she adopted you."

Her lip curled. "Those ridiculous people from the orphanage sent her to me, and after my father had paid them a goodly sum to keep quiet about your ancestry. I warned him it wouldn't work. As far as I know, there is only one effective way of silencing people."

Zeke could only stare at her, chilled not so much by her words as her manner. She was confessing it was all true, just like that, as calmly as though these facts of his life held no more meaning than reading off the social register.

"Then . . . then you are admitting you've always known about me—who I was?"

"My family managed to follow your progress, even when you ran away from the orphanage."

Did they? Zeke thought with a sudden sharp surge of bitterness. *They* had known when he had slept in the gutters, pawed through garbage in search of something to eat, fled for his life from the blades of some street gang. *She* had known.

"And my father too? Did he know what became of me?"

"I suppose he did, if you believe the dead can look down upon you." She sounded almost bored by the entire discussion. "What is all this sudden fuss about your birth, John? You never expressed much interest in your parentage before, at least not to me."

"I never realized you knew so damn much. Now I want the truth."

"Do you?" She had an odd glint in her eyes, her smile almost mocking. "I wonder . . . even someone as tough as you think you are. I wonder if you can take it."

"Try me," he snarled. "You might as well come out with all of it. You've as good as told me that Stephen Markham was my father. That makes you my aunt."

He fairly spat the words at her. To his astonishment, she laughed. He couldn't recall ever hearing her do so before. The sound left him feeling cold.

"Not your aunt, John," she said with one of those smiles he was coming to dread. "*Your mother.*"

She had to be lying, or else mad. She didn't know

what she was saying. He hadn't heard her right. Zeke sought every form of denial, but there was no escaping the truth reflected to him in the depths of those chilling, mocking eyes.

"My . . ." He couldn't bring himself to say the word, not in connection with her. "What the hell are you talking about? You mean that you and your own brother—"

He stopped, moistening his lips, feeling as though he would be sick.

"No." Her voice held a faint trace of amusement. "Stephen always took his pleasures elsewhere."

Zeke heaved a deep breath of relief. That made it better, but not much.

She continued, "Your father was one of the Irish grooms in our stables."

His incredulity must have shown on his face, for she went on quickly, "Everyone commits some indiscretion, and this was mine. That one hot July afternoon, I needed to know what it would be like to lie beneath a man glistening with sweat, calluses on his hands, passions as wild and primitive as the studs my father bought to breed his mares."

For a brief moment, a shudder tore through her, her features transformed by a look of ecstasy she quickly repressed. "The experience was every bit as loathsome as I imagined.

"Yet I made a fool of myself over that man. There's no saying where it would have ended before I came to my senses. Fortunately, one day Sean broke his neck, jumping one of the horses."

"How obliging of him," Zeke said darkly. He tried to summon some feeling of sorrow for the father he had never known, tried but couldn't. He couldn't help believing that the young groom was better off even descending into the regions of hell than within Mrs. Van Hallsburg's poisonous grasp.

Undaunted by his sarcastic remark, she said, "Yes, Sean was always a most . . . accommodating man. I might even have mourned his passing but for the legacy he left me."

Her gaze swept toward Zeke, her eyes icy splinters of

accusation. "You were already growing inside me, feeding upon my life's blood like some parasite. I would have aborted you, but I was too far gone before I realized. I was rather naive about some facts of life in those days."

Zeke couldn't credit it. Cynthia Van Hallsburg might have been many things in her youth—spoiled, selfish, fatally attractive—but never naive.

"So then what?" Zeke prompted when she fell silent, uncertain if he could stand to listen to any more of this, but strangely unable to turn away from her either, until he had heard every last wretched detail.

She sighed. "I had to pretend to leave for an extended visit to a friend's summer house, while actually I went to live in this miserable boarding house with only my maid Emma to attend me. You came into the world after midnight one April morning, not stillborn as I had hoped, but lusty and screaming."

Mrs. Van Hallsburg pressed her hands briefly to her brow as though after all these years, she was yet trying to shut out the sound of those cries. "It was your constant screaming that did it, drove me to abandon you on that refuse heap. I suppose if I had been thinking more clearly, I would have suffocated you, but the ordeal of childbirth had disordered my wits."

Zeke's mouth went dry, but he was too stunned to say or do anything other than regard her with loathing. She was so calm. That was the true horror of it—so calm as she explained why she hadn't managed to murder him at birth.

"You needn't look at me that way," she said. "As though I were some sort of villainess. When I heard later you had been found, taken to the orphanage, when I was far away from your cries, I didn't mind at all that you had lived."

"Thank you," Zeke said bitterly.

"No one would have known a thing about you, except that my maid betrayed me. She told my father, who insisted that something more had to be done. Such a stupid man. He paid the orphanage a large sum of money for your care, and to keep silent about who your benefactor was.

"And what good did that do? You never saw a penny of that money and it only put my reputation at risk. Luckily everyone believed you were just another one of Stephen's indiscretions."

Zeke wished he could have continued believing that himself.

"And that's what you told Sadie when she came to see you?" he asked.

"I started to, but it was so strange. Somehow I found myself confiding the truth to her. I knew she would never betray me. She was too terrified I might want you back. But I never found you the least interesting until you were fully grown."

The nature of her interest showed all too clearly in her eyes, that unholy light springing there again. Zeke took an involuntary step back, his gut wrenching. Now he understood full well why Sadie had never told him any of this, the painful knowledge she had tried to shield him from, why she had been so terrified when Mrs. Van Hallsburg had come back into his life.

As Mrs. Van Hallsburg approached him, he tensed, afraid of what he might do if she tried to touch him. He glanced down at that once-lovely face that suddenly seemed to be showing the lines of age, not a graceful aging, but one of decadence, a twisted soul too long kept hidden behind that timeless mask.

"Sadie tried to warn me once," he murmured. "She said you were evil."

"Evil? Simply because I desire my own son?" She drifted closer, her scent filling his nostrils, as cloying as the sickly sweet smell of too many floral offerings clustered round an open casket. "The trouble with you, John, is that you have a lower class mentality. You understand wealth and power, but not fully enough to know that they bring you freedom from the laws that govern lesser men.

"The Pharaohs of Egypt intermarried, mingled their own blood. Why not us?"

"My education must be lacking, but they sound like nothing but a passel of heathens to me."

"I forgot. Dear Mrs. Marceone raised you to be a good Catholic boy."

"Don't sneer at my upbringing," he said. "Especially when you never troubled yourself whether I lived or died."

The closer she came, the more his flesh crawled, and he knew he had to get out of there, get himself a good stiff drink. Maybe if he poured enough whiskey down his throat, it would burn, cleanse him of the taint of her.

As he made a movement to leave, some of her composure crumbled. She even looked a little desperate as she got between him and the door. "Where are you running to, John?"

"Anywhere away from you. You were right about me and the truth. I guess I can't take it."

"John, please . . ." Her rasping plea seemed to whisper over his skin like a layer of silt.

"Get out of my way."

"John, I understand. I should have broken this to you more gently. You are in shock, but when you have had time to grow accustomed to the idea—"

"Not in a million years, woman."

"But you may never see me again after tonight. When all the truth is known, I will be forced to leave the city."

"Not because of me. I'm not about to go boasting of the connection between us."

"I'm not talking about us, but that other matter, with your friend Duffy."

When Zeke regarded her blankly, she said with a tinge of impatience, "You must be the only person in New York who doesn't know about the extent of his investigation, how he's dragging me into . . ."

She hesitated, then rushed on. "I may as well tell you. I . . . I was Charles Decker's partner in his enterprises. When he made such a disaster of everything, I had to kill him, fake his suicide. Does that astonish you?"

"After what you've already told me tonight?" Zeke gave a harsh laugh. "Madam, nothing about you would surprise me. And so Duffy is onto you? Well, I wish you luck, because you're going to need it. He's damned persistent."

"I don't need luck," she hissed. "All I need is you." She clutched at his sleeve. "Come away with me, John. I have money deposited in Switzerland. We could live quite comfortably abroad. . . ."

But he barely heard her breathless flow of words as he stared at her hand, which no longer appeared so smooth, so elegant, but rather like skeletal fingers grasping at him, death tugging at his arm. Her skin seemed pulled so tautly across her face as to be brittle, levels of desperation and madness swirling in her pale blue eyes.

Despite his revulsion, he managed to grasp her wrist, put her away from him very deliberately. But when she tried to cast herself into his arms, his control broke and he shoved her back with more roughness than he had ever shown any woman. She staggered into one of the chairs.

"John," she cried. "We belong together. You are my flesh. It's my blood that flows through your veins."

"If I thought that counted for anything, I would slit my wrists," he said. Before she could regain her balance, come at him again, he strode out of the room, slamming the door behind him.

With a shrill cry, she started to go after him, only bringing herself up short as she reached the threshold, fighting for the familiar comfort that was her dignity, the icy shroud of her composure. What was happening to her? Never had she begged anything of anyone before.

Leaning against the door, she closed her eyes, trying to still the unaccustomed pounding of her heart. Instead she found herself looking back over the ruins of her life, wondering where it had all started to come apart.

Despite her youthful folly, she had always enjoyed the position in society to which her birth entitled her. And thanks to Charles Decker, she had had the wherewithal to sustain it. When John Ezekiel Morrison had strode back into her life and she had commenced the task of polishing him, making him a fit companion for her, everything had been perfect.

Until . . . until the day of that disastrous lawn party

when that girl had crashed on John's lawn. Yes . . . Mrs.
Van Hallsburg's mouth pinched taut. That was the day
when she had first begun to lose control of John, when
that girl had swept into his life.

Almost unconsciously she laced her fingers together as
though tightening them about a slender white throat. She
had never understood the concept of revenge before, considering it a meaningless waste of energy and emotion.

But as the image of Aurora Rose Kavanaugh's lovely
young features rose into Mrs. Van Hallsburg's mind, she
began to comprehend the allure of vengeance for the very
first time.

Twenty-one

✳ ✳ ✳

Early morning mists curled off the East River, rising slowly to assume the form of a woman, a flowing white gown hanging from her in tattered shreds, silvery hair tangled wildly about a face pallid as death, the eyes as empty as the black void of a grave.

Rory shuddered as that pitiless, unseeing gaze turned in her direction. She slashed frantically at the ballast bags weighting down the balloon, seeking to rise above the mist and that terrifying visage. But as the balloon lifted, soaring skyward, the spectral figure below let out a shriek of horrible laughter.

Stretching her arms upward, the white witch floated after Rory until her hands closed over the side of the gondola, her fingers more bone than flesh. Sobbing with terror, Rory sought to pry away those cold grasping hands, but at the first touch, she could feel that deathly chill spreading to herself. In horror she watched as her own hands began aging, decaying before her very eyes.

"No!"

With a loud cry, Rory sat up, wrenching herself awake. Bathed in cold sweat, it took her a moment to realize she was safe, sprawled on the sofa of her flat. The packages delivered by Altman's yesterday were bestrewn upon the floor, mingling with the cozy furnishings of her parlor . . . familiar, reassuring surroundings, and yet her heart thudded with fear. The dream had been so vivid, she took a trembling survey of her hands, relieved to find her skin smooth and warm, life yet thrumming through her veins.

She released her breath in a shivery sigh and raked her hands through her hair. Damn! She hated dreams like that. Go back to sleep and forget about it, her Da would have told her. He had always scoffed at the old superstitions of the banshee, been sorry he had ever let her head be filled with such nonsense.

Rory wished she could be equally as scornful, but in the past her nightmare had always been followed with a death. Whose might it be this time . . . her own?

Zeke had warned her she was going to break her neck one of these days. But she wasn't even taking the balloon up today. She had formed far different plans. The heavy ring of keys left lying on the parlor table reminded her of what she had to do, reminded her also of a future so bleak she didn't care if she crashed to her death or not.

That was a wicked thought, and Rory was quick to cross herself. All the same she did feel utterly miserable. Ever since Zeke had stormed out of her apartment, she had drifted into a state of lethargy, unable to do anything but replay their dreadful quarrel over and over in her mind. Furious and despairing by turns, her frettings had culminated in a sleepless night.

She had at last curled up on the sofa, eventually drifting off somewhere in the wee hours of the morning, falling asleep in time to have a nightmare. Just her luck.

Struggling to her feet, Rory pressed one hand to the small of her back, stiff and aching from the posture she had been sleeping in. She nearly tripped over one of the boxes. She would have to notify Altman's to have them retrieve the blasted parcels, or else have the whole lot packed up and sent to Zeke's mansion.

Her trousseau, Zeke had called it. But there could be no trousseau when there was to be no wedding. She had no doubt but that all was ended between her and Zeke. What he had done, trying to force her to abandon her dream, was dreadful, the words she had spoken to him more unforgivable still.

She could scarce believe she had been so cruel, even in the grip of her rage and anguish. But perhaps what she had said, driving Zeke away as nothing else could, would prove kinder in the long run. It should have been obvious from the beginning how unsuited they were for each other.

Even as she sought to convince herself, other memories intruded, of dancing until dawn, sharing stolen kisses in the little cottage by the sea, snuggling against Zeke's shoulder on the bench in City Hall Park while watching the sun set. Memories of how they had laughed, loved, even fought together, side by side, ready to take on the toughest of villains, the whole world. Memories that she had to suppress if she were going to make herself believe that she was better off without Zeke Morrison in her life.

Ignoring the stinging beneath her eyelids, she strode resolutely to her bedchamber. She had spent enough time moping. She needed to get dressed and go to the warehouse. Tony and the others would be expecting her to get ready for the return of the government contractor. It was going to be difficult enough to explain to them why they would be spending the day otherwise engaged without facing them all with reddened eyes.

Perched upon crates in the warehouse, Tony, Pete and Angelo faced her in varying postures of confusion and disbelief. She had finished explaining how Zeke Morrison had bought the warehouse, rendering it necessary for Rory to remove all her equipment from the premises.

"Wait a moment." Angelo scowled, scratching the back of his head, succeeding in making his cowlick worse. "Didn't you just say that Morrison left you the keys?"

"Yes, he did," Rory said, tapping her foot impatiently, not wanting to offer any more explanation than she had to. "And so?"

"Then the fellow must have changed his mind about tossing us out, right?" Angelo appealed to Pete, who shrugged but nodded in placid agreement.

Rory pursed her lips. "It makes no difference even if he did. I have no desire to be the recipient of Mr. Morrison's generosity."

"Resippy-what?" Angelo echoed. "What's that mean?"

Tony, who had listened in silence, his arms crossed over his chest, now spoke up, interpreting with aggravating clarity. "It means Rory and Morrison had some sort of a row and now Rory is being stubborn."

Rory glared at him. "Nothing of the kind. It's merely that I can no longer afford the rent here. So get up off your tails and start packing."

Pete and Angelo slid off the crates, still looking nonplussed, but preparing to begin. Tony, however, kept shaking his head in a way that made Rory want to hit him. As the other two shuffled off, he muttered, "I don't know what this is really about, Rory. But I can take a good guess and for once I sympathize with Morrison. If you was going to be my wife, I wouldn't want you flying the damned balloons anymore either."

That Tony would range himself on Zeke's side both wounded and annoyed her. "I'm not going to be anyone's wife, Bertelli. Now I would appreciate your getting busy."

"What do you think you're going to do with all this stuff?"

Rory hadn't thought that through clearly, but she blustered, "For now, I . . . I suppose I'll have to cram it all into my flat."

Tony rolled his eyes and opened his mouth to say something, then apparently thought better of it. With a snort of total disgust, he moved off to supervise the other two boys.

They all fell to their task in a manner less than enthusiastic, moving so slowly, exchanging so many superior male glances over the illogic of women that Rory could no longer bear to watch them. She stomped off upstairs to clear out her office.

But as the minutes ticked by, she packed very little, sitting behind her desk, staring up at the familiar cracks on the ceiling, wondering if she was, as Tony said, merely being stubborn.

Tony's ready sympathy for Zeke's position had disturbed her more than she cared to admit. Was she being unreasonable? She supposed . . . no, she knew Zeke was only trying to protect her in his rough way. But she couldn't accept his manner of doing things as though her feelings and opinions didn't count. He was so . . . so aggressive, bullying, maddening.

And she still loved him desperately.

The tears crept back into her eyes and she wiped them fiercely away. There was no sense sitting here thinking such things as that. She would only end up bawling. With a dogged set to her lips, she forced herself into movement, heaving ledger books, pencils, pens and ink bottles into a carton.

At noon she paused long enough to see how Tony and the boys were doing. They had made suspiciously little progress. Tony had gone off somewhere to fetch lunch back for all of them, and she caught Angelo, in his usual garrulous fashion, pausing to entertain a visitor.

Rory stopped on the last step, mildly surprised to see that bright beacon of red hair that marked the presence of Bill Duffy. She had no idea what could have brought the reporter down to her warehouse. Much as she liked the fellow, she approached warily.

Angelo sprang guiltily back to work at the sight of her, and Duffy grinned, doffed his derby. Rory studied the man, detecting something different about him today. The shine of his blue frock coat proclaimed it as brand new, and he had stuck a carnation in his lapel. Always jaunty, he seemed particularly smug and well pleased with himself.

"Good afternoon, Miss Kavanaugh," he said. "I couldn't resist coming by for a peek at the infamous balloon factory.

Anything interesting going on this afternoon? You all seem to be getting ready for something. Another flight perhaps?"

His fingers twitched, and Rory knew he would be reaching for his notebook in another moment.

"Nothing newsworthy," she said quickly to forestall him. "It's only . . . well, due to some setbacks, I am obliged to vacate the warehouse."

"Say, that's too bad. And Morrison can't help you? Lordy, the fellow's richer than J. P. Morgan."

Rory winced. "No, er . . . Mr. Morrison is not very sympathetic to my business interests."

"Well, you can smooth all that out after you are married. And speaking of weddings, I don't suppose you would let me cover yours as an exclusive?"

"You have been misled. There's not going to be any wedding."

"Oh?" Duffy rocked back on his heels. "Had a spat, did you?" he asked sympathetically.

The small sigh that escaped her said everything.

"Don't worry. He'll be back. I've never been bitten by the love bug myself, but I've seen it happen to plenty of other fellows. And believe me, Morrison has a bad case of it."

He coaxed a reluctant smile from her, but she really didn't want to discuss it any further, his words raising hopes in her she didn't dare to entertain. She tried to excuse herself on the grounds that she had work to do.

She hoped Duffy would take the hint and leave, but the man seemed incapable of being discouraged by anything less subtle than a club over the head. And Rory didn't have the energy for that.

She allowed him to trail after her as she returned to her office.

"Your marriage to Morrison would've made a good story. But I've been doing all right for myself in any case. In fact I just got a big raise in salary."

"Congratulations," Rory said. Out of politeness she added, "And how is your investigation into the Addison affair going?"

"That's what I'm talking about. Haven't you been reading my stories?" He looked almost insulted when she shook her head. "Well, it's just the biggest scandal since the days of Boss Tweed. I found out that Decker had a partner in his nefarious schemes. A woman. A real high-stepper. And you'd never believe who!"

"I haven't a clue," she said wearily.

Duffy seemed disappointed when she wouldn't even hazard a guess. "It happens to be none other than that blue-blooded pillar of society, the Ice Goddess herself. Cynthia Van Hallsburg."

Rory's head came up sharply at that, her eyes widening in astonishment. Duffy smirked, looking pleased to have provoked a reaction at last.

"Yessiree. And there's more. It looks as though Decker was shot by someone. Not that I think a lady like Mrs. Van H. could be capable of going that far."

Rory was troubled by a memory of cold hard eyes. "Yes, she could," she murmured, unable to repress a tiny shiver. She didn't know why she found Duffy's news so unsettling, but she did. Mrs. Van Hallsburg meant nothing to her, and yet something about the woman had always disturbed Rory, from the time the ageless beauty had once figured in her dream, taking the place of the banshee. An uneasiness sifted over her as enveloping as the mists of her recent nightmare.

"Do you think Zeke knows all this?" she asked Duffy anxiously.

"Morrison?" Duffy appeared surprised by the question. He shrugged. "If he reads the right newspaper, he does."

"Maybe he ought to be warned."

Duffy looked at her as if she had run mad. "Warned? About what? So Mrs. Van H. dirtied her hands a bit, investing in illegal activities. That hardly makes her dangerous. And even if she was," Duffy puffed out his chest, "she'd be more likely to come after yours truly."

Rory didn't agree, but she sought in vain for the words to convey her pricklings of fear. Duffy was a hardheaded reporter who dealt in facts. How did one begin to explain to him such intangible things as dreams, instincts, premonitions, without sounding a fool?

"I would just feel better," she said at last, "if you would go to Zeke and make sure he knows, or at least see if the police have taken Mrs. Van Hallsburg into custody."

"Well, sure, if you want me to." He pulled out his pocket watch and snapped open the case. "But I'm not certain at this hour of day where to find him or Mrs. Van Hallsburg."

"Say, Rory." Angelo's piping voice startled them both. "She's downstairs." He had poked his head in the office door obviously in time to hear Duffy's last remark.

"What?" Rory gasped, hoping she must have misunderstood the boy.

"That lady you were talking about, Mrs. Van Whatshername." Angelo jerked his thumb over his shoulder. "She's waiting below, wants to see you, Rory."

Rory exchanged a glance with Duffy, felt herself going pale.

"She sent up her card." Angelo gave her a crisp white rectangle of vellum now smudged by his fingerprints, yet not enough to obscure the elegant, arrogant scrawl. The faintest odor of cloying perfume drifted from it, and Rory's hand trembled as though she had just been handed some witch's charm.

Duffy let out a long, low whistle. "Well, speak of the devil. What an opportunity. Show her upstairs, kid."

Before Rory could intervene, Duffy had dispatched Angelo on the errand.

"Duffy," she protested. "I don't want to see her. I . . ." She was too ashamed to admit she had an almost supernatural dread of the woman. "I can't imagine why she would come here. Shouldn't we send for the police?"

"And miss the chance for the biggest interview of my career? Look, I know she won't even let me get near her, but you could help me, Miss Kavanaugh. Maybe just ask her a few questions."

"Like what?" Rory's laugh had almost an hysterical edge to it. "Have you been to tea with the Astors lately, Mrs.

Van Hallsburg? Oh and by the way, did you kill Charles
Decker?"

"Well, you'll have to be a little more subtle than that.
But I better get out of here. If she sees me, she'll turn
and stalk right out again." With a scrambling haste, Duffy
snatched up his derby, pausing only long enough to give
Rory's shoulder a pat. "Good luck."

"Duffy!" she protested. But the door was already closing
behind him. "Damn you, Duffy!"

The man had just set her up for a tête-à-tête with a
suspected murderess, then had the temerity to wish her
luck. Rory had to fight an urge to bolt the office door.
When the knock finally came, she nearly started out of her
skin. Struggling to be calm, she ranged herself behind her
desk as though that meager barrier could afford her some
protection.

"C-come in," she said, hating the way her voice shook.
The door inched open and a wraithlike shadow fell across
the room, a shadow that seemed to be all rustling silk and
regal posture. Mrs. Van Hallsburg stepped over the threshold clad in a dove-colored walking suit trimmed with black
braid, her white-gold hair swept up beneath an English felt
hat adorned with a jet pin and tiny feathers. She looked
so composed, so sophisticated, so very much the socialite,
that Rory felt a little foolish, as though all her fears and
suspicions were absurd . . .

. . . until she looked into the woman's eyes.

Hard, compassionless, colder than the winds of winter.
Rory shivered.

A faint, contemptuous smile curled Mrs. Van Hallsburg's
lips. "Miss Kavanaugh?"

Rory was surprised that the haughty dame even remembered her name. "Yes?"

"I assume I may sit down?"

Rory flushed, realizing she had been gaping foolishly,
making her nervousness too apparent. She nodded, indi-
cating a chair. Mrs. Van Hallsburg ran one gloved finger
over the wooden seat before deigning to lower herself
upon it.

Then she trained the full force of her regard upon Rory her stare steady and unnerving. Rory thought fleetingly o Duffy, all the careful probing he wanted her to do, but the only question Rory could think of was *What the hell are you doing here, lady?*

After a nerve-splitting silence, she managed to say "You . . . you'll have to excuse my astonishment, Mrs Van Hallsburg. Frankly, you are the last person I eve expected to see."

"Indeed." Mrs. Van Hallsburg slowly stripped off he gloves. "I was put to some trouble to find you."

Why did her soft-spoken words leave Rory with the harrowing impression of some sleek silver ferret relentlessl stalking its prey?

"I don't know why you would go to such bother," Rory said. "The few times we've met at Mr. Morrison's, I had the impression you found me beneath your notice."

"Let us merely say I didn't approve of your friendshi with John."

"What right did you have to approve or disapprove? Yo had no claim on him."

"I have more of a claim than you could possibly imagine my dear. The bond that existed between myself and Joh Morrison was something . . . special, irrevocable, at leas until you came along."

For the flicker of an instant, the winter in those pale blu eyes melted to become a blazing inferno, hellish flames c hatred, jealousy and thwarted desire. It was enough to mak Rory draw back, want to bolt from the room, but Mrs. Va Hallsburg was quick to veil the frightening expression wit a soft laugh. "I didn't seek you out to discuss John. I cam here for other reasons."

Rory frowned. "I can't imagine what they might be."

"Necessity compels me to leave New York. I nee to put distance between myself and the city quickly. I short, I need to avail myself of your unique services, Mis Kavanaugh."

"You . . . you mean you want me to . . . to . . ."

"Get one of your balloons ready immediately."

Rory stared, scarce able to believe the arrogance of the
woman, coming to her, of all people, and asking, no,
demanding such help. Her fear of Mrs. Van Hallsburg
was lost in a rush of indignation.

"Are the police after you?" Rory asked bluntly.

"Not yet, to my knowledge. That hardly concerns you."

"The devil it doesn't. I'm running a balloon company,
not an escape service for fugitives."

"Yet you aided John Morrison in his flight from the law.
I see no reason you cannot accomplish the same for me."

Only that Rory would have aided Jack the Ripper to
escape before she would have lifted one finger to help
Mrs. Van Hallsburg.

She pushed abruptly to her feet. "I am sorry, madam.
But you came to the wrong place."

"I don't think so." Mrs. Van Hallsburg cooly tugged
loose the drawstrings of her beaded purse.

Rory regarded her with scorn. "You may as well put your
purse away, Mrs. Van Hallsburg. There isn't any amount
you could pay that would induce me to help you."

"Oh, it isn't money that I mean to offer you, my dear."
With a thin smile, Mrs. Van Hallsburg drew forth a small
revolver and aimed it straight at Rory's heart.

Something was wrong. Duffy shifted uneasily, watching
from the shadow of the stairs the sudden flurry of activity
in the warehouse as the two lads hustled to ready one of
those mammoth balloons for launching from the dock.
Rory's interview with Mrs. Van Hallsburg seemed to have
stretched out to an interminable length. Duffy might have
rejoiced, only hoping that Miss Kavanaugh possessed a
good enough memory to recall all that was being said. But
his satisfaction was marred by that brief disturbing moment
when both women had appeared on the upper landing.

Duffy had kept out of sight while Rory shouted down the
terse command. "Prepare the *Seamus*. I'm taking it up."

When the boy named Angelo had sought to question this
order, Miss Kavanaugh had fair took his head off before
vanishing back into the office with Mrs. Van Hallsburg.

Duffy's own confusion was apparent in the two young men. hard at work, hooking up some kind of generator thing to the gas bag of the balloon.

"Geez, what's the matter with Rory, Pete?" Angelo was saying. "First she tells us to get a move on with the packing, now she insists she wants the balloon ready."

"I dunno," Pete replied. "I wish Tony would get back here. Rory always explains things to him."

"Not lately. Rory hasn't been right in the head since she fell in love with that Morrison," Angelo grumbled. "She doesn't even seem to remember she dropped the *Seamus* into the ocean, that the only balloon left fit for travel is the *Katie Moira*."

Pete's face lit up with sudden inspiration. "Hey, maybe that rich woman up there is giving her some kind of commission. Maybe we won't have to move after all."

"I guess so." Angelo's puzzled frown disappeared. "That must be it."

The boys appeared satisfied enough that they worked more swiftly. Only Duffy remained riddled with alarm. Maybe he shouldn't have left Rory alone with that woman. Maybe he ought to burst up there and see what was going on. But if Rory was learning anything from Mrs. Van H. his appearance would ruin everything.

Yet what would the girl want her balloon for all of a sudden? Duffy didn't believe for a moment Pete's naive suggestion that the Van Hallsburg woman wanted to hire one of the contraptions.

And yet who could guess what might be running through the lady's mind? Mrs. Van Hallsburg must be under a tremendous amount of pressure owing to his investigations. Duffy had seen people do some really crazy things when their world threatened to crumble apart, even ones as ice-blooded as Mrs. Van H.

His nervousness mounting, Duffy inched hesitantly toward the stairs just as the warehouse door creaked. He hoped it was that Tony kid returning. A little older, he appeared to have more sense than those other two boys. Maybe Tony could—

As the door inched open revealing a pair of broad shoulders, Duffy experienced a peculiar feeling of relief. Better than the Tony kid, it was Morrison.

Zeke didn't enter with his usual arrogant stride, but lingered on the threshold, as though unsure of himself, expecting to be tossed out on his ear. His clothes were so rumpled he looked as though he had spent the past few hours being steam pressed in hell. But that was nothing compared to the haggard expression on his face, the craters beneath his eyes, the clear signs of a man who had been on an all-night binge.

"Mother o' God, Morrison," Duffy called out. "What have you been doing to yourself? I've seen week-old corpses in better shape."

As he came forward, Zeke merely regarded him with a dull stare, not even barking out his usual demand to know what Duffy was up to. "Where's Miss Kavanaugh?"

"Upstairs," Duffy said with an upward motion of his thumb. "I'm glad you're here. Something funny's going on. Look, she's getting one of those blasted balloons ready and—"

"Son of a bitch." Duffy was cut off as Zeke swore, pacing off a few steps to glance through the open doors of the warehouse, back toward the dock, where a familiar loud hiss rattled the windows. The sight of the balloon straining skyward at least brought a spark back into Zeke's listless eyes.

"You don't even know the half," Duffy said. "That friend of yours, Mrs. Van Hallsburg, is upstairs with Miss Kavanaugh, and I can't begin to imagine what the devil—"

"Cynthia! Up there with Rory?"

Duffy grimaced with impatience. Wouldn't the man ever let him finish his sentences? Apparently not, for Zeke shoved Duffy out of the way, the line of his jaw hardening to granite as he started to rush up the steps.

But it was not necessary. Rory was already on her way down, Mrs. Van Hallsburg a step behind, but not far enough that Rory couldn't feel the muzzle of the gun jammed up against her ribs, the weapon concealed by the folds of her dress.

She had been stalling as long as she could, seeking a way to flee or overpower the woman. But it had been impossible as Mrs. Van H. never kept her gun more than a hair's breadth from Rory's side. One false move, and Rory knew she was dead.

As she descended the stairs, she forced herself to remain calm, to exhibit a bravado she wasn't feeling. Just wait until she got Mrs. Van H. up in her balloon, she tried to reassure herself. The sky was her world, the balloon's mysteries hers to control.

Intent upon her thoughts, Rory was halfway down before she realized a man was storming up the risers. Zeke's sudden appearance was so unexpected, her heart turned over. It was all she could do not to fling herself into his arms with a cry of relief and joy.

But close behind her she heard Mrs. Van Hallsburg's sharp intake of breath, then the hissed threat. "One move, one plea for help, and I'll shoot him directly between the eyes."

Would she? Despite Mrs. Van Hallsburg's icy facade, Rory sensed the woman was mad enough to do so. Rory shrank back from Zeke's approach, calling out. "Z-zeke. Damn you. Get out of here."

He frowned, but kept coming. "Rory, what in blazes is going on?"

"None of your business," she shrilled desperately. "Just go away."

"I've engaged Miss Kavanaugh's services," Mrs. Van Hallsburg chimed in. "We're going on a journey together."

"What! The hell you are," Zeke snarled. As he took another step, Rory felt Mrs. Van Hallsburg tense.

"Stay away," Rory cried. "I mean it, Zeke. Don't you dare to touch me."

The vehemence of her command brought him up short.

"I . . . I told you before I didn't want to see you anymore. Now you and Duffy just . . . just get out of here before I have you thrown out."

She tried to telegraph a far different message to Zeke with her eyes. She wasn't sure he understood, but after exchanging a glance with Duffy, he backed off enough to allow Rory and Mrs. Van Hallsburg to proceed down the steps.

Rory had an impulse to shout out a warning and run, but Mrs. Van Hallsburg's grip on her arm was too firm, her gun hand never wavering.

"How very touching that you came to bid me farewell, John," Mrs. Van Hallsburg sneered. "But it seems the least a boy could do for his mother."

His mother? In her astonishment Rory nearly forgot herself and jerked away. How crazed was this woman to say such strange things?

Not crazed enough, Rory thought, a dull ache lodging in her chest, compounded of horror and empathy for Zeke. She could see the truth of the woman's bizarre words upon Zeke's face, shame mingled with a loathing so strong he appeared nearly sickened unto death. Duffy's eyes fairly popped from his head as Mrs. Van Hallsburg continued to taunt Zeke.

"You are my son. I hope you never forget that." There was a deliberate cruelty in her voice as though she couldn't resist taunting him one last time.

"Maybe I won't, but I'm sure as hell going to try," Zeke said. He watched as Mrs. Van Hallsburg began tugging Rory toward the balloon.

"Damn it, Morrison," Duffy said. "Aren't you going to do anything? Let's grab that witch and—"

"You fool." Zeke grabbed Duffy by the coattails to halt his impulsive rush forward. He whispered harshly, "Can't you tell she has a gun jammed against Rory's side?"

"Then what are we going to do? We can't just let Rory go off with her. That woman's crazy."

Duffy didn't need to tell him that. But Zeke stood frozen, beset by the sick sensation of helplessness that had surged through him from that minute upon the stairs when he first realized the desperate peril Rory was in. What the hell could he do? There was no way to wrench Rory out of Mrs. Van Hallsburg's grasp without Rory being hurt, perhaps worse.

All he could do was follow, clinging to the wild hope that there would be one moment when Mrs. Van H. would be distracted, lose her grasp upon Rory—one split second when he would be able to act.

Yet it was almost as though Cynthia sensed the direction of his thoughts, for she didn't allow her concentration to waver for an instant, not even as she and Rory clambered into the gondola. Rory's assistants appeared too caught up in the launch of the balloon to notice anything amiss.

Rory's chin was raised in a valiant effort to conceal her fear, but the pleading look in her eyes seared itself into Zeke's heart. Was there a chance that Cynthia would let her go once Rory had served her purpose, helped her to escape? As the lines were being cast off, Mrs. Van Hallsburg shifted her gaze at last to meet Zeke's, her impassive features flushed with a taunting triumph. Zeke knew all hope was futile. Whatever Rory did, she was going to die.

As the balloon lifted off, he was seized with a blind panic. He charged forward. Shoving past the astonished Angelo, he grabbed onto a dangling rope, tried to hold the balloon earthbound. But he hadn't counted on the sheer power of the hissing behemoth above him.

The balloon yanked him up as though he weighed no more than a rag doll, his feet kicking nothing but air. He heard the startled shouts from below and made the mistake of looking down at the wooden dock spinning rapidly away from him. For a second, he felt a rush of dizziness, the familiar nausea, but he forced himself to look up. The rough rope cut into his palms as he strained to climb upward, pull himself into the basket.

Dragged down by Zeke's added weight, the balloon rose a few feet above the warehouse and no higher. Almost sick with horror, Rory peered over the side of the basket. She forgot her own danger in the face of Zeke's struggle for his life, fearing that any moment she would see his hands slip, his body hurtle back to smash against the docks.

She made a frantic attempt to tug on the rope, help pull Zeke up to safety. A hysterical and futile gesture. Idiot, she rebuked herself. The valve line, she needed to pull on the valve line, release enough air to lower gently, allow Zeke a chance to drop safely back to the ground.

But as she spun about, she was chilled by a burst of maniacal laughter from Mrs. Van Hallsburg. With a cry of dismay, she saw the woman striving to release some of the ballast so the balloon would surge even higher.

Rory leaped to stop her, but Mrs. Van Hallsburg brought her gun back to bear. Rory slapped the weapon aside, deflecting it just as it went off, the shot whizzing harmlessly past, singeing one of the ropes. The gun flew from Mrs. Van Hallsburg's fingers, vanishing over the side of the gondola. With a shriek of fury, Mrs. Van Hallsburg lunged for Rory's throat.

Rory fought with all her might to hold her off, but despite her brittle elegance, the woman seemed possessed of a demonic strength. Rory felt herself driven relentlessly backward. The basket pitched and Rory lost her balance. Mrs. Van Hallsburg shoved hard and Rory screamed as she fell, tumbling into nothingness.

She grasped wildly, her fingers barely managing to close over the side of the basket. For a terrifying moment, she thought she couldn't hold on. She heard Zeke roar her name, glimpsed him swaying on the rope just beneath her.

But she dared not look down, scarce dared breathe, seeing nothing but Mrs. Van Hallsburg's pale face hovering above her, the woman's length of white-gold hair blowing free in a witchlike tumble. Her eyes were pools of ice, utterly without mercy as she grasped Rory's fingers, her nails biting into Rory's flesh. Slowly, remorselessly, she began to pry Rory's hands away.

Rory let out a shuddering sob, her legs flailing against the tangle of her skirts. Her hands throbbed with pain as she felt her sweat-slickened fingers start to slip.

"Zeke!" she cried. Below her, she sensed his struggles to scale the rope, reach her in time. She felt her foot strike against his shoulder just as she lost her grip.

Her cry seemed borne away by the wind as she plummeted, knocking against Zeke. He grabbed for her, his fingers clamping ruthlessly about her wrist, arresting her plunge with a suddenness that nearly wrenched her arm from her socket. His other hand barely clutched the end of the rope, his incredible strength the only thing between them and certain death. His face was beaded with sweat, the cords of his neck muscles taut with the strain, and Rory knew he couldn't maintain this for long.

Above them she had a blurred glimpse of Mrs. Van Hallsburg, the woman's features contorted beyond recognition as she worked frantically to release the ballast, her smile inhuman, a hag's grimace, a witch's smile. The white witch . . . death.

Zeke gave a gasp of rage and despair. He suddenly stared downward as if mesmerized, and to Rory's horror, he let go the rope.

As Rory fell, she had no time to even cry out. She struck ground much sooner than she anticipated, slamming down, the breath driven from her lungs. She felt Zeke landing hard beside her, but for a moment was too dazed to comprehend anything more than that somehow, by some miracle, they had dropped to the roof of the warehouse. They were both still alive.

After gulping in a few painful breaths, she struggled to sit up, reach out to Zeke, see if he was hurt. But he was already drawing himself up to his knees, gazing anxiously toward her.

"Rory. Are . . . are you all right?" he murmured.

She managed to nod, and in the next instant, he swooped her into his arms, cradling her against him as though he would never let her go. Every muscle in her body ached, but she reveled in the feel of his strength, the reassuring thud of his heart thundering in rhythm with her own. The danger was past. She was safe, but to her astonishment, she burst into tears.

"Hush, darling. Don't cry. It's all over now," Zeke said, brushing the hair back from her brow in a familiar gesture, the rough texture of his fingers achingly gentle.

"It . . . it was so dreadful," Rory wept. "Like a nightmare. She . . . she . . ."

"She's gone, Rory. She'll never have a chance to hurt you again, curse her." He twisted his head, glancing skyward. Rory followed his gaze toward the vanishing speck that was the balloon. She knew it would have surged upward when she and Zeke dropped off, but not at such a rate as that. Mrs. Van Hallsburg had to be releasing the ballast like a madwoman, out of ignorance or design, propelling herself upward to those cold regions of sky where the air was too thin, where the heavens themselves could become a hell. Suddenly Rory recalled her dream of the night before and she understood its significance.

"I suppose she will manage to escape," Zeke said bitterly. "Get away with everything she's done."

"No," Rory whispered, a chill working through her. "There's no escaping the banshee."

Twenty-two

Some distance beyond the farthest reaches of Fifth Avenue, pavement and mansions gave way to farmland, rolling green fields that stretched out in rural tranquillity, trying to ignore the encroachments of the ever-advancing city. Late that afternoon, the balloon that touched down seemed just one more of these. Tom Grey, the farmer who owned the land, was less shocked by the strange object entangled in the branches of his apple tree than he was by the fair-haired woman sprawled on her back near the tree's base, her sightless eyes turned toward the sky from which she had fallen.

"Strangest darn thing," Farmer Grey remarked with a shudder to the police who had been summoned to remove the body back to the city morgue. "One of the warmest spring days we've had this year, and yonder she lies all stiff and cold, the blood fair frozen to her face. When I first came upon her, I was near sick. A horrible sight. I'll never forget it as long as I live. . . ."

Hours later, Zeke Morrison feared that he might not either. He stood outside the door leading into the morgue, uncertain he could cross that threshold and imprint upon his memory whatever grim scene lay beyond.

Duffy plucked at his sleeve. "Hey, Morrison, you going to be all right? You sure you want to go through with this? There are plenty of other people who could identify her. It's not exactly as though she was any relation of—" Duffy broke off suddenly, unable to meet Zeke's gaze. He reddened with embarrassment.

"I'm going in," was all Zeke said. It wasn't a question of wanting to. He had to. He had permitted enough of his past to haunt him without allowing Cynthia Van Hallsburg to become the most formidable ghost of all.

Shoving open the door, he stepped inside with Duffy following. Within moments, a young policeman moved to twitch back the sheet from the still, draped form resting upon the wooden table.

Zeke braced himself, but whatever horrors he had been expecting were not forthcoming. Any blood had been cleaned away, and those mocking cold blue eyes were closed forever, the rigid contours of her face retaining only a hint of the beauty she once had been. Gazing down upon her, it was almost impossible to believe any spark of life had ever animated those impassive features.

His mother.

No matter what Cynthia claimed, the word had no meaning when attached to her. Zeke tried to dredge up some emotion at her passing . . . pity, anger, relief. But he felt absolutely nothing.

He made the identification, then left the room as the police officer drew the sheet back over her face. Outside, in the hall, Duffy appeared the more shaken, although he was doggedly making notes.

"Thank God, that's over," he said with a huge sigh. "Now I suppose you'll be hurrying back to your Miss Kavanaugh."

Zeke nodded. Rory had wanted to accompany him to the police station, but he felt she had been through enough for one day. There had been so much he had wanted to say to her, but in the uproar that surrounded the aftermath of their narrow escape, the right moment had not presented itself.

Perhaps he was simply stalling, uncertain of her response, still fearing her rejection. It had been one thing to dash into reckless action, risk his neck to try to save her. A far different kind of courage was required to settle the differences between them, admit to her how wrong he had been, to ask her pardon.

Duffy seemed to sense some of his trepidation, for he clapped Zeke on the shoulder and wished him luck. "I have to be rushing off myself," he said. "They're holding the presses for me. I've got a helluva tale to tell. I only hope I got all the details straight." Duffy cleared his throat, suddenly appearing uncomfortable. "Uh, Morrison, I couldn't help wondering. That wasn't true, was it . . . all that nonsense Mrs. Van Hallsburg spouted that she was your . . . about your being her . . . her . . ."

"Her bastard son?" Zeke filled in dully when Duffy hesitated. "Yes, it was. You've always said you'd get your story about me. Well, now I guess you have it."

Duffy slowly folded his notebook and tucked it back into his pocket. "I don't know what you're talking about, Morrison. Everyone knows Cynthia Van Hallsburg died childless. As far as I'm concerned, there won't be nothing worthwhile to print about you until the notice of your wedding."

Zeke stared at him, astonished, more moved than he could say by this evidence of Duffy's friendship. He extended his hand in a gesture of real gratitude, but Duffy, never able to stay still for long, was already gone.

Twilight settled over McCreedy Street like a soft blanket of night being drawn over the sidewalk and the rows of tall brick houses basking in the last rays of the setting sun. The peaceful silence was only broken by the rattle of the occasional coach wheel or some straggling urchin being called into supper.

Rory sat on the front stoop of her apartment building, watching the moon rise. As a warm breeze tickled her cheek, she breathed deeply, appreciating as she never had before the sights and sounds of her street, not even minding the occasional yapping of Finn McCool.

After the madness she had lived through earlier, it was all so blessedly sane, so wonderfully normal. Rory wished she could simply lean back and fully enjoy the evening like any other girl on a Friday night, waiting for her beau to call.

But if Zeke did fulfill his promise to return, she knew he would be pulled down, wearied from his grim task at the morgue. Despite the way they had clung to each other upon the warehouse roof, the tensions from their previous quarrel yet remained.

That realization still did not prevent her from glancing eagerly down the street at every new clopping of horses' hooves. A wry smile touched Rory's lips as she couldn't help remembering Zeke's last grand entrance onto McCreedy Street. When he did come, he would likely bring Miss Flanagan rushing to her window again.

After an hour of waiting, the minutes began to drag by. Rory's pleasure in the evening began to fade before a feeling of mounting disappointment. Another vehicle turned the corner, but it was only a battered old wagon with two men perched upon the box. Rory regarded it with scant interest until it drew closer and she was better able to remark the outline of the second man, settled next to the driver. The narrow wagon seat seemed barely constructed to accommodate Zeke's broad shoulders and athletic build.

Her mouth flying open in astonishment, Rory shot to her feet as the wagon pulled over to the curb. Even more startling than Zeke's manner of arrival were the contents of the wagon. She stared in disbelief at the familiar shape of the gondola, the ropes and trappings of the *Katie Moira*.

When Zeke clambered down from his perch, her stunned gaze flicked from him to the balloon and back again. She had rehearsed many ways of greeting him upon his return, but now all of them flew out of her head as she gasped, practically babbling.

"Zeke. What the . . . I never expected . . . that is I don't understand. What . . . what is . . ."

"It's your balloon, Aurora Rose," he said with a flash of his old humor. He affected a careless shrug. "As long as I was down at the police station, I supposed I might as well see if there was anything left of the blasted thing. I lack your expert eye, but I think the gas bag can be mended. If you would give me the keys to the warehouse, I'll have it sent on there."

Rory was yet too dumbfounded by his gesture to respond. With great patience, he repeated his request until she finally groped in her pocket and handed the keys over. Zeke retrieved something from the front seat of the wagon before sending it on its way. When Rory followed the vehicle's progress up the street, still tempted to rub her eyes, Zeke asked, "Is something wrong? I assumed you would want the balloon retrieved."

"Yes, I would, I mean I am very glad you did. That is . . . I thought . . ." She hesitated, then blurted out, "After your experience today, I would scarce have blamed you if you had wanted to set fire to it."

"At one point, the thought did occur to me," he admitted. "But hell, the day might come when I actually will be able to get myself to go up again. Though next time, I'd prefer to be in the basket."

"M-me too," Rory stammered with a wavering smile, her wonder seeming to increase along with the sudden accelerated tempo of her heart, the wild hopes beginning to flutter inside her.

She could hardly believe she was hearing these things from Zeke. He appeared much the same, with his heart-stopping grin, the familiar inflexible line of his jaw, and yet she sensed a difference as well, a more thoughtful stillness in the depths of those jet-black eyes. Deep shadows rimmed them, only hinting at what he must have suffered in the past hours from Mrs. Van Hallsburg's cruel revelations.

Rory longed to stroke back the ebony strands of hair that drooped stubbornly across his brow, kiss away some of those shadows, but she felt suddenly shy. Perhaps it was the unaccustomed diffidence in Zeke's own manner that communicated itself to her.

She allowed her gaze to drop, for the first time realizing what he had fetched away from the wagon. Awkwardly clutched in one of his large fists was a small bouquet. When he noticed her staring, he thrust the flowers toward her.

"Here, you better take these. I'm beginning to feel a little foolish holding them."

It was a simple arrangement of violets and daisies, but Rory accepted it with delight, burying her nose among the blossoms, enjoying the faint, sweet scent.

"Goodness," she said. "I . . . I've never received flowers from a gentleman before."

"Haven't you?" he asked with a momentary rush of his former impetuousness. "If I had known that, I would have bought you an entire—" He checked himself with a self-conscious laugh, looking sheepish.

"These are just fine," Rory assured him softly, at last daring to meet his gaze. Their eyes met, locking in a sudden silent understanding that the rush of words that followed couldn't hope to match.

They both burst into speech at once.

"Rory, I want to tell you how sorry I am about everything. That's why I came to the warehouse today—"

"Oh, no, Zeke. It was all my fault. I shouldn't have gotten so angry with you—"

"You had every right to be. I was a pigheaded fool—"

"But all those dreadful things I said. I never meant any of them—"

"Everything you said was perfectly true—"

"No, I was cruel, unkind."

With each breathless rush of words, they inched closer, Zeke grasping one of her hands between his own. "Then you can forgive me for what I did? I'd give you the warehouse or . . . or it could belong to both of us if . . . if . . . Aurora Rose, could you possibly still consider being my wife?"

Rory doubted that John Ezekiel Morrison had ever made such a humble request of anyone in all of his life. Tears stung her eyes and she could barely whisper her response. "Oh, yes, Zeke. Yes."

She flung her arms about his neck, half crushing the bouquet, sending a shower of daisy petals raining down over Zeke's frock coat. His head bent down to hers, seeking her lips in a tender kiss that seemed to erase all the misery, the misunderstanding of the past twenty-four hours.

She clung to him, urging him to intensify the embrace with a passion that was at once both fierce and gentle. Lost in each other's arms, they scarce noticed the last of twilight deepening into darkness or the lamplighter making his rounds, setting McCreedy Street softly aglow.

Time no longer seemed to have any meaning and Rory barely knew how long she lingered with Zeke, whispering pledges of love in the darkened, rustling shadows. They sat side by side on her front stoop, her head resting against his shoulder, as they made plans for a future that now beckoned brightly with promise.

He told her all that he had done the night he had slammed out of her apartment, his walk back through his old neighborhood, his reunion with his family.

"I realized then," he said, murmuring the words against her hair, "that there were some parts of my past, no matter how painful, that I couldn't and didn't want to put behind me. Cynthia Van Hallsburg abandoned me to a life of hell. If it hadn't been for a woman like Sadie . . ."

He had to pause a moment before he could go on. "There's a lot of kids, a lot of people back there in the slums that weren't so lucky. I never really believed any of that misery could be changed; I thought that Addison's dreams were all a little cockeyed. But I've been doing some thinking. Hell, I'll never be any wide-eyed crusader, but I've always been a fighter. Maybe I could make a difference."

Rory gazed up at him, her heart full of a tender pride. "I know you could," she said. "I would help you. If . . . if you did run for mayor, I could drop pamphlets for you from my balloon."

He grimaced a little at that, but laughed and said, "I hope I can keep your feet on the ground for a little while, lady. At least until I take you home to meet my family. I have strict orders from Caddie to bring you to dinner. I only wish . . ."

His face clouded. "I wish that my mother could be there as well. Maybe Cynthia Van Hallsburg gave me life, but it was Sadie that made it worth living. There's so much I regret now, so much I wish I could have made Sadie understand, how grateful I was, how much I—"

When he broke off, unable to go on, Rory reached up to touch his cheek. "I have a feeling she understood more than you imagined, and wherever she is now, I am sure she knows."

Zeke pressed a kiss against her palm. "I'll have to take your word for that. My faith has always been shaky. I guess until it grows stronger, I'll just have to borrow some of yours."

"I'd gladly lend it all to you," Rory whispered, wanting to share everything with him—her faith, her dreams, the rest of her life.

Zeke tightened his arms about her, straining her hard against him. "That's one mistake I'll never make again with you, Aurora Rose, keeping my feelings all dammed up inside. You're always going to know how much I love you, never be left to doubt it a single day of your life."

Her heart too full to answer, Rory could only show him how much his words meant to her by upturning her face to receive his kiss. From a great distance, she could hear Finn McCool barking, the creak of Miss Flanagan's front door as it opened. But swept up in the heady sweetness of Zeke's embrace, Rory only tightened her arms about him, determined to give her inquisitive neighbor something well worth craning her neck to see.